INHERENT FATE

BLOOD SECRETS ✚ BOOK 3

ALICIA ANTHONY

ISBN: 978-1-7333624-5-0 (Print)

ISBN: 978-1-7333624-4-3 (Ebook)

Published by Drury Lane Books, Sedalia, OH USA.

Library of Congress Control Number: 2020912068

Keep up with Alicia online for up-to-the-minute news and reader extras:

www.AliciaAnthonyBooks.com

Cover Art by Paper and Sage. www.PaperandSage.com

 Created with Vellum

PRAISE FOR
BLOOD SECRETS

"Anthony's writing keeps the reader on the edge of their seat."

~RED HEADED BOOK LOVER

"Anthony writes with gravitas and edge to give you real goosebumps."

~BOOK_NOOKIE

"Love this series! Always keeps you wondering and wanting to read more."

~KRISTA S., AMAZON REVIEW

"Action, suspense, shocks, and twists make for a great read. The characters are intriguing and suck you in."

~LEAH H., NETGALLEY REVIEW

"Psychological thrillers with a bit of paranormal thrown in are my favorite books to read and this one did not disappoint. This will definitely be a series to follow."

~MOMS4MISSIONS, AMAZON REVIEW

ALSO BY ALICIA ANTHONY:

The Blood Secrets Series:

INHERENT TRUTH, BLOOD SECRETS BOOK 1
INHERENT LIES, BLOOD SECRETS BOOK 2

STAND-ALONE THRILLERS:

FRACTALS

Learn more at:
www.AliciaAnthonyBooks.com

For Jillian,
my favorite twist of fate.
Thank you for cheering me on.

You'll always be my favorite.

1

LIV

Something about death makes invisibility easy. After all the years I spent trying to disappear, who knew all I needed was a death certificate issued by the very government who did everything within their power to bury me?

I gripped the porcelain around the pedestal sink, my knuckles white. The gray-toned walls of the law office bathroom squeezed in on me. *Breathe*, I coached myself. *You can do this, Olivia Sullivan. You made it this far. He can't hurt you anymore.* That was a lie.

A soft knock sounded on the ladies' room door.

"Miss Allyn?" A man's voice broke the silence, the same man who'd waited for me outside Arrivals at Dulles International less than two hours before.

Tony Medici, as he'd introduced himself, was a tall, muscular brick wall of a man. His eyes were a muted hazel, almost gold, and he was close-shaven, his nose just a bit crooked. The result of an injury, I was sure, but too intimidated to ask.

His broad back and shoulders strained the seams of his dark suit. And he looked less like a go-fer for the US Attorney's Office and more like a mob boss. When I closed my eyes now, I could picture the sign clutched in one of his meaty paws, my new pseudonym printed in bold black letters–Olivia Allyn.

Tony cleared his throat from the other side of the door. "Ms. Rogers is waiting."

I swallowed hard and stared at the reflection in the mirror, wondering why the unaffected gaze of the woman in the mirror didn't match the rabbit race of my heart.

"Thanks, Tony. Be right out." I pushed the door open just enough for him to see a slice of my face, ensure I hadn't ducked out the window and ran. Not that the possibility hadn't crossed my mind in the five minutes I'd been holed up here, but it was dark. I wasn't familiar with DC, and everyone I'd once known on this side of the Atlantic thought I was dead. In short, I had nowhere else to go. Besides, how far could I get before the USAO tracked me down?

I washed my hands under lukewarm water and jerked a couple paper towels from the metal dispenser on the wall. Glancing back at the reflection, I wiped away the glaze of moisture on my palms. *You deserve a fresh start*, I reminded myself. *Fresh doesn't mean forgotten*, my inner critic chattered at me, the black-lettered sign surging back full-force.

Two months ago I was sitting in the back room of McGill's Pub, two miles from my grandmother's cottage on the shores of Lough Dan, fighting my way through dial-up internet to find an attorney willing to listen to my story. A story that implicated a high-ranking Bureau official in conspiracy against his own department, his abuse of power and misuse of government assets–namely me.

Assistant US Attorney, Michelle Rogers, wasn't even on

my list, but somehow, she'd found me–intercepted the email intended for one of the other prosecutors in her office. She was young, driven, and had an obvious hatred for men who used women as rungs on the ladder of power. And if Marcus Sowards' conduct over the course of the GenLink operation didn't fit that description perfectly, I didn't know what did.

She'd launched an investigation into his handling of the Skylar McCaffrey rescue and by extension, the GenLink operation. The evidence I turned over, coupled with the dirt she turned up on her own, was enough to convince Bureau Director, Cristophe Hamlin, to put Sowards on administrative leave pending further investigation.

Now, she was knee deep in building a criminal case against Sowards, while the Bureau itself launched its own inquiry. And for that, she needed Liv Sullivan in the flesh. There was just one problem. Liv Sullivan no longer existed. It was up to Michelle Rogers to bring me back to life.

The door to the bathroom breezed inward with a *thwap*, heels clicking across the tile floor. I tossed the paper towel in the trash between the sinks, catching the reflection of Michelle Rogers in the mirror. Blonde hair hung at shoulder length, streaks of well-placed lowlights proof it wasn't her natural color. Pale blue eyes locked on mine as she extended her hand in greeting.

"Michelle Rogers," she offered. "It's nice to finally see you in person."

I cleared my throat and smoothed travel wrinkles from my purple button-down, pulling myself up as tall as my 5'3" frame would allow before facing the lawyer and shaking her hand. "I apologize for keeping you waiting, Ms. Rogers."

Michelle smiled and shrugged, less like a lawyer and more like a friend–an observation that spiked an unanticipated blade of unease. "Please. It's Michelle. And I expected it." She retreated to the door and propped it open with the toe of her pump. "Come. We've got a lot to cover before Sowards' firing squad moves in."

2

RIDGE

The repetitive *thwack* of the lawnmower cut through the late spring stillness at Sullivan Farm, echoing against the line of trees at the edge of the woods. Ridge McCaffrey cut a straight path through the overgrowth of the side yard, just a few more passes and he'd be done–with this project anyway. He cut the engine when the silver Audi pulled in, swung his leg over the seat of the second-hand riding mower and hopped to the ground. He brushed stray blades of grass from his jeans and started toward the drive, watching his ex-wife lift Colton free from the backseat booster.

"Thanks for bringing him out, Bridget," Ridge said when he got within earshot. "I'll be done here soon and then we'll head back to my place."

Ridge ruffled the blonde curls on his son's head as Colton wrapped a hug around his leg, trotting off toward the overgrown flower bed along the front porch.

"New car?" Ridge tipped his chin in the direction of the tiny vehicle Colton clutched in his hand.

Bridget shrugged. "You know he won't let me leave the

grocery without one. Jeep this time," she said as Colton kneeled at the edge of the dirt and plowed his new toy through the vegetation.

"Of course," Ridge smiled, turning his attention back to Bridget.

"Try to hurry it up," she said. "You know I don't like him being out here." She glanced toward the old barn. "Especially since the storm. He could wander in that old barn and get hurt."

"I've already had the tree cleaned up, Bridge." He let his gaze drift over the hulking structure at the edge of the barn lot, the rear of the old dairy barn collapsed by the weight of an ancient oak.

Bridget sighed, frustrated.

"I'll keep my eyes on him," Ridge promised. "We won't be long."

"I don't know why you feel the need to do all this. It's been over six months, Ridge. It's not like you're living here. Just sell it. Beth would understand." She skimmed a hand down Ridge's shoulder. "A good buyer and Colton's college fund would be set."

Ridge was well aware of his ex-wife's opinions when it came to his inheritance of Sullivan Farm after Liv's death. Liv's mother had no expectations, and he knew Beth would understand if he ever made the choice to put the place on the market. But obligation didn't even break the top five on his list of reasons not to part with the place. He might not be able to bring himself to live there, but the chance of him moving out there someday wasn't completely out of the realm of possibility.

"I've got to figure out what to do about the barn before I make any decisions," he said.

Ridge had already called the local fire department who'd agreed to come out and destroy the barn as part of a training exercise. But keeping that tidbit of information to himself put off the discussion of his plans for the farm for another day, which had been increasingly difficult since Ridge had gone back to work, dividing his time with Colton between the farm and his apartment.

Bridget didn't like it when Colton rambled on about their adventures on the lake or in the woods. And while he wasn't sure if it was jealousy or true concern for their son's safety, he was certain of one thing. Bridget would never understand how he felt about this place. And he didn't expect her to.

The farm had become the one place he could visit after nearly seven months and still feel a connection to Liv. There were moments when he was alone that he could swear he'd heard her voice–her laughter–rustling in the trees. But he didn't share that with anyone, least of all his overly critical ex-wife.

Bridget fixed her thunderstorm eyes on his and gave up. "I know it's hard," she said. "But do something about the barn before Colton gets hurt." Her voice calmed into a smooth whisper. "You'll drop Colton off Monday after the zoo trip?" She popped the driver's side door of the Audi and climbed inside.

"After my day of fun with the PTO posse," Ridge confirmed, a smile tugging at his lips.

"Don't call them that," Bridget said, but the tilt of her own lips told him the nickname had hit its mark. Since Colton started preschool, neither one of them had managed to find a niche within the well-oiled clique of the St. Stephen's Parent Teacher Organization. "It's our first year. They're like this with all the new families."

Ridge gave Bridget credit for trying, but he'd seen the looks, felt the stares and heard the half-veiled comments at their monthly meetings. Unlike Bridget, he no longer felt the need to assimilate with a group of mostly women who treated him as either eye candy or damaged goods, depending on what they needed from him.

Ridge nodded. "See you Monday."

As Bridget disappeared up the driveway, Ridge turned to Colton. "How about a ride on the mower? You can help me steer."

Colton jumped up from his spot on the grass and ran across the side yard toward the mower, climbing onboard before Ridge could get there. The few passes that should have taken fifteen minutes took closer to an hour after a few misguided turns. But the rounds of giggles through the smile on his son's face made the extra time well worth it.

"Why's Mommy want you to get rid of the barn?" Colton asked as they stowed the mower in the newly erected lawn shed Ridge had built since the falling oak took aim at the old Sullivan barn.

"She's afraid it'll fall and hurt somebody," Ridge explained.

"Like Dewey?" Colton said, fixing his big blue eyes on his dad.

"Who's Dewey?" Ridge asked, preparing himself for a crazy explanation from an almost five-year-old.

"I'll show you," Colton said, running from Ridge toward the open mouth of the barn.

"Colton, don't–" Ridge hollered, but Colton held his hand up, stopping just short of the entrance, and kneeled in the dirt.

Holding his hand toward the black of the interior, he called, "Here, Dewey."

Ridge watched a small black and white cat creep cautiously from the darkness and right up to Colton, who scooped him up and carried him over to Ridge.

"This is Dewey, Daddy. Can we keep him?"

The little cat purred against Colton's chest as Ridge

kneeled, stroking the fur on the top of its head with his index finger.

"Sure," he said. Short of the possibility of a few fleas, the cat looked to be in good shape, which was remarkable considering he hadn't fed anything in that old barn since taking the key from Beth six months ago. "But he'll have to stay here until we find out if we can have a cat in the apartment."

Colton groaned. "Why can't we just move out here, Daddy?"

The question from his child's lips pressed an ache into his chest. It wasn't something he was sure he could answer for himself, let alone in a way a preschooler could understand.

"It's gonna take some time for us to figure out what the plan should be. I know that isn't what you want to hear, but–"

"It's 'cause you miss Livvie," Colton said, sounding suddenly much older than his four-and-a-half years. "But I like it here."

"Me, too, bud. Me, too." Ridge swung Colton onto his hip, Dewey in tow, and headed toward his Shelby. "Tell you what, I'll call the manager first thing in the morning. In the meantime, we'll stop by the store and grab some food, a bed, maybe a few toys and see how Dewey does at home tonight, okay?"

The glittering excitement in Colton's eyes as he snuggled the purring cat was all the reward Ridge needed.

3

LIV

Michelle Rogers sat in a burgundy wingback in a corner office, stirring sugar into a cup of tea Tony had just dropped off.

"Sugar?" she asked, nodding at the porcelain bowl on the tray.

"No, thank you," I said, pulling the second cup from the tray and hazarding a sniff of the barely steeped Earl Grey.

"You're settling in, then?" She smiled at me. A wisp of honey blonde fell over her left eye as she cocked her head to the side.

I'd been in DC a little over a month and Michelle continued to surprise me. She wasn't at all like I'd pictured from our interactions online. Granted, her interception might have been a stroke of luck, but I'd done my research after the fact. According to Google, she was the only female senior prosecutor with the US Attorney's Office in DC But for reasons I couldn't explain–my own preconceived bias, perhaps–I'd pictured a hardened Marsha Clark type, not the soft smiling blonde that sat before me now.

The same thread of anxiety that wove its way into my chest when we'd first met in the bathroom, returned with a renewed grip.

"I know I'm not what you expected." Michelle let the statement drift. "But have I disappointed you so far?"

I bit the inside of my lip and answered, "Of course not. To be honest, I'm not sure what I expected."

Michelle laughed softly. "Then that makes two of us, Olivia." She returned her teacup to the tray and leaned forward, elbows on her knees and hands clasped. "I have to say, though. I've always found being underestimated has its rewards."

She sat back, taking me in with scrutinizing eyes. "Sowards underestimated you in O'Malley's cabin, did he not? First, when you plunged that cigar into his neck to free Agent McCaffrey's sister. And now, as you prepare to testify against him?"

I swallowed, the stale cigar and mildew scent of McGill's back room still burned into my olfactory senses. "How long until he knows?"

"That you're alive?" Michelle smoothed her skirt. "Sowards was arraigned this afternoon. Was out on bond within the hour. My associate delivered the discovery packet this evening. Depending on when his legal team decides to involve Sowards is up to them, but I'd guess we can expect him to know everything by nine a.m."

Her eyes locked on mine, watery blue flecks sparking in the low streetlight filtering through the window. "Does that worry you?"

I sucked in a wobbly breath.

She reached for my hand and gave it a soft pat. I watched her fingers as they pulled away, wondering if I'd ever again feel the buzz of emotion that used to accompany every interaction.

"It's okay if it does. You're only human." Michelle glanced to the corner of the room where Tony stood. "That's what Tony's here for. Evan, too, for that matter. Their only job is to make sure you're safe."

"Sowards will retaliate." My words came out strong, belying the internal churn of anxiety that had been a constant companion since making the decision to return home. "I've stripped him of his power. Called his decisions into question."

"Yes. Decisions that should have been questioned long before any assets lost their lives." Michelle was good at keeping me focused. From the moment I handed over the list of names Cam O'Malley shoved in my pocket the night of the explosion, Michelle had been singularly focused on making Sowards pay. Her brows lifted. "What is it you're afraid of?"

"I'm not worried about me." I leveled a stare at Michelle. "I don't want him going after the people I–" I couldn't finish the statement.

"Love?" Michelle hesitated. She leaned back against the chair and crossed her legs. "Let's talk about that."

A slice of panic shredded my chest. "Did Sowards do something?"

"No, no, it's nothing like that. But I need to be straight with you. Just like you've been straight with me." Her eyes softened. "I've known you for a month now, Liv. And in that month you've never once mentioned what *you* hope to gain from this case. You've said you want your life back. But I didn't get where I am today without knowing everyone has limits. What I need to know now is, what're yours?" Michelle cocked her head to the side.

"I'm not sure I know what you mean," I managed.

"What's your safe word, Liv? What could Sowards do that would stop you from pursuing this case?"

Her question hung in the air between us. My heart thumping hard against my sternum.

"I know you want to go back to Cascade Hills, back to the life Sowards stole from you. What if I told you that could never happen? That your life outside of witness protection is over. Would you still pursue this case?"

I didn't answer. How could I? Her words ricocheted through me, echoing deep in my consciousness.

Her eyes skimmed me from head to toe, and I clenched my jaw against the pit of loss that pushed its way into my chest.

Before waking up in my grandmother's cottage, the side effects of Cam O'Malley's drug still rattling around in my lungs, I could have felt Michelle's reaction. My palms itched with the need to feel it now. I slid my hands down the thighs of my jeans. Being rid of something I'd spent my life coming to terms with–even hating–should've made me happy, but instead, I felt lost, unmoored.

Her voice lowered, full of soft regret. "You need to be prepared for the likelihood that you may never be able to go home, Liv. I have the resources to protect you and I can promise you a life. But I can't promise you *your* life. Do you understand?"

I swallowed the fingers of understanding that clotted in my throat. "Thanks to Sowards, my family thinks I'm dead. And if I show up in Cascade Hills, he'll find out–come after me. Whether or not I want it, I'm tied to GenLink. I have been since the day I was conceived, and I will be until the day I die. I've spent most of my life reacting to the consequences–being someone else's puppet. I've already sacrificed my life, Michelle. At least give me a chance to work the strings."

4

RIDGE

Sergeant Kyle Renner and his team were already in action at the farm when Ridge pulled down the driveway the following evening. He tucked his car alongside the few others on the grassy patch that ran along the eastern exterior of the house, farthest from the burn site. He hadn't planned to come, but even with a little boy and a new kitten distracting him, the nagging in his gut refused to let him stay away. Lucky for him, Brian stepped up to take Colton for a few hours.

"Thanks for giving us the go ahead on the old barn." Kyle headed toward Ridge and tipped back his face shield. "Makes for a perfect training burn."

"You're welcome," Ridge said. "Smells like you've already got it cooking." He smiled, but the sudden stab of pain in his chest inhibited the accompanying cough of laughter. Liv's mother had given her blessing, which had been important to Ridge. But the person he wanted most to clear it with was beyond his reach. A bubble of guilt in his chest expanded at the realization he was destroying what had once been hers.

"We started in the middle of the structure," Kyle explained pointing for effect. "Trying for a central-burn scenario. But we're dealing with old wood here. Should go up quick."

Somebody hollered for Renner from the back of the barn and he trotted off with a tip of his head. "Just watch the house," Ridge yelled over the hum of machinery.

Renner tossed a backward salute over his shoulder and disappeared behind one of two Cascade Hills Fire units flanking the lot between the barn and the house.

Ridge climbed the porch stairs and watched as the first signs of flame licked at the faded red exterior, swathes of paint bubbled and dropped under the heat of an orangey-red glow. The department was doing a nice job keeping the flames in check. And the cooperation of the wind blowing from the south pushed the smoke away from the house.

He lowered into one of the wicker porch rockers and leaned his head against the headrest. The first tendrils of heavy black belched from the opening between the main barn doors. Ridge closed his eyes, the scent ushering in a wave of unwelcome memories he wasn't sure he could take.

Images of his sister, Riley, trapped in their childhood home, unable to escape the result of his teenaged stupidity morphed into memories of the street outside Cohen's Guest House in Dublin, Ireland. His frantic search of the strangers lining packed sidewalks as the block went up in flames. The squeeze of panic that had constricted his chest in the aftermath hung heavy in his lungs now. Then it had been chased away by the relief of finding Liv, pulling her into his arms. Relief he'd never find again.

The memory forced him forward in the chair and he hung his head, elbows on his knees. *Failure.* Creeping pinpricks he'd come to recognize as the precursor to a panic attack started down his forearm. He rubbed the flesh, massaging until the marching buzz dissolved into nothingness.

Failure. Ridge could name the emotion now. It'd taken all of the last seven months–and countless hours of therapy–since the explosion at O'Malley's cabin ripped Liv from his life. But he'd gotten better at naming the emotions as they came, which his therapist assured him would help. But the barbed wire strands of guilt tangling through his gut on a daily basis never truly subsided. Although, they had grown less destructive.

The patter of small feet sounded from the side of the porch and he looked up to find Colton, Dewey tucked in the crook of his arm, running toward him. Brian heaved himself onto the porch from the side yard and strode across the decking, sliding into the second rocker with a sigh.

"There are steps you know," Ridge said to his friend, folding Colton into a hug, careful not to squeeze son and cat too tight. Ridge patted Dewey on the head.

"I wanted to make sure we didn't get in the way," Brian said, launching the chair into a gentle sway and adding an apology. "I made the mistake of telling Colton what you were doing out here. He was fascinated so I told him if he promised to stay close, I'd bring him out. Hope that's okay."

"Of course," Ridge said, ruffling Colton's curls and pulling him onto his lap. "Just don't tell Mom, okay, bud?"

"Kay." Colton released Dewey and the little cat jumped down, weaving his way back and forth around Ridge's legs, purring.

"You'd never know that was a barn cat," Brian said. "Friendliest cat I've ever seen."

Colton watched with big eyes for a few minutes as the fire men and women worked back and forth, hosing the fire like a well-oiled machine. Before too long, the orangey glow reflecting on his face had a soothing effect, coaxing his eyes closed. Within fifteen minutes he was curled, asleep, snuggled against Ridge's chest.

"You doing okay?" Brian asked once he realized Colton was out.

Ridge nodded in the firelight. "It's harder than I expected," he admitted.

"In what way?"

"The guilt, I suppose. Memories."

"She'd understand," Brian said.

"I know she would." Ridge shoved at the rush of emotion that surged with those words. Reminders of her loss were everywhere. From the expanse of empty mattress next to him each night to the silence after recorded voicemail messages he'd played and replayed more times than he could count. He sucked in a breath as the wind shifted, blowing a gust of fire-singed air toward the porch before settling back into its north-westerly flow.

"She'd also understand if you started putting yourself out there." Brian's voice was hesitant.

"Skylar put you up to this?" Ridge asked, careful to keep his volume low.

"She's worried about you. We all are. It's been six months, Ridge. All we're asking for is one date. No one would fault you for moving on."

"Seven," Ridge corrected. "Liv's been gone seven months and eight days, Brian. And if you think the reason I haven't dated is because I'm worried about what the town gossips might say, you don't know me very well." Colton shifted in Ridge's arms, forcing him to muffle the pulses of irritation that boiled through his blood and into his voice.

Brian stopped rocking, sliding one foot over a creaky floorboard and pressing with the toe of his shoe.

"You still planning to go to DC next week?" Brian asked.

Ridge nodded. "Adam's picking me up from the airport Tuesday evening. They have me scheduled for a deposition Wednesday afternoon." He waited for Brian to tell him what he already knew, that testifying for Marcus Sowards wouldn't bring Liv back, that he'd be reliving a tragedy for no good reason. He'd heard the same argument from both Skylar and his dad since telling them about the impending trial and Sowards' request for testimony.

"I just hope you know what you're doing, Ridge."

"Me, too," Ridge said, "but if I don't go now, they'll just subpoena me for the trial. It's not something I can avoid."

Testifying seemed like a way to gain some clarity, a chance to understand why Sowards pulled Liv into his showdown with Cam, and then left her there to die. To be honest, when he heard about the inquiry he knew he'd be called, he just thought it would be for the prosecution, not the defense.

He watched a plume of red flame lift from the burning remains, floating, ghost-like into the air. He wondered, not for the first time, how much of his life Liv could see. He'd grown up believing in heaven and hell–in something greater than the life we lived on earth–but when Liv died, he'd grown bitter, facing an uncertain future and irrepressible guilt he couldn't control.

Now, as he sat watching the final flames lick at the pile of debris that had once been the Sullivan barn, he couldn't help but wonder. Would someone who had extrasensory gifts in life have similar abilities on the other side? He was fully aware how crazy it sounded, which is why he'd never voiced the idea, not even to his best friend. Ridge glanced at Brian.

"I should get this guy home," he said, rising and carrying Colton from the porch to the cluster of cars at the corner of the house.

Brian collected Dewey, who'd made his own nest in a pile of nearby leaves leftover from the winter, and followed, tucking the cat in the back seat alongside Colton.

"Why don't you let me drive you to the airport on Tuesday," Brian said as Ridge slid behind the wheel. "Give us a chance to talk."

"Sure," Ridge agreed, urging the engine to life.

"You're not the only one who lost her, you know." Brian said, his comment almost lost in the rev of the V8.

Ridge nodded, swallowing against the stab of hurt that shot through his chest. He shifted into reverse, backing away from his best friend, heading toward Cascade Hills and the now-familiar comfort of his two bedroom apartment.

I picked up the cup of coffee in front of me and sipped, gazing out over the sea of faces coloring the careful neutral tones of the hotel cafe. Only two were familiar, Tony and Evan, the less-than-inconspicuous bodyguards Michelle had insisted follow me everywhere. Part of me wanted nothing more than to shake them, run off into the subway and jump trains until I no longer saw them whenever I looked over my shoulder.

I'd done it once, about a week after arriving. But it hadn't taken them long to catch up, and Michelle had been furious. Now, I'd succumbed to this new normal. The life I'd imagined before leaving Ireland was nonexistent. Instead, I'd become a poster child for witness protection–my days a revolving door of strict schedule implementation and daily visits with Michelle at the Department of Justice, interspersed by weekly court ordered psychiatric evaluations and hotel-hopping. I was beginning to accept the fate that my life and normal would never be used in the same sentence.

It had been a week since Michelle had delivered the news

that going back to a life in Cascade Hills was no longer an option. A week to settle into the understanding that I was Michelle's ace in the hole when it came to the case against Sowards. I'd been naïve to think that once Sowards was convicted I'd be able to go home again.

Evan flicked the newspaper, spread it wide in front of him and folded it closed. My signal it was time to go. I followed his gaze to the front desk of the hotel where a group of blue-suited lawyer types were checking in. I'd been at this hotel, a Marriott two blocks from the DOJ office for ten days, longer than I'd stayed anywhere since coming back to the States, and the constant moving around was worming its way under my skin.

I nodded at Evan and stood, fished some bills out of my purse to cover the check while Tony headed out of the lobby cafe ahead of us. No one spoke. Tony held the door of a black sedan while I slid into the backseat. I ran my hands over the cool leather of the seats, closing my eyes, hoping to pick up some remnant of energy–anything–but, as usual, nothing came.

"Ms. Rogers is waiting for you in her office, Miss Allyn," Tony said, glancing at me through the rearview mirror. "She wants to meet with you alone before Sowards' team arrives. Your deposition is scheduled for tomorrow at ten."

After a month of checking in and out of hotels, I'd gotten used to the name. Olivia Allyn, age 26. Hometown: Indianapolis, Indiana. Michelle Rogers shaved a few years off my age, but other than that, it was an identity without too many moving parts to get caught up in. I didn't need to worry about an accent, and I responded to the first name without thinking about it. It served the purpose. Although, I'd already overheard discussions about what would happen after the trial–once Sowards knew for sure I was the unnamed informant. And WITSEC, Michelle liked to remind me, had a much more significant learning curve.

"Will we be at the Marriott again tonight?" I asked.

Tony nodded, his eyes drifting to me in the rearview mirror. "It's a central location, a few blocks from the DOJ. Ms. Rogers thinks it would be best, at least through the end of the depositions. We'll be waiting for you–like normal–pick you up and drive you back once your meeting is over."

"Thanks, Tony, but I think I'd like to walk."

Evan started to refute, but Tony raised a hand to silence him.

"Understood, Miss Allyn," he said instead. Which meant they'd follow me on foot, but at least I'd get some fresh air. I stifled the wry smile that crept onto my lips and went back to staring out the window, watching my nation's capital drift by in a blur of traffic and congestion.

I closed my eyes, imagined the subtle jostle of the sedan was moving me down the tar and chip country road toward Sullivan Farm. The blare of a car horn in the lane next to us yanked me out of the fantasy and left a pang of regret in my chest. I'd chosen this life and Michelle had warned me. But I never really believed it would mean giving up the chance to go home, to see Sullivan Farm, smell the lilacs at the edge of the porch in the spring, crunch through the autumn woods, or dip my toes in sun-warmed Cascade Lake.

An involuntary clench took hold of my jaw as the people I'd left behind surged into full view of my memory. I'd grown accustomed to pushing them away. Trying not to think about Ridge–the life he was building without me–was the most difficult.

Thoughts of him, my mother, even Brian and Skylar moving on with their lives, memories of me left shrouded in a darkened past, became more and more tangible. Seven months was a long time. And not one of them had a reason to wait for me. A knot of loneliness settled in my chest, wrapping its arms around my heart and squeezing until breath became difficult. I'd wanted this, I reminded myself. Had fought for it, in fact. And Sowards was getting the punishment he deserved. But this wasn't the outcome I'd expected.

I swallowed, opened my eyes as the car slowed to a stop in front of a massive granite building, budding cherry trees flanked either side of a grand staircase. And Michelle Rogers stood at the top. Waiting. This is the choice I'd made. And there was no going back now.

"THANKS FOR COMING TODAY. I know this meeting wasn't originally on the schedule." Michelle ushered me into her office and gestured to the chair on the other side of her aged executive desk. "As you know, we'll be deposing the witnesses the defense plans to call just like his side will be deposing ours." Her eyes darkened, narrowed. "I received his team's final list this morning and I think you owe me an explanation."

She pushed a list across the desk between us. I pulled it into my lap, refusing to break her accusatory stare.

"Adam Miller?" I asked. I'd known he'd be called. Michelle and I had talked at length about his involvement, my non-existent memories of him pulling me from the cabin, and his reluctance to admit as much.

"For one." Michelle's pale blue eyes finally pulled away, freeing me. "Sowards was responsible for Miller's promotion, after all. And his job's on the line."

I glanced down at the second name on the list, breathed his name, "Ridge McCaffrey."

"I need to know, Liv. Have you had any contact with Special Agent McCaffrey since the explosion? Any at all?"

"Of course not." Last year I would've been able to feel the

pinpricks of her doubt. But now, I could only read it in her eyes. "You don't believe me."

She leaned forward. The jacket of her burgundy suit straining at the shoulders. "I do believe you. But what happens this week will dictate the course of this trial. I need to know there's nothing you're holding back. Silence breeds opportunity, Liv–not our opportunity–Sowards' opportunity."

I ignored Michelle's near accusation and let my eyes drift through the series of names–most unfamiliar.

She pulled back, adjusting her jacket and resting against her seat back once again. "How would it look if the significant other of our star witness testifies for the defense?"

"Excuse me?"

"What does he have, Olivia? You need to tell me what he knows."

"I have no idea what he knows. I was too busy being raped and drugged, remember?" The heat of anger simmered in my veins. "If you want his side of the story, you'll have to ask him yourself."

Michelle pulled back. A deep breath lifted her shoulders and chest. "I apologize. It's just...there's a lot on the line. A lot we still don't know."

There it was, another jab at my patchy memory. This past month had been a crash course in Criminology 101. So much of my side amounted to nothing more than hearsay. I could provide my own account of what happened inside O'Malley's cabin. But I'd been drugged, had admitted as much. The chance that my testimony would even make it to court, let alone hold enough weight to convict, was slim to none. We needed corroboration. And that was an area in which we were sorely lacking.

"What about us?" I asked. "Who are you calling for our side? Who will vouch for us?"

"Besides you, we've got statements from Michael Donaghey and Ashlyn Callaghan."

"That's it?"

"Our cross exam of Adam Miller could go either way."

Air burned hot in my chest. "And Ridge? What will you ask him?"

"I won't know until I hear his testimony. He's no longer with the Bureau. With any luck, whatever he has to say will swing in our favor."

She hesitated, waiting for a response from me that never came.

"Liv, you knew he'd be called. By one side or the other."

I nodded. Possibility was one thing. Knowing was another beast altogether. I forced the words through my throat. "Is he here? In DC?"

"His flight's due in tonight. He's being deposed tomorrow afternoon."

"Does he–" Panic constricted my lungs.

"Know you're alive?" she finished. "Not to my knowledge."

I swallowed the knot that rooted itself at the base of my throat, fighting through the burn behind my eyes. "But he will," I guessed. "They'll tell him...about me?"

"I can't control what Sowards' team will say. You know that. But I promise you, that information won't come from me. At this point I can't see any reason they would tell him. Acknowledging your existence would only make Ridge more hostile, would it not?"

I met Michelle's stare. Her eyes were hard, judgmental. "Hostile to who?" I managed. "Sowards or me?"

"We've talked about this, Liv. Does it really matter?"

More than you can imagine, I thought.

6

RIDGE

Bridget met Ridge on the porch of the Cape Cod Monday evening, watching as he lifted the sleeping child from the backseat of his Shelby and snuggled him against his shoulder.

"He's gonna outgrow that, you know?" Bridget said, nodding toward the car. "You need something more practical."

Ridge ignored Bridget's jab at his choice of transportation and passed Colton off to his ex-wife. "I should be back by Friday. Adam said the depositions wouldn't take more than a couple days, depends on what kind of questions they have, I guess."

"Do you need a ride to the airport?" Colton shifted in Bridget's arms, a matchbox car dropping to the cement with a clatter.

Ridge bent to pick up the toy. "Brian's taking me. But thanks." He tucked the toy into Bridget's palm and planted one last kiss on the side of Colton's head before descending the front stoop and heading back to his car.

As soon as he'd heard from Adam that Sowards' conduct

during the GenLink operation had been called into question, he'd known he would be asked to give a statement. He wasn't sure how much he could offer in the way of saving grace for his former boss, but if it would bring him answers to some of the burning questions he still had about that night, he was glad to do his part.

Ridge's suspicion for Marcus Sowards had only festered since Liv's death. She should have been his first priority, not the basement full of drugs he planned to use to reconstitute an already suffering intelligence program. That much seemed to be common knowledge among staffers, and as far as Ridge was concerned he couldn't see how any of that would help Sowards beat charges of coercion and misappropriation of federal resources. Ridge suspected saving Liv's life ranked well below the priority he'd given O'Malley's drugs.

He sighed as he turned out of Bridget's drive toward his apartment complex. Questioning, for the umpteenth time, what difference involving himself in this deposition would make in the grand scheme of things. His dad had called just last night. *"It won't bring her back, son."* As if Ridge wasn't painfully aware of that fact.

ADAM MILLER UNFOLDED himself from the corner booth when Ridge entered Broderick's Bar and Grill just outside his hotel lobby. Adam wrapped his arms around Ridge, clapping him twice on the back before letting go. Ridge hadn't seen his former partner since Liv's memorial service last December. Adam had been reassigned by the Bureau within days of the explosion at O'Malley's cabin and had flown back from DC for the occasion. They'd been mostly out of touch since.

"Good to see you, man," Adam said as he pulled away,

motioning Ridge into the booth. "How's civilian life treating you?"

"Good." Ridge stretched the truth. "I've been spending more time with Colton. Been pulling a few shifts for a freelance security company. Sowards was generous with his severance package. Just trying to decide where to go from here."

Ridge could feel Adam studying him. Scrutinizing every word as he wrangled with what to say, struggling through small talk. Moisture built on the palms of his hands as they talked.

"Got any possibilities?" Adam asked. His eyes scanned Ridge's face, watching for hints of deception. Ridge shook away the irritation with a shrug. Whatever job opportunities presented themselves were no one's business but his own. Ridge exhaled, reminding himself, *he's just trying to be nice.*

"Wallace asked me to come back to Cascade Hills PD as a consultant."

"You gonna take him up on it?"

"Not sure. Bridget is all for it, of course. I just don't know if I need to be back in the game, yet. Even if it is just part-time."

"Sure." The corner of Adam's mouth tipped downward. "I get it. It must be hard staying in Cascade Hills. All the memories." Adam's voice trailed off. Miller had never been good when it came to rehashing feelings. Ridge thumbed the glass of water in front of him. Who was he kidding? He could hardly be considered a pro.

"It's alright," Ridge said to break the awkward silence. "I'm better off there where I can be with Colton."

"How's Bridget?" Adam asked.

Ridge smiled. "Bridget's still Bridget. She's working in Columbus now. Seems to enjoy the small town vibe of Cascade Hills. Schools are good, so I think she'll stick around a while."

Adam paused, the question he wanted to ask seemingly poised on the tip of his tongue. To anyone else it might look like a random hesitation, but Ridge had learned to read the signs. Pity, laced with some other emotion–judgement, usually–at the fact that he was wasting his life dwelling on the past. Everyone had an opinion. Adam was certainly no different. *"Move on,"* he imagined Adam wanted to say. *"Start dating, find someone to share your life with."* Ridge only wished it could be that easy.

What most people didn't understand was that the memory of Liv never left him. He woke up with her on his mind, and he fell asleep the same way. Could still feel the pressure of her lips on his, the heat of her body molded to his own. Vivid dreams played out in his subconscious, and there were moments the memory of her felt so real he questioned his grip on reality. But regardless of what happened in the privacy of his own home, he still couldn't look at a woman without comparing her to Liv. At this point he wasn't sure he'd ever be ready for that next step. For some reason, he'd hoped Adam might be able to understand.

Ridge forced himself not to bring up the drop on O'Malley's cabin. The idea that Adam had been so close to the action but hadn't been able to bring Liv out haunted him. It didn't make sense. He'd run over the possible scenarios in his mind more times than he could count. They were friends–partners in the field. He trusted Adam with his life. He just wasn't sure he should have trusted him with Liv's. Ridge wiped his hands along his jeans. The waitress's arrival offering a momentary reprieve.

"The meeting should be fairly cut and dry," Adam said as they ate. "Bill Bishop, Sowards' lead attorney, will meet with you first, then the lawyers from both sides will call you in around one tomorrow afternoon. You have the address, right?"

"For the Department of Justice?" Ridge couldn't help but smile. "Yeah." The DOJ offices were a couple blocks south of his hotel, an easy walk.

"Just be ready for whatever they throw at you."

"Got it," Ridge said. "You know I've done this before, right?"

Adam smiled and apologized, going back to his food.

Ridge watched his friend eat. The artery below Adam's jaw ticked, pulsing in rapid succession. "What's going on, Adam? You afraid they're going to tell me something I don't already know?"

Adam let out a high pitched, nervous chuckle as he shoveled the last bit of food from his plate. He scrunched his brow up as he swallowed, meeting Ridge's stare. "Damn. The Bureau took a hit when they lost you."

Ridge waited him out.

"No, it's nothing. It's just, you know how lawyers are. They like to open old wounds." He hesitated. "Create new ones."

"What exactly do they have on Sowards, anyway?" Ridge asked. "I gotta be honest. I'm not sure there's much I can say that's going to help his cause."

Adam leaned back in the booth, his eyes flicked around the bar as he shrugged. "Just tell them what you know. Let them decide. You know as well as I do that op at O'Malley's cabin was bound to go bad. The prosecution suspects there was more to it than that. They think Sowards might have conspired to have it go down the way it did. Might have set Liv up."

Ridge's jaw ached, a firm reminder of his own role in Liv's death. If Sowards was responsible, then so was he.

"Hey," Adam interrupted his thoughts. "There's nothing you could have done differently, Ridge. Don't beat yourself up over this, okay? And don't let the suits in that room tomorrow afternoon get under your skin."

Ridge sucked in a lungful of air. That would be easier said than done, he was sure.

"Look," Adam checked his watch and waved the waitress over. "I've got to get going, but before I do, how about a drink?"

Ridge nodded. Even under the circumstances it had to be better than staring at the gray-tone walls of an empty hotel room for the next fourteen hours.

"Bring us two glasses of Macallan, neat, would you?"

Ridge swallowed against the rock that took root beneath his sternum.

"I figured this is kind of a special occasion, right?" Adam asked.

"What? The chance to figure out why they destroyed her?" Ridge allowed a wry smile to twist the corners of his lips. "I guess it is."

"You wouldn't believe the change in the Bureau since they suspended him."

Ridge laughed, "If we're all the defense they have, it doesn't bode well for Sowards."

Adam smiled, but his eyes remained dark, pained. "You know the way this works, Ridge. In a courtroom, perception will always be more important than truth."

Ridge leaned back as the waitress placed the glass of amber liquid in front of him. It'd been six weeks since his last drink. He twisted the glass between his thumb and middle finger. A pang he'd come to recognize as loss thumped through his chest.

Adam held his glass in the air between them. "A toast. To old friends—and to Liv."

Ridge hoisted his highball. "To Liv." He knocked back the liquid, praying the burn of alcohol would numb the ever-present pain of grief.

7

LIV

The men seated at the conference table across from me shuffled papers, whispering amongst themselves while storm clouds thickened and billowed outside the plate glass windows behind them. Part of me knew I should be nervous. I'd told my side of the story. It was their turn to clarify anything they didn't understand, call into question my testimony. But the twitch of nervousness that accompanied me into the office that morning, had since vacated, leaving me with an overwhelming feeling of loneliness.

"Just a couple questions." The lead attorney's gaze bounced from his papers, to Michelle, before finally landing on me. "The first is simple. What is it you hope to gain by bringing these accusations against my client?"

I waited for the court reporter's fingers to stop, hovering, waiting. I twisted my fingers into a knot in my lap. The nervousness was back.

"Answers," I finally responded. "Sowards was responsible for the assets in the GenLink program. I want to know why he didn't do more to protect them. Why did he abduct Skylar McCaffrey? Was it just to get me to O'Malley's cabin?"

"There's no evidence my client abducted Miss McCaffrey."

"That doesn't mean it's not true." My chest tightened. Squeezed by the memory of Ridge's sister curled on the hand-sawn planks of O'Malley's cabin. The way she'd writhed and fought as Sowards held her down, prepping to plunge a syringe-full of Cam's drug into Skylar's delicate system. *She's fine, Liv*, I reminded myself. *She's home, exactly where she needs to be.* I breathed through the panic.

The panel of lawyers, dressed in uniform navy blue suits, exchanged glances.

"Miss...Sullivan, is it?" The lead attorney scrutinized me over his too small reading glasses.

"You know her name, Mr. Bishop," Michelle said, her own voice tight.

"You were in a relationship with former Special Agent Ridge McCaffrey, were you not?"

"I was."

"How would he feel if he knew you were here today?"

Instinct forced me to level a stare at the man across the conference table.

"What would he think?" Bishop leaned forward, voice low, threatening.

"What is this, Bill?" Michelle broke in. "These proceedings have nothing to do with the witness's personal life."

"Don't they? If the information I have regarding their relationship is accurate—and I believe it is—I have a hard time believing that Miss Sullivan would allow this length of time to go by without reconnecting with the man she admits is..." He rifled through the papers, stopping on one and reading, "...one of the main reasons I contacted the US Attorney's Office."

He looked at me, flopping his glasses onto the table in front of him. "What's changed, Miss Sullivan? Afraid he'll be able to tell you're not the *real* Olivia Sullivan?"

A smile broke at the corners of Mr. Bishop's lips as blood raged against my eardrums.

Michelle stood, leaning over the table, her finger pointed at the offending lawyer, while he aimed his smug smile at me. "This is blatant intimidation, Bill. Unless you have some kind of evidence to share, I suggest you strike your last comment from the record."

"Relax, Michelle. We aren't in a courtroom. This is an informal proceeding." He pushed a folder to our side of the table.

"What is this?" I watched her eyes skim the lines of text. I could make out the seal in the corner of the cover page–FBI Laboratory Division.

Mr. Bishop cleared his throat before continuing. "Defense submits that the witness claiming to be Miss Sullivan is not who she presents herself to be. This, in consideration of the fact that remains located at the site of the explosion have been positively identified as those of one Olivia Grace Sullivan, deceased."

"That's impossible." The words came without effort.

"Is it?" Bishop said. He looked relaxed, one arm draped over the back of the neighboring empty chair. "Science doesn't lie."

Michelle was looking at me now, eyes wide, accusatory. "I need a few moments with my client."

"Of course." Her gaze never left me as Sowards' team gathered their belongings and made their way out of the conference room.

She waited until silence settled. "What the hell is this?"

I fought the wave of panic induced tears that threatened at the backs of my eyes. "I don't know. He's lying."

"How, Olivia?" Michelle nearly screeched. She tucked her head to the side and checked herself, the next words quiet, deliberate. "They have remains, Liv." She pushed the paperwork toward me and pointed to the lab report. "A mandible. He's right. This isn't some woo-woo science. This is DNA. A jury will find it irrefutable. Do you understand?"

Even without my former abilities, it was clear Michelle was livid. Hate burned from her eyes.

"This is a criminal offense. You'll go to prison."

"You took blood samples when I got here. Can't you use them to disprove this?"

"How?" She read from the cover letter, "After further analysis, and with 99.9% accuracy, it is the opinion of this laboratory that the DNA extracted from remains uncovered at the site in question are indeed a match to the genetic profile of GenLink Asset #32, Olivia Grace Sullivan."

The air in the conference room felt heavy and thick. "This is retaliation, Michelle. It's Sowards' payback for dragging him under. What can I do?"

Michelle slid slowly back into her chair. "We'll bring the suits back in. I'll file a motion to have an independent lab review their findings."

"What about Ridge? What will they tell him?" Bishop's words still spun in my skull, *"What would he think?"*

Michelle's stare shot up to meet mine. "That's the least of your worries right now, Olivia. Go back to the hotel and don't move until you hear from me. Understood?"

"Understood." I sat in silence as the team filed in, their strides loose and cocky. Every step sent a pulse of rage through my core.

Michelle addressed the group. "For the record, Miss Sullivan refutes the defense's claim that she is not the same Olivia Sullivan who was attacked and left for dead by the defendant. Our motion to suppress this evidence until it can be verified by a third party lab will be forthcoming. In the meantime, Miss Sullivan will be exercising her fifth amendment rights and will not be answering any further questions this morning."

"Seems premature considering your client has not been accused of any crime." Bishop hesitated. "Yet." He pulled his eyes away from Michelle and onto me.

"Miss Sullivan, are you sure there's nothing you want to say? No message you'd like me to deliver to Special Agent McCaffrey?"

"Why are you doing this?"

"Liv, not now," Michelle cut in. Her fingers wrapped around my forearm in an angry clench.

I jerked away. "Ridge has nothing to do with this. He wasn't in the cabin that night. And you know those remains don't belong to Liv Sullivan. Sowards knows I'm alive and he'll do what it takes to end me, just like he did last November."

"That's it. This meeting is over." Desperation crept into Michelle's voice. She left her seat and opened the door, a firm signal that no more words were to be spoken.

I stared at the glossy table. The reflection of Bill Bishop, the last to leave, leaned down, his voice a whisper as he passed my chair. "My client is a powerful man, Miss Sullivan. If he'd wanted you dead, you would be."

I TROTTED down the steps from the Department of Justice, sucking in a breath of the spring breeze, pregnant with the second wave of the impending storm. I stepped around a sleeping homeless man on the sidewalk, a sign propped against his knee that read, "Help me get my life back."

I paused and dug a couple ones from the bottom of my purse and tucked them into his hand. He roused, tired eyes combing over me as the, "Thank you," rolled off his tongue. I smiled and carried on, ignoring the ever-present company of Evan and Tony lurking a few feet behind. My eyes shifted to the nearby subway entrance. I could make it if I was fast enough. I walked faster, the first tears shooting to the backs of my eyes. I launched into a run as Tony swung forward, a human wall in the path of my escape route. He gripped my arm, pulled me to face him as the first droplets of rain landed in cool splats against my face.

"Now's not the time to be careless."

I shoved Tony away as Evan came close, his back to us as he scoured the surroundings. "Don't you get it? Everything I came back for, Sowards is stripping it away. Michelle doesn't even believe me. I should have stayed locked up in my grandmother's cottage, Tony. This isn't what I wanted."

"You knew what to expect going in," Tony said, his voice firm but gentle. "Regaining a life comes with a price."

"I'm tired of hiding, Tony. I don't just want *a* life–I want *my* life."

Thunder ricocheted through the sky, cold pellets of rain slicing across exposed skin. The downpour erupted around us as I squinted up at Tony, jerking my arm from his grip.

"Liv?" The voice pierced the pounding hum of the rain. The familiar baritone sunk through me, pulling like taffy at emotions I'd stuffed away for the last seven months.

Breath caught in my chest and Tony shoved me to the side, shielding me from the man on the sidewalk, but his name came anyway, a breath on my lips, "Ridge."

Evan jerked the hood of my raincoat up and over my face.

His hand planted over my mouth. Hard hands shoved me toward the waiting sedan.

"Olivia Sullivan?" Ridge spoke again. Louder, closer this time. I fought against Evan's unyielding hold. The fabric of my rain-slicked coat added a layer of protection against the bodyguard's reach as I paused, taking in the man on the sidewalk.

Ridge stood frozen to the pavement. The umbrella he carried hung haphazardly from one hand, no longer shielding him from the pelting rain. Evan's grip tightened, his palm pressing on the top of my head, forcing me into the Lincoln and shutting me inside. I pulled at the silver handles, screaming and cursing at the impenetrable child locked doors.

I watched through the darkened window as Tony approached Ridge, made a comment I couldn't hear, and turned away, striding purposefully toward the driver's side door.

Ridge stepped back. The crease between his dark brows etched in concern—or maybe confusion. His eyes, the same blue that haunted my dreams fixed on the passenger window of the car—on me—as the sedan pulled away from the curb with a screech.

The whole interaction couldn't have lasted more than a few seconds, Evan pushing me to the car, shielding my face while Tony intercepted Ridge. My breath was still coming in short huffs when I spoke, breaking through the heavy silence as we pulled into the underground parking garage of the Marriott.

"Go back." The words were barely audible. I repeated them louder. "You have to go back."

"Not a chance." Tony turned in his seat to face me. "Remember what I said out there, Liv. This is just the beginning. If Sowards can find a way to hurt you, he will. That includes going after McCaffrey."

I lurched toward Tony. "Why would you say that?"

Evan and Tony shared a veiled glance as Tony turned back around. "Poor choice of words, Liv. I didn't mean anything by it. But I do have experience. And experience tells me McCaffrey is safer if he thinks you're dead."

8

RIDGE

Ridge stood in the street, the chill of the rain soaking through his jacket and onto his skin, just as it had the night he lost Liv. The hiss of the cars in the street threaded into the background as the scene replayed in his memory. Her hair, longer than he remembered, but undoubtedly her.

The way she spun to face the man, her chin tipped upward in defiance. He'd born witness to that very expression more than once in their time together. He'd been too far away to see the color of her eyes, but from a distance, the almond shape of them was the same.

He pulled his collar up around his neck and walked toward the steps leading to the Department of Justice building, dragging his gaze away from the taillights of the black sedan as it disappeared down the block and around the corner. Instinct burned the license plate numbers into the back of his mind.

"You're a lunatic, McCaffrey," he mumbled to himself, ignoring the urge to text Adam right then and there, have him run the plate. His mumbling caught the attention of the homeless man huddled under the stairwell. Ridge paused as the man nodded. Some unspoken brotherhood he wasn't sure he wanted to share.

"You ever see that woman here before?" Ridge asked gesturing to the sidewalk where he thought he'd seen Liv.

The man's soft brown eyes squinted into focus.

Ridge shook his head. "Sorry. Here." He pulled two fifties from his wallet and folded them into the man's hand. "Get yourself a room. It's supposed to rain all afternoon and evening." Ridge slipped from the stairwell and started up the steps. Stopping, on second thought, to pass off his umbrella to the already drenched man.

It wasn't her. It couldn't have been. The thoughts ran on a loop through his mind. This certainly wasn't the first time he'd sworn he'd seen her. The first time was less than a week after her death. He'd been driving from Murphy's Pub to his apartment. The woman had been walking along the side of the road. He'd turned around and driven by twice. The second time by she'd stopped walking and faced his slow moving coupe, yelling obscenities from a mouth that, at close distance, bore no resemblance to Liv's.

Four steps up, he heard the drifter's voice. "Wait."

Ridge turned to face the older man, dingy skin mapped by deep lines, the needleless tattoo of years spent on the street.

"That lady you're askin' about? She gives me two bucks every day. Enough for a coffee. But it's not what ya think."

Ridge took the steps slowly, returning to the sidewalk. "What is it I think?"

The man's lips curled into a smile revealing a row of shockingly white teeth. "Most people don't see me, but I see them," he said. "You? You're the protector type. Right? The fixer?" He paused, but Ridge didn't answer. "Don't worry, he ain't gonna hurt her. Been here every day for the past ten days or so. Those dudes are her muscle."

"Protective detail?"

The man shrugged, matter-of-fact. "Way I see it."

"What for? Do you know who she is?"

"I look like I'm up on current events?" the man shot back before stooping to gather his belongings.

Ridge stuck a hand up in apology. "I appreciate the information." He started up the steps again before giving voice to the question gnawing his insides raw. "Just one more thing. You said she gave you money?"

"That's right."

"Did you happen to notice the color of her eyes?"

The skin around the man's eyes crinkled and his lips pulled back into another grin. "That's an easy one. Green. Color of the grass at Arlington."

A knot of something–hope, fear, loss, excitement–or a combination of all four punched its way into Ridge's chest.

"Can I go now?" The man asked, as if he needed Ridge's permission to leave.

Ridge nodded. "Of course."

The man walked away, raising a hand in farewell. "Thanks for the room," he hollered above the hush of rain against wet pavement.

Ridge stood motionless, a buzz of uncertainty crawling through his veins. *Ten days.* He said he'd seen her every day for the last ten days. Logic battled the well-spring of hope that unleashed in his gut. *You've done this before,* his inner critic reminded. *You're imagining things. Just like you imagined the girl on the road or the woman at Starbucks last month. Let it go, McCaffrey. Liv's gone.*

Ridge glanced down at his shoes, wet and rooted to his spot on the pavement. *"Sorry sir, I'm sure you're mistaken.*" The bodyguard's words played on a loop through his mind.

He gripped the handrail, forcing uncooperative feet up the steps of the DOJ building. The soaking downpour cooled the sizzle of white hot hope, a prelude to dull reality.

"YOU'RE EARLY." The first words out of Michelle Rogers' mouth when he pressed open her office door was almost as telling as the pull of barely restrained panic in her pale eyes.

"I grabbed a bite of lunch near the Mall, was hoping to make it inside before the rain started," Ridge said, shaking his jacket over the umbrella stand inside the doorway.

"Looks like you didn't make it."

"Not even close," Ridge said, forcing a smile. "Thought I'd just wait here until the suits were ready for me. I can leave if it's a problem."

"It's no problem. The suits, as you call them, took a break for lunch, but you're up next when they return."

Ridge hung his coat and focused on the woman in front of him. A woman whose tells proved she knew more than she was letting on. "May I ask you a question, Ms. Rogers?"

Michelle nodded, her eyes narrowing on Ridge.

"Why was the inquiry against Sowards filed?"

"I'm not sure what you mean." Michelle propped herself on the edge of the massive desk, crossing her arms over her chest.

"I just mean, did someone come forward with information? Accusations against Sowards?"

The corner of her mouth tipped into a hesitant smile. "It was an internal investigation. The end of any Bureau program, particularly one that went down in a blaze of glory like GenLink, warrants an inquiry. It's protocol. You know that."

"And the inquiry turned up what? Procedural offenses?" He was fishing, and by the twitch at the corners of Rogers' mouth, she knew it.

"Some. But our investigation focuses more on the human side of things." Michelle slid into a chair. She looked tired.

Ridge could feel her eyes on him as he walked toward the window and looked out onto the sidewalk below. "The assets—like Liv."

Michelle nodded. "Liv. And the others."

Ridge adjusted the chain around his neck, fingering the Claddagh ring he'd found in the cooling rubble of O'Malley's cabin. He pressed it hard against his sternum. "They never found her, you know. Liv's remains."

Michelle sucked in a breath in the quiet of the room.

Ridge turned to face her. "Did you know the human body incinerates at between fourteen hundred and eighteen hundred degrees Fahrenheit?"

He waited for the lawyer to shake her head.

"Gold melts at nineteen hundred and forty-eight degrees." He pulled the chain from underneath his shirt and let it drop against his chest. Michelle's eyes caught on the Claddagh. "There were accelerants at the cabin. But you've got to admit, not a lot of wiggle room there."

"The ring was Liv's?" Michelle asked.

Ridge nodded.

"Look. I'm sorry for your loss, Ridge. Truly. I know what it's like to lose someone you love. It's one of the reasons I took this case. I'm doing everything in my power to make things right."

Ridge let his lips tip into a smile before turning back to the window. "Sometimes I think I see her—in a crowd, at a bus station..."

Michelle moved from her chair and propped herself against the front edge of the massive desk.

"Even on the sidewalk outside of this building." Ridge turned in time to see Michelle swallow, her hand dropping to her side.

"Our brains have a funny way of mocking us sometimes," she said.

Ridge fixed his eyes on hers. She was doing a damned good job trying not to appear nervous. But not that good. They were still standing there, facing each other when a parade of navy-blue suited lawyers pushed through the door, voices loud and grating.

A white-haired gentleman stopped as the rest of the team disappeared through the door of the adjoining conference room.

"You must be Special Agent McCaffrey," he said, extending his hand. "Bill Bishop, lead attorney for Special Agent in Charge Marcus Sowards. My client has had good things to say about you. Pleasure to make your acquaintance."

Ridge bit back the venom that clotted at the back of his throat and shook the man's hand.

"Are you ready to get this business over with?" Bill asked with an unaffected smile that stoked the brew of hatred in Ridge's chest.

"I've never been more ready."

9

LIV

Evan's hand wrapped around my upper arm in a hard grip as he pushed me into the basement elevator in the parking structure of the Marriott.

"I need to see Ridge." I pulled against him. "He needs to hear the truth from me." My fingers clawed at Evan's thick digits, working to loosen their bruising impact on the flesh of my bicep.

"Take it easy," Tony said to Evan as the doors closed.

"We have our orders," Evan responded through gritted teeth.

"Our orders don't include injury, Thurber." Tony laid a hand on Evan's arm, his gaze laser focused on his partner.

Evan released me and I moved to the far corner of the elevator, rubbing the assaulted arm.

"You okay?" Tony asked, his eyes softened as the elevator doors opened onto the sixth floor. Evan brushed past and into the hall, scanning, as usual, for whatever threat he was trained to see.

"I'll be better if I never have to see him again." I jutted my chin in Evan Thurber's direction as he scouted the empty hall ahead of me and Tony.

"I'll put in a word with Michelle. See what we can do. In the meantime, try to forget what happened today, okay? It'll only cause more harm. Michelle will figure this out. She's good at what she does."

I shook my head against the anger boiling up inside and tucked my head low, pushing into my room and closing the door before Tony could work his way inside.

"Liv," he said from the other side. "You know we need to do a device check. It's important. Especially tonight."

"Tonight, I need to be alone. If you want to protect me, get rid of Thurber." My blame was misplaced, but it was the only thing in my control.

I could hear Tony sigh on the other side of the door. "You couldn't have predicted this, Liv. No one could."

"I should have told him." I rested my forehead against the interior of the door. "Long before now. It shouldn't have happened this way."

"Liv." He didn't follow it up with anything, but I could tell he was still there.

"Get something to eat, Tony. I'm in for the night."

I lifted my head to focus on the fisheye perspective of the hallway. Tony and Evan headed toward the bank of elevators, each of them checking the almost imperceptible cameras they'd installed when we arrived.

I turned away as the two men disappeared. The image of Ridge danced in my consciousness. Rivulets of rain dampening his mahogany hair, grown out just a touch from the last time I'd seen him. His eyes stunned wide with awe, maybe disbelief. I should have fought back, pulled out of Evan's grip, wriggled away from the veil of that raincoat hood.

I shrugged out of the confining garment and tossed it onto

the floor. Following it down, I sunk onto the plush carpeting with my back against the door. *Why hadn't I fought back?* I growled through a knot of frustration. Ridge hadn't been the only one in a state of shock.

The possibility of passing Ridge on his way to his own deposition had registered in my brain when Michelle confirmed he was on the list. But the likelihood of it, especially considering the careful scheduling of my day to day activities, seemed unlikely ... impossible even. But he *had* seen me. And I couldn't pretend it didn't happen.

Chances were high Sowards' team would fill Ridge in on the details, and what would they say? Tell him there was a woman impersonating Liv and making false accusations against his former boss? That's exactly what they'd say.

I slipped the government issued cell phone from my pocket and opened a search window, typing in, "How many hotels are in the greater DC area?"

If the US Attorney's Office had made the arrangements, Ridge's hotel wouldn't be far. And today, he'd been walking.

A hot spike of anxiety pushed up my spine, ending in a tingle at the base of my skull as I skimmed the list on my phone. The name of the Marriott was third on the list. What if he was here? Sleeping under the same roof? And instead of going after him, I was sitting in damp clothes on the floor of my suite, feeling sorry for myself and hating Sowards even more than I'd hated him that morning–if that was possible.

Tony was right. Seeing Ridge could be dangerous. Sowards wasn't above hurting others to get what he wanted. That was clear. And pulling Ridge in gave Sowards another target. But knowing he was close and not being able to see him caused an ache in my chest that rivaled the pain of O'Malley's drug. I needed Ridge to hear the truth. And I needed him to hear it from me.

I pulled myself off the floor and picked up the room's telephone receiver. My index finger trembled as I pressed the zero.

"Front desk, this is Stefanie, how can I help you, Miss Allyn?"

"Hi, Stefanie. I'm expecting a friend from out of town," I lied, "and I was hoping you could tell me if he'd arrived yet."

"Of course. What's the name?"

My throat closed. Breath trapped in my lungs.

"Miss Allyn?"

I closed my eyes, forcing a stream of air through tight lips. "McCaffrey. Ridge McCaffrey." His name grated over my tongue, settling into caramel.

The click of keys peppered the silence of the line as she typed his name into the computer. "Ah. Here he is. Room 362. Would you like me to connect you?"

"No." The word came out too fast—too forceful. I backpedaled. "No, that's okay. I'll touch base with him later. Thank you."

I dropped the receiver into its cradle. How was I going to explain any of this? Up to now, I'd convinced myself I wouldn't have to. I'd been living in a dream world where he'd only find out if I got my life back on track. But now I was backed into a corner.

Maybe he was sitting in Michelle's conference room right now, listening to Sowards' team tell him their version of the truth. And if they did, he'd hate me for it. Clarity reared its ugly head. Even if he believed I was Liv Sullivan, how could he not hate me? I should have called him from the back room of McGill's Pub. Why hadn't I? That question circled my mind like a buzzard.

Keeping my existence a secret—for any reason—was an unforgivable offense. And now he'd be forced to decide whether the woman in front of him was telling the truth or claiming to be someone she's not for some nefarious purpose. I wasn't sure I'd ever be able to fully explain how I ended up here, willing to spend the rest of my life in hiding if it meant punishing Sowards. But one thing was clear. It was time to do this on my terms.

Ghosts, and the memories of them, would no longer dictate the direction of my life. I'd come back to the States to convict Sowards–to make things right for the assets that came before me. And if I could no longer regain some semblance of a life for myself, the least I could do was make sure Ridge knew the truth. I'd earned that chance. I only hoped I wasn't too late.

10

RIDGE

Ridge lay on the hotel room bed, staring at the television screen. He had no idea what show was on. Didn't care. He was satisfied with the mindless white noise as he replayed the afternoon's deposition. It had lasted a little more than an hour. Question after question about Liv's disappearance, Skylar's survival, and his role in it all. Not once did any question verge on the possibility that Liv may still be alive. Instead, the meeting had been a not-so-gentle reminder that if different decisions had been made, Liv would still be alive.

"Where were you when the team moved in on the cabin, Agent McCaffrey?" The lawyer's question seeped through his memory, nullifying what small bit of peace he'd been able to conjure up over the past half year. And as far as he could tell, neither side of the legal team was taking the possibility that Sowards had been using Cam—just as he'd used Liv—seriously. Yet another reason his dad was right when he'd told him not to get involved. It only bred frustration.

Ridge allowed the memory of Liv's death to play out in

his mind, the familiar pangs of guilt now somehow comforting. But this time the images were interrupted by flashes of the woman he'd seen on the street that afternoon. The barely perceptible kernel of guilt he'd watched fester in Michelle when he confronted her. Neither brought him any peace.

Seven months ago he should have gone in O'Malley's cabin with the rest of the team. And today he'd told the lawyers as much. To hell with the promises he'd made to Adam and Sowards. Liv had counted on him and he'd let her down in the worst way possible. He'd left her entombed with a killer.

Even today, whether what he'd seen playing out on the street was real or not, he should have intervened. Asked more questions. Demanded to see the face of the woman they'd shoved into that car. It wasn't enough he spent every day reliving Liv's death, now he'd be regurgitating this scenario right along with it.

Liv's face danced in his subconscious, his last memories of her from the recordings O'Malley had streamed. Images meant only for him—hair matted with blood, eyes red-rimmed from drugs and abuse—that now would be shared with both legal teams and a jury. Even in death he couldn't protect her.

He spun Liv's ring around the tip of his little finger. The chain wrapped around his wrist like a snake—circling, releasing—hanging suspended between the gold band and mattress.

He slipped the chain back into place around his neck and grabbed his phone, punching in Adam's number.

"How'd it go today?" Adam asked, his tone a touch too jovial for Ridge's current mental state.

"Fine," Ridge managed. "I need a favor."

"Anything, brother. What is it?"

"I need you to run a plate for me."

There was hesitation on Adam's end of the line. "Mind if I ask, why?"

"Nothing." Ridge did his best to sound underwhelmed. "Curiosity, really. Can you help me out?"

After a lengthy pause, Adam's voice finally cut through the line. "Sure. Of course. What's the number?"

Ridge rattled off the combination of six letters and numbers he'd committed to memory. "How long you think it'll take?"

"Just owner information? Give me a couple minutes. You wanna hang on the line?"

Adam yammered on about the Bureau, the trial, and his own deposition, before growing silent.

"What is it?" Ridge asked.

"Where'd you say you got this plate number?"

"Saw it on the road. Who's it belong to?"

"It's a black MKZ registered to the US Attorney's Office. They've got a whole fleet of them."

"Any way to tell who's assigned to this particular car?"

"That information is internal. I don't have access to their fleet records."

"Right. Thanks anyway, Adam." Ridge sensed Adam's uncertainty and hung up before he could ask any more questions. It's not like he had the answers anyway. A car registered by the US Attorney's office parked outside the DOJ. No crime there. Not even suspicious. Ridge groaned and laid back against the stack of pillows.

Ridge was running through yet another self-deprecating scenario when the knock sounded on his door a few minutes later. He lifted his head and swung his legs to the floor. He'd declined Adam's earlier dinner offer and called less than ten minutes ago for room service. *That was fast,* he thought, grateful for the distraction as he dug his wallet out of his back pocket, pulling a few bills out to give to the server.

He didn't bother looking up as he swung the door inward, propping it open with his knee.

"That was qui–" Ridge's sentence cut short by the black-suited man filling the doorway.

"Expecting someone, Agent McCaffrey?" The man's brows lifted as Ridge stepped backward into the room.

"You were on the street today." Ridge said, scouring the man in front of him for signs of intent. His eyes were dark, full of purpose, but not malice.

"Name's Medici, Tony. I work for Ms. Rogers. May I come in?"

Ridge's breath hung tight in his chest, aching with the swirl of possibility and pain. Ridge pushed the door open wide and stepped out of the way as Tony entered. He glanced around the room, a well-practiced skim of his surroundings. Ridge couldn't help but wonder what he was looking for.

"First of all, Ms. Rogers wants to offer her sincere thanks for your candor this afternoon. She knows it wasn't easy for you." Tony turned to face Ridge.

"I was called by the defense," Ridge said. A bead of irritation seeping into his voice.

Tony cocked his head to the side, studying. His mouth crooked into a lopsided smile. "I know." He hesitated a beat before thumbing to the nearby easy chair. "Mind if I sit?"

"Only if you plan to tell me why you're really here."

Tony's grin broke into a full-fledged smile, complete with chuckle. "Really? That's what you want to ask me?" He groaned as he eased into the low-backed chair.

Ridge played the question in his mind before lending it voice, knowing full well how crazy he sounded. "Liv's here, isn't she? She's alive."

"That's better," Tony said. "I was beginning to think you

might disappoint me." He dug a hand into the inside of his jacket and pulled out a pack of gum.

Tony peeled the end from the unopened Big Red package and tossed it into the wastebasket before folding a stick into his mouth and offering the pack to Ridge.

Ridge shook his head.

Tony gestured to the desk chair a few feet away. "You should maybe sit."

Ridge did as Tony asked, skimming his fingers along the beveled edge of the Queen Anne style desk as he lowered in front of it.

"The short answer to your question is yes. But I think you already knew that considering she called downstairs to get your room number this afternoon."

"She's in this hotel?" The words came through Ridge's lips, but the pounding pulse behind his eardrums drowned out the sound.

Tony leaned forward, elbows on his knees, fingers laced. His eyes planted firmly on Ridge for any sign of deception. "You mean to tell me she has not contacted you? Not by phone, text, or any other means since you've been in DC"

The tremor started in Ridge's right hand and he rubbed it against the thigh of his khakis, hoping the burn of friction would stall the progression of the impending panic attack. When that didn't work, he tightened his fingers into a fist. "What makes you think she'd want to see me?"

A streak of some emotion flicked across Tony's face—sorrow, regret maybe.

"I only ever let her down."

"Maybe. But she begged me to turn back today. After we saw you on the sidewalk. You deserve to know that much."

"Why are you telling me any of this?"

"Because Sowards is retaliating against Liv's testimony. We

need to make sure we have all our loose ends accounted for, if you know what I mean."

"How?" Ridge asked.

"Pardon?"

"How is Sowards retaliating?"

Tony was silent.

"Fair enough." Ridge knew when to cut his losses. "So, you thought–" The words stung. They thought she'd contacted him, maybe even arranged to see him. But she hadn't. Which could only mean one thing–Liv didn't *want* to see him.

"Don't beat yourself up, McCaffrey. There could be a thousand reasons why she hasn't called."

"Right," Ridge huffed through a forced smile. "Seven months isn't long enough."

"Look, Rogers is with her now. She scheduled a meeting with an intake rep from WITSEC. By this time tomorrow, Liv Sullivan won't exist and you can pretend I never showed up here tonight."

"Wait. You're not with WITSEC?"

"Nah," Tony stood, hesitating a moment. "Independent contractor."

"So you just showed up to tell me the woman I believed to be dead for the last seven months is very much alive, but I can't see her, and she doesn't want to see me?" Ridge tamped down the threat of anger bubbling in his gut.

Tony shrugged and popped his gum. "Can't get on board with that last assumption, but the first two are true enough. Rogers asked me to make sure she hadn't contacted you."

Ridge worked the buzz of anxiety from his hand while Tony eyed him, brushing past and heading for the door.

"I need to see her." Ridge brought his gaze up to meet Tony's. "Just once."

"My job is to make sure she's safe, Agent McCaffrey.

Allowing her to see you is a risk to you both. None of us want a repeat of what happened last fall."

Tony's words registered. "I'm not a threat to her."

"This is a legal decision."

"Because of whatever Sowards is doing?"

Tony stared him down without an answer.

"You know what haunts me the most about last fall?" Ridge asked.

Tony stopped, mid-reach for the door handle.

"It's not the scent from the blast or the heat of the flames, it's what I said to her the last time we were together."

"What was that?" Tony's voice was quiet, reflective. Ridge detected the note of regret floating just beneath the surface of the bodyguard's rough exterior.

"I drove to her mom's to say my goodbyes after Sowards' ultimatum. Either way, I was damned if I left and damned if I didn't. Breaking up would at least give her a chance to live life without the constant meddling of the government. She deserved that." Ridge skimmed both palms down his thighs and sat up, taking in the other man in the room. "Still does."

Tony dropped his head.

"Anyway, my dad called, interrupted us. That's when I found out Skylar was missing. But Liv and I weren't finished. I needed more time. She needed to know I loved her. So I said, 'We'll finish this.' Those are the words I replay in my mind. 'We'll finish this.' My last words, one more promise I failed to keep."

"You had no way of knowing what would happen."

"No." Ridge shrugged, his gaze finding Tony's. "But I could have taken her with me. If I had she never would have been in that hotel, never ended up—"

Ridge paused. The memory of watching another man's hands on Liv's skin, the slice of leather across her back, invaded. The word, *raped*, swam in his skull. But he didn't know how much Tony knew. Ridge wasn't about to share that pain with a stranger. Instead, he took a breath and shook the word away.

"Imprisoned?" Tony finished instead.

Ridge nodded. "One tiny insignificant choice. We make a million of them every day. That one changed my life–and hers–forever."

Tony's phone buzzed from his pocket. He pulled it out and glanced at the screen. "I've gotta take this."

Ridge motioned him away and rose from the chair. The slight buzz of the staved off panic attack tingled through his arm as he walked toward the window. He ignored the click of the hotel room door as Tony exited. But the commotion that followed, swift footsteps, the rumble of loud voices, the *thump* of something heavy against the hallway wall not far from his door, was impossible to ignore.

I struggled to put myself in Ridge's shoes. If he'd died in the M.E.'s office and reappeared months later, out of the blue, what would my reaction have been? Anger? Betrayal? Fear? Love? The possibilities swirled in my brain. But I was out of time. That became clear when Sowards' team passed a doctored lab file across the table this morning.

I could play the ostrich—stick my head in the sand and pretend I was okay with Ridge believing I was a fraud. I could convince myself he'd moved on. Had a new life. I could even pretend it was out of my control. But those were choices the old me would have made. And I was done being the victim.

The decisions I'd made since waking up in my grandmother's cottage were far from perfect. And I'd gladly start over. Worry less about revenge and focus more on rebuilding the only piece of my life that mattered. But that opportunity had passed. Now, I could either hide or make right what little I could.

I finger-combed my hair and twisted the shower-damp curls

into soft waves. Staring at the reflection, I wondered if Ridge would see the same tired, scared, heartbroken woman who stared back at me. So much had changed since I started this journey.

I wasn't the same woman who'd driven Route 33 across three states to help find Ridge's sister. But there was equal comfort in the fact that I doubted he was the same man who'd left me in his rearview mirror, pretending the decision he made was best for me.

I flipped the bathroom light switch and grabbed the door handle, jerking it open. The hall was quiet. The ever-lurking presence of Evan and Tony conspicuously absent. But the button eyes of the cameras were still there–watching. I made my way toward the bank of elevators. My heartbeat outpaced my steps, the hope I might be able to make it to the third floor without interference, thundering in my chest. I shoved my knuckle onto the down button and waited while the illuminated numbers above the door ticked upward.

I felt Evan before he appeared from the opposite side of the hall. The claustrophobic clutch in my lungs the first signal I was no longer alone. A phenomenon I'd once attributed to psychometry but now realized was just a normal sensory capability.

"What are you doing here?" I asked.

"I could ask you the same thing," he said, planting his size twelves a touch too close as the elevator doors slid open.

Michelle stepped forward. A few strands of her hair tipped down over her left eye as she reached to stop the mechanical doors from sliding closed too soon. Her glance rebounded from Evan to me before she stepped out of the metal box and waited for it to disappear.

"Going somewhere?" she finally asked.

"Thought I'd go down to the bar for a bit." The lie came out practiced, believable.

Michelle nodded. "I could use a drink myself," she said. A hint of tired discomfort colored her voice. She nodded toward the hall, her hand on my shoulder guiding me away from the elevator and toward the corridor of empty rooms. "But let's order in. We need to talk about what happened today."

I followed Michelle. Evan fell in step behind us, expecting me to bolt, I was sure. The lawyer talked—Michelle was good at that—telling me she'd set up a meeting with an intake counselor from WITSEC first thing tomorrow morning.

"It's time," she finished, stopping a few feet from my hotel room door. "Sowards is coming on strong. You know that. We need to get this lab report under control, figure out how—"

"Do you trust me?" I asked, cutting Michelle off mid-sentence.

Her silence was all the answer I needed.

She sighed. "We can't wait any longer, Liv. I've given you as much time as I can. Remember, we're doing this for your own safety."

I pretended to dig in my pocket for my room key, shifting my feet closer to the fire exit a few feet behind me.

"What difference does WITSEC make if Liv Sullivan is already dead?" I pulled the keycard free and handed it to Michelle. Her gaze met mine.

"This is the process. You know that."

I waited until she turned toward the door and shuffled backward one final step. The cold steel of the door pressed hard, unyielding against the small of my back. With as much momentum as I dared, I shoved the exit door open—and ran.

I'd only made it to the second of six flights of stairs, two for each floor, before Evan's footfalls echoed in the cement surround. I extended my leaps from three steps to four, praying not to twist an ankle.

Michelle's and Evan's voices tangled in the percussive space, angry and uncertain. And with them, doubt. Evan's heavy footsteps closed the gap between us, gaining momentum as we neared the third floor landing. He reached out with a grunt, his fingers grazing my shoulder. I leaped away, glancing back as he landed on all fours in the landing. The swing of the fire door muffled his curse as I blasted into the third floor hall.

My lungs burned, a reminder that I hadn't fully healed from the side effects of O'Malley's version of truth serum. The incessant need to cough came next, and I doubled over just as a man and woman exited their room a few doors from the bank of elevators. They paused, looking me up and down while I sucked in jagged lungfuls of air, struggling to stifle the coughing fit.

I glanced at their room number, 326. Ridge's should be down the hall and around the corner, one of the last, if the back-of-the-door fire escape plan was an accurate representation.

I listened for Evan as the strangers disappeared toward the elevators. He was walking now. And he'd waited for Michelle. I could tell by his slowed breath. But he wasn't far behind. His voice echoed low in the corridor. A one-sided phone conversation.

Michelle's voice broke in alongside his. "Tell him to stay there. Watch for her. Don't let her go in. We'll figure it out."

I huffed on, launching into a modified sprint to the end of the hall and around the corner. Maybe if I hadn't been breathing so hard I'd have heard Evan come up from behind. But instead, I only felt the jerk as his fist tightened in my hair, yanking me backward.

Tony's concerned expression as he exited a room at the end of the hall flickered in my line of sight before Evan's grip moved from my hair to my arm, propelling me sideways and thumping me face first against the nearest wall–one door away from Ridge.

12

RIDGE

The unmistakable *thunk* of a body. The involuntary exhale of someone having the wind knocked out of them–female, if Ridge had to guess–was audible even from the window side of his hotel room.

"Christ, Evan, watch yourself." Tony's voice, loud and unmistakable, filtered from under the doorway as Ridge moved toward the door. "She's not the enemy."

Tightness gripped Ridge's chest and he pushed the desk chair out of his way, toppling it to the floor as he brushed past.

"This was your choice, Olivia." The words stopped him cold–the chill of the metal door handle colliding with the heat of his fingers sent a spiral of anxiety up his spine.

"You knew there'd be consequences. You can't change your mind now. It's too late."

Ridge pushed the balloon of air from his lungs and rested his forehead against the faux wood veneer above the peephole. He forced reason to join the ranks of uncontrollable hope that swelled in his chest.

"No one ever said this would be easy," Michelle continued. Only she and Tony were visible from Ridge's fishbowl view.

"Let. Me. Go." That voice, those words punctuated by restorative breath, stole every fiber of logic from Ridge's body. He swung the door open and stepped into the hall.

His breath caught as he met her gaze. *Real. Tangible. Here.* A thump of blood rushed against his eardrums, silenced by the breath of her name sliding across his lips. "Liv."

"McCaffrey—" There was a warning note in Tony's voice, and Ridge was suddenly aware of himself moving toward the second bodyguard.

The man's hands—the same ones that had forced her away and into the sedan that afternoon—gripped the soft flesh of Liv's arm. She twisted against the bite of his fingers as the bile of hatred bubbled through Ridge's core.

"Take your hands off her," Ridge said, words muffled by the clench in his jaw.

The bodyguard's brown eyes checked in with Michelle and Tony before dropping his lock on Liv. No one moved. The silence of the hall caved in. Ridge dragged his gaze back to the woman he'd mourned for the last seven months. The thump behind his eardrums surged and the corridor walls blurred—breathing to life.

He forced an exhale and reached for the metal trim around his hotel room door. Something solid to steady himself as the first barbs of panic cut in at the base of his neck and traveled down his right arm. It was too much. There were too many people. Not enough air. His eyes danced, skimming from one body to another. All with some form of shocked trepidation streaked across their face.

Michelle was the one to finally speak. "Fine. I suppose we owe you this much," she aimed her words at Liv, but she hadn't moved. Hadn't taken her eyes off Ridge since he'd stepped out into the hall. "But you have one hour. You know what's next."

Liv dipped her chin once, waiting while Tony ushered the group down the hall and around the corner. Ridge blinked and pressed his shoulder against the doorframe, bracing against the emerald eyes staring back at him. His heart jumped as she stepped closer, pounding an uneven arrhythmia in his chest. Porcelain skin, with a spatter of freckles across the bridge of her nose. Long auburn curls kissed by the sun.

"Should we go inside?" Her voice sent a knot of unwelcome emotion to the back of his throat.

He closed his eyes tight, fighting the tickle of paranoia that unwound from deep in his brain. *She's dead.* His mind replayed the explosion. *It's a delusion*, the voice said, an echo of words his shrink had used more than once. *This can happen when you're under stress.*

He forced an even exhale and nodded, opening his eyes. She was still there. Close enough to touch. The sudden ache to feel her pulsed through him. His hand shook as he pulled the keycard from his back pocket, jamming it against the front of the lock. A red light blinked defiantly at him.

"Here, let me." Liv slipped the card from his hand and hovered the rectangle of plastic just above the sensor until a mechanical click registered in the silence, the green light fully lit as she pushed the door inward and stepped through.

Ridge stood in the doorway. His eyes locked on the woman now standing in his room. The gentle part of her full lips. The sloping curve of her jawline. The soft twists of her hair. She slid the keycard onto the credenza, turned to face him. She hadn't changed. She was the embodiment of the memories he allowed to play out in the quiet of the dark. Except now, she was here.

Liv looked away, toward the floor, scuffing the toe of her

tennis shoe across the burgundy carpet. "I don't really have a speech prepared." She sucked in a jagged breath. Her lungs still recovering from whatever happened in the hall. "Please say something."

Her voice was a punch to the gut, unleashing hot ribbons of emotion. Pleasant waves of relief warred with the slicing knife of blame. Suddenly aware that he was shaking his head, he forced himself still. He stepped to the side, waiting for the door to swing closed sealing them alone–together.

"I heard you hit the wall. Are you okay?" He could already see the slight oval of pink developing along her cheekbone.

She nodded, pressing her fingers against her cheek. "Evan gets a little carried away sometimes. But he's harmless."

Harmless. The word echoed. Of course. Nothing like what she'd already been through–what he'd put her through. The reminder forced him back a step. Another beat of silence passed between them before a single tear cut loose from her eye, skimming down her cheek to her jawline. He reached to brush it away, but hesitated, and she palmed it away herself– hard and unyielding against her bruised cheek. Fingers of skepticism climbed through him, tempered by the ache of loss.

"I'm so sorry I wasn't the one to tell you. I never wanted to wait this long." Her eyes drifted downward again, and she tucked the corner of her lower lip between her teeth.

He couldn't stop watching. The muscles in his core tightened, a reminder of the nights they'd spent tangled in each other's arms. She released the hold on her lip and his gaze gravitated to it, ripe and swollen.

"Can I touch you?" It was all he could think of to say.

Her eyes sparked up to meet his, a barely perceptible nod.

He reached out a hand and she stepped into him. Tucking her cheek against the curve of his palm. A suck of air caught in his chest, pressing hard against the knot of resentment he'd carried since November. His fingers trembled against the warmth of her skin. Pinpricks of panic disintegrating. A second tear slipped from her eye. The wetness of it on the pad of his thumb tangible proof of her existence.

He folded her into him in a slow dance, tangling his hand in her hair and breathing in her scent. It was different now. Better somehow. Beachy coconut traded for hints of vanilla and something fresh and sweet–strawberries, maybe. He twisted a curl. Soft and silky, her hair slipped in a circle around his index finger and fell away. She closed the remaining space between them, her body molding to his as if she'd never been gone.

He closed his eyes against the spin of the room. Her breath fell in hot wisps against his neck, raising gooseflesh. They stood locked together in silence until she drew away. Far enough to let her hand skim from his neck, down his chest, fingering the lump of her ring against his sternum.

Almond shaped eyes peppered with flecks of pain that he'd played a part in putting there, searched his, pleading for forgiveness she'd never need. She tugged the gold band from its hiding place beneath his cotton t-shirt and turned it over in her fingers.

"I never thought I'd see that again."

His stomach spiraled as she let go of the Claddagh, smoothing it against his chest.

"Where'd you find it?" she asked.

Ridge felt for the ring, tracing the circle of it with his index finger.

"In the ash at the cabin." Ridge paused. "I watched you die, Liv." The words were harsher than he expected, fueled by a fire of unresolved guilt that had smoldered for too long.

"I know. I'm sorry," she whispered, stepping away.

His body cooled where hers had been, and he ached for the warmth she provided. "Tell me this is real."

"It is," she said, but her eyes told a different story.

He reached for her, but she slipped away, dragging a finger over the top of the desk before bending to right the chair he'd knocked over on his rush to the door.

"I never meant for you to end up in the middle, Ridge. I only wanted to settle the score with Sowards, get my life back." The pain permeating from the woman in the room intensified as she fumbled for words, cutting into Ridge's gut like a knife. "But now–" She hesitated, unable to finish.

"You don't need to apologize," Ridge said. And he meant every word.

"I can't stay."

Something snapped in him then, a hot ache he hadn't felt since the night Sowards forced him away from the still burning cabin.

"You have a life to go back to. But it can't be with me." She looked at him, her eyes full of the same familiar pain he'd seen in his own reflection. "You have every right to ask me to leave."

Ridge shook his head. "Why would I do that?"

"Because tomorrow I–" A clot of hurt constricted her voice.

"WITSEC. Tony told me." A sudden rod of understanding plunged itself through Ridge's core, followed by the returning slow creep of anxiety. He opened and closed his fist, staving off the hot burn of panic.

He caught her watching, and he stopped. But she came closer, tucked his hand into hers and laced their fingers together. He sucked in a breath as she pulled his fist to her lips, kissing his fingertips.

"When I saw you this morning, it all came back. Everything I'd been missing. My reason for coming back here in the first place. I lost sight of that. Got caught up in making Sowards pay.

And now–" She dropped his hand and slid her palms down his chest. "I need you to believe me–trust me–no matter what they tell you."

"I will always trust you, Liv. Always." He hadn't, though. And that was on him. Ridge traced her arms with his fingertips, feeling his way toward her shoulders, her neck, the soft skin of her cheek. His body responded, his voice soft when he asked, "I just need to know how–"

He didn't know how to finish. *How, what?* How she'd made it out of that cabin alive? How she ended up in DC tonight? How she slept knowing everyone who cared about her believed she was dead? How she'd waited half a year to see him? He didn't mean for the last two questions to stick in his consciousness, gnawing their way into the moment. But there they were, just the same, a raging plague with no vaccine. He forced the strangled choke of a chuckle from deep in his chest.

"I know," she said, her fingers caressed his jawline, pushing the nagging tendrils of blame away. "I waited too long."

Ridge shook his head and pulled her close. "But you're here, now."

The softness of her curves molded against him. The heat of her body–breaths shallow and affected–was more than he could take. Her hands skimmed his shoulders to the back of his neck, tangling in his hair. God, how often had he imagined this? His body quaked as she pressed closer, backing him against the credenza. He wanted her. Not just tonight, but always. And no amount of time or blame could change that.

Shifting, he turned their bodies as one, so that she was the one now propped against the table. One hand cradled the face that haunted his dreams. He kept his eyes open, fixed on hers as he bent for her lips, tasting her sweet saltiness. The other hand followed her lead, skimming over soft warm flesh, his thumb teasing a physical reaction as she arched against the hardness of him.

Her breath caught, hungry, as he leaned deeper into their kiss. Heat seeped from her body into his, loosening the knot of resentment he'd carried away from Cam's cabin. The hollow numbness in his chest at last replaced by a glowing ember of hope.

13

LIV

I got lost in the heat of him. Familiar need traveled from my core and along my extremities as we kissed–long, hard, deep–combating the surge of guilt that sliced upward through my chest, splitting me in two.

"Stop." At first I wasn't sure the word had been mine, but Ridge's reaction assured me that it was.

He stepped away, eyes scouring mine, searching for understanding.

"I can't do this."

Ridge returned a gentle hand to my cheek. His words all calm understanding. "Okay. Whatever you need."

The rich baritone in his voice spiked unsatiated need along with a thread of guilt. I pushed away from our connection and headed for the wall of windows.

"Why aren't you angry with me?"

"What are you talking about?" Confusion permeated Ridge's voice as I turned. He stood frozen to the spot where I'd left him. "Do you want me to be?"

"You haven't asked where I've been. What I've been doing

for the last seven months. Why I never even called you." The tears of self-loathing I'd buried for seven long months now clawed at my throat.

"I didn't ask because it doesn't matter." The muscle in Ridge's jaw ticked. "You're alive, Liv. You being here is all that really matters."

"You're supposed to hate me." The truth of those words became suddenly clear. I was so good at justifying my actions, telling myself that the decisions I'd made came from a place of honor. Vengeance for lost assets. The punishment of a man who destroyed all the good in what my grandmother created. But the truth of it was, I came here tonight because I *needed* Ridge to be angry, to push me away. It was the only way to escape the guilt.

I sank to the floor, a puddle of ragged breath and ugly tears, and still Ridge came. He kneeled beside me, pushing tendrils of tear-damp curls from my face. He wrapped me in his arms and I curled against him.

"Would that make it easier for you?" There was no blame in his voice. Only sadness.

"None of this has been easy," I refuted.

"No," Ridge agreed, settling onto the floor. He laced his fingers through mine. "But there's enough guilt to go around. Let's run the tape back, shall we?"

I exhaled slow and heavy as Ridge listed ways he'd failed me in our time together. Lack of trust, keeping secrets, leaving me to fend for myself against the man hell-bent on destroying the Sullivan fortune. As he talked, my muscles ached, the exertion of the chase catching up to me, or maybe the fear of losing what was right in front of me. At this point I couldn't be sure.

"If I'd taken you with me to Charlottesville, none of this would have happened." Ridge fell silent for a moment. His thumb skimming arcs along the back of my hand. "I know about guilt, Liv. Every moment without you I earned."

"I never blamed you." I said quietly. "Not once. Maybe I should have, but I could see you–feel who you were–and I needed that person in my life."

"What do you feel now?" Ridge asked pulling our interlocked hands against his chest.

I shook my head, afraid of the word, "Nothing."

I wasn't ready for this conversation. Hadn't even considered the possibility it would come up. But I saw the pulse of panic behind his eyes.

"What are you saying?"

I shrugged, fighting the downward tip of my lips. "It's gone. The dreams, psychometry, all of it."

Sowards hadn't only taken my freedom and the lives of assets. He'd destroyed the one way I'd had of connecting with Ridge without words. Sowards had stolen a part of my soul.

Ridge shifted to face me. He opened his mouth as if to speak, but no words came. What was there to say?

"It's fine," I managed, filling the silence. "I'm getting used to it."

Ridge settled against the wall again. "Is that what you came to tell me?"

I pushed a breath of laughter out that settled into a sigh. "I thought you'd already know."

"Just tell me." Ridge pleaded.

"According to Sowards' legal team, they found remains at O'Malley's cabin. Mine."

Ridge's eyes locked on mine, swirling with some version of panicked fear that unleashed another bubble of nervous laughter from my throat.

"Don't worry. You're not crazy. I am really here."

"So what's that mean?"

"It means Sowards is holding all the cards. Unless Rogers can get the evidence suppressed somehow, Sowards will go free."

"And you'll—"

Thump. Thump. Thump. "Hour's up," Tony's voice filtered in around the edges of the doorway.

"Disappear," I said, standing.

"No," Ridge's voice was strong, demanding as he caught my hand, stopping me. "The last seven and a half months of my life have been a living hell." Ridge let go. He stood, dragging a hand through his hair. "I can't let you walk through that door. Come home with me, Liv."

"It's not that simple, Ridge. I don't exist, remember?"

"We can figure out a way to fix that. Please." The words hung in the air between us, the power of them injecting us both with enough hope to make us careless.

Ridge pulled me into him, hungry lips on mine, and my body responded. The balloon of need expanded in my chest. I inhaled. His scent stoked the smoldering fire of want as I pushed away, backing toward the door.

I kept the security lock in place as I opened the hotel room door. "I need till morning," I said. I thought I noticed a hint of understanding in Tony's eyes, but it disintegrated, settling into disappointment.

Running my tongue across my lower lip, I could still taste Ridge. I heard him approach from behind. Felt him push my hair off the back of my neck, his gentle kisses tingled along my spine pooling into a pulsing ache deep in my core. It was all I could do not to slam the door in Tony's face and let Ridge take me right there.

"Six a.m.," Tony finally said. "No games, Olivia."

I nodded and closed the door with a click, forcing a steady breath before turning to face Ridge.

"Think you can make up for seven long months in the next eight hours?"

Ridge's lips tipped into a smile until his dimple appeared. I thumbed the indentation in his cheek as he reached for me, untucking my blouse in a slow rhythm.

"I'll give it my best shot," he said. Raising my hands over my head, he tugged my shirt free. Fiery kisses melted against my skin as he rediscovered me. My hands explored, pushing his shirt over the taut muscles of his abdomen, coaxing him out of his t-shirt between kisses.

His body was exactly as I remembered it, the addictive cuts of muscle flexed under the golden tan of his skin. His hands dipped lower–teasing–sliding the denim of my jeans over my hips. He tugged them over my feet and tossed them to the side. Eyes on mine, kisses singed the insides of my thighs as he worked his way back up. My hungry moan escaped without warning, eliciting a smile.

Ridge hoisted me into his arms, tight and strong, guiding my legs around his waist. His eyes glittered in the low light as he lowered me onto the mattress and stepped out of his khakis. He slid under the sheet, hovering over me–a silent request for consent.

I arched to meet him, our bodies a tangle of heat. And for the first time in what seemed like forever, I let myself go. Gave myself permission to feel what Sowards had torn from me. I matched Ridge's rhythm, savoring his groan as my own body shuddered.

14

RIDGE

Ridge's fingers skimmed over Liv's naked shoulder and down her arm. He bent, tasting the hollow above her collarbone. His breath came back hot against his own lips as he whispered, "Don't ever leave me again."

He glanced at the alarm clock on the nightstand. An hour and fifteen minutes and he'd be forced to deal with whatever Rogers and her team had planned for Liv's future. But after last night, one thing was certain. There was no way he'd let her face any of it alone.

The mattress shifted with a squeak as he rose from the bed, and he winced in the quiet. He turned to see if he'd disturbed her, only to meet Liv's sleepy smile. Her fingers reached for his. He ran a thumb down her cheek as the smile tickling the corners of her lips spread.

"What time is it?" she asked.

"Four forty-five," Ridge said, clenching his jaw against the immediate evaporation of her smile. "I'm going to grab a quick shower. Why don't you order some food? We can talk over breakfast."

"Eggs and bacon?" she asked.

"Perfect."

He'd be a damn poor agent if he didn't notice the immediate wall that slammed down behind Liv's eyes at the mention of a talk. But he chose to ignore it, planting a kiss on the side of her head before closing himself inside the confines of the bathroom. The first tendrils of panic snaked through his arm—a reminder of what was at stake. He clenched and released his fist, willing the unwelcome sensation away.

The hiss of the shower drowned out the first thump from the other side of the bathroom door. But the second one, Ridge heard. He scrubbed the last of the shampoo from his hair and turned the water off, listening.

Two more thumps on the hotel room door. "Ridge? You in there?" Adam hollered from the hall. "Wake up."

Shit. Ridge wrapped a towel around his waist and swung open the door. Liv sat on the edge of the bed, wrapped in the bedsheet, an unmistakable look of horror stretched across her face.

"I didn't know what to do," she said.

Ridge's heart seized. Liv's fear driving a straight line in and cracking him open.

He held the door to the bathroom open. "Just grab a shower. I'll take care of Adam."

Liv nodded and slipped inside, but her eyes never left him. He could feel her watching as he tugged on a pair of jeans, gathered her clothes from the floor, and handed them over.

"I'm sorry," she said as he lumped the garments into her waiting arms. Again, the expression on her face wounded him.

"I'm not." No words had ever carried more truth. He traced

the line of her jaw with his index finger before leaning in for a kiss.

He nodded and closed the door, listening for the squeak of the shower knob that accompanied the first rush of water. Soft rustling as Liv unwrapped from her sheet triggered a rush of adrenaline and the first nagging tendrils of uncertainty.

Ridge swung open the door before Adam could knock again.

His former partner gave Ridge a once-over. His usual grin was missing, replaced by a grave expression of horror. "I have some news. I'm not sure how to tell you, but you need to sit for this."

A thump sounded from the bathroom, and Adam turned toward the sound. "That's what took you so long to answer?" His usual ornery grin returned. "You've been here two nights. Really?"

"First, all anybody ever says to me is how I need to move on, and when I do I get the third degree?" He was kidding, of course, but there was bitterness lurking in the tone. "Not sure my personal life is any of your business, but thanks for your input."

Adam sighed, the hint of a smile playing at the corner of his lips. "Actually, I think it's great. Maybe it'll make what I have to say easier." Adam held Ridge's gaze for a moment, opened his mouth as if he was about to say something else, but thought better of it. He twisted his lips into a grimace and sighed. "Forget it. Ridge, have a seat." Adam's brown eyes flicked to the unmade bed. "There's been a development."

"I'm gonna need a little more than that," Ridge said, studying Adam.

The nervous twitch of Adam's thumb and forefinger slowed as he waited for Ridge to follow his command.

Ridge crossed his arms across his chest. He had no intention of sitting. "Whatever you came to say, just say it."

Adam scratched his temple, cocking his head to the side and lifting his gaze to meet Ridge's stare. "They found remains, at O'Malley's cabin."

Ridge blinked at Adam. A rush of adrenaline, absent when Liv had been the one to tell him, emptied into his gut. Another soft thump sounded from the bathroom. "Whose remains?"

"Just one bone identified so far—a mandible." Adam handed Ridge his phone, the lab report cued on the screen. "Preliminary testing matches Liv's profile."

Silence filled the space as Ridge skimmed the results. He swallowed the knot of uncertainty that began rebuilding in his chest as he returned Adam's phone.

"The forensics came into the Bureau yesterday, but I just found out. Ridge, it's her."

"What was the method of ID?" Ridge asked, his throat closing on the words. Liv was right. Sowards was out to destroy any chance Liv had at reclaiming her life.

"DNA extraction. I didn't tell you before because I–"

"That's not possible," Ridge cut him off.

"You saw the records, Ridge. The markers match."

A bubble of nervous laughter erupted from Ridge's throat in place of words.

"Come on, brother. I know this is hard, but you knew this was coming. It's always been a matter of time." Adam stepped forward, clamping his hands over Ridge's shoulders, forcing Ridge to face him.

"No, Adam." Ridge kept his voice calm, even. "It's a fabrication. Sowards' play to discredit the case against him."

"Ridge," the word was condescending, a drop in the bucket of pity Ridge had been forced to carry since Liv's death. Ridge's skin crawled as he cringed against it.

"Liv's not dead." A pent-up breath followed Ridge's admission. The words hanging like honey on his tongue.

Adam stepped away, dropping his hands from Ridge's shoulders. "I shouldn't have encouraged you to come. The stress is—"

"Too much?" Ridge cut Adam off, pushing away the thread of irritation. "She's on the other side of that door, Adam." Ridge tipped his chin in the direction of the bathroom.

Both men looked. The hiss of water now silent. A few muffled bumps sounded from the other side as Adam's eyes drifted back to Ridge.

"This isn't some delusion, Adam. It's real."

As if on cue, the latch disengaged with a click and Adam faced the slab of ebony separating the bathroom from the rest of the space.

The door popped open with a whine, and Liv stepped from the cloud of steam, blue jeans neatly in place while wet ringlets dripped damp splotches over the shoulders of the purple blouse Ridge had enjoyed removing last night.

"Hi, Adam," Liv's voice sizzled through the air between them.

Ridge wasn't sure what had happened in the seclusion of the shower. But the fear he'd seen before was gone, replaced by vibrant strength, or at least the appearance of it.

Her green eyes skimmed Ridge, and a pulse of warmth slid through him as she came closer, lacing her fingers through his. Ridge watched Liv's gaze shift to Adam, narrowing in a silent challenge. "Nice to see you again."

15

LIV

"Liv–" Every hint of color drained from Adam's usually tanned complexion, leaving him pale and scared-looking. "What the actual fuck?" Barely more than a whisper, Adam's words filled the space with every ounce of the tension that I'd felt since my sister fingered him as the man who'd pulled me from O'Malley's cabin before the explosion. The details of which had never been clear.

"Did you think I'd just disappear? Sorry to throw a wrench in your plans."

His eyes shifted from me to Ridge, then back to me. "I thought you were dead." He was telling the truth. I didn't need to be psychic to know it.

"You pulled me from O'Malley's cabin, Adam. You knew I didn't burn. Just like you know those remains can't be mine."

"Wait," Ridge cut in. "Are you telling me you *knew* Liv was alive?" Shock roughened the edges of his voice. "All this time, you watched me grieve. Watched my life fall apart and you never said a word?" Ridge's voice cracked with the punctuation of pain and for the first time since waking up in that cold bedroom on the shores of Lough Dan, a tickle of heat sparked at me from his skin.

I forced the accompanying clutch of breath from my lungs in an even stream, focusing instead on the man in front of me–my one time friend–who was now perpetuating Sowards' lies.

"I couldn't tell you." Adam said to Ridge, then aimed wide, accusatory eyes at me. "You shouldn't be here."

Ridge broke his hand free from mine and stepped toward Adam, running a frustrated palm over still damp hair.

"What gives you the right?" Ridge's voice escalated, louder now. "She shouldn't be in DC or she shouldn't be with me?"

"Neither," Adam shot at Ridge. "You want to know what happened that night at O'Malley's cabin?" Adam locked in on Ridge, but Ridge didn't back down.

I had somehow become the onlooker in a testosterone-fueled pissing match. But Adam was the first to give way.

"Fine." Adam sunk to the edge of the mattress, refusing to make eye contact with either of us. "But you have to promise me one thing. None of this goes further than this room."

"You stole seven months of my life," Ridge said. "I don't have to promise you anything."

Adam glanced at me, eyes softening. Ridge's intended blade of guilt hitting its mark.

"Two days before the drop I got a letter. No return address. No prints. There was a stamp, but it hadn't been mailed so I couldn't even trace the postal registry. Fifty grand to make sure Liv got out of that cabin alive."

Ridge pulled the desk chair toward the side of the bed as if to sit. But he never did. Instead, he paced the space between Adam and me. His jaw clenched and released in an angry pattern I'd seen only once before.

"It was a no brainer, you know?" Adam glanced at me. "I'd

do whatever it took to get her out of that cabin, for free. You know that."

"So why didn't she make it home?"

"The directions were clear. I had to take her to a safe house. Leave her there. Ended up being some 10x10 hunter's shack about fifteen miles from O'Malley's place. I couldn't get her help. And I couldn't tell anyone what I'd done. Especially you."

Adam's cell buzzed from his jacket pocket. He reached for it, but Ridge caught his hand before he could pull it free. Adam raised his palms toward Ridge in a gesture of submission.

"Who was at the cabin?" I asked. I only remembered bits and pieces. Millisecond memories I had trouble piecing together–the sensation of cloth against my skin, a strange woman's face, tender fingers dressing my wounds, the *thwump thwump* of helicopter rotors. But of all those snippets, not one contained Michael or Ashlyn, who were the only two taking care of me by the time I regained full consciousness in my grandmother's cabin. I was tired of missing fragments of my life.

Adam swiveled his head from Ridge to me. Shook it slowly from side to side. "No one. All I've known is that you were alive when I dumped you at the cabin." Adam hung his head. "Barely."

"You left her there to die?" Anger heated Ridge's voice.

"My instructions were to head back to the scene before anyone could miss me. Truth is, all this time, I thought she was dead." Adam's eyes shifted from Ridge's to mine. "You could hardly breathe. I did what I could, Liv. I swear. The back of your head was gashed up–a bloody mess. I wrapped it before I left."

"How chivalrous," Ridge chucked at Adam, eyes blazing.

"She had bruises–handprints–around her neck. I took pictures. I know Sowards did that to her. I had the pictures processed by the lab, but they were inconclusive, no way to run a print from them." Adam's eyes darkened and his lips twisted downward. An expression I wasn't used to seeing on him. "Her lungs rattled when she breathed. I could barely feel a pulse." He fell silent for another moment. "I'm sorry, Ridge. I knew what would happen if I left her there alone, and I did it anyway."

Adam looked at me, "I'm truly sorry."

"You did this for money?" Ridge's hands balled into fists at his sides and I felt the electric spark again, this time in the air between us.

Adam shook his head. "Do you know what it's like to live with that guilt? Knowing your actions caused someone else, someone you cared for, to die? Staying quiet gave her a chance, but how could I ever admit to what I'd done?"

"So make it up to me." Ridge said. "To her."

"How?"

"Tell Rogers what you did. Convince her those remains don't belong to Liv."

"You don't know what you're asking," Adam said.

Ridge lunged. Jerking Adam from the side of the bed, he spun him around and pinned him against the wall. It happened so fast, I couldn't even reach for him before he had Adam's service weapon out of his holster and rammed against his head.

"Ridge, don't." Repercussions of anger I hadn't felt in months rolled off Ridge in waves. I blew through the unexpected jolt of energy. "Please, think about what you're doing," I whispered, pushing my body against his back and wrapping my arms around Ridge's shoulders. I couldn't pull him away, the vibrations of energy told me that, but I could remind him I was still there.

A glint in Adam's eyes caught my attention, the awareness

of one who truly believed he deserved whatever vengeance Ridge was about to dish out.

My words must have somehow wormed their way into Ridge's conscience, that or the reality of the situation finally struck. But Ridge stepped away, lowering his partner's Sig and giving Adam room to breathe.

Adam doubled over, hands on his knees, pulling in long drags of oxygen. Ridge turned, pulling me into his embrace. The weight of the gun still gripped in his hand pressed against my back.

"How long have you known?" Adam's voice cut through the quiet.

Ridge didn't turn from our embrace, just answered. "Since last night." His breath against the top of my hair soothed the vibrations of anger, betrayal, still roiling through him. I bit back the urge to pull away.

"How?" Adam asked. "Did Rogers say something at the deposition?"

Ridge looked down at me, as if he was leaving this question up to me. But before I could answer, Adam sucked in a breath and pulled himself up to his full height, realization dawning across his face.

"You did this, didn't you?"

I shifted to put Adam in my line of sight.

"You filed these charges against Sowards."

I didn't need to answer.

"That's what this is about." Adam ran both hands through his hair. He paced a few steps each way, stopping in front of me as I shrugged out of Ridge's embrace. "You don't understand what you've done."

"Enlighten me," I said, a ribbon of defiance building in my core. "This is my life, Adam. I've been hiding long enough."

Adam's gaze skipped around the room, into corners and on nightstands.

"He'll crush you, Liv. You've got to know that. He'll destroy everything you came back for."

"Who?" Ridge asked. "Sowards? Then testify against him, Adam. If we get enough ammunition, they won't need Liv to prosecute."

Adam shook his head. "Maybe it's Sowards, maybe not. I don't know. But it's never been about the money, Ridge." Adam reached for his sidearm and Ridge handed it back. "You should know me better than that."

"Then why, Adam? What could possibly be worth leaving the only woman I've ever loved to die alone?"

Ridge's words cut into my core, cracking me open like a fault line and exposing the magma beneath.

"Ridge," I breathed, but he ignored me, waiting for Adam's response.

"I'm sorry, but I can't tell you. Not yet."

"Jesus, Miller." Ridge cursed under his breath, lunging toward Adam.

I stepped between them, skimmed my fingers down Ridge's arm, pulling him back.

"Sometimes there is no black and white when we make a decision, Ridge. There are only shades of gray. What I did wasn't right. But I couldn't bear to watch you suffer through the alternative."

"Which was what?"

Adam's jaw tensed, his eyes flicking to me. "Lose them both."

Ridge hesitated. "Don't try to pretend you did this for the right reasons, Adam. Liv's future—my future—was not your choice."

Ridge brushed past me, forcing Adam to retreat toward the door.

"Your job was to report, turn the letter over to proper authorities. Let them decide how to handle it."

Adam pivoted on his heel and lunged for Ridge, their faces only inches apart. "Think about that, Ridge. Who would that have been? Sowards. The same man who spent his final moments in O'Malley's cabin threatening to drug your sister and choking the life out of your girlfriend? Is that really what I should have done?"

The two men faced off, eyes blazing at each other. Adam's usual smile was long gone, a ghost I feared I'd never see again. A sliver of guilt trickled into my core. Ridge's build easily overpowered Adam's thin frame, but neither of them moved. Neither spoke.

I slipped between them, wedging my body against Ridge, my palm flat against his chest. The hardness of the Claddagh pressed against my fingertips. "I'm here now," I whispered the gentle reminder. But Ridge's eyes burned with the fire of blame.

"Whoever's behind this will never let her stay," Adam cut in.

"You took an oath, Adam. Your job has always been to find a way to do the right thing, not skim your cut off the top like a common criminal."

Adam disengaged. "I didn't spend a dime of that money, Ridge. It's in a trust. A trust I set up for *your* son."

Ridge pulled back. "What are you talking about?"

"It seemed like the least I could do," Adam said to Ridge, smoothing his jacket and swinging open the hotel room door before turning his attention to me. "You shouldn't be here, Liv. Rogers can't protect you–not now. And this time, the blood will be on your hands."

16

RIDGE

Ridge pressed the door closed behind Adam. He couldn't help but glance at the clock as the revelations tumbled in his brain. 5:30 a.m.

"How much of that did you already know?"

"I knew he was the one who pulled me from O'Malley's. That's all I knew."

Ridge's bare feet sunk into the carpet pile as he walked from the entryway to the edge of the bed. He pulled Liv close, breathing in her freshly washed scent. "How do we fix this?"

"I don't know that we can." Her voice was calm, resigned.

"I won't let you walk out of my life, Liv."

A bead of panic settled, then burst in his chest. He forced a breath through the tightness, focusing on the sensation of Liv's hands as they tangled through his hair. But her silence said too much.

"Say something. Promise you won't leave me." He'd never said those words to anyone. And he hated the note of desperation that seeped into every syllable.

"That's the last thing I want," she said, her voice wavering. "But—"

"No." Ridge pulled away, his gaze on hers. "No buts. I'll convince Adam to testify about the letter."

"He could go to jail, Ridge. What he did wasn't right, but if he hadn't pulled me out, I'd be dead. You can't forget that."

"Do you think Adam acted on Sowards' order?" Ridge asked, pulling Liv closer. He needed the heat of her, would climb inside of her if he could. Desperation clawed him from the inside.

"I don't know."

But she did. Ridge could feel it in the way her muscles tensed against his. He pushed his fingers up into her hair and pressed her close, his lips against the skin of her neck–tasting, exploring.

"No one else needs me like that." Her voice was no more than a breath, but it stopped him cold.

"That's not true," Ridge said, forcing her to look at him.

"I just mean..."

Her eyes clouded with sadness, stabbing like a dagger straight through his heart.

"He had means. Opportunity." She shrugged, her hands skimming over Ridge's bare shoulders. "Motive." Her eyes darkened. "Who else could it be?"

Liv peeled herself away from Ridge and walked away, pulling the discarded duvet from the floor and folding it neatly at the foot of the bed.

"And now he'll go free." Liv's words were punctuated by demanding thumps on Ridge's hotel room door. They both glanced at the clock. 5:59. "I have to go," Liv said, thumbing toward the door.

"When can I see you?" Ridge said, catching her arm before she could make it to the entryway.

Liv shook her head. Her brows scrunched together. The corner of her lips wobbled before tipping downward. She was fighting tears. "Thank you."

"For what?" Desperation pricked at him, tightening around his chest.

"You could have pushed me away last night, but you didn't. For that, I'll always be grateful."

Liv slid a hand down his chest, fingering the circle of gold still hanging on the chain.

"Here," Ridge said, moving to take it off.

"No. Keep it."

The thumps returned. "Just a minute," Liv hollered.

She tucked her lower lip under her teeth and turned back to Ridge, eyes wet.

"Don't do this." Every emotion he'd experienced over the past seven months slammed through him. "Let me help you."

"This is my life, Ridge. It's up to me to face this. I'm not taking anyone else down with me." She tilted up on her tiptoes to plant a quick kiss on Ridge's cheek. His skin burned where her lips had been.

She reached for the door and swung it open. "I'm ready," she said, stepping into the hall without looking back.

"Liv." Ridge forced the word through uncooperative lungs and lunged for the door.

Tony stepped forward, blocking his exit. "We'll take care of her," he said.

Ridge retreated, letting the door drift closed on its hydraulic hinge before his body gave up. He sank to the floor, legs buckled at the knee. The benign tingle in his right arm now omnipresent–ants crawling over his scalp and down into his chest. A lead weight descended on his lungs. Ridge leaned forward, forcing a growl through gnashed teeth in a fight for control.

Tony was quiet on the way up to the sixth floor. I hung back as he swept the room for devices.

"I trust you had a nice evening last night," he said, moving from one corner of the room to another.

I didn't answer.

Tony took the hint and didn't say another word until he was finished. "This can't be easy." He stood in front of me in the entryway of my suite.

"The hardest thing I've ever done," I admitted, staring at the diamond pattern on the carpet beneath our feet.

"Michelle should be here around nine."

He reached around me and unplugged the hotel phone from the wall, tucking it under one arm. He held out his hand next. "I'll need your cell, too."

I pulled it out of my pocket and handed it over.

"It may not feel like it now, but you're doing the right thing."

"Am I?" I lifted my eyes to meet Tony's. His were

surprisingly soft, sad. I fought the choke that surged in my throat. "Tell that to the man in room 362, okay?"

Tony's shoulders rose and fell with a resigned breath. "WITSEC will ensure your protection. That's worth it to Ridge."

I looked away from the heat of Tony's stare. I wasn't sure he was right about that–not anymore.

"They pulled Evan," Tony continued. "Things will change from here. This might be the last you see of me for a while." He swallowed and glanced toward the open door. "I've enjoyed our time together."

"Me, too," I managed. The first fingers of witness protection reality snaked their way in.

"Take care of yourself, Liv."

Tony left without another word, pulling the door closed behind him.

ADAM WAS WAITING outside my room when I came back with a bucket of ice less than an hour later. I glanced both ways up and down the hall. But Tony's calming presence was absent.

"Why are you here, Adam?" I asked.

"I just want to talk, Liv–about what happened at the cabin."

I nodded, ignoring the spike of uncertainty welling up in my core. "I've got a meeting in just a few minutes. My lawyer and some WITSEC agents."

"You don't need to be afraid of me. I'm not here to hurt you," he said, that familiar smile tickling the corners of his lips.

Adam waited while I swiped my keycard and pushed inside. The ice bucket was still in my hand when he pressed the door closed behind us, sliding the security bar into place with a *shink*.

"Do you remember what happened?" Adam's voice was low, almost threatening.

"Only bits and pieces," I admitted, sliding the bucket along the top of the credenza.

"What about before you got to O'Malley's cabin?"

Flashes of moments I wished I could forget flickered like misremembered movie scenes through my mind. The rough fabric of a musty couch against my cheek, my arms bound behind me. The sound of a belt ripped from the waist of my attacker's jeans. The stinging *swack* as leather found sensitive flesh. I leaned forward on the credenza, hands splayed against the smooth top, praying the next image wouldn't invade.

"I remember enough." I swallowed and turned to face Adam.

"Did you know there was a camera?" Adam stepped closer, propped himself next to me. "Sowards showed Ridge the whole thing."

Breath caught in my chest.

"I'm guessing he didn't mention that last night."

The clutch of anger solidified, burning in my lungs.

Adam leaned close. "I guarantee he was thinking about it."

I shoved Adam away. His lower back caught on the corner of the credenza and he let out a groan as I yelled, "Go to hell, Adam."

Adam swung around and lurched toward me, his hand gripping my shoulders and forcing me backward, away from the credenza and against the nearby wall.

"Do you know why I agreed to pull you out of that cabin?" he asked, dark eyes drilling into mine.

"Why?" I asked. My lungs seized. Fear-laced breaths coming quick and panicked as I fumbled a hand along the wall, toward the desk, grasping for the edge of the lamp–anything that I could use as a weapon.

Adam readjusted his grip, thumped me against the textured wallpaper, his forearm firm against my neck. He reached to the right, sweeping the desk clean.

"I need you to understand. I did what I did to protect Ridge. I knew you'd save Skylar. You'd never let her die, never let Ridge suffer the loss of another sister."

I didn't have a response. Adam was right. I would have done anything to get Skylar out of that cabin alive. "Let go of me," I forced the words around the tightness in my throat. My fingers clawed at Adam's arm, leaving thin red streaks.

"Stop fighting," Adam seethed. Spit settled on his bottom lip. His forearm shifted. His right fist closed around my throat.

"They have info on Ridge. Information that could destroy him. But you and I are the same. You won't let them hurt him. Not if you can do something to stop it. Which is exactly why you are going to do what I tell you."

Tears burned behind my eyes. Adam stared into me with fury-dark features–waiting for my submission. I blinked, tipping my head in a nod.

Adam's grip loosened.

"Tell me what they have on Ridge." I rubbed at tender skin along the base of my jawline.

Adam didn't answer. Maybe he didn't know.

"What about WITSEC?" I slid away from Adam. "Rogers will prove those remains aren't mine. You know that. And then what happens?"

Adam lifted a shoulder in a shrug. "You'll be gone. And by that time, so will he."

"He? You mean Sowards?" The words barely made it through the clench in my jaw. I hated Adam right now. Hated what he'd done. Hated the idea of money changing hands–the price my life was worth. And I hated his weakness–his refusal to come clean and testify.

"Didn't you wonder why no one was in the hall when you went to get your ice?" A smile pricked at the corner of Adam's mouth as he closed the distance between us. Skimming a hand down my arm, he wrapped his fingers around my wrist. "I'm guessing there's usually a thug or two out there...waiting."

"They'll be back any minute." I heard the lifted squeeze of panic in my voice, and I despised it almost as much as I despised Adam.

His grip around my wrist hardened. "Criminal Psychology 101, Liv. Know who you can trust."

18

RIDGE

Michelle Rogers swung through Ridge's hotel room door and propped herself against the front of the desk, blue eyes locked on his.

"Aren't you supposed to be meeting with Liv right now?" Ridge asked, returning to the side of the bed where he was packing for his flight back to Cascade Hills.

She didn't answer. "Agent McCaffrey, it's important we're honest with each other during this process. It's the only way to keep Liv safe."

Ridge glanced at Rogers, could feel the thread of skepticism working its way up his spine. "I've been nothing but honest."

"Tell me what you know about Adam Miller." Michelle's words stopped Ridge. He tucked the shirt into the suitcase and turned to face Michelle.

"He's my former partner. We worked GenLink together."

"When's the last time you saw him?"

"He came to my room with the lab results...this morning."

"Was Liv with you?"

"She was. Why do I feel like I'm being interrogated right now?"

Michelle shifted positions, turning to retrieve a paper from her briefcase. She held out a photo, printed on standard printer paper, toward Ridge. It was Adam, standing in the hallway outside a hotel room door.

"In case you can't tell..." Michelle swapped the picture for another. "This is outside Liv's door."

Ridge's chest tightened with the image in front of him. Liv, carrying an ice bucket as Adam approached.

"To your knowledge, did Adam know of Liv's whereabouts before this morning?"

"No," Ridge answered. "What's going on?" The words bit at his tongue.

"Look, I know this is strange. You were called by the defense and here I am questioning you. But I need to know what Miller said to you–both of you."

Ridge sucked in a breath. At this point, what did he have to lose?

"Evidently, Adam had an attack of conscience when he saw Liv. Decided to spill his guts. Said he received a payout before the drop on O'Malley–some kind of insurance policy to make sure Liv got out alive." Ridge attempted to keep the seething anger from his voice but was fairly certain he hadn't succeeded. Michelle's wry laugh was proof.

"Good," she said.

"Good?" Ridge asked. None of this seemed even remotely good to him.

"I plan to file charges against Adam Miller within the week. I'll need your testimony. Once we have him in custody we'll be able to go through every correspondence, find out exactly what he knows–run a proper trace."

Ridge lowered to the edge of the mattress. He slid his palms down the front of his jeans. Another life down the drain in his wake.

"You didn't expect that." Michelle stated her accurate observation. "Look Agent, believe it or not, I have one ambition here. To make sure when this is all over, Liv Sullivan can walk out of the courtroom to whatever life she wants to live. It's been pretty clear to me from the start that life includes you. But we need to tread carefully. We don't know what Sowards is capable of. He's under tight surveillance, which only proves he's got help from the outside. Miller's a wild card. I'd lay money on the fact that original letter was penned under Sowards' direct order. And it's our belief Miller received another one early this morning."

"Another letter?"

Michelle nodded. "A concierge delivered an envelope to his room between two and three a.m. A couple hours after the lab report came in. When he left his room, he came straight to yours."

"You're tailing all of us." A smile played at the corners of his lips. He should have expected it—a case this high profile, she didn't need any surprises.

She shrugged and lifted herself from the wingback. "It's my job."

"Is Miller still with Liv?"

An insistent knock sounded on the hotel room door before Michelle could answer. She excused herself, slipping out into the hall, leaving Ridge to sit in silence, his mind spinning. But even as the possibilities took flight through his skull, a thread of hope wound itself around his heart. Rogers was good. Thorough. If anyone could make sure Liv got out of WITSEC, had a life to go back to after Sowards' conviction, it was her.

"Agent McCaffrey, we're going to need to postpone the rest of our meeting if you don't mind."

Ridge laser focused on the clench of her jaw and the blanch of her face. "What's wrong?"

"Stay here. I'll be in touch." She took her briefcase from the desk and headed for the door.

Ridge stood, but he didn't make a move to intercept her. "Tell me what's going on. Seven months is long enough to stay in the dark."

Michelle stopped, her eyes grazing over Ridge, judging his worthiness. "Miller left the Marriott with Liv. Possibly at gunpoint. Someone hacked into the surveillance. Been sending us images of an empty hall for the last few hours."

"Hours?" An involuntary crash of emotion in Ridge's chest must have shown on his face, because she closed the distance between them, rested her hand on his shoulder.

"Don't worry, Agent. We've already got a team tracking them. We just have to make sure Miller doesn't panic—doesn't do anything he can't undo."

The implication hit Ridge full-force. A wave of heat followed by the squeeze of panic. Before this morning, it'd been months since he'd had a full-blown attack. But the vise-clench of his lungs didn't lie. It had taken Ridge over an hour to recover from the episode this morning, and the last thing he needed was a second wave, this time with an audience.

His breath hitched and he slid back onto the mattress, digging his fingers into the duvet. His heart banged an idiosyncratic rhythm against his chest. He squeezed his eyes closed, focused on pushing air out and pulling it in on counts of three, fighting his way through the attack.

Michelle gave a nod to the team huddled at the door and they slipped out. She kneeled in front of Ridge.

"Breathe," she coached quietly. Inhaling and exhaling in calm waves. Ridge shifted his focus away from his internal counts and onto her. The watery pools of her eyes, inches from his, shone nothing but worry.

"I'm sorry," he managed once the wave had passed.

She shook her head. "When's the last time you had one of these?"

"This morning," he admitted. "After Liv left."

"And before that?"

He shook his head. Wondering why it was any of her business. "A month–two, maybe."

"You need to take care of yourself Ridge."

It wasn't lost on him that she used his first name in that moment. Pansy-assed panic attacks had a way of making it easier to come off the "Agent" bandwagon.

"I've got a therapist who'd be happy to meet with you. Talk through what's going on."

Ridge pushed up off the mattress and worked his way toward the door. "I'm good, Counselor. Thanks."

He held the door open as Rogers stepped through. He wanted to ask if he could help but knew better. The tingle still eating away at his arm from the inside was proof he was a liability not an asset.

"Just bring her back to me this time, okay?"

"You have my word," Michelle said as Ridge pressed the door closed behind her.

"I'm supposed to trust you?" My voice lifted out of desperation and into anger. A switch I was happy to take.

"They promised you wouldn't do this, Liv. I never would have helped you get this far if I'd known all you were going to do was come back here and threaten everything we worked for."

"Never would've helped me get this far?" I repeated, pulling against him as he guided me toward the other side of the room. "So, you'd have left me in O'Malley's cabin to burn? Is that it?"

I tugged harder, ignoring the burning pain at my wrist. "Besides, who's *they*?" I shot Adam an accusatory stare. "I get that your career is on the line, but if you know who's doing this, you *have* to come forward, Adam. You can get out from under this. Do what's right. Rogers will cut you a deal."

"I'm trying to do what's right," Adam yelled. His face inches from mine, eyes wide, full of a fear I didn't understand. "And you can't do this to Ridge. They'll come after both of you."

"Ridge saw me on the street, Adam. I had no choice. He needed to hear the truth."

"The truth?" Adam's voice rose, desperation clawing at his words as he cornered me against the credenza. "And what exactly is the truth, Liv?"

I only wished I knew. My silence gave him his answer.

"That's what I thought. So what's your plan? Go back to Cascade Hills, pretend to be the happy couple again?"

"We were a happy couple, Adam–once upon a time." I stepped out of Adam's reach while he stared at me. His face reddened, fear or frustration coloring his features. "Besides, it's over. I said my goodbyes. If you're trying to get rid of me, consider it done. I'll be in WITSEC. No one will know I was ever here."

"You don't get it. You're a threat, Liv. And he already knows–everything." Adam pulled his shoulders back and turned on his heel, escaping the conversation. "You can't run from this."

Adam pulled a folded envelope from his back pocket and shoved it against my chest.

"I wasn't going to show you this–either of you. Found it slid under my hotel room door this morning."

He pulled at his hair with frustrated fists, turning a complete 360° turn before returning to his position in front of me.

"I knew this would happen, Liv. When they launched the inquiry against Sowards, I knew. I played my part in Ridge losing you, and I regret that. But this is bigger than you, or me, or even Ridge. Hell, it's bigger than GenLink."

I unsheathed the note from the envelope, my fingers trembling as the cocktail of fear swirled through my veins.

"Life is a gift, but all decisions breed consequence," I read aloud the first line, stopping as my eyes skimmed the rest of the typewritten font. Adam was right. Going after Sowards had been selfish. Instead of gaining justice for assets who no longer had a voice, I'd only put more lives at risk.

Adam returned to stand before me as I reread the letter for the third time.

"There are no prints. It's totally clean, envelope, too. Just like the last one. Security footage shows the hotel concierge delivering it about three a.m."

"This has to be from Sowards." I said, not taking my eyes from the text in front of me.

Adam's shoulders sagged and he shook his head. "Does it matter?"

I refolded the threat and passed it back.

"Keep it," Adam said, his eyes boring into mine. "In case you need a reminder."

The lines of the letter were already singed into memory. *"Life is a gift, but all decisions breed consequence. We had an agreement, and betrayal is expensive. Can you live with the blood of Ridge's son on your hands? Undo this."*

Adam and I stared at each other. His eyes were dark, desperate, panicked.

I sunk onto the edge of the mattress and smoothed my fingers over the comforter. "Undo what?"

"I don't know," Adam admitted. "I thought the case, but this came after the lab results were released."

"You don't really think they'd hurt Colton, do you?"

"Are you willing to take that chance?"

He waited for me to respond, so I shook my head. "Of course not."

"You need to disappear, Liv. Without WITSEC. Any kind of government program and he'll find you."

I swallowed against Adam's demands. "What about the trial?"

"Let it go. Colton didn't ask to be pulled into this mess, and I sure as hell won't let Ridge lose his son because of you."

His words landed like daggers. "And you?" The words erupted without warning. "Who made you his protector, Adam? Why'd they choose you?"

Adam's jaw clenched and released. His eyes dark and angry. "Don't ask questions you don't want the answers to Liv. We're leaving. Now."

"I'm not going anywhere. Not yet." I brushed past Adam and headed for the door. I'd never had neighbors, the whole floor always reserved for me, but Tony had to be back by now.

Adam grabbed my wrist and twisted, shoving me against the wall face first. I opened my mouth to scream. The first syllable of Tony's name ricocheted off the walls before the cold steel of Adam's sidearm against my ribcage silenced me.

"I don't want to have to do it this way, but I will."

My heart kicked into an uneven rhythm. The steel pressed into my side as Adam moved me from the entryway toward the closet and released my arm.

"Pack a bag, Liv."

He started pulling shirts off hangers, throwing them onto the mattress. His aim never wavering. He jerked a roller bag from the bottom of the closet and shoved it into my arms. His eyes caught mine. Fear-bred hatred seeped from them.

"You've lost your mind Adam. We can turn this around. Go to the authorities. Together we can end this."

"Shut up and pack." The barrel stabbed between my shoulder blades, and I winced. Memories I didn't want to relive danced in the distance, on the cusp of taking hold.

I leaned over the mattress and packed what I could. I pulled the letter from my jeans pocket, pretending to shove it deep inside the exterior compartment of the roller bag, but instead watched as it slid silently to the floor at my feet. I swept it into the under-bed darkness with the toe of my tennis shoe. Adam jerked the bag from my hand and wrapped a fist around my upper arm, shoving me into the empty hallway.

20

RIDGE

Ridge stabbed the down button of the elevator over and over. He gave up on the slow-ass machine and flung open the nearby stairwell door. His footsteps echoed in the space as he made his way to the main floor. He slipped through the fire door, closing it quietly, before weaving through a clutch of new arrivals toward the front desk.

He stood in line, shifting his weight impatiently from one foot to the other. Why hadn't he thought to ask Liv what room she was staying in? She'd given him her cell number but every call was going directly to voicemail, and each time it did his anxiety heightened. It took every ounce of his energy to keep parallels of what happened half a year ago from screaming into his skull and taking over, clawing him from the inside out.

He never should have let her walk out of his room. At the very least, he should have demanded to go with her. If he had, she'd be in his arms right now, not with Miller who was apparently in the midst of some psychotic break. Ridge glanced around the heads of the people in line ahead of him, waiting to speak to the clerk, identified only by "Stefanie" in block print on the name tag attached to her pinstriped vest.

"Can you tell me what room Olivia Sullivan is in, please?" he asked as the traveler in front of him stepped to the side, gawking left and right for the bank of elevators Stefanie had already pointed out twice.

"Just one moment, sir," Stefanie said, punching an array of keys before screwing her mouth into a sideways frown. "I'm sorry, but we don't seem to have any guests registered under that name."

Ridge thanked the clerk and turned to survey the open interior of the hotel. Strangers sat at tables near the Starbucks kiosk. A few older businessmen clutched newspapers in their fists while downing what was left of their morning coffee. Most of the patrons milling about had their heads buried in their phones, meandering obliviously. Helplessness started a slow creep up his spine. If he wasn't careful, another panic attack would be next.

Ridge swung around to face Stefanie, who waited for his next request. "How about Ashlyn Callaghan? Anyone by that name?"

It took the clerk a couple seconds to search the database before coming up empty. "I'm sorry, sir."

Ridge reached in his back pocket, dragging out his wallet. He flipped open to the green eyes and auburn hair he'd held in his arms just hours before.

"I'm looking for this woman. She may be using another name."

Stefanie's eyes softened. "Oh, that's Liv Allyn." She shrugged. "I mean, I think it's her. She's been with us a couple weeks." The expression on Stefanie's face grew guarded. "I mean, it could be her."

Ridge's heart jumped in his chest. "Can you tell me what room she's in?"

"Actually, she's one of our VIP guests. I'm not allowed to distribute that information." Stefanie handed Ridge his wallet. For the first time since tendering his resignation to the Bureau, Ridge longed for the badge. That ID had a way of opening doors that were otherwise closed. And right now, he needed a set of master keys.

"Please," Ridge lowered his voice. "She's in trouble. I need to get into her room, see if there's anything that can help me find her." He slipped a fifty dollar bill out of his wallet and slid it across the desk toward Stefanie. "I know you're just doing your job, Stefanie. But Liv's life is on the line here."

"I'm sorry," Stefanie's eyes were wide. She glanced both directions before flattening her hand over the fifty. Ridge recognized the part of her lips, the building empathy. Stefanie liked Liv.

Ridge made one last ditch effort. He leaned in. "I'm an undercover agent with the Bureau. I'm here to keep her safe. Please, help me find her."

When the clerk picked up the phone, he thought for sure she'd call security to have him removed. But instead, she pushed the bill toward Ridge and listened to the other end of the line.

Stefanie laid the receiver gently into its cradle. "No one's answering in her room."

She pushed a keycard across the smooth veneer, glanced down the long front desk toward the second associate who'd popped out from the back to assist with the growing line. Ridge followed her gaze, but her colleague wasn't paying any attention.

"Room 617. Just drop this in the keycard box in the lobby when you're done."

Ridge nodded. A breath of relief accompanied his, "Thank you," as he fought the urge to launch himself over the desk and hug her.

THE SIXTH FLOOR hall was quiet when he stepped off the elevator. He checked for the cameras. Older model white units hung in the corners in the common area around the lifts, standard hotel security. It took a closer look to see the tiny black button eyes staring back at him every ten feet or so as he made his way down the hall toward room 617. His growing respect for Michelle Rogers and her team solidified.

Ridge pulled the keycard from his pocket and waved it at the lock, the green light blinked, ushering in a thread of relief. Liv's room was a corner suite, bigger than his. Her layout the mirror image. Bathroom on the right, a small kitchenette–absent in his unit–the wardrobe and credenza to the left opposite a king sized bed.

A pile of discarded clothing lay heaped on the carefully made bed. A taunting reminder of where Liv had spent last night wound its way around his gut and squeezed. He couldn't–wouldn't–lose her again. The wardrobe doors hung open, hangers empty. He snapped a picture of the scene and sent it to Michelle.

A ping from his phone caught his attention–a text from Michelle.

Michelle: Get out McCaffrey. It's under control.

Ridge typed back: Just trying to help.

Michelle: Contaminating a crime scene isn't help.

Ridge sighed. She was right. He had no law enforcement authority. He'd just make it easier for the perp–Adam–to get off once they caught up to him. The thought caused a lead weight to sink through his gut. *Adam.*

He should turn around, get out of that room and do what Michelle had asked. Wait for her call. The call that would tell him that Liv was safe and secure. But he'd done that once–waited for others to do the job that should've been his. He scrubbed his hand down his face and to the back of his neck, rubbing at the tight coils of tension running down his spine.

The air conditioning in the unit kicked on with a suck of air as he skimmed the scene one last time. The flicker of motion from under the bed caught his attention. He kneeled, lifting the edge of the duvet. A flap of paper lay under the bed like a crumpled wing. Ridge snapped a picture before pulling a ballpoint pen from the nightstand. He used the non-inking end to slide the paper free from its hiding spot.

He was still reading, his eyes skimming the words for a second time, when the sound of the door unlocking ricocheted through the silence behind him. Tony stepped into the room.

"Let's go," he said. "You've got to let us do our job." His words were forceful but kind. With gloved hands, he removed the letter from the floor in front of Ridge and ushered him outside toward the elevators. Tony didn't speak again until they were alone in Ridge's third floor room.

"You know, I've been working for Ms. Rogers about four years now. Been on the Sullivan case since the first email came."

Ridge swallowed, words from the note he'd found on Liv's floor still swimming in his mind. "Email?"

"That's how Liv first contacted Rogers. By email. I was part of the verification team. We tracked down leads, made sure her story added up. I'll give you one thing, Liv's got one for the books." He snorted a chuckle, lowering into the easy chair in the corner of Ridge's room. Ridge copied Tony and sat on the bed.

"You didn't believe her?"

"Didn't say that," Tony said, holding an admonishing finger in the air. "But it sure wasn't easy. Not at the beginning anyway."

"Tell me you found her."

"Enterprise is helping them track Adam's rental." He reached in his pocket and pulled out another pack of Big Red, holding it toward Ridge in offering.

Ridge declined, wondering how many packs Tony went through in a week.

Tony checked his watch. "I'd say they're pulling in behind him as we speak."

He folded the stick of gum into his mouth and pocketed the rest.

"You don't have to babysit me," Ridge said.

Tony looked amused. "This isn't babysitting, McCaffrey. You know your place in all this. And frankly, I'd say we have the same end goal, wouldn't you?"

"How long have you known there's still a threat?"

The glimmer of humor in Tony's eyes darkened. "We watched Sowards while Rogers stayed in contact with Liv. He placed an overseas call two days before we could get the documents in order to get Liv back to the States. Told whoever was on the other end to 'eliminate her.' Used those words. Those next forty-eight hours were hell."

Ridge felt the clutch in his chest. The sudden realization he never would've known the difference if Sowards had made his move while Liv was still in Ireland. "Why didn't he kill her at O'Malley's cabin? Why let her go?" He clasped his hands in front of him, rubbing the faint scar along his knuckles.

Tony shrugged. "Your guess is as good as mine. But there's

more to this McCaffrey. There's a reason Adam's taking her to the bus stop and not putting a bullet in her head. We just don't yet know why."

"And the letter?" Ridge nodded toward the envelope Tony had shoved in his pocket. Tony's eyes softened.

"A son, huh? I got one of my own. He's ten now, lives with my ex in Virginia. But I get to see him a few times a month." Regret passed over Tony's rough exterior. "What's his name?"

"Colton," Ridge answered. "He'll be five next month."

Tony smiled, exposing a crooked eye tooth. "Four's a fun age." He hesitated, stood. "Call home. Talk to him if it'll make you feel better. I'll be just outside."

A spiral of worry unleashed itself in Tony's absence, winding around Ridge's gut with sudden force. He couldn't wrangle his phone out of his pocket fast enough to satisfy the rabbit thump of his heart.

"Bridget?" he said as soon as the line clicked open. He coughed to hide the note of panic in his voice. "How's Colton?"

"Nice to talk to you, too," his ex-wife responded, feigned irritation seeping through her words. "But he's fine. I'm waiting in the pick-up line at school."

The knot of fear gripping Ridge's chest loosened. "What do you two have planned for this afternoon?" He tried to sound unaffected, a concerned dad just checking in on his son. But life had already stolen too much from him. The fear of losing more hovered over him, tipping like a Jenga game on the brink of collapse.

Bridget sighed in typical exasperation. "What do you want, Ridge? Need a ride from the airport or something?"

"No, I'm good." Ridge scrubbed a hand over his face, scratching at the stubble on his chin. "Just wanted to hear the little man's voice." The knot in his throat thickened, threatening to choke him. He checked his watch and glanced at the hotel room door. The shadow of Medici's shoes still visible. The last twenty-four hours rolled through his memory like the blur of a freight train.

"Hang on a sec. Here he comes." Bridget's words carried across the line, soothing some of his panic.

Colton's breath, his mouth shoved too close to the receiver, reached him first, giving way to the angelic symphony of his son's four-year-old voice.

"Daddy, when you coming home? You said Jeremy could come meet Dewey when you got back."

Ridge released the pent up breath that had been caged in his lungs. "It might be a few more days, buddy. But as soon as I'm back I'll pick you up at Mommy's and we'll invite Jeremy over, okay?"

"'Kay," Colton chirped agreeably. "Mommy says I get to stay with Aunt Sky and Uncle Brian. We're going to the movies and I'm gonna get the biggest tub of popcorn you ever saw."

Colton's excitement penetrated Ridge's wall of worry. Colton was fine. The letter was nothing more than some bogus attempt to get Liv to drop the charges, drive her out of the picture. But why Adam? To save his own skin? The implications behind Adam's involvement warred with the buzz of worry already churning in his gut.

"Have fun, buddy. And be good. I don't want any bad reports."

"I will Daddy. See you later."

Before Ridge could get the good-bye across his lips, Colton had disconnected. Ridge plunged the phone back into his pocket, counting through two even breaths before the *click-whirr* of the door lock engaged, depositing Tony back into the confined space.

21

LIV

The crunch of still-wet pavement under the tires of Adam's SUV echoed in my ears as he steered into the near-empty parking lot of the Greyhound bus station. He drove the whole route with one hand on the wheel, the gun positioned low, never straying from its intended target—me. That weapon, and Adam's obvious ability to use it, was the only reason I hadn't popped open the passenger door and taken my chances with the asphalt.

"What about the trial?" I asked.

"As soon as they introduce that jawbone as evidence, everything will be thrown out. You know that."

I swallowed. I did know, and it was exactly why leaving was not an option. It was up to me to fight for the truth, even if I had to do it from the confines of WITSEC.

"Tell me why he's threatening Colton. You know more than you're willing to admit, Adam. What does Sowards want from me?"

Silence in the car built around us. Nothing I could say would change Adam's mind. My job now, was to survive. Get on a bus to who-knows-where and disappear just long enough to get Adam, and whoever he was working for, off my tail. I glanced at the man I'd once trusted, his dark eyes fixed on the Greyhound sign atop the squat building at the far end of the lot.

"Open the glovebox," Adam instructed.

I engaged the lever-action release, exposing the hunk of paperwork stashed inside. Adam reached over me and jerked the top envelope off the stack, shoving it at me. "Here. It's part of Colton's college fund, but it's enough to get you out of here. Find a little town somewhere, Liv. Somewhere he can't find you."

I wasn't sure if Adam was referring to Ridge or Sowards, but in the end, I supposed the result was one and the same.

"Why are you doing this?"

Adam ignored my question. "Just take it and go, Liv. If you won't do it to save yourself, then do it for Ridge. Do it to save Colton."

"Ridge knows I'm alive, Adam. You can't change the past twenty-four hours."

Adam's eyes locked on mine. "If it comes down to a choice between you or his son, which one do you think he'll choose?"

I choked back the curse that rose in my throat. How had I never seen this part of Adam before? How blind had I been?

"Go, Liv. Get as far away as you can. No phones. No contact. Cash only."

"What am I supposed to do when this runs out?" I held up the envelope of cash.

"You're smart. You'll figure something out."

A slither of hate slipped up my spine as the realization hit. "How long have you been working with him?" I sucked in a breath when Adam didn't respond. "You're not doing this to save Colton. Sowards' interests are limited to GenLink, and Colton has nothing to do with that."

Adam looked away, out the driver's side window.

"Tell me, Adam. Why? What can you possibly hope to gain?"

"The less you know, the better. I won't let Ridge lose his son. Now get out." He prodded me with the barrel of the gun. "And don't try anything stupid in there. Get on the first bus out of here. Don't think I'm not watching your every move, Olivia."

I popped open the passenger door and slid out into a harsh spring breeze. My hair whipped across my face, blinding me as I hauled my carry on out of the back seat. I could feel Adam's eyes on me as I started around the car toward the office. The stench of diesel engines permeated the air, prompting an eruption of coughs from my scarred lungs. I hesitated to catch my breath, lowering the bag to the ground.

Adam stepped from the car, slipping around the front of the still-running rental. "You're doing the right thing." His voice was soft, the Dr. Jekyll to his previous Mr. Hyde. He pulled my hoodie up over my head, tucking in a few stray curls.

I picked up my luggage from the wet pavement and walked away without another word, disappearing into the bus station. Adam's car was still idling in the lot when I turned to the ticket agent.

"Where to, Miss?"

The agent, a tired looking grandmotherly type, didn't even make eye contact as I approached. But the cameras behind her caught everything. I lowered my hoodie, just enough for at least one of the eyes to catch a full view of my face.

"Where's the next route headed?"

The odd answer was enough to make the cashier pause, give me a once over. She leaned forward, cocked an eyebrow. "You're awful well-groomed to have no place to be. Runnin' from something?" Her lips pulled back into a nicotine-yellowed smile.

"Time for a fresh start," I said, shooting a nervous sideways glance toward the parking lot. The ticket agent followed my gaze. Her hand slipped beneath the surface of the counter for a moment before she turned her attention back to me.

"Next route's boarding now, leaves in five minutes. Nashville."

I nodded and dug the fare out of the envelope I'd shoved in my hoodie pocket. "Those backpacks for sale?" I asked, nodding toward a row of Greyhound labeled bags on a shelf behind her.

She nodded.

"I'll take the blue one."

She turned to grab the bag and handed it through the small access hole at the bottom of the safety glass. I thanked her and stepped to the side, out of the way while I shoved the most important items from my carry-on inside.

Her pinhole stare bored into my back as I finished reorganizing and exited. I checked for escape routes, but Adam wasn't stupid. He'd planned this well. The entire lot was caged by chain link fencing, topped with barbed wire to keep criminals from sneaking in at night. It was also highly effective at keeping law-abiding citizens in. So much for slipping away.

I made my way through the bays, checking for placards that read Nashville. I was about to force myself back inside the ticket office to ask for directions, when I checked one last stall. An idling, sludge-grimed bus marked *Hashville*, waited for me. The N transposed to an H by a yellow pixel lit in the wrong place.

"Nashville?" the driver asked, moving forward to take my bag.

I flashed a smile before handing him the carry-on. Slinging

my newly purchased backpack over my shoulder, I trudged up the too tall steps. If I did get a chance to run, I'd need a few things, and I didn't want to be slowed down by a too-big carry-on full of useless relics from a life I no longer lived.

I glanced out at the parking lot one final time as I made my way down the aisle. Adam's SUV sat motionless. I saw him inside, watching me, the expression on his face unreadable. The bus growled forward from the bay, exiting the lot with a hiss and groan.

22

RIDGE

Dark descended on DC before Ridge was able to sneak down to the restaurant, away from Tony long enough to call Brian and let him know he wouldn't be home on the red-eye that night.

"What's going on, Ridge?" Brian asked. "And don't tell me nothing, I can hear it in your voice. Did something happen at the deposition?"

Ridge half choked on the words, forcing them out in a whisper. "It's Liv. She's alive."

The silence on the other end of the line was proof Brian had heard. If it hadn't been for the background noise in the kitchen of Brian's pub, Ridge would've sworn they'd been disconnected.

"Did you see her?" Brian's voice wobbled into the dead air between them. "Is she okay?"

Ridge nodded, as if Brian could see him. He scrubbed a hand down his face and pushed out a breath. "She was."

"What do you mean, 'She was?' Jesus Ridge, spit it out. What the hell is going on out there?"

"Adam took off with her. The lawyers' private investigators tailed them to a Greyhound station just north of the city. They plan to arrest Adam. Think he might be in on whatever new conspiracy theory Sowards is cooking up to get out from under these charges. They're supposed to bring Liv back once Adam's in custody."

"But that hasn't happened yet?"

"It's been hours, Bri," Ridge's voiced dipped lower into worry-clipped syllables. "They won't tell me anything."

"You need me to come out? Call someone?"

Dishes clinked in the background. Ridge closed his eyes, wishing he was back in Cascade Hills instead of holed up in a hotel with Tony the Not-So-Terrible.

"Nah." He forced a semblance of nonchalance into his tone. "Thought I'd call Dad, maybe rent a car and head out there for a day or two once they bring Liv back. We'll just drive home."

"She's coming home?" Brian asked. His voice was a whisper.

Deep down Ridge knew it could never happen that way. But it was easier to lie, pretend there was a chance at restoring his own imbalance. And a visit with his dad might be just what he needed.

"That's the plan." Ridge forced the lie across the line. Besides, if Brian thought he was stuck out here alone, waiting for a woman who was supposed to be dead, he just might plan an impromptu visit–invitation or not.

"Thought you and Sky had a night out tonight?" Ridge said, praying for an easy change of subject.

Brian sighed. "Had to postpone till tomorrow. We're actually taking Colton to see a movie. New job's been sucking away most of her extra time, but she seems to enjoy it, so that's all that matters." There was a flatness to Brian's tone that Ridge didn't like.

"You don't need to spend your one night out taking care of my kid, Brian." Ridge meant it, but under the circumstances he was glad they'd agreed. "You should know, I called in a few favors at the PD. Just someone to watch the house, keep an eye on Colton."

"I talked to Bridget a couple hours ago. She mentioned that. This is because of Liv?"

Ridge didn't know how to answer that, and the silence stretched again.

"Anything I can do?" Ridge managed. "About Sky? I could talk to her if you think it would help." From five hundred miles away and in his current emotional state he wasn't sure he'd be capable of anything in the way of support, but if he could make a phone call, talk some sense into his little sister, he owed Brian all that and more.

"I think the wedding's making her a little nostalgic, you know? Feels like she's missing out, not having your mom or sister around to give her pep talks. I try to help, but I'm not much force on the family front."

Brian had lost both his parents young. Had been in the system since elementary school. If he hadn't gotten tangled up with Ridge, the chances of graduating straight from one system to another–foster care to reform–all before he turned twenty-one was high. But instead, Ridge had caught his fall, seen too much of himself in Brian.

"It's worth a call. I'll talk to her, see if there's anything I can do," Ridge said, noticing Tony's melt-iron stare as he reentered the hotel restaurant. "Look, I gotta go. The PI is back. Maybe there's news."

"You keep me posted, okay, man?" Brian hesitated. "If you see Liv, tell her–"

"Yeah," Ridge interrupted. The weight of what he'd admitted to Brian suddenly crushing him. "Don't mention this to anyone. I'm not sure I'm supposed to be saying any of this. It's all new." He fingered the condensation on the water glass in front of him. "I needed to tell someone–to make it real."

"You've got my word," Brian answered. "And Ridge? If she's with Adam, she's safe. He won't hurt her."

"I hope you're right." Ridge ended the call and tossed the handset onto the table in front of him. Tony sidled up to the booth and slid in.

"Who was that?" Tony asked.

"Just a friend."

"Right now, McCaffrey, you have no friends. Until we get Liv back and under surveillance, friends are not in our vocabulary. Got it?"

Ridge nodded.

"We'll need your friend's name and number, just in case." Tony pushed a pad of paper, like the one Ridge used to carry himself, across the table. Ridge scrawled Brian's information across an empty sheet and slid it back.

"I thought your guys had a tail on Adam. What's taking so long?" Ridge asked, determined not to sit around in waiting mode any longer. The last time he'd done that, it hadn't ended well.

Tony leaned against the wooden seat back and flagged two fingers in the air. The waitress bobbed up to the table with a smile. "Scotch on the rocks," Tony said, glancing at Ridge with one eyebrow raised.

"I'm good, thanks." Ridge said before the waitress walked away.

He'd been down this road before and wasn't proud of the spiral he'd plummeted through the last time around. He'd be damned if it happened this time. Right now, clarity was his friend, and the combination of anti-anxiety meds and alcohol didn't do anybody any good. The waitress checked in with a nearby table before turning her attention to the bar.

"So?" Ridge prompted Tony.

Tony tapped his fingers on the table. "Unfortunately, the takedown wasn't as clean as we'd hoped."

Ridge could feel the cord of tension running along his spine thicken. "Meaning..."

"Ticket agent activated a silent alarm, which summoned local PD who holed Miller up in his vehicle. By the time we got there, situation had escalated."

Ridge leaned forward in the booth, his grip on the glass in front of him tightening.

"Miller fired on the officers, which shut down the block and initiated a SWAT situation."

The pinpricks of ice against the heat of Ridge's skin threatened.

"Don't worry, though. Liv's safe on a Greyhound to Nashville and Miller was apprehended about a half hour ago." Tony shrugged. "He's been less than forthcoming, but we'll get Liv. Buses make easy targets."

"Nashville?" Ridge echoed. He could think of no good reason why Liv would go there.

Tony nodded as the waitress returned, positioning the glass of amber liquid in front of him. Ridge's mouth watered. Now, he needed a drink.

23

LIV

T he bus lurched to a stop, my temple thumping against the cool glass of the window, ending the faint pretense of an unsettled nap. I checked my watch, it'd been three hours since we passed the "Welcome to Virginia" sign, which, by my calculations, should put us somewhere smack dab in the middle of nowhere.

I pinched the bridge of my nose, hoping to stave off the headache growing behind my eyes. Craning my neck, I peeked under and over the heads of other passengers, searching for a sign of life beyond the dark windows of the bus. I was about to give up when the gas station marquee finally came into view.

I shifted in my seat, pushing against the shoulder of the hulk of a man who'd taken up residence in the aisle seat. I'd counted fourteen empty seats on this bus before we pulled out of the station, and this guy—the last one on—had to pick my row. I pressed again on his shoulder, dislodging a snore that rattled from his sinuses.

"Just wake him up, sugar. He ain't got no business trapping

you in there like that. A girl's gotta do what a girl's gotta do. You know what I mean?"

I shot a careful smile at the woman standing in the seat behind me, popping and cracking a jaw-full of gum while waiting for the aisle to clear.

"Go on," she urged, flicking the man on the back of his balding head as I said, "Excuse me," as loud as I dared.

The man started to life, his body jiggling out of sleep in stages.

"Thanks," I managed as he grunted and gathered his jacket, making his way into the aisle.

I shot a grateful look at the woman and pushed out of the row ahead of her, backpack in tow.

"Do you know where we are?" I asked once we were out of the virtual cattle chute and on solid ground. Moist spring air clung to my nostrils, similar to the air at the farm–fresh, clean, unpopulated.

"Well it ain't the bright lights and big city." She shrugged and wandered off, guitar case in tow.

The interior of the gas station was bigger than I expected. All fluorescent lighting and white linoleum opened into an attached diner that seemed to be a happening place for the truck drivers who made their way from the rigs out back. I pilfered through the first aid aisle, grabbing a handful of individually dosed Tylenol before heading for the snacks.

"Where are we...exactly?" I asked the cashier who looked at me like I'd just dropped from Mars.

"You're at a freeway truck stop," he said.

I shot him a less than amused look as I dug some cash from the envelope stashed in my Greyhound backpack.

"'Bout five miles outside Bishop's Hollow...Virginia," he added, his lip curling in some form of teenage mockery I'd lost familiarity with.

My chest tightened. Bishop's Hollow was Ridge's hometown. The irony of this bus's stop wasn't lost on me.

"There any place to stay in town?" I asked, scooping my unbagged snacks and Tylenol from the counter between us. He looked me up and down before answering.

"There's an old bed and breakfast on Main Street." He paused to check my response, but I forced my face into what I hoped was an expressionless void. He leaned over the counter with a glance in both directions. "A Motel 6 on the other side of the overpass if you're into the hourly crowd."

His index finger brushed mine before I could step away from the counter. "Thanks. Think I'll stick with the B and B," I fired the words as I backed away, the smirk across cashier boy's lips unspooling a thread of unease through my core. In my rush to put space between us, I shoved through the swinging glass doors and straight into a mammoth of a man.

"Easy there," he said with a heavy drawl–West Virginian, maybe–I apologized and kneeled to scavenge the array of pain relief packets and Cheez-its from the gravelly pavement.

The man's oil-stained hands pushed and pulled at the bags, likely crushing the twenty or so crackers inside. I fought the wave of panic as the man eyed me. Tugging his ball cap down in a minuscule salute, he nodded and disappeared into the station.

I took a moment to shove my purchases into the top of my backpack before rounding the corner of the block building toward the commercial end of the parking lot. The kid's cigarette smoke reached me first. A fresher version of the smoky staleness that accosted me from the other side of the cashier's counter less than five minutes ago.

"So, B and B, huh? I get off work in fifteen. I could give you a lift."

I narrowed my eyes at the kid's sallow complexion. He couldn't have been much more than eighteen–twenty, tops.

"I've got it under control, thanks." I said, moving away. I felt him turn to follow me. Noticed the bus in the lot beyond lurch to life.

"Looks like your ride's gonna leave without you," a second man said. Stepping from the shadows near the back corner of the building, he blocked my path. In the dim light I could tell this guy was older, more ragged, but he had the lanky build and toothless grin of drug addiction.

The men closed in, one from the front, the other from the back, obscured from the parking lot by a massive dumpster in a cement surround. I opened my mouth to scream and the cashier grabbed me from behind, covering my mouth with his nicotine-flavored hand. I bit. Hard enough to taste blood. And the kid squealed a curse, jerking his hand from my mouth and cushioning it between his legs.

I screamed.

The second man grabbed me by the shoulder, shoving me against the cinderblock surround of the dumpster, knocking the wind from my lungs and marking the end of my scream. His heavy body pressed against mine, stale breath hot against my skin.

I craned my neck for a look at the bus lot. The now familiar *squeak-groan-hiss* that shifted the mammoth vehicle from idle and into first-gear reached my ears.

"Girl like you doesn't take off on a Greyhound adventure empty handed. Where you hiding it, sugar?"

"Get the fuck off of me," I said, turning my head to the side to avoid his stench. His forearm shoved harder, locking my arms above my head.

"If you ain't got money, we'll have to take our payment another way."

Black eyes reflected the light of the gas station marquee. Hands groped, clawing for the waistband of my jeans under the too-big bulk of my sweatshirt. The button popped as his face morphed into one I'd seen before–the man from O'Malley's cabin. My lungs seized, the panic of abuse taking over.

His fingers reached their target, and he groaned, rough digits sliding against soft skin as he ground against me. He worked to loosen my jeans between thrusts, and I scrunched my eyes closed, searching for escape. Breath returned to my lungs and I screamed. But his massive hand planted against my mouth. He spun me sideways, grinding the side of my face against knives of jagged cinderblock.

"Check her bag," the kid from the station said from a few feet away. "Come on, man. I didn't sign on for this. Take the cash and let's get outta here."

"Shut-up and keep watch," the second man growled, hardening against me.

The sound of his own fly buzzed through the quiet of the night, too loud for my oversensitive ears. A rush of panic sliced through me and self-preservation took over. I shoved off the wall. Every last ounce of hot strength seeped through my veins. His body smacked against the dumpster behind us as I regained my footing.

He staggered, lunging for me as I pulled at the dislodged waistband of my jeans. His fingers clawed my shoulder and I swung my backpack. The solid contact knocked me off balance, my body teetering in a slow motion dance to the side.

A sick *thwack* followed, echoing off the building. I glanced back. His head ricocheted off the side of the dumpster surround, depositing a round circle of blood amidst the mural of graffiti before he went limp, landing in a heap of arms and legs on the pavement.

I shrugged my bag onto my shoulder launched jellified legs into a run as a group of bystanders trickled into the area.

"Whoa, whoa, whoa, slow down, honey? You okay?" Firm hands wrapped around my biceps, halting my momentum. Kind eyes studied mine, no doubt still wild and panicked from the attack.

"What's your name?" He tried again. I glanced behind him at the spot where my bus once stood. He followed my gaze, returning to me as the distant rise and fall of a siren replaced the thump of blood in my ears.

24

RIDGE

Tony found Ridge outside the front door of the Marriott, standing a few feet from a group of smokers. "You smoke?" he asked.

Ridge shook his head, "Just needed some air."

"There's better air around the corner," Tony said as a ribbon of smoke drifted their direction. "Let's take a walk."

Ridge followed him down the block and around the corner before either of them spoke.

"Rogers called," Tony started, ignoring the fact that Ridge had left the dining room without so much as a see-ya-later.

Ridge turned to survey Medici's face. No sign of the irritation he knew he'd caused by leaving the table a few minutes ago. An opposite reflection, he knew, of the emotion streaked across his right now. The guy was well-trained, Ridge would give him that.

"Miller lawyered up. We got nothing from him." Tony shrugged. "Except for the fact that his biggest concern seems to be the safety of you and your son. Any idea what that could be about?"

"I have no idea," Ridge managed before the panic took hold. He bent forward, hand on his knees. "Jesus Christ, I can't do this."

He didn't mean for the words to escape the way they did–a string of anxiety manifested in a weak-ass phrase. But whether he wanted to admit it or not. It was true. He wasn't sure he was capable of losing Liv again. He'd barely made it out on the other side the first time around, and he was damn sure the second time would be worse.

Right now, he couldn't process why Adam had done what he'd done, not seven months ago, and not now. All Ridge could think about was how Liv had felt in his arms, the music of her laughter in his hotel room, the one night of pleasure that somehow repaired achingly long months of loneliness.

"I know, which is why we're cutting you loose. Go home. Be with your son. We'll contact you as soon as there's any news–Liv or otherwise."

"How am I supposed to do that?" Ridge pulled his eyes up to meet Tony's.

Tony's gaze softened. "Go take care of Colton, Ridge. It's the one piece we can't figure out. Right now it seems like nothing–a way to get your attention, Liv's attention. But somebody should be there. Just in case."

The muscle in Ridge's jaw contracted, sending a shooting pain into his temple. He rubbed it away. "Be straight with me, Tony. Is there a threat or not?"

"We think it's unlikely. Seems more likely whoever is doing this–"

"Sowards," Ridge cut in.

"Whoever." Tony nodded. "Knows Liv would protect Colton, would give up everything she's worked for to make sure he stays safe."

"That's what you think this is?" Ridge stood upright, forcing himself to his full height, a couple inches taller than Tony. "You think Adam convinced Liv to leave? To take herself out of the picture to protect Colton?"

Tony licked his lips and surveyed the street around them. "It wouldn't be the first time she's risked herself for one of your family members."

The words crashed into Ridge, cutting through what little appearance of normalcy he'd been able to muster. "But you'll find her. You're following the bus, right? Buses make stops. You'll catch up before it gets to Nashville."

"Rogers feels it's best that we allow Liv to think she's alone. Let her drop off the radar for a bit until we figure out why Sowards–if that's who this is–threatened your son."

"That's bullshit, and you know it." Ridge spat, punching a finger into Tony's chest. "I won't leave her. Not this time. I won't sit back and watch because someone else claims to have it under control. I lost her that way once. I won't lose her again."

"This is about your son, McCaffrey. Liv's resourceful. She's proven that. Go home. At least until we can figure this out. Rogers doesn't want a little boy's blood and a parent's worst nightmare on her conscience."

Tony's words registered, plummeting through Ridge's chest until they tangled in a knot of frustration in his gut. He slid down the stone facade of the hotel, squatting in a low balance. He tipped his head to the starless sky.

"So this is a choice," Ridge said, meeting Tony's gaze. "I have to choose between bringing the woman I love home, and the life of my little boy."

"Until we know more...yes."

Ridge released the pent-up exhale from his lungs. The pain of the choice manifested in his lungs, squeezing them until they refused function. Tony's arm wrapped around his shoulders and pulled him to his feet.

"Come on, McCaffrey. I won't make you say the words. But let's get back inside, get you packed."

25

LIV

The man lay sprawled at the base of the dumpster while two medics performed CPR. The cashier was nowhere to be seen.

An officer's gaze skimmed to the back of the squad car where I sat, held a moment as he took statements from customers who had crawled out of the woodwork. He broke eye contact to scribble something in his notebook.

I let my eyes wander back to the man who attacked me. The medics had left him now, were gathering their supplies and loading them back into their van.

The interior light of the cruiser blinked to life as the driver's door opened. The same officer who'd taken statements slid inside.

"How you doing back there, Olivia?" His eyes caught mine through the rearview mirror. "Unless you want to hang around this place, I think we'd best continue this at the station, don't you?"

"Am I under arrest?" I asked.

He shook his head. "Nah, just need to clean up a few loose

ends that's all. Take your official statement, file a report. Ask you a few more questions. See if we can't lock down what happened out here tonight."

I swallowed the knot of anxiety. I'd already told him what happened. Every bystander that stuck around and gawked had given their version of events. But I needed more than a story. I needed a life. Why was I here? Where was I headed? And the question that was bound to raise a red flag: Who the fuck was Olivia Allyn? The officer waited for me to nod in agreement before turning the key in the ignition. I shivered as the eight cylinder engine roared to life.

The ambulance pulled out of the parking lot in front of the cruiser in silence, its once whirling emergency lights dark. The police car rocked, pulling onto the near empty road as a bubble of bile threatened from the pit of my stomach. I coughed, cleared my throat to choke it away.

"Is he dead?" I asked quietly.

The heat of the officer's stare hit me again from the mirror.

"Yes." He stated it matter of factly without an ounce of emotion in his voice. I swallowed. A wave of heat flushed up from my core, heated my cheeks.

I sucked in a wobbly breath and pushed it out through the words, "I didn't mean to kill him."

The officer didn't respond, but I could tell he heard. His eyes shifted from me to the road in front of him. We rode in silence for the next fifteen minutes until the cruiser turned into the parking lot of a gray block building on the outskirts of town.

The officer offered his hand to help me out of the car and followed me inside the station. Within minutes I was seated at a table in what looked like any normal conference room. The chairs were padded and the walls painted a trendy dark gray. If it wasn't for the camera tucked high in the corner, I might've believed this wasn't an interrogation.

"Evening, Miss Allyn." An older gentleman wearing a lopsided tie and beige blazer stepped into the room. "My name's Detective Charles and this is Officer Toops." He motioned to the officer who stepped in behind him, the one who'd driven me from the gas station. "We'll be taking your statement tonight. I know you've already relayed this to Officer Toops, but can you tell us again what happened? For the record? Start from the beginning if you don't mind."

I relayed the scenario, from walking up to the cash register, to running into the truck driver outside the door, to the moment I swung the backpack at my attacker's head.

"Officer Toops said you refused medical care, is that correct?"

"I'm fine, Detective. I'm not hurt." The tickle of a memory from the last time I'd refused medical treatment at a crime scene toggled loose.

"You mentioned the cashier, but he wasn't on scene when we arrived. Can you describe him for us?"

"Tall, skinny. His clothes looked too big. Smelled like cigarettes. I bit him. Should have tooth marks on his hand."

Detective Charles stifled the smile that tugged at the corners of his lips. "We'll make sure to track him down, have an officer get his statement as well."

"Any idea why those two would single you out?" He shrugged innocently. "Ever seen them before?"

"Never," I answered as the door to the interview room popped open.

A third officer handed Detective Charles my backpack with a low, "It's been processed."

"You mind?" the detective asked, his attention back on me.

He placed the bag on the table between us. Tiny spots of blood spatter sprinkled across the running Greyhound emblem. He waited for my response.

I considered telling him it was private property and unless he planned to arrest me, he could go to hell. But the conformist in me complied.

"Go ahead," I said, doing everything in my power to keep the surge of panic from churning my insides into a rippling wave of nausea. Officer Toops stood by as Charles rifled through my backpack, chucking the Tylenol and Cheez-its onto the table.

"These come from the store?"

"Yes," I said.

"Stolen?" he asked. One sandy eyebrow raised in suspicion.

"Bought and paid for," I shot back.

He pawed through my clothes until he came upon the passport and Indiana driver's license courtesy of Michelle Rogers. He glanced at it, eyeing me before handing it off to the assisting officer.

"Where you headed?" he asked.

"Nashville," I said. That part would be easy enough to check out.

"Got family there?"

"Friends," I lied, just as his hand landed on the thick white envelope Adam had given me.

He opened it, fingering through the cash inside. He shot the officer a sideways glance before handing it over.

"Where'd this come from?"

A slice of panic plummeted through my chest and into my gut. "Been saving." I nearly choked on the lie.

The need to tell Detective Charles how I ended up on that bus grew like a seed sprouting roots in my stomach. How I was a witness for a federal case. How the defendant had managed to scrounge up phony evidence and was now threatening the life of a little boy I loved. Even as the thoughts ticked through my brain, I realized how crazy it sounded.

"Give us a minute, will you?" Detective Charles asked Officer Toops. "Take this out to the lockers with you." He piled my belongings into Toops' arms and waited while he left the room, the door clicking closed behind him.

He stood at a self-service beverage kiosk. "Can I get you some water? Coffee?"

I shook my head, wiped my palms on the thighs of my jeans as he poured himself a cup of black coffee and returned to the table.

"What is it you're running from?" he asked, his voice low, sympathetic.

I swallowed, twisted a nonexistent ring on my right hand, a nervous habit I'd yet to shake. Colton's blue eyes taunted me, his laughter a near constant echo in my memory since reading the note Adam had shown me. *You wouldn't believe me if I told you,* I wanted to say.

"Look, we got a dead guy, 24 years old. His wife, pregnant by the way, will have to come identify his lifeless body."

"He attacked me," I asserted.

Charles nodded. "That's clear. And I don't want you to think I'm victim blaming or any of that bullshit, but the fact remains we still don't know why."

"Because he thought he could," I said, fighting the wave of emotion clawing at the back of my throat.

"Guess you showed him." He waited. Tired, bloodshot eyes scoured mine, waiting for a reaction. He sighed in the silence and leaned in. "I know your name's not Olivia Allyn. Database flagged it as soon as we ran it."

The flicker of panic that pinched my brows together came on too suddenly to mask. Charles didn't miss the tell. One eyebrow lifted in confident curiosity.

"You're safe," he added for good measure. "Whoever you're running from, they can't get to you here."

I shook my head. He had no idea. "Sullivan," I said. An unexpected bubble of relief accompanied the release. I didn't realize how much I'd missed it. I pulled myself up taller in the chair, spoke louder this time. "My name's Olivia Sullivan. I'm a witness in a Federal case against a former FBI Special Agent in Charge."

Charles' eyes squinted, a momentary blink that meant he wasn't sure he believed my story. I shrugged it off, the hum of relief at using my real name far outweighing the possible fallout. When he prompted, I relayed the short version of the story. Abduction to O'Malley's cabin, waking up in Ireland, fighting my way to get back home only to lose my identity once I did. The detective scrawled furious notes as I talked. The first page of the yellow legal pad in front of him was full by the time I finished telling him about Adam–the threat against Colton.

Charles thrummed his pen on the paper, skimming his notes before pushing himself up from the chair. "You sit tight," he said. "I'll be back in a bit." He paused at the open door. "If there's someone you need to call..." he let the statement hang, motioning down the hall. "The receptionist can help you use the station phone up front."

Bugged, no doubt. But I didn't care. For the first time I could remember, I had absolutely nothing to hide.

26

RIDGE

Ridge lay on the yet-to-be-made sheets of his hotel bed. Tony's departure, and thoughtful addition of the Do Not Disturb sign to the outside of his room, a welcome reprieve. He pulled the second pillow to his nose, inhaling what was left of Liv's scent. The sugary sweetness, now mixed with his own scent, stirred simultaneous desire and fear-induced frustration. He growled into the pillow and tossed it away, staring wide-eyed at the ceiling. In less than six hours, he'd be on a flight back to Cascade Hills. And all of this may as well have been a dream—or nightmare—he wasn't sure which.

His eyes were just beginning to get heavy when a vibration from the nightstand shook the exhaustion away. He snatched the phone and checked the number. A Bishop's Hollow area code stared back at him from the screen. *Dad.* Anxiety plunged through the hole in his gut.

"McCaffrey," he answered.

A female voice crackled across the line. "This is the Bishop's Hollow Police Department, I have a witness in custody calling for Ridge McCaffrey. Can you confirm?"

He bolted upright. "This is Ridge McCaffrey."

"Hold, please." Ridge's heart thumped against his sternum as he kneaded the edge of the duvet.

"Ridge?" A wave of relief melted through him at the sound of Liv's voice. "I think I'm in trouble."

The shot of adrenaline at the content of her words launched his heart and lungs into overdrive. "Liv, what happened? What are you doing in Bishop's Hollow?"

He didn't care. He was already stumbling around the room, pulling on clothes one-handed while he listened to Liv retell snippets of what he imagined was a much longer story.

"I don't know. Ridge—" It wasn't the words that stopped him cold, but the fear in Liv's voice. The quiet desperation that clawed its way through the line. "I killed someone." The whispered words forced him back to the edge of the mattress. "I don't know what they're going to do to me."

Before he could form a response he heard a woman in the background chirp, "Wrap it up, Sullivan."

His lungs clenched in an involuntary vise. They knew who she was. Whether that was good or bad he had no idea, but he wasn't about to let her face the fallout on her own.

"I'm on my way, Liv. But it'll take me some time to get there." She didn't respond, but he could picture her, phone pressed to her ear, words trapped in a choked sob. "Dad's fifteen minutes away. I'll call him. You shouldn't be there alone."

Only when the line went dead did he realize what he'd promised. He shrugged into a hoodie and flipped it over his head, leaving his room and exiting down the stairwell in the opposite direction of the elevators. By some miracle, he made it out the door of the Marriott and into his waiting Uber without laying eyes on any of Rogers' investigative team.

"I need the closest open car rental, please." Ridge said to the driver. He checked his watch.

"It's one a.m., sir. I'm not sure any of the rental dealerships are open right now."

Ridge started stabbing his fingers at his phone, hoping at least the one at Dulles would be open for business. No such luck.

"Any chance you could drive me to Bishop's Hollow, Virginia?" Ridge allowed the bead of hope to color his voice. He waited as the driver punched the destination into his GPS. Ridge knew full well what he'd find.

"That's six hours away, man." The young driver, probably a college student, eyed him from behind the wheel.

"It's a family emergency," Ridge said. "I'll pay twice your rate and an extra hundred if you can get me there inside of five hours. Cash."

Ridge had made the drive more times than he cared to admit. He knew it was possible to shave almost an hour off the drive. But it took commitment, and an eye for state troopers.

"Twice the rate?" The kid parroted back at him.

"Yes."

The next few seconds dragged like minutes as the kid weighed his options and finally shrugged, "Let's go, man."

The next call Ridge made was to his dad. This one wasn't going to be easy, he expected that, but it was a necessary step to make sure Liv had someone in her corner until he could get there.

His dad's sleepy voice met him from the other end of the line. "Ridge, you okay?"

"I'm fine, Dad. Just need some help."

"It's after one, what could possibly be so important that it couldn't wait until morning?" With every word George McCaffrey spoke, the sleep hangover diminished from his voice. "Did something happen at the deposition? Jesus, son, I knew it was a bad idea for you to go out there. You're not–"

"Please, Dad, just listen." Ridge cut his father off. "You can ask questions later, but right now I just need you to get in your car and drive to the BHPD."

There was a moment of silence on the other end of the line before George spoke again, his voice low, insistent. "What happened, Ridge?"

The tension in Ridge's jaw migrated into his temple. He raised his hand to his head and rubbed the ache. "It's Liv, Dad. There's been some kind of accident and she's there. Alone," he added, as if it might make a difference.

The soundlessness between them grew, echoing like a drum chorus in his head.

"Please, Dad. I'm on my way, but it'll be a good five hours before I can get there." He hesitated, emotion creeping up the back of his throat and constricting his vocal cords. Ridge caught the driver eyeing him from the front seat. "I left her to fend for herself once. I can't do it again."

"I–" George started. Ridge expected the barrage of questions. And his father had every right to ask them. But instead, Ridge heard a resigned exhale. "I'm on my way. See you soon, son."

The car screeched to a halt. The kid in the front seat uttered a curse. Ridge scanned the road, a familiar black MKX parked in the middle of the lane ahead, blinkers flashing.

"You know this guy?" the kid asked as a dark suited man made his way to the rear passenger door.

Ridge nodded. "Unfortunately, yes. You can let him in."

The kid unlocked the doors and Tony slid in beside Ridge. "Nice try."

"She's in trouble," Ridge said. "I can't leave her."

Tony nodded and leaned toward the front seat.

"Montgomery County Airport," he said. The kid glanced at Ridge before putting the car in gear and pulling away from the curb.

Tony looked at Ridge. "I've got a helicopter waiting. Assuming you want to get there before daybreak."

"Why are you helping me?"

Tony looked out the window as the lights of the city flashed by. "If anyone asks, I'm not."

27

LIV

Detective Charles flopped a folder onto the desk between us when he returned to the interview room. He lowered his body into the chair with a resigned sigh.

"You sure aren't making this easy for us, Miss Sullivan."

I locked eyes with the detective. His rumpled beige jacket was gone. The sleeves of a worn blue button down rolled up to the elbow. Sandy hair, beginning to gray at the ends sprinkled along his bare arms. He pushed a piece of paper toward me, and I glanced down at the document.

"Seems Olivia Sullivan passed away last year, rather tragically I might add."

I skimmed the death certificate to the box labeled cause of death, "Declared death in absentia."

"I've asked a colleague to consult with me on your case. She'd like a few minutes with you if you don't mind."

"Am I being arrested?" I asked for the second time that night.

"No, we just need to know what we're dealing with. Need

to make sure everyone gets their due process. I'm sure you understand."

"I have a friend on the way. He can help clear this up," I said, remembering the nearly eight hours I sat on that Greyhound bus before it dumped us out in the armpit of Bishop's Hollow. My only hope was that Ridge could get here faster than that.

"Good," Charles said, watching me. "In the meantime, I'll give you a few minutes with Dr. Talbott. Got nothing better to do to pass the time, right?"

Charles' jovial façade was grating on my nerves. The Good Cop persona dripped off him like he'd been dipped in it. But I agreed, allowing myself to be led down a long hallway toward a cluster of offices at the rear of the complex. Charles knocked twice before turning the handle.

"Dr. Talbott, this is the witness I spoke with you about, Olivia Sullivan?" His voice tipped up at the end as if he'd asked a question.

"Yes, of course." A slight woman not too many years older than myself made her way around the desk to meet me. She extended a hand and I took it, the cool of her skin sent a chill along my spine and raised the hairs on the back of my neck. "Please, have a seat." She gestured to an overstuffed chair in one corner of the boxy room and took a seat in its twin, her knees inches from mine.

"Detective Charles tells me you were attacked this evening." She cocked her head to the side, brown eyes soft and sincere. "Would you like to talk about that?"

"No," I said. The word tight on my lips.

She smiled. "He also said that you took another life in order to save your own. Would you say that's an accurate representation of the evening's events?"

Disinterest colored her words with a flat tone, a harsh

opposite of the practiced concern that shone from her eyes. I choked back the growing lump of emotion in my throat. Someone with less experience might believe her feigned sincerity. But I answered anyway, "That's accurate."

"You have someone coming for you? A friend?" she asked.

I nodded.

"Good," she smiled. "Now, let's forget about what happened at the gas station."

The comment unleashed a wave of nausea in my gut. *Forget?* She'd obviously never had her face shoved into a rock while her pants were around her knees. I took a breath, pushing away the ongoing threat of anger still simmering beneath the surface.

"Why don't we start with what prompted your trip to Nashville in the first place?"

Trust. She was asking for something I had no idea how to give. And she hadn't earned even a smidge of it. She was a stranger, employed by the city of Bishop's Hollow, and housed in the local police station. Trusting anyone after the last year was an increasingly insurmountable challenge I was still coming to terms with, but trusting *her* was the worst decision I could make. At least I had the awareness to admit it. The clock on the wall ticked, marking the silence between us.

"Where were you staying before your trip?" Dr. Talbott asked, brown eyes sparkling at me innocently.

"I'm a witness in a federal case against a former FBI agent." I repeated the same line I'd given Detective Charles, but I watched the corner of Talbott's glossed lips tip down. She didn't believe me. "It's why the ID in my bag doesn't match what I've told you. They were trying to protect me from the agent I filed charges against."

Talbott scribbled something across the pad in her lap. "Were you traveling for the case?"

"I left for personal reasons."

She waited. A knock on the door my only saving grace.

"Dr. Talbott, I apologize for the interruption." Officer Toops filled the doorway, hands at his belt. "Miss Sullivan's *friend* has arrived." Suspicion dripped from the word friend.

Dr. Talbott glanced at me. Heat flushed my cheeks as a spike of worry shimmied down my spine. An arrival this soon meant George McCaffrey, Ridge's father, was standing in the lobby of the police station, waiting for his son's dead girlfriend to rise from the grave.

"You look worried," she said, standing. "I can accompany you up front if you like."

I'm not sure what would make her think that's what I wanted, but maybe it was protocol to ask. Either way, I declined. Peeling myself from the oversize chair, I followed Officer Toops down the brightly lit hall toward the front of the station.

When we turned the corner, I saw him. His eyes, an aged version of Ridge's, focused on the thin pane of wired glass in the door between us. His jaw dropped a little and his eyes widened as Officer Toops led me into the station house lobby.

"Ridge called. Asked me to come," George managed, still without averting his gaze. He blinked twice and slid a comforting hand down my arm. "Let's get you out of here." He turned to Officer Toops. "She's free to go, I assume."

Toops nodded. "We'll need to keep the backpack for now, but you can pick up the rest of your belongings from the officer at the desk."

He tipped his chin in the direction of the front desk, waiting, as I approached the same woman who'd begrudgingly helped me phone Ridge less than a half-hour before.

Minutes later, I was sliding into the passenger seat of George's Mercury. Once inside, he focused his attention to the key in his hand, running his fingers over the angular crevices.

"You didn't have to come," I said. The tap of rain joined my words, echoing against the roof of the car.

"When Ridge called I thought he'd–" George's voice thickened, stopped.

"Lost his mind?" I offered, picking at the hem of my sweatshirt. "I've got the patent on that, I'm afraid." I tried to smile, but my lips twisted, turning down into a fear-tugged frown.

George shifted in his seat to face me. "I have so many questions."

"I don't have all the answers," I admitted. "But I promise, I'll answer what I can."

WE PULLED into the driveway of an older two-story frame house. Instead of the cookie-cutter vinyl sided kind you'd find in any suburb across the expanse of this country, this home only existed in the older nooks and crannies of this nation, still sided with wide, white asbestos shingles. George noticed me taking it in. He chuckled.

"I know it's not much to look at. This was my dad's house. He passed away about ten years ago." He shrugged. "It's where I grew up."

I smiled at George as he worked the key in the front door. "The kids used to love to come out here. There were hardly any neighbors then. Nobody close meant they could pretty well do as they pleased." He chuckled. "That was just what Ridge lived for."

A stab of guilt worked its way through my chest. *Colton.* The name swam in my skull. "Do you know if Ridge has talked to Colton today? Yesterday," I corrected, realizing the sun would soon peek over the horizon.

"The call was short, but he didn't mention it, why?" A ribbon of worry worked its way through George's voice and I immediately regretted asking.

"Just curious," I said, tamping down my own bubble of anxiety.

George led me into the family room, taking the plastic bag of belongings from my arms and setting it on a nearby desk. I trailed an index finger over the family room mantle, set with an array of family pictures. Ridge and Skylar in all stages of life, some with their sister, Riley, and some without. I paused at a family photo taken when Ridge was about six.

"You have a beautiful family," I said.

George thanked me and moved closer. "Those were happier times," he said. "When we were all together."

"It must have been hard, raising three kids on your own."

George chuckled. "Riley just about raised 'em for me. Don't know what I'd have done without her in those early years."

Silence in the room thickened. I hadn't grown used to it— the sound of silence. Before there'd always been a low hum of vibration, even in quiet moments. Some indication of the mood of the people or place around me. But with that gone, it was hard to judge the best way to react. Maybe, if that ability hadn't left me stripped bare, I'd have reacted differently to the attack at the gas station. If I'd known he just wanted the stash of money, I'd have given it to him instead of smashing his head against a cinder block wall. I swallowed against the memory. Felt George's hand on my shoulder.

"You must be exhausted. It'll be hours before Ridge gets here. Come, I'll show you where you can get cleaned up. There's an extra bedroom. You can catch some shut-eye if you like."

He rambled as I followed him up the stairs to the second floor.

"Sorry you had to get tangled up with some of Bishop Hollow's finest citizens. Doesn't leave a very good impression of the community, now does it?" He paused in front of an open door and nodded inside. "Make yourself at home, Liv. Bathroom is across the hall, towels in the linen closet over there."

"Thank you." The words weren't enough. I still had too much bottled up inside. "George?" I called as he headed back down the hallway. He turned. "I killed a man tonight."

George's eyes widened, but he didn't speak.

"At the gas station, someone is dead because of me."

George closed the distance between us and wrapped his arms around me, squeezing me into one of his bear hugs. The pressure of his body against mine rocked loose a choked sob I'd been fighting since the moment I'd heard the crack of bone against brick.

George held me, smoothing my hair with one giant paw while whispering the words I needed to hear more than any other. "It's okay, Liv. You did what you had to do." He sighed into my shoulder. "Everything's going to be okay."

28

RIDGE

Ridge thanked the pilot and climbed out of the chopper. A tan sedan waited by a nearby hangar, lights on, ready to take him wherever he needed to go, thanks to Tony's instructions.

Ridge rattled his dad's address off to the driver and watched familiar surroundings flash by the window as they made their way from the south end of Bishop's Hollow to the north-west side of town–his dad's corner of the world.

The front door cracked open as the car jostled down the gravel driveway. His dad stepped onto the stoop, wiping his hands on a kitchen dish towel. Ridge couldn't get out of the car fast enough.

"That was fast," George said, flipping the towel over his shoulder and folding Ridge into a hug.

"Is she okay?" It was all Ridge cared about at this point. That and the fact that Colton was sound asleep in Brian's loft–which he was, according to Brian's return text, time stamped within minutes of landing.

George nodded. "I think so. Asleep, finally."

Ridge started to push past his father and into the house, but George planted a hand firmly on his chest. "Are you sure you know what you're doing here?"

Ridge stepped back, caught the pained spark of worry in his father's eyes.

"I'm not sure this is healthy, son. She ran for a reason. You were starting to get past this–moving on. Maybe it's time for you to let her go."

Ridge pulled himself up tall, besting his father by at least three inches, and sucked in a long combat breath. "She didn't run, Dad. She was forced onto a Greyhound bus–by Adam Miller, of all people." The last bit he added under his breath, barely audible through the painful clench of his jaw.

George stepped back and followed Ridge into the house. "Liv and I talked. When she couldn't sleep. She told me she'd made a mistake, going to you at the hotel. Said she never should've come back."

George slung the dish towel onto the kitchen island before returning to the living room. He settled onto the sofa, as Ridge headed for the stairs, listening for signs of life from the second floor.

"She's afraid of hurting you–again."

"There's a lot more to it than that," Ridge said, drifting away from the landing and back to the living area.

"Ridge–" The tone of his father's voice said what words never could.

"There's been a threat against Colton. That's why she left. She's trying to protect him."

"What kind of threat?"

"That's what Liv's legal team is trying to work out."

"Ridge if this is serious, why are you here? Why aren't you

in Cascade Hills?" A note of terror bubbled up through his father's voice, raising the octave.

"Colton's okay, Dad. I talked to Bridget. She took him over to Brian's. He's asleep as we speak. I'll get back later this afternoon, as soon as I can." Ridge lowered onto the couch with his dad. "He's my first priority. I'm not going to let anything happen to him."

"But?" George said, anticipating Ridge wasn't through.

"But I can't leave Liv to battle this on her own."

George's immediate refute was shut down by the buzz of Ridge's phone. Ridge answered, refusing to justify whatever excuse his father was about to come up with. "McCaffrey."

"Tony says you're in Bishop's Hollow?" Michelle Rogers' voice hummed through the line, free of niceties.

"Just got here," Ridge answered. "Liv's asleep."

"I'm sending a team out. Got a call from a Bishop's Hollow Police detective. She killed a man, Ridge. We can't risk the fallout from this. Not now. WITSEC is taking her under."

Ridge scrubbed a hand down his face, stared at the green and black flecks in the Oriental-style rug under his feet. "There's got to be another way," he said.

"It's too late. Until we can prove Sowards is behind all this it's the only way. Are you willing to risk the life of your child for her?"

The question hit Ridge square in the chest.

The moment of silence was all Michelle needed. "That's what I thought."

"So the threat's legit?" His throat tightened around the words, pinpricks of heat climbed up through his core. He pushed off the sofa.

"I know this is hard to swallow. But my job is to provide legal protection from an enemy we don't yet understand."

Ridge allowed the silence to filter through the line.

"I'm sorry, Agent McCaffrey, but this is no different than when Liv left your room yesterday morning. You have to let her go. I'll do what it takes to keep her alive. You protect your son until we can prove Sowards is at the center of this."

Ridge ended the call and tossed his phone onto the coffee table with a clatter. Hearing Rogers admit that she thought Sowards was to blame was a step in the right direction, but it wouldn't make him whole. He prayed his father would refrain from whatever argument he was about to make for a few more moments, at least until he could get the creeping tendrils of panic under control.

George's eyes drifted up to meet his before Ridge heard a familiar squeak on one of the old stair risers.

"Let me guess. Michelle?" Liv's voice slipped over him like a warm tide, washing away the dregs of hate and frustration that had pummeled him for the last three hours. He turned from his position opposite the couch and pulled her from the bottom step and into his arms, all in one lithe movement.

"I'm sorry," she breathed into his chest. Her fingers clawed at the back of his shirt, as if no matter how close they were, she wasn't close enough.

He exhaled into her hair and pulled away, his eyes searching hers. "Are you okay?"

Liv nodded.

Ridge smoothed his hand over her head, sliding his fingers through silky bed-mussed curls.

"I won't let them take you away from me." The heat of an uncertain breath ricocheted off her skin and back onto his.

"I'll start some coffee," his father said, but Ridge ignored him, pulling far enough away from Liv to scan her from head to toe. She had an abrasion along the side of her cheek, the skin scuffed and red. She appeared fine, but the pain behind her eyes told a different story. He skimmed his thumb just below the reddened area along her cheekbone.

"Come on," Ridge wrapped Liv's hand in his and pulled her along behind him, ascending into the shadow of the second story. He let her take the lead from there. Liv pushed the door of the guest bedroom open and slipped inside, Ridge followed, closing the door behind them.

She looked in the dresser mirror. "I didn't know that was there until now." She pressed her fingers along the painfully red scuff on her face. "I guess it's from the cinderblock."

Ridge sucked in a breath, the memory of her brutalized by another man, rushed back.

"He had me pinned against the wall. I fought him off. But he came back at me. I swung the bag." Her eyes met his through the mirror, pleading. "I just wanted to get away. I never meant to kill anyone."

Ridge cringed against the implication of guilt in her voice. He wrapped his arms around her from behind, his voice a whisper. "You did what you had to do, Liv."

"It all came back," she said through the sob in her throat. "Everything that happened in the cabin. His hands on me. His breath. The way he looked at me. It was all the same. Like I was prey to be devoured."

Ridge held her while she talked. Listened while she dumped memory after memory of nights spent trapped at the hands of a rapist. Her words stoked the fire of his own anger, but he forced it away, chained it into the darkest depths of his soul where it couldn't hurt her.

He was all too aware of the scars Liv's ordeal left on his own psyche. He had no clue how she'd managed to function with the experience of them wrapped in the recesses of her brain.

"I'm sorry," she said finally. Tears spilled from her red-rimmed eyes, soaked through his shirt and onto his skin.

"This is not your fault." He wrapped her tighter and she melted into him. "I never should have left you."

Yesterday, seven months ago, last year, she could take her pick. He'd done enough leaving to last a lifetime and in that moment he swore, no matter what the consequences, he'd never leave her again.

29

LIV

R idge's fingers traced the length of my arm as I sat curled against him. As the shock wore off, pain trickled in—both physical and emotional. As hard as I worked to keep them at bay, monsters lurked in my subconscious. Monsters born of ghosts and fed by abuse, trauma, and lack of control. Ridge was the antithesis of those monsters—warm, safe, and gentle. Everything I wanted, but nothing I deserved.

"Michelle wants you in witness protection," Ridge said. "She's on her way to Bishop's Hollow. I thought you should know." Ridge's breath was hot against my scalp as he spoke. "It's your choice, though. The feds require consent for WITSEC, they can't force you in."

I let my fingers drift down his arm and laced my fingers through his. The simple act sent a spike of emotion from my stomach and into my chest, tightening around my lungs—desperation.

"No one else will die because of me."

"You are not responsible for what happened in GenLink,

Liv. That's on Sowards. Losing those assets was the result of a madman with too much power, and agents like me who didn't ask more questions."

I pulled my gaze up to meet his. That was the first time I'd ever heard him share blame for the destruction of GenLink.

"They threatened Colton, Ridge." The words burned a hole through me.

"I know," he said. "I found the letter. Michelle has it now." Ridge tugged my hand to his lips, kissing the tips of my fingers. My eyes combed over him, searching. "Colton's fine. He's with Brian. I'm keeping tabs on him."

I nodded and Ridge brushed away the tear I didn't know I'd shed.

"They arrested Adam. I don't think he's saying much."

I shook my head, pulling my hand from the warm security of his. "What are you going to do? Hire 24/7 security? It's not realistic." A note of panic crept in and I coughed it away.

"We'll make it work," Ridge said.

I forced my eyes onto his, desperation shone from their depths. A sudden vibration spiked between us, shooting a note of helplessness along my spine.

"I'm signing the papers, Ridge. Let the government keep me under lock and key until they can figure this out. There's a chance we can work this out. Figure out what Sowards is trying to do. I could get my life back."

"If it doesn't happen that way?" The muscle in Ridge's jaw tensed.

"Then I'll disappear." I could hardly believe the words had passed through my own lips, but the lurch in my gut, the threatening wave of sickness, was proof.

After all Ridge and I had been through, the thought of giving it all up was physically painful. He was here, for me, sitting silently at my side, his eyes fixed on his fingers as he stroked my hand. The heat of his skin on mine melted into my core.

"Would you take it all back?" he asked. "If you could?" Ridge lifted his eyes to meet mine.

"Take what back?"

"Us? Saying yes when I asked you out?"

The bubble of laughter erupted without warning. "Well, if I remember correctly, you only asked me out because I was your target–part of the operation." Somehow I managed to smile.

"Liv–" It was a plea. He needed to know.

"No." Honesty felt good. "I might change some details, but Ridge McCaffrey, you'll always be my one."

Ridge breathed a heavy sigh. Relief.

"What about you?" We weren't going to have much more time for ridiculous conversations like these, so I might as well take advantage of the moment.

"I'd take back my involvement in GenLink, without a doubt." Ridge tucked my face against his hand. "But I'll never regret falling in love with you."

"I'm sorry I've made this so difficult."

Ridge's gaze combed over my face. Pain dulled the cerulean sea of his eyes. He shifted his hand to tuck an unruly curl behind my ear. The corner of his mouth twitched, as if he was deciding the weight of his words. By the time he spoke it was little more than a whisper.

"Stay. Please."

Another vibration–desperation–sparked at me as his thumb traced my jaw. I jerked away on instinct and Ridge dropped his hand in surrender.

"No," I shook my head, trying to help him understand it wasn't his touch I'd pulled away from. "Touch me again," I whispered.

Ridge lifted his hand to graze my cheek once more, his eyes scouring me for signs of unease. I closed my eyes to his touch. At first, nothing but the warm security of his hands against my skin seeped through. But as his thumb started down my jaw, the spark hummed, this time with confusion and pain. I fought the reactionary exhale for as long as I could, absorbing his energy. But the moment it came, he knew—and I felt it.

"I can feel you," I whispered. He leaned closer, absorbing the words into the depths of his kiss. He tugged, pressing closer as a spike of heat from low in my belly ignited into flame.

I closed my eyes, expecting to see a monster's face. But it never came, driven away by the buzz between us. I wanted his skin against mine, needed the sensation of his own desire meshing with my own—proof I wasn't damaged beyond repair. Electric sparks of desperate need danced along exposed skin.

Ridge lifted me from the edge of the mattress, his lips never leaving mine. He tossed the covers back, repositioning me toward the head of the bed. He left me there, holding up his index finger in a wait-a-minute signal while he returned to the door. Shoving a nightstand in front of the unlockable slab of wood, he stepped back to admire his handiwork.

"Nice," I admired, unable to contain the giggle bubbling into my chest. "You act like you might have done this a time or two."

Ridge shrugged. "What? The door? Just twice actually, and not for the reasons you think." He unzipped his hoodie and pulled it from his arms, depositing it on the floor at his feet before tugging the white t-shirt over his head, ruffling the deep mahogany waves of his hair.

I propped up onto my elbow to enjoy the view as he slipped in next to me.

"Is this okay?" he asked.

I nodded, a choke of memories I'd just as soon forget

taunted from the recesses of my brain. He took my hand, planting my palm over his heart, chasing them away. His eyes burned into mine. Electric sparks buzzed through my hand and into my arm, like the touch of an electric fence.

"What do you feel?" His voice slid like caramel through me, coating dregs of irrational fear. I focused on the churning emotions vibrating through my hand. The harsh knives of anger, frustration, and loss dulled into pinpricks by overwhelming hope. Love dueled with desperation below the surface, dusting all the other emotions with thin layers of skepticism and worry.

"Worry," I breathed. "Hope. But, Ridge, I can't stay."

"Shh–" Ridge lifted an index finger to cover my lips. "Right now, you're here. In this moment. In my arms. And I never thought I'd get that chance again."

The heat of a tear gathered at the rim of my right eye, the clutch of emotion in my chest.

"No matter what happens next–what decision you make– we have this moment." His words raised gooseflesh along my arms and he leaned closer, his lips trailing from my mouth southward until he broke contact, tugging the t-shirt I'd borrowed from George off over my head. His eyes asked for permission, searching mine.

"I'm okay," I said. My hand drifted from Ridge's chest to his waist. And that's when I realized, as long as I had him, I would be. I loosened the belt at his waist and unfastened his pants, pushing his jeans toward the foot of the bed.

He turned away to kick out of them and climbed back under the covers, rolling to hover over me, his lips teased and tasted as flickers of vibration hummed through my skin, heightening every sensation. I guided him onto his back, tossing my own jeans onto the floor.

I straddled Ridge, and the corner of his lips tipped in

appreciation. His eyes followed his hands as they skimmed sensitive flesh. I lowered against the warmth of him, delivering a trail of kisses up his torso until the low growl in his throat ignited a spark of insatiable want. I sat up, the hardness of him pressed against me, chasing the monsters away.

30

RIDGE

idge padded down the steps in his dad's house in bare feet, avoiding the risers that creaked out of habit, not necessity. His father sat on the couch, coffee in hand, television blaring some mid-morning news program.

"Coffee's ready," George said. A tiny smile tugged at the corner of his mouth. "Might be cold by now, though." He took a sip from his own mug.

"Thanks, Dad. I'll brew a new pot if Liv wants some." Ridge slipped around the railing and sank onto the couch next to his dad.

"You're playing with fire, son." George spoke after several seconds of silence, the background peppered by the local weather report.

"Last year you were all for this relationship. What changed your mind?"

"She's carrying an awful lot of baggage. She needs time to heal, to find herself, before jumping in with both feet."

"So you're concerned about *her* well-being?"

"And yours," Ridge's dad answered. He tipped forward, elbows on his knees, and stared into his cup of coffee. "She'll need help to get through this. Therapy."

Ridge knew his father was right. He'd seen evidence behind her eyes, scars on her back she wouldn't allow him to touch. "I can get her that."

"Maybe. But after everything that's happened, do you have the patience to weather this storm?"

"It's *because* of what's happened that I can help her through this, Dad. I can't let her go."

"And Colton?" George narrowed his gaze on Ridge. "I won't let you put my grandson's life at risk. Not for Liv. Not for anyone."

Ridge swallowed the knot of defiance that pulled in his chest. "Colton will be fine, Dad. I can make sure of that. I'll hire security if that's what it takes." A bead of anger percolated to the surface. "Why are you making this difficult? Why can't you be happy for me?"

Instead of answering Ridge's question, George gathered his mug and stood, disappearing into kitchen. Ridge followed. He propped himself against the countertop, arms crossed across his bare chest.

"What do you remember about when your mom left, Ridge?"

"Mom?" Ridge shrugged, the retaliatory teen he once was creeping back to the surface. "Not much. I came home from school and she was gone. I know she'd been holed up in her room for what seemed like days. But I was a kid. I remember you sitting the three of us down the next day, telling us she'd left." Ridge hesitated, stubbed an unsocked toe against the hardwood floor. "Sky didn't cry until she asked when Mom would be back, and you told her she was never coming home."

Ridge let the memory filter through his mind, his little sister's tears landing with a splat against her bare, summer-tanned legs. "Why are you asking me this?"

"Your mom didn't run away, Ridge. She didn't leave us. She was unstable."

His father's words prodded at Ridge, picking at the scabs left by his mother's disappearance all those years ago. He opened his mouth, to clarify, question, refute–he didn't yet know–but nothing came out.

"Liv and I talked a lot last night, Ridge. She doesn't want to stay. She's scared, afraid Colton will get caught in the middle. There's nothing you can do to make that fear go away."

The heat of desperation started a slow crawl through Ridge's veins. "I can sure as hell try."

George sighed, leaning against the countertop. "There's something about her story, her need to escape–the belief she's at the center of it all. It reminds me of your mother. Liv can't help the demons in her mind Ridge, but neither can you. She'll have her ghosts to keep her company, son. But you'll end up like me. Alone."

"Are you saying you think Liv's crazy?"

Ridge waited for the slight dip of his father's chin.

"Liv's story checks out, Dad. I've talked to her legal team. She's not making this shit up. I was there. I worked this op. And I'm sorry if what you said about mom is true. I know she had faults, but Liv is not Mom. She's scared, yes. Rightfully so. But she's not crazy."

Ridge felt Liv's presence before he saw her, leaning against the doorway, watching. She combed her fingers through a mess of disheveled curls. "I'm sorry to interrupt. I was just looking for some coffee."

Ridge slid from his position at the counter and grabbed a mug from the cabinet. "I'll brew a fresh pot," he said, shooting a dagger stare at his father who excused himself, slipping past Liv without so much as an apology.

Fingers of ice threaded through Ridge's gut as he busied himself with the coffee maker. He breathed through the urge to send the empty mug careening off the counter and onto the floor. Liv's hand grazed his bare arm, sliding up and over his shoulder.

"Cut your dad some slack. He loves you. He's just trying to protect you."

Ridge turned to face her. "How can you say that? My father thinks you're insane. I'm just supposed to be okay with that?" Ridge felt the anger twist his words, carving the air between them.

"You don't think I've questioned my own sanity over the past seven months?"

The sad smile playing on Liv's lips shot straight to his heart. He slid an arm around her waist and pulled her close, breathing in the familiar scent of his dad's drug store shampoo.

"I know how crazy all of this sounds–claiming to be the target of a man who took an oath to serve and protect. Your dad's not the first to question me. He won't be the last."

The heat of her breath danced against the skin of his chest. She pushed out of his embrace and grabbed the carafe from the coffee maker as it sputtered its last drops.

"Want some?" she offered.

Ridge reached for another cup and slid it her direction, watching her pour. He wondered how much longer he'd be able to enjoy little moments like these. She handed him his mug and took a sip of her own, her eyes smiled at him as she sipped.

"Hungry?" he asked. As if on cue, the doorbell chimed and Liv's face dropped. A spike of regret tore into his chest as he peeked out the nearby window.

Two vehicles, a black sedan and deep gray SUV parked in the gravel driveway behind his dad's aging Mercury. Ridge listened as his father answered the door, speaking in hushed tones as Michelle Rogers and her team descended on his dad's little suburban house.

31

LIV

Quiet commotion from the other room sent prickles marching along my spine. Ridge watched me, sadness reflected in his eyes. I wondered what he saw. A fearful woman–scarred, broken, and running away–or a strong one, sacrificing everything she ever wanted for the safety of the people in her life. I turned away from the heat of his gaze–banking on the former.

George had been right to tell Ridge about his mom's mental state. I had no idea how true any of it was, but George had no reason to lie. Besides, Ridge would have to process it in his own way–research, interrogation, evidence, conclusion. At least, that's the way it had always been. Stripping a badge doesn't change the man.

"Ready?" I asked, forcing myself tall, I tipped onto my toes to deliver a quick kiss.

"Now or never." The mask of a smile played on his lips as he grasped my hand and led me out of the kitchen. On instinct, I braced against his vibrations, but I let down the wall, opening myself to the fear-laced worry humming through my fingers.

Four heads, George's included, swiveled to face us as we slipped through the doorway and into the family room.

"Miss Sullivan," Michelle started. "You know Tony." She gestured toward him before introducing the stranger. "This is Special Agent Amanda Lombardi. She's here to go over some of the–" Michelle's gaze flicked from George to Ridge. "–the details of our next steps." Her eyes locked on mine. "I was very sorry to hear about the incident at the gas station." She pushed forward, her hand skimming from my shoulder to my wrist. "The detective said you refused treatment?"

"I'm fine," I pushed the words through guilt-tightened lips. Ridge squeezed my hand, his thumb grazing mine.

Michelle's gaze drifted to Ridge, taking him in from head to toe before settling a moment too long on his bare torso. "Agent McCaffrey." She nodded. "Nice to see you again."

The tip of her head and twist of her lips cracked open a nugget of undeserved jealousy in my chest.

"Wish I could say the feeling is mutual," Ridge said. My envy soothed by the addition of his hand to the small of my back. I sucked in an even breath.

"Fair enough," Michelle said. "As you know, we were able to apprehend Adam Miller after a somewhat lengthy standoff. There is quite a bit we need to go over before we discuss protection. Is there somewhere we can sit?"

George offered up the dining room and excused himself, heading upstairs.

Ridge whispered, "I'll be right back," pressing his lips hot against my temple. He followed George, taking the steps two at a time before disappearing onto the second floor.

"Can I get you some coffee?" I offered, showing everyone into the adjacent dining room.

I poured a cup for Special Agent Lombardi and Michelle before joining them at the seventies-era wood-laminate table. Ridge returned, a faded Nirvana t-shirt stretched over his chest. Amusement tickled the corners of my lips as he planted a kiss on the top of my head and slid into the chair next to mine.

"Left my clothes in DC," he said in a whisper, squeezing my leg under the table. "It's a little small, but this was the best I could do."

I lost control of the smile as it broke out over my face, catching Michelle's attention.

"Something funny, Miss Sullivan?" The accusation in Michelle's words sucked the humor from the moment.

I shook my head, glancing at Tony who stood like a bouncer in the corner, eyeing me while Michelle dug a legal pad out of her briefcase.

"First, I'll start with the good news. The judge approved our request to have an independent lab run their own tests on the remains found at O'Malley's cabin. They'll do their own DNA extraction and will return the results to us. Is there anything I should know about that key piece of evidence before we move on?" Her right eyebrow cocked in suspicion.

"No, the bone they found does not belong to me." It sounded asinine to say it. I was sitting right here, very much alive, in a kitchen where Ridge had eaten Cheerios as a kid.

"So there is no way our lab will find any trace of DNA belonging to you, Liv Sullivan, in that specimen?" Michelle prompted.

"Correct," I confirmed, unsure why she was going out of her way to make me confirm my identity in front of a group of people who, to my knowledge, hadn't questioned it.

"Now, on to the bad news. We've done some digging on your assault at the gas station. It's clear Miller knew you were on the Nashville bus, which means he could have known the bus would pit in Bishop's Hollow."

Ridge tensed in the chair next to me. "You think she was targeted?"

"It's a possibility." Michelle held Ridge's gaze a beat too long before returning her focus to me. "We're pulling Miller's phone records. See if we can pin down any contact between him and the men at the Stop-n-Go."

I slid my hand down Ridge's thigh. "Go check on Colton," I said. His eyes on mine sent a stab of pain into my chest. Barely concealed panic clipped his voice as he excused himself, dialing as he strode away.

"Miller wouldn't do this," I said.

"And you're sure because..."

"Because he thinks he's doing the right thing. He's trying to protect Ridge and Colton."

"By sacrificing you?" Michelle's tone carried implications I didn't like.

"Adam's just as scared as I am. Find out who's doing this to him, and you'll find the person behind everything."

"And you believe that person is Sowards."

I nodded.

Michelle tucked her pen alongside the yellow legal pad and glanced through the doorway. "I assume you've talked with Ridge about what this will mean?" Michelle's voice was cautious.

"Not in detail," I admitted.

"That conversation needs to happen," Agent Lombardi cut in. "Within the next twenty-four hours." Lombardi hadn't spoken anything other than a quiet hello at introductions, and the power of her voice startled me. Firm. Decisive.

"What happens in twenty-four hours?" I asked.

"Ms. Rogers and her team will tape your testimony against

Former SAC Sowards. We'll also conduct recordings based on events during Miller's abduction and the assault at the Stop-n-Go. Those recordings will be used at trial. Considering recent events, it's too dangerous to wait. Keeping you in plain sight through the trial, which could be six months away at this point, could prove disastrous." Her eyes caught mine and held, her voice dissolving into kindness. "Your life is not something any of us are willing to risk right now."

Lombardi's eyes were soft and sincere. I liked her. Trusted her. Maybe more than Michelle.

She pulled paperwork from her own briefcase and slid it in front of me. "This outlines the benefits of Witness Security. But the costs, for many people, are a brutal adjustment. You have to be fully committed. It's not easy to leave everyone and everything you've ever known and become someone new."

I leafed through the packet. I'd done the research. Knew what was involved. But that was before Ridge had seen me. Before I'd inserted myself back into his life. Before he'd brought back a part of me I'd lost. I wanted to regret that decision. But I couldn't.

Ridge's quiet baritone filtered in from the other room. He was talking to Colton, chatting about the superhero movie he'd seen and whether or not he'd been good for Brian and Skylar. My heart squeezed.

"What will Sowards be told?" I asked.

The two women glanced at each other. Michelle spoke first. "I won't lie, Olivia, by coming forward to Ridge, you made our job difficult. But the incident in Bishop's Hollow ups the ante. We have a group of people who still believe you're dead. And a select few who know you aren't. We'll have to ensure Sowards believes you're truly deceased. How we'll do that is still being discussed." Another glance at Lombardi.

"Tragic accidents often work well," the agent said. "Ms.

Rogers and I will give the two of you some time to talk."
Lombardi checked her watch. "We'll grab a bite to eat and be
back to confirm."

She slid her hand over to cover mine. After what happened
with Ridge that morning, I expected warm rivulets of
compassion. But there was nothing. Just the smooth emptiness
of her skin against mine. She gave my hand a pat and drew
away, passing Ridge on his way back into the dining room.

Ridge pulled out the chair beside me and sat. "Colton's
good," he said. "What happens now?"

I forced myself to look at him. Pained eyes framed by fine
lines of grief reappeared on the man I once thought could
handle anything. I refocused on the papers in front of me.

"I never should have pulled you into this." Emotion crept
from deep inside, stoked by anger, desperation, and guilt. "It
would have been easier for you if I'd stayed away. Tony told me
it'd be safer if you thought I was dead. He was right." A tear
slid down the bridge of my nose, landing on the pamphlet in a
perfect puddle. "I'm so sorry."

Ridge slid his hands up my arms to either side of my face,
forcing me to face him. "I'm not," he whispered. "I'll never be
sorry."

His eyes flicked to Tony, still standing in the corner, head
bowed. "Give us some time alone, would you?" It was more
demand than question. Tony nodded and Ridge watched him
exit, likely just to the other side of the doorway, but at least the
façade of privacy was in place.

Ridge took a breath before starting again. "In those first few
weeks after the explosion, all I could think about were all the
things I'd done wrong. All the ways I'd betrayed you, kept
secrets from you, lied to you."

His thumb traced my lip before he pulled back, breaking
contact to watch me.

"I told myself it was my fault, that your death was my punishment. After that, I got angry. At myself, the Bureau, God," his voice dipped. "Even Skylar for a while, for surviving what you couldn't."

"Ridge–" I started.

"Please, let me finish."

I nodded.

"Started drinking again." A curl of emotion tugged at Ridge's lips. "Lost more than my fair share of time to drunken tirades. Until Brian stepped in. Lured me to some survivor's support group that met at a church on the west side of Columbus. And I spent my first visit listening. I listened to people tell these terrible stories about what happened to their loved ones–their mother, brother, sister, significant other, child–and I realized for the first time in almost three months that I wasn't alone. I wasn't the only one with a sad story, and I had so much to be grateful for–Colton, Skylar, Brian, my dad... the time I did get to spend with you." Ridge swallowed, eyes returning to mine. "You changed me, Liv. You taught me to trust."

Ridge sucked in a breath, his chest expanding under the too small t-shirt. "I guess what I'm trying to say is, the last few days have been an unexpected miracle." A chuckle bubbled up through Ridge's words. "Although, I did think I was losing my shit when I saw you outside the DOJ."

His smile melted into my core and a laugh of my own escaped in a huff.

"But then you risked everything to come to my room. You could have slunk away–should have, maybe–let me believe I was losing my mind. But you didn't. You trusted me to keep your secret."

Ridge shook his head and stood, ruffling a hand through his hair as he paced a circle in the room.

"Now I have to trust you to make a choice."

"I didn't start all this to turn tail and run away," I said, tears creeping up the back of my throat. "I can't let him get away with what he did."

"I'm not asking you to." Ridge returned to the table, wrapped his arms around me and pulled me into his chest.

His heart thumped against my ear, soothing the frustration that seeped through my veins.

"I'm asking you to let me help. I will do whatever it takes to keep you and Colton safe. This is my second chance, Liv. Please don't take it away from me."

"I can't—"

"I know this is your decision," Ridge cut in. "And making your own choices is something that's been taken from you for long enough. I'm just asking you to choose me."

"Jeopardizing Colton's life isn't a risk I can live with."

Ridge's face crumpled under the weight of my words. I reached out for him, a thread of panic seeping through my core.

"Don't—" He shifted away, sucked in a ragged breath and smoothed his hands over the tabletop. "I told myself I could take it, either way." His jaw clenched. "I was wrong." Ridge stood. "I can't stay here, hold your hand and watch while you throw our future away. Bye, Liv."

32

RIDGE

Ridge slipped into the living room, past Lombardi and Rogers who were asking George for restaurant recommendations, and out the front door. He could feel their eyes following him as he yanked the door closed with a solid *slam*.

He hopped off the side of the cement porch and turned the corner, rounding the side of his father's house. Obscured by the unused and dilapidated garage, he leaned back against the siding and looked up at the sky. Sun glittered through the trees and onto his face, its warm hopefulness the antithesis of the cold desperation that surged through his gut like a freight train with no end in sight.

His heart raced, pounding irregular thumps behind his sternum. He could hear the pulse of blood rushing against his eardrums as hot irons of panic stabbed his forearm. He leaned forward, trying to keep from falling off the edge of desperation into the vat of terror that waited to sink its claws into him once again.

He heard Tony before he felt his presence, boots crunching

against old leaves clustered in corners against the house. He joined Ridge in silence, holding an outstretched hand toward Ridge, the familiar pack of gum now almost empty. This time, Ridge took a piece. At least the gum could buffer the grind of frustration between his molars.

"Are you really okay with this?" Tony said, his voice low, conspiratorial.

"It's not my decision," Ridge countered.

"Isn't it?" Tony looked at Ridge, his gaze pulling Ridge's from the ground. "She's scared, McCaffrey. This isn't like your girlfriend's leaving you because she doesn't love you. She's making this decision out of fear. You've got to know that."

"It doesn't matter why she's making it. She's spent her whole life trying to live up to other people's expectations–her parents', her grandmother's, GenLink's, even mine. This needs to be her choice. I owe her that."

Tony exhaled. "Why do you think I didn't stop her in the hall outside your hotel room that night?"

It was a question Ridge had wondered. Liv might have been the one to fight for it, but Ridge knew they could have ended that visit before it ever began. Evan had certainly tried.

"I've spent a lot of time with Liv," Tony said. "It's clear why she came back to the United States. It might be easier for her to put a name on it–revenge, retribution, whatever–but her return has never been about that. Not at the core."

"What's your point?"

"She came back for you. Are you really willing to let her walk away? To live the rest of your life knowing she's out there. Maybe in another man's arms?"

Ridge shook his head and stepped away, increasing the distance between them.

"There's a chance, once Sowards is away, she could come back."

"You know of any instances where that's worked out, Agent McCaffrey?"

Ridge swallowed. He didn't. Because there weren't any. He sucked in a breath and squared himself against Tony. "Why do you care?"

"Because maybe you aren't the only one who's lost someone. Maybe when I see someone with the chance to make things right, I can't help but interfere."

Ridge closed his eyes, the memory of his hand tangled in Liv's hair, her skin against his as he clutched her to his chest, so vivid he could almost feel it. He forced himself to breathe evenly, to calm his racing heart and limit the flashes of an uncertain future that flickered like old movie clips through his mind.

"This isn't about giving her the freedom to choose. It's not chivalry. And you want to talk about what you owe her? Then give her what she came back for, even if she won't admit it. She's doing what she thinks is best for your son. And you're trying to be the bigger man. And that, my friend, will destroy both of you."

Ridge pulled himself up and stared at Tony, the gum clutched tight between his teeth.

"Stop her," Tony said. "Now. Before it's too late."

33

LIV

S pecial Agent Lombardi was the first to peek her head around the corner into the dining room.

"What did you decide?" Lombardi pulled a chair away from the table and sat, her soft eyes combing over me with delicate scrutiny.

"I'll sign your papers." My voice sounded deceivingly strong against the pain of Ridge's judgement. "I'll do whatever you need me to do in terms of the trial."

"You understand that if we initiate this process on your behalf that you can never return to Cascade Hills? That you can never again see Ridge McCaffrey–never?"

I swallowed and sucked in a lungful of uncertainty. "I understand."

Lombardi twisted the packet of papers she'd given me earlier and thumbed through them, she folded it open to a new page. Her index finger tapped at the empty signature line across the bottom as she pushed the contract toward me.

I skimmed the typewritten page, my breath clinging tight in my chest. The basic contract stripped me of any identifying information that had ever been mine—Social Security number, birth certificate, driver's license, all financial information—every bit of it would be turned over to the Bureau and reprocessed into an identity that would suit our purposes.

"The declaration of your death after the explosion makes things easier," Lombardi said. "You've got no assets to worry about."

I reached for the pen with shaky fingers, hesitating. "Who owns Sullivan farm now?"

Lombardi exchanged glances with Michelle as the lawyer lowered onto a chair.

"Never mind. It doesn't matter." A plunging sense of regret rushed through me. "Whose name should I sign?"

"Sullivan," Lombardi answered.

The front door creaked as I looped the O onto the page in front of me. Hard fast steps on the living room floor followed. Michelle turned. I looked up as Ridge appeared in the doorway, pausing before the double loop of Ls in my last name.

"Stop." His voice echoed around the quiet square of the room. "Liv, don't do this."

The sight of him in the doorway—tall, broad shoulders, dark hair, the crystalline blue of his eyes, the tiny line of concern pressed between his brows—sucked the air from my chest. Another swirl of regret plummeted through my stomach. I glanced down at the nearly completed signature scrawled across the bottom of the paper. Lombardi's "*Never*," rang in my ears, and my fingers shook.

"You're making the right decision," Michelle said from across the table. "For everyone."

Ridge stepped forward and his eyes locked on mine, cerulean seas of hope-laced fear.

"Liv, this is *your* decision," Lombardi added from my left as Ridge moved from the doorway to my side.

He pulled the pen from my trembling fingers and tugged me to the side, kneeling beside my chair.

"I need you," Ridge started. "I can't go back to Cascade Hills and pretend nothing happened. I can't live the rest of my life knowing you're out there and not be able to be with you."

"It's too big a risk, Agent McCaffrey," Michelle's voice cut in. "At least she'll be alive."

"Fuck your promises, and fuck Sowards." The words from Ridge's mouth fell on the room with percussive whacks.

Lombardi and Michelle shifted in their chairs. "You can't promise he won't find her." Ridge leveled a dark, accusatory glare at Lombardi and Rogers. "Tell me you can guarantee Liv's safety—put it in writing—and I will walk out of this room right now."

The women were silent for a beat before Lombardi answered. "You know as well as I do, there are no guarantees. But we do have resources."

Ridge ignored her and turned back to me, his eyes now soft, imploring. "He took you from me once, Liv. There's no way in hell I'll let him take you again."

"This isn't about me." My voice wobbled in the air between us.

Ridge pulled my hands into his, his voice softening. "Colton is my son. And I will protect him with my life. But he needs a father who's whole." Ridge's gaze held mine. "Don't sign those papers. Don't throw away what we have together."

His skin sparked hope into me, gentle pulses sending a throb of need through my core. He was right. Regardless of the secrets, the lies, there was a connection between us that I'd never understand. I swallowed. The anticipation in my lungs heavy and thick. I broke eye contact with Ridge as he made one final attempt.

"Please." It was more breath than word, overpowered by

the nervous shifts and quiet comments of Michelle and Lombardi as they whispered to each other in the background. Ridge skimmed his thumbs over the backs of my hands, his voice a quiet whisper. "I know you can feel this, Liv. Don't give up on us. Don't walk away."

I closed my eyes. I couldn't let my own desires get in the way of this decision. I couldn't risk a little boy's life for a relationship that any outsider would claim had been doomed from the start.

"This can't be about us," I said.

"It already is about us." Ridge's voice sunk deep, penetrating the darkest recesses of my core. "It always has been. You fought your way back here. You came to my hotel room. I don't give a shit about Sowards' last ditch effort or his threats. This is about you and me and building a life for ourselves without GenLink ruling our every decision. This is your chance to choose your own path, Liv. You came back here to be free. And you're so close. Don't let fear stop you now."

34

RIDGE

As Ridge kneeled in front of Liv, her hands in his, desperation clawed its way to the surface. He'd said everything he could think of to say and the longer Liv remained silent, the deeper her refusal would cut. She leaned into him, her head against his chest, and he pulled her close. Was this her way of saying goodbye?

"Don't leave me," he breathed into her hair before emotion cut off his ability to speak.

He felt her shudder against his chest, the moisture of tears permeating the t-shirt he'd thrown on in the interest of decency. His heart seized.

"I can't do this," Liv said, breaking the silence. She cleared her throat, looked from Ridge to Michelle and Lombardi. "Ridge is right. I came back for a reason. Running only gives Sowards more power."

The exhale that ripped through Ridge's lungs was long and hard, followed by a huff of relief. He gripped her against his chest with so much force she had to push him away. She swiveled with a sideways smile before making eye contact with the women on the other side of the laminate table.

Ridge rose from the floor, grabbing a nearby chair and pulling it up beside Liv.

"Now what?" he asked. A quick scan of both women showed bitter disappointment. A stark contrast to the glee he had little hope of masking.

"Fine," Lombardi said. "But the longer we can keep you under the radar the better." She shuffled the protection contract into a pile and returned it to Michelle.

"I think the original plan, videotaping any further testimony, would still be our best option. If you're out of the DC limelight, perhaps Sowards will assume you're underground," Michelle added.

"What about Miller? What will he be told?" Ridge asked.

"He's under investigation for his role in Liv's abduction. He won't be informed of any of this directly. Chances are good his lawyer will argue mental instability. So unless we find anything that proves a connection with Sowards or the attack at the Stop-n-Go, he'll likely get a deal," Michelle replied.

"Are you watching Sowards accounts?"

Lombardi cleared her throat. "With all due respect Agent McCaffrey, we are doing our job."

"I didn't mean–" Ridge started the apology before Lombardi cut back in.

"But the answer is yes, and at this point, there's been nothing out of the ordinary."

Ridge thanked her and relaxed against the kitchen chair. The warmth of Liv's skin against his own tethered him to the hope snaking through his gut.

"Of course, we'll continue the protection detail, at least through the trial," Lombardi continued.

"If I'm going back to Cascade Hills I'd rather do it without Tony." Liv's words snapped Ridge to attention.

"That's out of the question," Michelle cut in, her voice hard.

"I agree," Ridge said. "At least until we know more about what happened at the gas station."

The muscle in Liv's jaw contracted. "I was an easy mark, Ridge. I had a wad of cash. That's what happened at the gas station."

Ridge laced his fingers through hers. "I need to know for sure," he said, dragging her hand to his lips.

Her eyes locked on his, a cocktail of the fire he loved so much and the fear he'd work day and night to take away.

"Fine," she said, finally. "But I want Tony focused on Colton, not me. Discretely, if possible."

"Olivia, I don't think that's the best use of our resources," Michelle cut in.

"I don't care," Liv countered. "I need to know Colton's safe. Maybe that letter meant nothing. Maybe it was just a way to get me out of the way, to force me onto that bus. But I can't take that chance, not with him."

Ridge stayed silent, the hot threat of emotion built in his throat as he dragged his eyes over the woman next to him. The woman giving up what little protection remained in order to ensure his own son's safety.

Dregs of guilt filtered through his veins, all the times he'd kept the truth from her, abandoned her when she needed him the most. He'd blamed the badge. But it wasn't that. Hours of group therapy broke down those excuses. Everything that had come between them in the past boiled down to one thing—his inability to trust. A quality he was going to have to continue to work on if he intended to keep Liv in his life. He owed her that, and so much more.

Afternoon dragged into evening, with Lombardi and Michelle peppering Liv with questions Ridge was sure had been asked a zillion times before. He and his dad remained sequestered in the kitchen as the team interrogated Liv. Ridge eavesdropped through the semi-open floor plan while his father watched him, a twist of insecurity plastered across his face.

"Do you have someone you can talk to about what's happened so far?" Lombardi asked Liv.

"I can talk to Ridge."

"Olivia, you'll need to see a professional. Someone who can keep tabs on you. Make sure your mental health stays where we need it to be."

"And where exactly is that?"

Ridge could hear the clipped note of irritation in Liv's voice. She was reaching her limit.

"Are you sure this is for the best?" His father cut in, distracting him from the conversation in the other room.

"There's no question in my mind, Dad."

George studied him, the heat of his gaze melting into Ridge's skin. He nodded. "I am on your side, son. You need to know that. But there's been so much–too much." George may be having trouble processing through the scars of loss left by his own history–a history his dad would rather forget–but loss was one emotion Ridge was intimately comfortable with.

"It's okay, Dad. I get it. But Liv isn't Mom."

"Even after all this, you think she's capable of moving past everything? All the conspiracy. That boy's death?"

"He was a twenty-four-year-old attempted rapist, Dad. Hardly a boy." A bead of anger pulsed through his core.

"It's still a life, Ridge. She's got to learn to cope with that. Lombardi's right. Who's going to help her do that? You?"

Ridge took the last sip of iced tea and slid the glass across the countertop toward his dad. He exited the kitchen without a response to his father. The simmer of anger still roiling in his gut.

"I think that's enough, Lombardi. If you need more from her, you know where she'll be." Ridge moved beside Liv and gestured toward the door. "We've got our own plans that need to be made, so if you don't mind."

He caught the small smirk that twisted the corner of Tony's lips as Michelle and Lombardi gathered their things. Ridge ushered the group from the living room and out onto the sidewalk. The trio was already loaded in their vehicles before Liv joined him on the stoop.

Sliding up behind him, she reached up on her tiptoes. Her hands skimmed his shoulders as she planted a kiss between his shoulder blades. She wrapped her arms around his midsection, her breath hitting hot against his back, "Thank you."

He waited for the gray SUV to exit his father's drive and accelerate toward the center of town before turning to face Liv. He cupped her chin between the palms of his hands.

"You know I'll do whatever it takes to make sure you're okay, right? Not just physically, but—"

"You're gonna make sure I don't turn crazy?" The corner of her lip tipped in a teasing smile, unleashing a ribbon of relief through his core.

Ridge slid his hands down her arms and around her waist, pulling her close. "You did the same for me. Least I could do is return the favor."

35

LIV

After Michelle and her crew disappeared into the night, I tugged Ridge off the stoop. I backed down the driveway holding both his hands while he stepped slowly toward me looking more than a little confused.

"Where are we going?"

"This is where you grew up. I want to see what there is to see of Bishop's Hollow."

"At nine o'clock?"

I hesitated at the end of the drive and waited for him to catch up. "I need to get out of that house, Ridge." His hands wrapped around my waist and pressed us together, kicking a tickle of heat loose from deep in my core. "Besides," I whispered, staving off the effects of his body against mine. "I want to see where you lived. Where you hung out."

Ridge's tongue darted out to moisten his lower lip before he leaned in, the heat of his mouth on mine. I smiled as we broke contact. Everything in that moment was right. Ridge in his too-small t-shirt, his hands on me, losing ourselves in each other, even if it was to stave off reality–at least for a little while.

"You taste like cinnamon chewing gum," I said.

Ridge met my grin and laughed as he took my hand, leading me up the sidewalk in front of his father's house. "Big Red," he said. "Tony's a fan. He gave me a piece earlier. Turns out it really does calm frustration." Ridge tipped his head to the side. "Why, does it taste bad?"

"No, I like it." I stopped him on the cement walk for one more kiss.

"The house I grew up in is about three blocks from here. Another family lives there now, but we could walk by."

A knot surged into my throat. I hadn't thought about his house. I guess I just assumed they'd lived somewhere else after Ridge's sister, Riley, was killed in the fire. I processed the implications going back to that house must have had on an already guilt-ridden teenaged Ridge as we walked.

Before long, he pulled me to a stop and nodded at the two-story Colonial perched atop a knoll. The anxious suck of breath came before I could stop it, and I could feel Ridge's eyes on me.

"It's just like I remember from my dream."

"You sound surprised." Ridge squeezed my hand. "Once the insurance money came through, Dad had it rebuilt nail for nail, just like it was before the fire. It was like he was trying to erase the memory of her." Ridge drew in a breath of his own. "I hated him for it at the time. But I get it now."

Ridge's voice sunk low and quiet, like fog settling over a valley. The need to apologize for leaving him alone all those months clawed through my chest. But Ridge stopped me before it could rise.

"And don't even think of saying you're sorry, Liv. I didn't mean that as a reflection of what happened between us." He turned me to face him. "Besides, I got to spend those months believing you loved me. That's more than I did for you."

Guilt surged through Ridge's skin, pricking at my

fingertips. "I knew. I wouldn't be here if I thought otherwise. You did what you had to do."

Ridge shook his head, his gaze planted on our interlaced fingers. "No. I followed an order–a bullshit order at that. I should have put a stop to Sowards' demands after Jason's death. Instead, I waited. Let them take you to Ireland–train you for a psychic intelligence program. I knew it wasn't right."

His eyes rose to meet mine, chasing away the memory of my ex-fiancé shooting himself in Sullivan barn. Ridge's thumb grazed my lip.

"This is bigger than you, Ridge. I was born into this, remember? You didn't have the power to put an end to GenLink."

"I should have tried. Look at what I put you through."

Hot spikes of guilt-laden rage filtered into my skin, pricking at me like iron fresh from a flame. I clenched my jaw against it, but it refused to let go.

"Where's the 7-Eleven?" I asked, hoping for a distraction.

Ridge tilted his head, an uncertain expression clouding his features.

"Skylar told me you used to ride your bike down there."

The pulses of rage slowed into pinpricks as Ridge refocused on a happier memory. He pointed down the street. "About a mile up the road that way. It became a Shell station after the 7-Eleven, but they tore that down five or six years ago. I think it's a Subway sandwich shop now." He hesitated. "Skylar told you that?"

"We shared some childhood memories. It was one of her favorites," I said, smiling.

I glanced at the grassy spot in front of the white Colonial as we walked away. I could almost still see the huddled family waiting on the lawn for the firefighters to find Riley, the lick of flames against the house, the stench of burning insulation.

"I'm sorry about what happened to Riley."

Ridge nodded and squeezed my shoulders, turning back in the direction of his father's house. "We should get back. We've got to figure out how to get home tomorrow."

"Lombardi wants me to stay another day," I said. "They want to bring in A/V equipment to videotape more testimony."

Ridge didn't say anything right away, but I could feel his frustration. We'd gone almost another block before he spoke. "I'll call Bridget and tell her I can't make Colton's concert."

"No. Wait, Colton's going to be in a concert?" I paused, my feet rooted on the cement.

"He started preschool. His first spring concert is tomorrow night."

"You have to go," I said. "He needs you there. Besides, I'm perfectly capable of driving myself back to Cascade Hills."

Ridge didn't answer, but his jaw pulsed as he walked next to me. I skimmed my hand up and down his arm, my own thoughts tumbling in the silence.

"What do you think he'll say?" I asked as we approached George's drive.

The question pulled Ridge out of the depths of his own silence, the pulses of worry lightening against my skin.

"Colton?" he asked.

I nodded, and Ridge laughed, a smile breaking out over his face.

"He's four. He'll probably just be glad he can raise his cat at the farm instead of our tiny apartment."

His words sent me back a step. "It's not mine anymore, Ridge—the farm, my grandmother's inheritance. Nothing is."

"You don't know, do you?" Ridges eyes combed over mine as we stood in the driveway. Light from his father's front porch cast a long shadow on his face. "Your mother came to see me after the memorial." He swallowed, as if the memory was painful. "She gave me the keys to the farm, signed it over to me a few weeks after that. All the money's in a trust now. Plan was to fund a scholarship program, maybe something for photography students through the arts college in Columbus. We never got that far."

Snippets of unvoiced thought tumbled through my brain—a continuous loop of oh-my-Gods, thank-yous, and don't-lie-to-mes. None of it worthy of the words Ridge had spoken. But he seemed to understand, pulling me close.

His breath warmed the top of my head as he said, "You're going back to Sullivan farm, Liv. You're coming home."

36

LIV

I f death made disappearing easier, coming back from the dead had the opposite effect. I sat with Ridge on George's overstuffed sofa the following morning, listening as Lombardi and Michelle outlined the minutiae of how best to get me from Bishop's Hollow to Cascade Hills without arousing suspicion from anyone who might be linked to Sowards. Every word out of their mouths heightened the discomfort already rolling off Ridge in waves.

"Does it really matter?" I asked.

The women's eyes flicked to me, ready to scold me like an insolent child.

"I'm serious. I'm going home. Sowards will find out, and that's on the off chance he doesn't already know. You've questioned Adam. Is there really any possible scenario where Sowards is kept in the dark, here?"

Both women fish gulped their way through insufficient arguments. I'd made my point.

"You're brave," Ridge said when I finally forced him and

George out of the house around noon, knowing it would take time for Ridge to pick up the rental and get on the road.

The last thing I wanted was for him to miss Colton's concert.

"Standing up to them like that."

"It doesn't take bravery to call out stupidity." I gave Ridge's chest a gentle shove, pushing him into the passenger seat of George's Mercury. "I'm not naïve enough to think Sowards doesn't know where I am."

"I can stay, Liv, if you're worried."

"You will not miss your son's first concert, not on my account. I'll be fine. Trust me, they won't leave me alone." I glanced up at the picture window, complete with two curious sets of eyes watching our goodbye. "Besides, I'll see you tonight."

Ridge tugged me lower, tangling his hand in my hair and pulling me in for a kiss that left me breathless. George cleared his throat a little too loudly, ending the moment. Ridge released me, tugging the door closed with a smile.

IT WAS ALMOST six thirty before I climbed into Lombardi's SUV, mentally exhausted from a day of testimony. She and Michelle had insisted a flight would be safer than a road trip, and I was fresh out of motivation to argue. Lombardi jabbered as she drove from George's house to the local airfield.

"Tony will be waiting for you when you land," Lombardi said, passing me a coffee. She navigated away from the Starbucks drive-through while I gazed out the window, focused on the flash of cars buzzing past as we merged back onto the main road. "He'll help you get safely from the airfield to

Cascade Hills. You didn't talk to Ridge about when you'll be there, right?"

"Right," I lied. The past few days had given me a taste of what freedom might feel like. I'd lived under someone else's rules and regulations for the better part of a year, and I was more than ready to break free, in spite of all the what ifs.

"Good." She hesitated. "Have you considered how you're going to handle this?"

I swiveled my head to meet her gaze before she refocused on the road ahead. "Going home?" I asked.

"Explaining your absence," she said, matter-of-factly. "You were declared dead, Olivia. There's legal work that goes along with bringing you back." Her voice softened. "I took the liberty of contacting Jack Reynolds. Agent McCaffrey mentioned you'd done business with him in the past. I've apprised him of the situation and he's agreed to help you petition the court to have the declaration of death nullified—quietly."

Honestly, the legal ramifications of being declared dead never once occurred to me. I was more concerned about the emotional impact my reappearance would have on my mom, Skylar, and Brian—maybe even Colton.

The possibility I wouldn't be able to provide adequate answers to the questions I knew were headed my way created underlying anxiety. But not once had I thought about the logistics—my name, identification. The sudden realization that there was a granite stone in the cemetery next to my grandmother—one with my name on it—ignited a renewed pulse of worry.

"What do I say to my family?" I asked, finally, as Lombardi pulled to a stop in the open airfield parking lot.

She shifted in the charcoal leather seat to face me. "Tell them what you remember. That's all you can do."

"They'll wonder why I never called. From McGill's Pub, I

could have called any of them. But I didn't. Ridge never asked, but I know he wonders."

"You had a lot to process, Liv. Your family will feel the same way Ridge does. They'll just be glad to have you home."

Agent Lombardi pulled an envelope from the console and handed it to me. "Here," she said. "Your confirmation number is in there as well. It's a private charter, but they might ask for ID. You only have to be Olivia Allyn for another hour and a half."

I pulled the familiar passport and driver's license from the envelope. I ran the pad of my thumb over the hard plastic photograph and unfamiliar name and address, swallowing a knot of hesitation before sliding the card back inside.

"Thank you, Agent Lombardi. I know you and Michelle wanted me to choose differently. I haven't been easy to work with. You could have made this decision very hard on me and you chose not to. I appreciate that."

Her soft eyes landed on mine. "Please, call me Amanda. Besides, you're the one who has to live with the consequences of the life you choose, Olivia. Fear drives many people to WITSEC. It takes a strong person to face that fear and spit in its face." She smiled. "Besides, some people aren't cut out for federal protection. Better to know now than to find out later."

She popped open the center console and slipped a business card and a pen from the space inside.

"Here's my card." She scrawled a second number on the back and handed it to me. "Call me anytime. About anything. Having someone to talk to that might remotely understand is half the battle."

She slid a hand down my arm. My skin prickled as she reached the bare flesh at my wrist. A flash of memory surged through the contact—a dark cabin, her cool hands positioning an oxygen mask over my face, the *thwack* of helicopter rotors in the air above us. And in that instant, I found clarity.

"You were there," I said. "That night, after the explosion."

The light huff of a laugh crept through her lips, but she didn't answer. "I admire the choices you made, Liv. You fought your way back here and you deserve to live *your* life, not someone else's."

An odd sorrow pricked at the air between us, the first atmospheric pulse I'd felt with anyone other than Ridge.

"Come on," Amanda said, opening the driver's side door. "Let's get you in the air."

I gathered the backpack George had dug out of a closet to replace the one I'd left at BHPD. My original carry-on now almost certainly in a Nashville Greyhound station's lost and found.

Lombardi slammed the driver's door, the jarring metallic *thunk* sending another spiral of anxiety up my spine. We walked in silence through the small terminal toward the charter desk where she gave me a quick hug. "Take care of yourself, Olivia. I'll be in touch."

She hung back as I approached the counter, a man in a coat and tie took my information. But Lombardi never moved. Still standing a few feet from the counter–watching.

"Is it too late to change my flight?" I asked as quietly as I could.

The man on the other side of the counter stopped typing into his computer and tilted his head at me, his lips lifting under a graying mustache. I glanced over my shoulder and the ticket agent's eyes followed mine.

"I'd just like to make sure I'm the only one who knows the details of the flight plan."

I was fully aware how paranoid I sounded, and I expected him to laugh at me. But instead, his eyes narrowed at Lombardi and he resumed tapping at the keypad. "Let's see what we can do, shall we?"

Lombardi was still watching when the agent led me back a hall to the private waiting area. The addition of a doorway between us cooled the raging heat of frayed nerves.

"Do you want me to call someone, Miss Allyn?"

I declined his offer and thanked him, wondering what kind of things he'd seen in the course of duty that made it perfectly reasonable that a woman would show up and want to change every aspect of her flight, down to the pilot, due to a severe case of paranoia. I shook away the thought. It didn't matter what he, or anyone else, thought. I knew what I'd seen.

I pulled the newly purchased cell from my pocket and turned it off, dropping it in the trash receptacle at the end of a row of chairs. I needed a form of communication, but Michelle had provided that phone, and I'd be damned if I gave them a homing beacon.

37

RIDGE

"**Y**ou're different," Bridget said as Ridge stood with her outside the auditorium at St. Stephen's, waiting for Colton and his class to come pouring from the backstage hall and into their parents' arms.

"What are you talking about?" Ridge said, giving Bridget a smile.

"That, right there. That smile. Where'd that come from?"

"I just watched my son wiggle back and forth on stage for the first time, Bridge, isn't that reason enough for a smile?"

It might have been a decent excuse, but he was well-aware of the good vibe he'd been putting off since returning to Cascade Hills that afternoon. Of course, other than Brian and George, no one else knew about Liv's intended return, and he planned to keep it that way until she was ready. He'd had too much to do with her death, he was more than happy to leave the coming back to life up to her.

"No, you've been like this all night. If I didn't know better, I'd say you're seeing someone. What gives?"

"I'm happy," Ridge said with a shrug. "Can't a guy just be happy?"

The cluster of kids fighting their way through the crowd saved him. He kneeled and waved at Colton who barreled over, launching himself into Ridge's arms.

THE THREE OF them were sitting in Murphy's an hour later when Brian came up to the table. "Heard you were the star of the show, little man," he said to Colton, flashing Ridge an unreadable glance. "Ridge, can I see you in the back a minute?"

Ridge excused himself and followed Brian through the kitchen and out the back door. Outside, parked along the curb, sat a gray SUV. Brian nodded toward the picnic table and Tony stood. Ridge searched Tony's face for some sign of news, but the PI remained expressionless. A lead weight of worry spiraled through Ridge's gut.

"What's wrong?"

"There's been an incident," Tony said. The first signs of unease cracked the stone of his face. "Lombardi took Liv to the airfield this afternoon. She was supposed to land at County Airfield an hour ago. She didn't make it."

Ridge could feel himself blinking. Could sense the weight of trapped air in his lungs. Brian's hand on his shoulder. A familiar wave of grief crept from the depths of his soul, overtaking him.

"We've been unable to establish contact with the aircraft."

"No." It was the only word Ridge was capable of speaking. His body swayed before his legs gave up, sending him to his knees on the damp earth behind Murphy's Pub.

Tony rushed forward. "This isn't the end, McCaffrey. Our

team vetted the charter, the pilot, everyone involved. There's weather over West Virginia. We're hoping the pilot rerouted."

"You said there's been no contact," Ridge said to the earth below, fighting to restrain the choked sob that threatened from the back of his throat.

"Correct."

"Aren't charters required to report modified flight plans?" Brian's voice cut in.

Tony gave Brian a once over, clearly judging his worthiness to be part of the conversation. "Yes. But it doesn't always happen."

Tony was trying to make this better, but nothing short of Liv standing in front of him right now could deliver Ridge from the searing panic that slit through him like the blade of a knife.

"Listen to me, Ridge. We'll find her. And when we do, you'll be the first person we call."

Tony was calm, a stark contrast to the overwhelming urge to pummel someone that coursed through Ridge's veins. Ridge gripped at the grass under his fingers to stave off the urge, but it didn't work. His arms and legs buzzed with electricity as he launched himself off the ground, landing a satisfying right hook against the unsuspecting bodyguard. Ridge shook the pain from his hand as Tony stumbled backward.

Brian's voice calling his name fell into the distance as blood rushed against Ridge's eardrums, muting sound. He swung again, landing a solid blow to Tony's gut, before the man defended himself, coming at Ridge with an uppercut that glanced off his jaw and into his nose with a slice of white hot pain.

Ridge swiped at the blood with the back of his hand before Tony regained enough breath to speak. "I'm not the enemy, McCaffrey."

Ridge grabbed Tony by the collar and shoved him against

the side of the SUV. "Then who is?" he seethed. "Who did this?" The unmistakable coppery taste worked its way to the back of his throat.

"Lombardi put her on the craft. That's all I know."

The words registered and Ridge released his grip, stepping away from Tony. "You think she did this?"

"I don't know." Tony smoothed his rumpled jacket, pressing the pads of his fingers against his cheekbone, testing the function of his lower jaw. "I think it's possible. That's what I came here to tell you. I found something."

"Ridge?" Bridget's voice cut the silence. "What the–"

But it was the higher-pitched, "Daddy?" that sent a snake of regret through Ridge's churning gut, pulling him down from the metaphoric ledge. Ridge glanced back. Colton held Bridget's hand, an expression of shock tattooed across his son's innocent face.

"Hey, little man." Brian swept between them, pulling Colton onto his hip and away from the scene. "I got some of those Sour Patch Kids left over from the movies the other night. You want some?"

Colton nodded, wide-eyes still focused on Ridge, as Brian carried him up the back steps and into his second floor apartment.

Ridge stumbled to the picnic table and sat, tipping his head between his legs as drops of blood puddled in the grass beneath him. The cool of Bridget's hands found the back of his neck before she spoke again.

"What the hell happened out here?"

"It's nothing, Bridget," Ridge tried as Bridget forced his head up, inspecting the result of his injury.

"Who the hell are you?" she added, spitting the words at Tony as he pulled a wad of napkins from inside the SUV and handed them to her. She pressed them against Ridge's face, sending a slice of pain into his skull. Ridge took them from her and scooted away, blotting the blood from his own nose.

"Tony Medici," Tony said, extending his hand in Bridget's direction.

"You'll forgive me if I don't shake the hand of the man who beat up my husband," Bridget said.

One of Tony's heavy eyebrows arched in a question mark.

"*Ex*-husband," Ridge clarified, ignoring the blast of ice Bridget shot at him. "And he didn't beat me up."

"Right, well he looks fine and you're the one with blood all over you so—"

Tony laughed, cutting off the rest of Bridget's sentence. "Yep. Definitely ex."

Bridget leveled a stare at Tony. "Fine, *Tony*." She stretched his name out in two sarcastic syllables. "What are you doing here?"

"I just needed to talk to Ridge."

"Does this have something to do with the whole happy-go-lucky vibe he's been sporting all evening?"

Tony stayed silent.

"Kind of," Ridge said. He pulled the wad of napkins from his nose, the bleeding slowing to a trickle.

"Well?" Bridget stood between Ridge and Tony, hands on her hips, waiting. Ridge glanced at Tony, who lifted a shoulder in a shrug.

"Liv's alive. I found out when I was in DC"

Bridget stared at him. The reflection from the parking lot lights illuminated the shock in her thunderstorm eyes. Her hands fell from her hips. Her gaze ping-ponging between Tony and Ridge.

"Why didn't you tell me?" Her words had lost their edge, concern replacing sarcasm.

"She's supposed to be on her way home tonight. Tony came

to tell me that she's late. They've lost contact with her flight."

Bridget cursed lightly under her breath. She kneeled at Ridge's side, scanning his face for signs of the weakness she'd borne witness to after Liv's death. Her fingers combed along the back of Ridge's scalp.

"We're doing everything we can to find her, Ms. McCaffrey." Tony held out his phone, pressed play on the cued image that filled the screen. "This is parking lot footage from the airfield where Lombardi dropped her this evening. Check her body language as they exit the vehicle."

Ridge squinted against the grainy image, but damned if Tony wasn't right. Her arms stayed close, hovering around her midsection as she walked, glancing back at Lombardi more than normal.

"I'm going to try to enhance the video as soon as I get to the hotel. I've got software that should help. But I think Lombardi said something–something that made her uncomfortable."

"You think Liv knew she was being set up?"

"*If* she was set up." Tony reminded him. "We don't know that, yet. But I plan to find out. I'll touch base when I know more." Tony's eyes shifted to Bridget. "I'm sorry for what your little boy had to see, Ms. McCaffrey. It won't happen again."

"Call me Bridget," she said, extending her hand. Tony smiled and returned the gesture.

"Bridget," he repeated. "Get this guy to the hospital, have that nose checked out. Don't let him tell you he's fine." He narrowed his gaze on Ridge. "You don't want a crooked nose the rest of your life. Trust me." Tony indicated to the slight offset bump along the bridge of his own nose. "How do you think I ended up with this?"

Ridge huffed what could pass for a laugh. "Call me," he said. "With anything." He lowered his voice. "I can't lose her again."

38

LIV

Passengers and flight crew filtered in and out through double doors in the waiting room that emptied down a hall toward the tarmac. The agent who helped me stayed in the room, watching a bank of screens for a customer to approach the ticket counter outside. He spoke and laughed with several other employees, but his eyes kept flicking to me. Suspicion or worry, I couldn't tell.

I took another sip of the coffee and jerked my backpack from the seat next to me. I scanned the walls for a restroom and found one in the far corner of the room. The agent watched as I strode across the room and ducked inside. The white porcelain of the space, brightly lit by bars of fluorescent bulbs tucked into the ceiling, sent a pulse of ache behind my eyes as my vision adjusted.

I checked under each stall to be sure I was alone before staring at myself in one of the over-sink mirrors. "What are you doing?" I mumbled under my breath at the reflection staring back at me. The fear in my chest manifested in wide green eyes. My pupils dilated, and I squinted my lids closed. A light wave of nausea worked its way from my gut as I processed the snippet of memory tugged loose by Lombardi's touch.

If she had been there, in that cabin where Adam left me to die, then what did that mean? She saved my life, that part was obvious. But why? And how did any of that fit into what was happening now?

An image of Colton and Ridge at the farm flashed in my mind. I couldn't do this. Neither of them deserved the baggage that accompanied Liv Sullivan coming back from the dead. No matter how much Ridge claimed to want it. No matter how much *I* wanted it.

I exhaled a groan and braced myself on the sink surround, blowing out a shaky breath. *You're paranoid.* The words came unbidden into my consciousness. *Fear is making you crazy.* And I had no means of refuting my inner critic's argument. I'd dumped my phone, rearranged an entire flight schedule, complete with a switch in both aircraft and pilot, and now was considering not getting on the plane at all.

The bathroom door swung open, surprise forcing me back a step. The woman shot me a smile and disappeared into a stall while I washed and dried my hands longer than necessary. The thin skin on my hands pursed and crinkled under the high powered forced air of the dryer. The stranger gave me another curious glance as she skimmed her hands under the water and shook them dry. I stayed rooted, hands planted in the waves of the other dryer until she exited.

One thing was for certain. Whatever I decided, I couldn't stay holed up in here forever. I glanced again in the mirror, and the image shifted, distorting. I flattened both hands on the counter, waiting for the wave of vertigo to pass. The door *thwapped* open a second time, giving way to a familiar face–the agent from the charter counter.

"Your flight is ready, Miss Allyn." His body stiffened. "Is everything okay?"

The wobble of him, my inability to focus on his features, should have been my first clue, but I answered with a short, "Yes," following him from the ladies' room, through the waiting area, to a door where a pilot greeted me.

He introduced himself, giving my shaky hand a forceful pump. "Should be a quick flight. You ready?"

"Let's go home," I managed, the words sticky in my mouth. I swung my backpack onto my shoulder and followed the pilot out onto the darkened tarmac, using every ounce of concentration to stay upright.

39

RIDGE

Ridge sat on the exam table in the emergency department of Memorial Hospital, his head tipped back as a nurse shoved bullets of gauze up each nostril.

"Doctor should be here in just a minute with the results of the x-ray," she said with a glance toward Bridget.

"I'm fine, Bridge. You don't need to babysit me." He rolled his eyes at the sound of his own voice. The nasal congestion mimicked either a severe head cold or a nerd from a 90s sitcom.

Bridget smiled. "I'm staying."

She allowed the soundtrack of the triage department to filter through the curtains before standing up from her chair and moving closer to the bed. "You should have told me." Her words were quiet as her hand skimmed his shoulders.

Ridge didn't bother with an apology.

"I know things are sometimes rocky between us, but we have a son together, for God's sake. You can't keep stuff like this a secret, Ridge."

"I was waiting for her." Ridge couldn't bring himself to say

Liv's name. "I didn't know how she'd want to handle it–coming back," he clarified.

Bridget nodded. At least she pretended to understand. "Are you going to be able to handle it if she doesn't come back?"

There it was, the question he'd forced himself not to consider for the past hour since he'd left Murphy's.

"No." Ridge fought the constriction of emotion in his throat. It may have been the most honest thing he'd said to Bridget in months.

Bridget leaned forward and pressed her lips against his temple. "I love you, Ridge. I can't watch you spiral like you did last time. Promise me you'll get help, talk to someone before it takes you over. If not for me, for Colton."

"Promise," Ridge managed as the curtain slid back with a *shink,* exposing the face of a young doctor with an iPad.

"It's broken," he said, showing Ridge the films on the handheld device. "But the good thing is, everything's in place. With a splint you should heal with no lasting signs of trauma."

Ridge let Bridget do the talking, stayed silent as the nurse returned to clean and splint his nose. She handed Bridget a packet of instructions and a prescription for pain meds before sending them on their way.

Tony was standing outside Ridge's apartment when he pulled in, grinding the Shelby to a halt in front of his corner unit.

"How's the nose?" Tony asked as Ridge lifted himself from the car.

"Broken," Ridge said shortly. "Like a lot of other things in my life right now." He slammed the car door and passed Tony, headed for the stairwell and his fourth floor apartment. Tony fell into step behind him.

"I spoke to the charter agent who worked with Liv. Said she had some unusual requests."

Ridge stopped on the landing and sucked in a breath of the cool night breeze. His grip on the handrail tightened as he let the words sink in.

"Can we talk about it?" Tony eyed him, waiting for permission before following him any farther.

Ridge nodded. "Fourth floor," he said, continuing on.

Ridge left the door open for Tony and went straight for the kitchen. He tore into the bottle of naproxen and reached in the fridge for a water, downing two of the pain relievers before Tony ever got inside.

"Sorry about that." Tony closed the door behind him and gestured to Ridge's face, which was just starting to take on a colorful red and purple hue. "I really am."

Ridge ignored Tony's apology. "Tell me what you know."

"Charter rep claims she acted scared. Kept looking over her shoulder at the woman she'd come in with, who we know was Lombardi. Wanted to change the entire flight plan. Pilot, plane, whole works. So they did. New plan was to get on a Cessna out of the Virginia airfield. Planned landing on a local strip just north of Cascade Hills."

Something in Ridge's chest snapped, cracking open and leaking a trickle of hope to counteract the all-consuming desperation he'd felt since Tony tracked him down at the pub. "When?"

"Tonight. Around two a.m."

"What are we waiting for?" Ridge asked, glancing at his watch as he made his way around the bar. If he left now he could be there by the time she landed.

"She dumped her phone. We've got no way to track her without that device." Tony hesitated. "There's more."

Ridge waited for him to drop whatever bomb he had straight onto his heart.

"Rogers sent me an email. Our lab came back with results on the mandible this evening. The extracted DNA matches Liv's."

Ridge reached for the nearby recliner to steady himself.

"Who else knows?"

"You, Michelle, Lombardi. I haven't told them about the flight, though. I'm putting them off. They know something went bad, though. But Ridge, we weren't there. What if this is their plan? Their way of making her disappear–to get her into WITSEC?"

"She wouldn't do that."

Tony lowered onto the couch across from Ridge. "Dumping her phone means one of two things. Either she's trying to hide from Lombardi's surveillance. Or–"

"She's trying to hide from me." Ridge finished Tony's statement. He clenched his jaw against the possibility that had already run through his mind more than once. "But according to her revised flight plan, she was coming home, to Cascade Hills."

"That's the plan she filed with the TSA." Tony said.

"Then we go to the airport, find out exactly where she is." Ridge checked his watch. It was already 1:30. He forced his legs to support his weight and pushed away from the chair. He studied the man standing in his living room. "I know I've asked you once before, but it bears repeating. Why are you helping me, Medici?"

"I told you in Bishop's Hollow."

"This goes beyond vicariously repairing a relationship, Tony. Somebody tampered with federal evidence, someone with access, which means we're verging on the edge of conspiracy theory, now. Are you comfortable with that?"

"I'm tired of watching the government destroy lives to advance their own agenda. I've seen it happen too many times, under the control of too many different people."

"Whose agenda is this?"

Tony shrugged. "Hell if I know."

"How do I know I can trust you?"

Tony lifted one eyebrow and opened the door. "Do you have a choice?"

40

LIV

The flight was hell. We were barely off the ground when my skin flushed, prickling into uncontrollable waves of alternating hot and cold. My vision spiraled, and I could swear the pilot, now asking if I was okay, had suddenly sprouted a pair of horns.

I nodded in response, keeping my eyes low, my hand gripped around the shoulder strap of my backpack as if it was some kind of life raft. It was in those moments, hurtling through the sky, that the thought stormed through my brain. *She gave you something.* I tried to focus, piece together what or when Lombardi could have drugged me. But the jostle of the plane, coupled with my inability to process the reality around me, made it impossible.

"Storm's worse than we thought," the pilot said through the headphone speakers meant to silence the sound of the twin engine jet. Silence was a strong word. Muffled was more accurate.

The throb of the Cessna hummed through me, vibrating every muscle as we rocketed through the turbulent sky.

"We're within fifteen minutes of Cascade Hills. But it's gonna be a rough landing."

The churning in my gut doubled. A wave of panic, activated by some primal fight or flight response, ate through me. A buzz washing up and down my arms and legs.

"Let me out of here," I heard my voice, but I didn't remember saying the words. My hands shook as I clawed at the three point harness, trying to make my fingers work against the clips of the belt. Fuzziness threatened my already altered vision.

The pilot's voice pulsed as the plane tipped. "You can't do that. Ma'am, are you okay?"

My breath came in short huffs and I heard the pilot on the radio, the letters and codes he rattled off too much for my drug addled brain.

I braced against the dash, my body hummed as a hot wave plunged through me, unleashing a churn of nausea through my gut. The pilot reached a hand for mine. His voice far away.

"Take it easy, we're almost there."

I felt the scream rise from within–at him, at myself–the gravel of the aftermath clotted in my throat as the plane pitched, plunging into what I was sure was a one-way trip to hell. If it hadn't been for the raucous bounce and screech of tires, I might have believed that was exactly where I ended up.

The space around me went suddenly quiet. The pilot reached over and put his hand on my arm. "Back on earth," he said, hopping from the plane. I blinked into the dark space around me. Forcing focus that wouldn't come.

The pilot moved around the front of the aircraft, and I watched as the rain poured over his jacket, his body morphing from man to monster and back again before settling into a gray blob of movement as he approached the passenger door.

Don't look at him, I coached myself. *What you think you see is not real.*

The door popped open. Night air pricked at my skin, cooling the sheen of clamminess. I shifted my focus slowly from my lap to the door, giving reality a chance to seep alongside hallucination.

The distance from the plane to the ground was every bit of three feet, more if I let the irrational creep in. The ground bucked and rolled in my maladjusted vision.

"Just give yourself a minute," he said, his voice inhumanly loud. "Help's on the way." He reached for me. His hands morphed into claws, snapping and pinching as he pulled me from the cockpit.

"No," I managed, shoving with unnecessary force.

"Okay, okay." He held his hands up in surrender, and his face changed, morphing from innocent pilot to the monster at the Stop-n-Go.

I shook my head, and a wave of nausea worked itself loose.

"I just don't want you to fall." The words exited his mouth as my gut churned. I shoved him out of the way just in time to spew vomit out the open door and onto the rural tarmac.

The rigidity in my muscles relaxed into a full body tremble. Tears streamed from eyes I could no longer trust. I ignored the feel of his touch as he helped me down, careful to keep us both out of the puddle of puke gracing smooth gray pavement.

"Where are we?" My voice was small, weak.

"County Airfield, outside Cascade Hills. I called the number on your backpack. I didn't know what else to do."

"When?"

"You passed out. You don't remember?" I shook my head, regretting the decision as soon as it was made. I attempted to stand but wobbled to the side.

"Whoa, whoa, just take it easy. He'll be here any minute."

I managed to turn the backpack over on the ground next to me. Skylar McCaffrey was written on the name tag, and under it a number I didn't recognize. The numbers fuzzed and jumbled together. I hunched over my knees, waiting for the next wave of nausea to spike.

The pilot strung an arm around my waist, helping me stay upright as we navigated the tarmac toward a small hangar. Each step took more effort than I had to give, and even with the young pilot's coaching, it was difficult to put one foot in front of the other.

Lights swung in, illuminating us before I ever saw him. A shadowy silhouette jogging toward the tarmac–toward me. Another surge of sick roiled in my gut and I pulled my escorting pilot to a stop, releasing his hand and lurching to the side. I lost my balance, falling to my knees as another wave of nausea tore through me.

"It was a rough flight." The pilot's voice echoed as footsteps slowed and came close. "But that's not what this is."

"Liv." Ridge's voice reached my ears, but my mind couldn't process any more than my name. His hand found the small of my back as I hugged the ground. This was not the reunion I'd had in mind. The thought barely entered my head before my stomach lurched, but this time, there was nothing left to spew. I coughed. Pinpricks of light danced in my peripheral vision as I sunk lower, reaching for earth that now resembled a watery abyss.

The sky split as lightning carved a jagged bolt against black clouds, briefly illuminating the grounds around us. Rivulets of rain poured over me–onto my scalp and down my neck and face. I shivered in spite of Ridge's arm around my shoulder.

"Can you stand?" Ridge's voice outspoke the rain.

I shook my head as another tilt-a-whirl took flight inside my skull.

"How long has she been like this?" The words sounded far away.

"Most of the flight. She was combative for a bit. Thank God that part's over. She passed out after that. She's gotta be on something. I checked her bag. There's nothing—"

A clap of thunder cut short the pilot's words and sent a shudder through my core. My lungs spasmed—some version of oxygen deprived panic—and I fought for breath. Ridge tried to coach me, asked me to look at him. But I knew better than to set the monsters free.

Another full body shiver took hold and I felt Ridge's grip tighten. The weeds in front of me turned colors—red-gold, green, and black again—the reflection of what I only later learned was an ambulance.

41

RIDGE

"What's her name?" The medic jumped from the front of the unit and made his way toward them.

"Liv," Ridge shouted over the pouring rain. "Liv Sullivan."

His heart hammered in his chest as the medics took over. Liv lay crumpled on the ground, extremities locked in a full body shiver manifested by either the chill of the rain or whatever substance was coursing through her system. The pair of medics moved her from the wet ground and into the back of the van within minutes. Ridge remained outside, watching, as they took Liv's vitals and strung an oxygen mask across her face.

"What did she take?" the second medic asked, moving to the rear of the van to address Ridge.

"I don't know." Ridge felt the first squeeze of panic tighten around his lungs.

"History of drug use?"

"No," Ridge said, unable to lock his memory before images

of her drugged and helpless in O'Malley's cabin rose to the surface.

"What about you?" The medic nodded toward Ridge's face. "You okay?"

"Fine," Ridge said, ignoring the pulsing throb behind his nose and eyes.

The medic gave him a once over before speaking again. "We're transporting her to County Memorial. You're free to follow, if you like."

Ridge managed a nod, forcing his legs into motion as he ran across the tarmac and back to his car.

By the time Ridge parked and navigated his way past the nurse's station and into the emergency department, his panic attack was in check, thanks, in part, to another dose of Xanax.

"I'm here to see Liv Sullivan. She was brought in by medics a few minutes ago."

The nurse typed into a keypad, while Ridge fought to keep the anxiety at bay. When the wooden doors sprung open next to the nurse's station he slid through, ignoring the nurse's pleas for him to stop.

"We'll need some information about the patient," the nurse said, trailing behind Ridge as he searched the triage bays where he'd been less than two hours before. He located Liv in the final one, fully conscious now, the medics helping her from their gurney and onto the hospital bed.

Ridge blew out a sigh of relief and took the clipboard from the nurse, realizing in one glance that he was incapable of filling out most of the information required. He tossed the clipboard onto the foot of the bed as the medics slipped out, leaving them alone with the triage nurse who was now taking vials of blood from Liv's arm.

Liv shifted her gaze from the needle in her arm to Ridge, overlarge pupils making her jade green eyes appear dark, inhuman. The nurse peppered them both with questions. Where had Liv been? What had she taken? Who had she been with? Could she explain the symptoms? How long had she been feeling ill?

Ridge remained mostly silent as Liv forced one word answers, her light-headedness clearly firmly intact.

The nurse finally let up, indicating the vials of blood she'd taken when Liv arrived. "I'll send this to the lab and be back in a few minutes."

Ridge nodded as she exited, leaving the mint green curtain open behind her.

"Your face." Liv's voice was slow and deliberate. "What happened?"

Ridge's hand went instinctively to his nose. Only now was the painful throb reregistering in his brain.

"Just an accident," he said. "It's nothing." He forced his lips into a smile that Liv tried to return before the heaviness of her lids won the battle.

The race of his heart calmed as he sat with her. The nurse returned twice, once to hook up an IV in hopes of flushing out whatever had taken over her system. And the second time to tell him they'd be admitting Liv for observation.

"We will need this information." The nurse indicated to the clipboard Ridge had left untouched at the foot of Liv's bed. "If there's someone better able to provide it—"

"I'll take care of it," Ridge said.

It was after three a.m. before Liv finally got to a room, and Ridge still hadn't worked up the nerve to call Beth. The last time he'd called Liv's mother with news about Liv had been from another hospital. But that time, Skylar had been sleeping peacefully while Ridge relayed Liv's death over cellular waves. That night, the silence on the other end had turned to deafening wails.

He turned back to Liv, now sleeping off whatever had pulled her under, and tapped Beth's contact in his phone.

"Ridge?" Beth's sleepy voice crackled through the line. "What's going on? Are you okay?"

The loop of questions knocked him off his game and he cleared his throat. "I'm sorry to wake you, Beth. But it's about Liv."

Ridge could hear movement from the other end of the line, the hush of sheets being tossed aside.

"Where are you?" Beth's voice was strong now. Worried. He'd given her plenty of reason to be over the course of the last seven months, and although he was ashamed to admit it, this wasn't his first middle of the night call to Beth Sullivan. The only difference was this time he was sober.

"County Memorial." Ridge sucked in a breath. He turned to the bed and skimmed his hand down Liv's arm, folding her hand into his. "Liv's alive."

42

LIV

The soothing warmth of my mother's hand on mine woke me. It took a few orienting blinks to understand where I was, that she was really here.

"Mom?" I pushed her name through lips dulled by the dregs of drugs and exhaustion. She smiled, wiping at red-rimmed eyes with the tissue wadded in her other fist. Behind her, Ridge stood by the window, head bent, his badly bruised face looking painful.

"How are you feeling?" she asked.

I pulled myself into a sitting position and sucked in a deep breath, clearing the leftover confusion. "Better," I said, letting my eyes comb around the room–free from memory-fueled monsters. "How did you know–"

I barely got the question out before Ridge stepped forward. "I called her. The hospital needed information and I didn't know..." He paused, a flash of some emotion–inadequacy maybe–clouded his eyes. "I'll give you two some time alone."

Ridge slunk through the doorway, closing it behind him.

"He told me about DC, the case against Sowards. About what you're trying to do. Liv, I–"

"You don't think I should be in the middle of it," I finished for her, sinking back onto the mattress with the next wave of exhaustion.

"I can't tell you what to do. But look where you are. We lost you once, Liv. I don't think either of us could take losing you again."

"I don't know what happened," I admitted, redirecting my mother's concern. "The flight was rough." I wasn't naïve enough to believe what happened on that plane was airsickness, but with my mother sitting in front of me, pleading with me to be careful, it seemed like the best option, whether she believed it or not.

My mother's hazel eyes landed on mine, full of emotion, a silent plea. She smiled and pushed a piece of hair from my forehead. "Please be careful."

I nodded, reaching for her as she enveloped me in a long, desperate hug.

The door creaked open and Ridge reentered. "The doctor's on his way in." My mother pulled away to stand at my bedside, making room for Ridge.

Ridge's eyes spoke more than his words ever could. Combing over me, checking for signs I was still under the influence of whatever put me here. Remnants of panic danced in his eyes.

"What's the other guy look like?" I forced my lips into a teasing smile.

Ridge laughed, releasing a lungful of pent up air. "Better than this," he admitted. "I think I might've lost my edge."

I laughed and reached for him, lacing our hands together. This was it. This was the fresh start I'd been looking for. I just never thought it would include an overnight stay in my hometown hospital.

Ridge tugged the nearby chair to the side of my bed, close enough for me to skim my hand up his arm and onto his face.

He closed his eyes, lips parted with a breath of relief.

"There she is." The doctor strode in, giving all of us a quick once-over. "Well, do you want the good news or the bad news first?"

"Bad," Ridge said, while I voiced the opposite.

The doctor chuckled. "Patient's choice." He stood close enough to rest a hand on the foot of the bed. "The good news is, you're free to go. Keep drinking plenty of fluids–water–for the next few days."

"And the bad news?" I asked.

"Your labs indicate high levels of Phencyclidine." The doctor's eyes shifted from mine to Ridge's. "Better known as PCP." He waited, eyeing us both for a beat before continuing. "Any idea how that might have gotten in your system last night?" The doctor's voice was light, friendly, but I read suspicion in his eyes.

"I've never taken PCP," I said.

"That was fairly obvious. Your levels were low compared to those of a frequent user." He glanced at Ridge again, clear blame etched on his features. "Experimentation can be as dangerous as addiction–more so, in some cases."

"I wasn't–" The squeeze of Ridge's hand on mine stopped me.

"Thank you, doctor. We appreciate the care you gave Liv. I assure you, this won't happen again."

The doctor nodded, narrowing his gaze on Ridge before smiling at me. "Take care of yourself, Miss Sullivan."

My mother followed him out to the nurse's station to gather the discharge paperwork, while Ridge helped me dress.

"Why didn't you let me explain? Now he thinks I'm some kind of drug addict." A thread of angry indignance seeped alongside my words.

"Do you know what happened?" Ridge asked.

"I know Lombardi did this. I don't know how or when. But she did this."

I bent to pick my shirt up off the chair, and the room spun. Ridge reached his arm to steady me, pulling me close. He took the shirt from my hand and slipped it over my head. I closed my eyes to his touch as his thumbs skimmed my sides.

"Doctors are mandated reporters, Liv. If you make an accusation like that, they are required to inform the police. That's the last thing we need right now."

I nodded and his lips pressed hot against my forehead.

"Come on, let's go home."

43

RIDGE

Ridge hung back while Beth wrapped Liv in a hug outside a nearby Olive Garden a few hours later.

"Take care of her," Beth said to Ridge over the roof of his car.

"You're welcome to come back with us, Beth," he said.

"Thanks for the invite, but I think you two need some time." She smoothed a hand over Liv's hair. "Call me tomorrow, okay? We'll go for a mani-pedi."

Liv laughed, and the clench in Ridge's chest returned. She was perfect, in every way that mattered to him. Losing her had broken him–physically and emotionally. But it wasn't until this moment that he realized the fear of losing her again made loving her almost as agonizing.

Ridge slid into the car and waited for Liv to join him.

"That was perfect," Liv said as she pulled the passenger door closed.

"You were hungry," Ridge countered. "It wasn't *that* good." He turned to meet the heat of Liv's gaze.

She was smiling, her eyes clear, happy, until she looked at

him. Her smile faltered, tipping at the corners, leaving him to wonder what she saw.

"Are you having second thoughts?" Her voice was soft, unsure.

"What? No. Why would you think that?"

She tucked her lip under her teeth, slowly freeing it before turning to face the dash. "Just a hunch, I guess."

The ache in his chest solidified into a hard knot and he pressed a breath through it, gripping the leather-wrapped steering wheel with both hands.

"I would understand." Liv's voice filtered in as he fought the building pressure in his chest.

He shook his head. The prickling vibration in his forearm turned to an unrelenting tremor, eating its way along the entire right side of his body.

"Ridge?" Her voice seemed far away, muted by the pounding pulse behind his eardrums. But the note of worry was unmistakable. He fought for breath, sucking in tiny gulps with nowhere for it to go. He moved a shaking hand from the steering wheel, keeping his eyelids clutched tight, and fumbled with the latch on the console storage compartment.

"What do you need? Ridge, please. Talk to me."

He flicked the compartment open and wrapped his hand around the orange bottle inside. He should have taken one hours ago. *Stupid.* The pills inside rattled as he pulled it out of the console with a shaky hand. It dropped to the floor with a clatter.

He bent to retrieve the bottle, his forehead colliding with the steering wheel harder than he'd intended. Liv fished the prescription off the floor, checking the label before withdrawing an elliptical blue pill. She shifted closer, easing his head off the wheel.

"Open," she said.

He did as he was told. His entire body hummed, his lungs locked in an immovable vise. His vision blurred with a slurry of involuntary tears. He felt the water bottle at his lips, Liv's hand cradling his head as she tipped the bottle back.

"Listen to me, Ridge, breathe." She held onto him, her hands like fire on his skin, coaching his breath until the grip on his lungs loosened.

Once Ridge was able to take a full respiration, Liv clicked open the console compartment and replaced the bottle of Xanax. He forced his eyes in her direction as the last of the devouring ants along his arms and legs disappeared.

"I never meant for you to see that." It seemed like the only thing to say. He kept his eyes focused on the scuffed knuckles of his right hand, still planted on the wheel.

"This is because of me?" There was a heat in her voice he couldn't quite interpret.

"The panic attacks started after the explosion. But they're not your fault."

"What triggers them?" Liv slid her hand onto his, pulled it from the steering wheel and kissed the red and purple scuffs.

"Fear, I think. Lack of control."

"How often do you have them?"

"I was actually doing pretty well until–" He stopped himself. The repercussions of what he almost said already written on Liv's face.

"Until I came back."

"That's not what I meant."

"But it's a fact, right?"

"There's just been a lot going on–a lot to process."

"Tell me how to make it better."

Ridge released a pent-up huff of laughter. "I get this isn't what you signed up for. I'm broken, Liv. Just, don't lose faith in me."

Liv leaned over the console, her breath hot and sweet against his face. "We're both broken, Ridge. But I've always had faith in you."

Her lips found his, and he sank into her kiss, mutual need soldering together like shards of broken glass.

44

LIV

Tony was waiting for us in front of Ridge's apartment building when we arrived that afternoon, his gray SUV semi-conspicuous among the array of colorful cars in the complex lot.

"Glad you made it safe and sound, Miss Sullivan," he said, before climbing in the driver's side of his rental. "We were worried about you."

"It's Liv, Tony, and I'm fine. Thanks."

"I thought he was supposed to be watching Colton," I said to Ridge as we headed for the stairwell.

"He heard what happened. He's just doing his job," Ridge said.

"I'll pretend you didn't just side with the lurking bodyguard." I let a smile tickle the corners of my lips. Tony had always been good to me. "Nice place," I added as Ridge took my backpack and leaned in for a kiss. His lips were soft against mine and I couldn't help the instinct to slip my arm around his waist and press my body close.

"Thanks," he answered, pulling away as a neighbor and his

dog rounded the corner about fifteen feet from the path where we stood. He tipped his chin in the direction of the open stairs. "Stairs or elevator? I'm at the top."

"Stairs," I said, following him up four flights to the top of the multi-apartment unit.

He stopped in front of the farthest apartment, a brass 1400C shining from the dark blue four panel door.

"Two things," he started. Worry pricked at the space between us. "One, you've got to promise not to think I'm six shades of crazy when you see the view." His eyes locked on mine.

"And two?" I asked.

"We have company."

A shot of adrenaline electrified my veins. I'd hoped for an evening with just the two of us, a chance to talk through the bombshells of the last 24 hours. Not to mention, figuring out a plan to tell the other people in our lives about my reappearance. No such luck.

"I'm sorry. I told Brian when I was in DC. Thought he should know considering Colton...and Sky–"

"Found out when the pilot called the number on the backpack," I finished. I skimmed a hand down his arm and he studied me, looking for signs of disappointment. I smiled up at him, ensuring he'd find none. "It's okay, Ridge."

He turned the door handle slowly and pushed it inward with a gentlemanly gesture for me to enter. A man and a woman sat on stools at a breakfast bar to my right. They swiveled at the light creak of the door, but no one said a word.

A lump surged into my throat as Brian's deep blue eyes latched onto mine. He slid off the stool and closed the distance between us, locking me in a giant hug as the breath of a curse slid past my ear.

My eyes blurred, tears coming without warning as I looped

my arms around Brian's shoulders and pulled him close. We stood that way, clinging to each other until Skylar's soft voice penetrated the silence. The warmth of her arms wrapped around us both as Brian drew away to let her in.

"I can't believe you're here," Brian said as the three of us broke contact and slid away from one another, finding places to sit in Ridge's living room.

"Congratulations," I muttered once the initial wave of emotion subsided. "Ridge told me about your engagement. I'm so happy for you."

Skylar stuck her left hand in my direction, "It's beautiful, isn't it?" She glanced at Brian whose cheeks flushed a rosy shade of pink.

I took her hand to examine the ring. "He did good." I smiled, ignoring the pang of what I could only identify as remorse churning in my gut. In another universe, it could be us planning a wedding instead of figuring out how to navigate a world where enemies lurked and evil seemed to be one step ahead.

"Will you be in the wedding?" Skylar asked suddenly. "Be a bridesmaid, Liv. Please. None of this could have happened without you."

I glanced at Ridge, who'd taken up residence along the wall to my left, near a panel of closed French doors. A tiny smile tugged at one corner of his mouth, but his eyes were careful, apprehension shining from their depths.

"Maybe." I dulled Skylar's glee with just one word.

"Give her a chance to settle in, Sky. She just got back." Brian, as usual, rescued me. And Skylar shot Brian a dagger stare.

We chatted for hours–about their upcoming wedding, the pub. Questions I'd worried would come, never did, friendship winning the battle between skepticism and relief. Maybe that's why Ridge never asked why it had taken me so long to get in touch. Sometimes, when the impossible happens, questioning it seems like tempting fate.

I spent the rest of the afternoon watching them. Skylar's excitement over their upcoming nuptials seemed genuine, but her interactions with Brian were standoffish. The couple I remembered from last fall, draped all over each other at Murphy's, was gone. Sky went rigid with every touch.

"Come by the pub, Liv. There's something I want to show you," Brian said as he and Skylar headed for the front door that evening, the scent of Chinese takeout still heavy in the air.

"It's ranking pretty high on my agenda, Bri." I smiled as Skylar slipped through the door without waiting.

"You know, the offer still stands. The space next door is begging to be a photography studio. It's still yours, if you want it."

I leaned in and hugged the man in front of me. All kind words and wit. I couldn't wrap my head around the obvious rift growing between Brian and Skylar. Even if she wasn't ready to admit it to herself, her energy spoke for itself.

The notion smacked me like a slap across the face. Her energy, pinpricks of frustration and hurt, had pulsed in the air around me. Not Brian's, just Sky's. I shouldn't have been able to feel her. But I could. I swallowed against the realization.

"Take care, Brian. I'll see you soon," I whispered and pulled away, watching him trot down the stairs.

"So?" Ridge asked as I closed the door. "Was it as bad as you thought it might be?"

"Of course not," I said, moving toward the French doors

while Ridge finished gathering the takeout boxes. "But I'm dying to see this crazy man's view you told me about."

Ridge wiped his hands on a kitchen towel and navigated around the breakfast bar and into the living room, making short work of the space between us. He slipped an arm around my waist, pulled me to face him while he unlocked and opened the door.

"Okay, but remember, I was trying to heal." A smile played on his lips and I lifted onto my tiptoes to cover his mouth with mine. We stepped in sync, our bodies moving as one onto the fourth floor balcony. He groaned playfully as I pulled away to take in the view.

Across the main road and the strip of trees beyond, a full moon shone over Cascade Lake, reflecting off the water and sending a ghostly sheen over Sullivan Farm.

"Ridge." His name came out in an exhale and he pressed closer from behind, his arms wrapping around my midsection. I skimmed my fingers along his forearms, unable to tear my eyes from the view ahead.

"I spend way more time out here than I should admit," he said, breath tickling my ear.

"And it's yours?" I asked, still in disbelief.

Ridge released me and padded off into the living room, returning a moment later. "Hold out your hand."

He held my gaze and pressed something cold and hard against my empty palm. A buzz of indecipherable electric energy vibrated through my hand and into my arm. I looked down onto the square key from the farmhouse door.

"It's yours." He stopped talking, swallowed. "I was never able to bring myself to move in."

"Why not?" I tugged away to study him. "Why are you living here instead?"

Ridge sighed and pulled a glider from the corner of the

balcony, dusting it off before sitting. "I couldn't." He ran a thumb over the knuckles of his right hand. "It didn't feel right. Not without you. I go over and check on the place, mow the lawn. A tree came down on the old barn. So, I cleaned that up. The fire department razed the barn," Ridge sucked in a breath. "I hope that's okay."

Ridge was right. He was broken. But the pieces had fused back together in the best possible way. I smiled as he kept talking.

"I tried to teach Colton to skip stones a few weeks ago after the weather broke." Ridge smiled, a dimple appearing in his right cheek and crinkling the bandage on his nose. "He's gonna need more practice."

A faraway look fell over Ridge's features.

"How is he?" I asked, turning the key over in my hand.

"Good. I talked to Bridget a few minutes ago. Told her I'd be over in the morning to pick him up. Grab breakfast before I take him to school."

I moved from the rail toward the gilder where Ridge sat.

"You can come if you want." His hands drifted lightly up my legs as I stood in front of him.

"I'd like that." The key clicked against the glass top of the nearby table as I placed it on top. "Thank you for taking care of the farm for me," I whispered, tucking my knees along his sides, I straddled him on the glider.

The pent-up emotion of Ridge's exhale sent a spike of heat through my core, intensifying as the line of kisses I delivered was returned. The heat of gentle lips singed sensitive flesh as the cool breeze of evening washed over us.

45

RIDGE

R idge lay under a tangle of sheets watching Liv sleep. Of all the nights they'd had together, last night had been the best–every moment a spiral of pleasure. If it hadn't been for the painful pulse behind his eyes, it would have been perfect. Of course, he had no one to blame for that but himself.

He'd spent the last fifteen minutes watching Liv, contemplating why last night had been so perfect, finally coming to the conclusion that it had less to do with their physical compatibility, and everything to do with trust.

For the first time in their history, he was holding nothing back. She'd now seen him at his worst. There were no secrets to keep, no operation to protect, no lies to be told. They had problems to figure out, sure–Sowards, Lombardi, his own son's protection. But they were in this together, and his future was here–with her. He only wished he'd realized a year ago the impact trust could have. He'd never have risked decimating the one good relationship he'd ever had.

He pushed a curl off the side of Liv's face, and she stirred.

Her eyes blinked open onto his, her lips curling in a sleepy smile. He reached over and kissed her, long and tender. She sighed as he pulled away, that perfect smile returning to her lips.

"What time is it?"

"Early. A little after five. I've got to take care of a few things before we pick Colton up."

Liv's eyebrow quirked up. "What do we tell him?"

"The truth," Ridge said, throwing the covers back and slipping into a pair of boxers. He turned to check Liv's expression. "He's four. He'll ask a lot of questions and I can promise some of them won't have anything to do with your miraculous reappearance."

"I can do truth," Liv said with a laugh, tucking her lower lip between front teeth, sending a flutter of lust straight to Ridge's core.

"Speaking of truth, can I ask you a question?" Ridge said, tamping down the surge of want. This was a conversation that had to happen. One that flirted along the edges of his subconscious, never fully disintegrating.

Liv nodded. "Of course."

Ridge perched on the side of the mattress. "Why did you wait so long?"

The smile on Liv's face fell, her eyes focused on the navy blue duvet as her fingers traced the stitched pattern.

"I wish I knew. I wanted to call, tell you. I think I was scared."

"Of what?" Ridge held Liv's gaze.

"After everything that happened between us—you leaving, Lyle's attack, all the lies. Part of me wondered if..." Liv stopped. She sat up against the headboard and tugged the comforter up to her shoulders.

"You can talk to me, Liv."

Liv sucked in a breath and fiddled with a dangling thread on the corner of the duvet. "When I found out Adam was involved, I thought you might have been part of it, too."

Heaviness returned to Ridge's chest. "Jesus, Liv. No." He slid closer, pushing another rogue curl away. His thumb lingered, stroking her cheek. "I could never hurt you like that." Anger started a slow creep from deep inside as flashes of what happened to Liv raged in his memory.

"I know that now. It just took me a while to figure it out."

Ridge scrubbed a hand down his face.

"It was a mistake, Ridge, to wait. I'm sorry."

"You were protecting yourself." That was experience talking. All the self-loathing and self-medicating he did while Liv was gone made him a bit of an expert. Time had been Liv's alcohol. And he couldn't blame her.

Liv shifted on the bed, leaning into him. "The night we met, I knew there was something between us–some spark I couldn't explain. Over time, you became more. More than the hidden motivations, the man checking my arms for track marks, leaving me to face Lyle alone..." She paused, skimming a hand over his shoulder. "...or telling me you wanted to forget me after the IED in the woods."

Ridge's shoulders slumped at the reminder. It wasn't his finest moment, that was for sure. A spike of regret unleashed in his core. He whispered an apology that Liv brushed away.

"Those things never matched the energy I felt from you. But some moments did. Like our first date at Murphy's, your panic in the hall at the Marriott when you thought Jason hurt me. The way you looked at me on the street in DC." She ran a teasing finger along his jawline. "The way you're looking at me now. That's the real Ridge McCaffrey. The brother who took his little sister to the 7-Eleven in spite of neighborhood bullies. The teenager scarred by guilt when his big sister didn't make it out of their burning house. The man willing to sacrifice everything to give his girlfriend a second chance at life."

Liv leaned forward on her knees and the covers dropped, exposing soft curves. Her lips covered his with a sweet heat he'd never tire of.

"That's the real you. That's the Ridge McCaffrey I fell in love with. And it's the one I came back for."

Ridge let his gaze crawl over Liv, light freckles sprinkled over creamy shoulders. The intensity of her eyes locked on his. His chest tightened.

"What happened with Lombardi? Why'd you change the flight?"

Liv's shoulder lifted into a shrug. "She was there. In the cabin where Adam left me. When she took me to the airport I saw it."

"She touched you?"

Liv nodded.

"Did she drug you, Liv?" Ridge folded a leg under and scooted closer to Liv on the mattress.

"I can't be sure. All I had on the way there was coffee. Maybe none of this would've happened if I'd agreed to witness protection."

Ridge lurched forward, his hand finding Liv's jaw and urging her to face him. "There's something I need to tell you." He dropped his hand and sat back, holding Liv's gaze. "The report on the mandible came back. The independent lab confirmed the DNA is a match." The words choked Ridge.

"That's impossible." Liv's eyes latched on his.

"I know. Tony thinks it's a set up. But we can't prove it."

"If they dismiss the charges, what happens to us? Colton?"

"I don't know." Ridge pulled her into his chest, his hand skimmed along raised scars lining the middle of her back.

She twisted away from his touch. He'd wanted to ask about

them since their first night together. But he already knew where they came from. The image was emblazoned in his memory just as the pain was inscribed on hers.

"I swear to you, I won't let anyone take this away from us."

Liv nodded as Ridge rose from the mattress, slipping around the corner and into the bathroom. He watched through the mirror reflection as Liv leaned back against the headboard.

"How will you stop them?" Liv said to the empty space.

She folded her hands around her midsection as he listened from the open doorway. Her words cut into him, slicing through the hope that ran like an underground river through his soul. He didn't have an answer.

46

LIV

Ridge was still in the shower, but at least I was dressed by the time Tony showed up at the apartment. I swung the four-panel entry door open with a steaming cup of coffee in one hand.

"I understand I might not be the person you want to see right now," Tony said, casting his eyes toward the floor. "Ridge told me what happened with Lombardi. But I want you to know, I don't work for Lombardi. I'm on your side."

"It's okay, Tony. I appreciate what you've done for us so far. I know you're not the enemy."

I backed away and swung the door wide enough for Tony to come through.

"I found something. It involves both of you." He glanced down the hallway. "I thought it only right that we talk it over–together."

"Ridge is in the shower. I'll let him know you're here." I closed the door and slid my full coffee cup onto the counter, motioning into the kitchen. "There's coffee if you want some. Help yourself."

By the time Ridge and I made it back to the living room, Tony had poured himself a cup of coffee and was rummaging in the drawers for a spoon. Ridge slid a teaspoon out of the corner drawer and handed it to Tony.

"I thought we were going to meet outside," Ridge said.

"You're both going to want to see this." Tony traced his steps around the breakfast bar to the coffee table where he'd left a closed manila folder. He unfolded the metal clasp and slid out a thick blue file folder, passing it to Ridge.

Ridge checked the tab before the heat of his gaze glanced off me. "Are you sure about this?"

Tony nodded. "Under the circumstances it was the least I could do." He looked at me. "It's your un-redacted Bureau file. Goes back quite a ways, before any of Sowards' involvement."

I shifted closer to Ridge on the sofa, peering over his arm to catch a glimpse of a history I still hadn't been able to fully piece together.

"How'd you get this?" I dragged my eyes away from the file to meet Tony's.

"I've got a trustworthy contact in Bureau archives. He snagged it for me."

"Archives?" I asked.

"When assets go off grid or are released, their files are stored in the archives. Believe it or not, they're just now starting to digitize everything. My friend works on the IT side of things. He was able to pull this for us."

"Jesus Christ." Ridge slid a hand through his hair.

Tony sucked in a breath and refocused his attention on Ridge. "This explains why Sowards went to such lengths to plant that mandible. I'd say it'd be reason enough to pay Adam off, too." Tony shrugged. "He can't kill her."

Ridge passed a paper to me.

"This is my grandmother's handwriting." I skimmed

lines of text followed by a table of genetic code, circles and boxes around specific combinations, most of it beyond the high school chemistry that marked the limit of my scientific pursuits. But the last paragraph caught my attention.

GenLink asset #32, code mutation indicates probable 2x ability carryover to offspring. Psychometric and telepathic abilities genetically confirmed. Guaranteed early asset ability without intervention. Note: Offspring viability uncertain without carrier match.

"What does this mean?" I asked.

"It means Sowards was never after O'Malley's drugs." Ridge started. "That was nothing more than a ploy to engage a man who knew too much. He needed a way to get Cam out of the way, Liv. From the beginning, he was after you."

"Adam was right." The words came out in a rush. But that wasn't the reality that plagued me most. I read the line of text again, the final sentence sinking into my core with cold finality. "And the threat against Colton?"

"We still don't have a grip on that just yet. But I promise you. He's safe." Tony was trying to soothe frayed nerves, but the fact they hadn't been able to validate the letter, attribute it to Sowards directly, only told me one thing. He was planning to use Colton to get to me.

"How can I get in touch with Adam Miller? Is he still in custody?" Ridge's voice broke through my thoughts.

"As far as I know, he is. Without tipping off Rogers and Lombardi, though, I'm not sure it's possible."

I glanced down at the paper in front of me. "Except, it's not really me he's after, is it?"

"What do you mean?" Tony asked.

"It's the next generation he wants. Not me. GenLink part two. And my kids will have the genetic code to make that possible." I handed the paper back to Ridge and stood. The flip in my gut intensified. "I can't do this right now."

I made it to the bathroom before the heat in my cheeks collided with the panic seizing my insides, doubling me over. *Get yourself together, Olivia*, my inner critic warned. I braced against the countertop until the wave of anxiety subsided, splashing water on my cheeks to dim the flushing effects of paranoia.

I stared at my reflection in the mirror. I'd promised Ridge a future, but my past was too tangled. I was bred for a purpose. And if I understood my grandmother's notations in that file, I'd never be able to give Ridge the future he craved.

If Tony was right, and Sowards needed me, it only meant one thing. The threat was real. My return to Cascade Hills had put Colton directly in the line of fire.

47

RIDGE

Ridge pressed his hand against the cool of the bathroom door. What could he say to undo the damage written in plain English in Liv's file?

"Liv?" He tried the handle, but he'd heard the click of the lock when the bathroom door swung closed. "Talk to me."

The door cracked open a moment later. Liv's red-rimmed eyes stared back at him from a pale face. "I'm fine. I just need a minute."

"Whatever this means, whatever he's after, we can stop him. We'll get through this together." Instead of lightening her emotional load as he'd intended, Ridge watched as the muscles in her face tightened. A shadow of fear clouded her eyes.

"I'll be out in a minute." She closed the door between them.

"She okay?" Tony asked when Ridge returned to the living room.

Ridge nodded, sliding onto the sofa across from the near

stranger who had somehow become a confidante. "It's a lot to process."

"I hate to say it, but there's more," Tony said, holding up his phone. "I just got word that Sowards' petition for dismissal was granted. Charges were dropped with prejudice."

Ridge's brain spun and the ache behind his eyes intensified. Having the charges dropped with prejudice meant Sowards could never be charged with Liv's abduction again, not to mention the lighter charges of conspiracy and fraud brought by the Department of Justice. Ridge fisted a hand through still damp hair.

"He'll go after Colton to get to Liv." Ridge picked up Liv's file and fingered the pages, on a hunt for something that might help him hold his family together.

Tony sucked in a breath, his voice dropped. "Maybe. But if that's the case, he won't hurt Colton, at least not until he gets Liv. And we know he won't hurt her, which buys us some time."

Ridge shrugged. That was little comfort in the midst of rebuilding a normal life. "Liv's got a twin. Ashlyn." He lifted his eyes to meet Tony's gaze. "Why is Sowards so focused on Liv? Wouldn't twins be genetically identical?"

A hint of guilt spiraled through him. He had no intention of throwing Ashlyn to the wolves, but if there was a way to distract Sowards, it was worth exploring.

"I thought you might ask that. As soon as the lab report came through, I did some checking. Thought maybe the mandible was hers."

A blip of tempered hope pulsed through Ridge.

"It wasn't. Ashlyn's alive and well in Dublin, Ireland, right where Liv left her." Tony tugged another, thinner file free from the manila folder and passed it to Ridge. "Ashlyn Callaghan."

Ridge compared the genetic code from Liv's file to Ashlyn's. "They're not the same."

"Grace didn't use names, but every participant in the program was numbered. There's a page near the back of each file. Looks like a family tree."

Ridge laid both folders in on the table in front of him, digging through each until he came up with the document Tony was talking about. He smoothed them side by side, his eyes combing over the stacks of numbers on Liv's page.

Asset #32 was listed in a bracket on the bottom. That bracket branched into two–Liv's parents, Ridge assumed. The number on the left matched the number above Ashlyn's asset number.

Ridge pointed. "So this is Aimee Callaghan, right? Liv's birth mother?"

"Far as I can tell," Tony responded, moving to sit next to Ridge on the couch.

Ridge drew a line from Aimee's number over to the connected block where the father's number should be listed. His jaw clenched as understanding crashed over him. "They have different fathers."

"Question is, which number belongs to Stephen Sullivan?"

"Grace Sullivan's value to the Bureau was in her ability to create assets with heightened abilities. In order to do that, she needed to breed a female, in this case, Aimee Callaghan, with a male who had the right genetic mutation running through both lines. We know Grace was psychic. Her son, Stephen, would have been the most likely choice."

"The most convenient, anyway," Tony added.

"I saw a picture of Liv and Ashlyn with Aimee and Grace. It was taken within a few days of their birth. If they didn't have the same father how could–"

"Surrogacy?" Tony lifted a shoulder at the idea. "I mean,

speaking from a purely scientific perspective. She needed a control, right? All other things being equal? So, fertilize two eggs, each with a different donor. It can be done."

A fist of panic took hold of Ridge's chest. "Twenty-eight years ago?"

"She would have been one of the first," Tony admitted.

"Ashlyn has abilities of her own, Tony. Liv's not the only one."

"Right, but just like blue eyes can show up as a recessive trait, whatever gene is responsible for psychic ability is likely to show up every now and then."

"How do you know what all this means?" Suspicion started a slow creep up Ridge's spine.

Tony shrugged. "I was a biology major. Entered the Army right after. Worked on combatants to biological warfare. Most of this genetic stuff makes sense to me."

"That's convenient." Ridge didn't mean for the words to drip with quite so much accusation.

"The genetic aspect of Liv's case is why Michelle Rogers asked me on board. I'll admit that. But I'm not here for Michelle." Tony locked eyes with Ridge. "I'm here for Liv. They're using her, and I've watched too many innocent lives destroyed in my life. If I can keep one more from falling victim to government greed, I'll do what I can to make that happen."

Ridge remained silent, processing the information.

"You know they actually test biological weapons on people?" Tony said.

Ridge swallowed and looked away.

"Sometimes the effects don't show up for a generation or two. Do you know what it's like knowing you played a role in the suffering of some poor kid twenty years down the line? That's guilt, my friend. In its purest form."

Ridge apologized, moving back to the papers in front of him.

"Liv's situation is no different. Her children will have to live with the effects of what the Bureau did to her."

"Which is what, do you think?" Liv's voice from behind startled them both.

Ridge stood, making his way around the couch to Liv, who took a step away before he could get close enough to touch her.

"I don't know," Tony admitted. "I have a friend from the service. He dabbles in parapsychology. There's a chance he could give us an idea of what we're dealing with here."

"Call him," Liv said. The corner of her mouth tipped down, fighting the emotion evident in her voice. She moved her gaze from Tony to Ridge. "I called an Uber. Could I have the key for the farm?"

"Of course," Ridge moved to the door and pulled the square key from its peg. "But let me take you."

Liv shook her head. "No, you two stay. I just need to go home for a while."

Liv snatched the key from Ridge's outstretched hand and swept through the door, closing it with solid finality.

"How long was she standing there?" Tony asked once she'd gone.

"Long enough." Ridge exhaled a curse as he grabbed his keys, taking off down the stairwell. He watched from the second floor as Liv's Uber pulled away from the curb.

48

LIV

The crunch of tires on gravel sounded behind me as I stood at the edge of the ash left by my grandparents' burnt out barn. The thunk of Ridge's car door, once ricocheting off the tall wooden structure, now dissipated, swallowed by the line of trees at the edge of the woods.

"Storm about a month ago took down that big oak." He pointed to the stump in the grass behind the charred swath of land. "The back of the barn came down with it. Didn't know what else to do."

"It looks so different." They were the only words I could think of to say that had anything to do with the lost barn. My mind twirled, fixating on the information in that file–on problems beyond my control.

"Your car is still here. Parked over at the side of the house. The keys are inside on the secretary. I had to move it when the fire department came to raze the barn."

"You've done a nice job with the place," I managed, the image of overgrown ivy and weeds from the night we'd first met hung thick in my memory.

"I lined up a friend of mine to come bury what's left, level it so we can reseed—" Ridge paused. "Or, whatever you want to do."

I kicked at a clump of burnt wood at the edge of the blackened grass.

"Did you and Tony solve any of the great problems of the world?" I turned from the scorched earth to face Ridge. He stood a few feet away, hands shoved in his pockets, chin tipped down—that James Dean look I loved so much.

"At least we know Sowards won't hurt you."

Just like he didn't hurt me last year? The sarcasm-laced words flitted through my brain, but I refused to lend them voice. "Where's that leave Colton?" I asked instead.

My words landed with force against Ridge, his eyes skimming from the gravel to meet mine.

"And how do you know we can trust Tony anyway? He worked hand in hand with Michelle. Michelle brought in Lombardi. What makes you so sure he's not feeding them information?"

Ridge unpocketed his hands. "He's got clearance I can't get anymore, Liv. Besides, everything he's done since DC has helped us stay together."

"Like?"

Ridge stepped closer, closing the distance between us. "Like helping me realize I couldn't come back here without you." Ridge sucked in a breath, blowing it out in a thick stream. "He thinks the Colton threat was arranged to scare you, get you somewhere Sowards could keep tabs on you."

"Under Lombardi and Rogers' watch?"

"Lombardi's, anyway." Ridge reached for me, the back of his hand brushed wind-blown curls from the side of my face.

"So Adam was trying to help—trying to get me away from Sowards by putting me on that bus."

"It's possible," Ridge said. "We'll figure this out, Liv. And no matter what's written in those files, your grandmother never wanted this for you. She wanted you to live the life *you* wanted, not under some government dictate. I may not be sure of much, but there's no doubt in my mind about that."

"Thank you for that." I released a pent-up exhale and tucked myself against Ridge. "Whether or not it's true, it helps to have something to hold onto."

His warm arms closed around me, pulling me close. And for the first time that day, the thought that all of this would turn out okay flirted with the edges of my consciousness. I closed my eyes as we swayed in the driveway, the thump of his heart soothing beneath my cheek.

"I've got to pick up Colton. That offer for breakfast is still on the table."

The smile tugged at my lips even through the anxiety that tightened into a knot in my chest. "Sounds delicious." I pulled away and laced my fingers through Ridge's. "I can't wait to see Colton and hear all about that concert I missed."

Ridge smiled, a pulse of happiness throbbed from his skin to mine.

"What if my grandmother's right?"

Ridge's eyes skimmed mine, all wary hesitation.

The heaviness in my chest weighed on me, making normal breath difficult. I sucked in a lungful of the sweet farm air, my heart pounding. My grandmother's loopy scrawls at the bottom of the typewritten page burned into my memory. I repeated the scrawl. "Offspring viability uncertain. If she's right, what does that mean for us? Our future?"

Ridge and I had only ever talked about having a family in passing. We'd never been stable enough to give it serious thought. But coming back to Cascade Hills, starting over, made space for the conversation.

Ridge turned me to face him. "We don't know what that means. No matter what, it doesn't change how I feel about you."

"What if it changes how *I* feel about me?"

The vibrant blue of Ridge's eyes set against the reddish-purple bruise across the bridge of his nose was more than I could take. That injury was only one of many he'd endured during our time together, and no matter what excuse he gave, I knew this one was a direct result of not telling him about my last minute flight change.

"I'm twenty-nine years old."

Ridge smiled. "Not for four months."

"What if I can't have kids?" I whispered. "Can you live with that?"

A hard vacuum of silence sucked at the space between us. I forced my eyes up slowly, dragging over his body until I reached his face.

"What kind of question is that?" Hurt stretched across Ridge's features.

"You used to talk about it. I don't want to be the reason–"

"The reason I get to spend the rest of my life with the woman I love? The reason I can fall asleep at night and for the first time in seven months, *really* sleep? I love *you*, Liv. Not some idealized version of a maybe future. But *you*. Here. Today."

"Say that again." Water lapped at the lakeshore in the distance.

He stepped forward slowly. Gravel crunched under the soles of his shoes as he reached for me. "I love *you*, Liv. Only you."

His hands slipped around my waist. Looping his fingers through my belt loops, he tugged me closer.

I rested my palms against his chest, fiddling with the lump of my Claddagh ring still tucked on its chain.

"Do you think Sowards knows?"

Ridge grew suddenly serious. "I don't know," he admitted. "But I don't plan to give him the chance to find out."

49

RIDGE

There was nothing Ridge could say to make the wheels in Liv's brain stop turning as they drove into town from the farm. He'd do anything to wipe the fear from her eyes. But he'd also seen the hint of happiness. And if he had to find ways to remind her how much she meant to him every hour of every day for the rest of his life, he'd do it.

"Does Bridget know I'm back?" Liv asked, rolling her head from her gaze out the passenger window.

"She found out the night of the concert," Ridge answered. "She was a bit worried I might fall off the deep end again after what happened with Tony." Ridge waved a hand in the direction of his face.

"So, that's what happened?" The sweet sound of humor colored her voice. "You got in a fight with a trained bodyguard?"

"I was with the Bureau for eight years, Liv, and in the Corps before that. I can handle myself, you know."

A ribbon of giggles permeated the interior of the car. "Obviously not," she said.

He glanced her way, bottom lip tucked under top teeth, eyes glittering, trying her damnedest not to smile too big in the wake of her insult. He couldn't help but laugh in spite of himself.

"Fine. Point taken. I'm out of practice, okay?" Ridge downshifted to pull into the driveway of Bridget's Cape Cod. He pulled to a stop, leaning over the console to wrap Liv in a kiss. Life, in this moment, was perfect.

Bridget stepped onto the front stoop before he could reach the door, "You're late," she said, hands on her hips. Everything was back to normal.

"Love you too, Bridge," he said with a wry smile.

She returned his grin and skimmed a hand over his temple. "How's the nose."

"Still feels like it looks, but it's fine. Thanks for taking care of me, Bridget. I appreciate it."

"I know." Bridget's voice filled with a quiet awe as her eyes tracked behind him. "It really is her."

Ridge glanced back at the Shelby as Liv slid out from behind the open passenger door, closing it behind her with a *thunk*. His ex-wife descended the stoop to meet Liv. A warm trickle of some emotion pooled in his gut as Bridget wrapped Liv in a hug it was obvious even Liv didn't expect.

"I know we've had our differences, Liv. I haven't always treated you with the respect you deserve, and I'm sorry. But you need to know that I'm genuinely happy you're here. It may have taken me a while, but I know how much you mean to him."

Bridget's words halted Ridge's approach.

"Livvie!" The squeal came from behind as Colton leaped off the front porch and passed Ridge, aiming straight for an unsuspecting Liv.

"Easy buddy," Ridge called after him, running forward to

catch up just as the little boy launched himself off the pavement and into Liv's arms.

Liv stumbled back a couple steps, but caught him, righting herself as Colton buried his head in her shoulder.

"Where have you been?" he asked. "You missed my concert."

Bridget tossed a glance at Ridge and for the first time he knew everything would be okay. Death had a way of changing perception. Bridget had grown over the past months–they both had–enough to ensure the family they shared could expand to include Liv.

"Your daddy told me. I'm sorry. But I promise I'll be there for the next one, okay?"

"M'kay," Colton answered, sliding from Liv's hip and trotting to Ridge.

"Ready for breakfast?" Ridge asked.

"Pancakes!" Colton jumped up and down and clapped his hands. "With Livvie, too?"

Ridge nodded, a clot of emotion clogging his throat. He kissed Colton on the forehead and helped him into the booster on the back seat of his car.

Liv thanked Bridget and slipped inside the Shelby with a wave.

Ridge sat in the front seat a moment, his gaze flicking from the little boy in the back seat to the woman by his side. In spite of looming threats, he was without a doubt a truly lucky man. Ridge backed the car out of the drive, hesitating to look at his son in the rearview mirror when Colton addressed Liv.

"I'm glad you're back, Livvie. Me and Daddy really missed you."

LONG-FORGOTTEN warmth seeped through Ridge's chest as he stood in line at the local diner, watching Liv and Colton talk and play while he waited for the cashier.

"Cute, those two," the gray-haired woman said, his cue to step up to the counter. He smiled and handed her the ticket. She punched numbers into the cash register and announced his total.

Ridge handed her the cash from his hand.

"She reminds me of someone, though." She snapped her fingers as if the action would jar the information loose in her brain. "The Sullivan girl, that's it," she announced with a flourish, tucking the bills into the drawer and drawing out his change. Her brown eyes drifted back to meet Ridge's gaze. "You know, the one who was killed in that explosion last fall?"

She was waiting for a response, so Ridge nodded. "I heard about that."

"She was good friends with my niece, before..." The cashier lifted one shoulder and ended the sentence without completing the thought. "Spittin' image, that one."

She tipped her chin in Liv's direction and counted a few bills and some loose change into Ridge's waiting hand.

"Bet she's heard it before, too. She local?"

"Just back." Ridge forced a smile to tamp away the tickle of worry. "If you don't mind me asking, what was your niece's name?"

"Andrea Chase." The woman smiled up at him with a crooked-toothed grin that disappeared as quickly as it had come. "Killed when she was seventeen–prom night if you can believe it. Only news rivaled it was all that hullaballoo at Sullivan farm last year." She huffed a chuckle and looked Ridge in the eye. "Out of towners think Cascade Hills is just a sleepy little burg. But let me tell you something. This town has secrets. And she doesn't give them up easily."

Ridge walked slowly back to the table. Liv's smile dropped as soon as she saw his face.

"Something wrong?" she asked.

"Nope." Ridge brushed leftover crumbs from Colton's shirt.

"Can we stay at the farm tonight, Daddy? Liv said it was okay. Can we?"

"Sure, buddy, but we've got to get you to school, remember?"

"Oh, yeah!" Colton hopped up and down excitedly, looking at Liv. "Jeremy's my best friend. I'm going to his birthday party on..." Colton screwed his face into confusion.

"When is it?" he asked Ridge.

"Saturday," Ridge said. A smile tugged at the corner of his lips, his son's enthusiasm catching.

"Yeah, Saturday. He's going skating. I've never been before, but Daddy says it's not hard, he'll teach me."

"Oh?" Humor colored Liv's voice as they walked down the sidewalk toward Ridge's car parked a few blocks down. "I didn't know Daddy could skate."

The smile she aimed at Ridge caught him right in the chest, a bloom of heat spreading despite the cashier's words still flirting with his memory. These were the moments he'd missed. The moments that made every worry, every tragic possibility, worth the risk. Colton skipped ahead, his blonde hair bouncing. Liv slipped her hand in his and he glanced away from his son, just long enough for the squeal of tires to register in his ears.

50

LIV

I caught the blur of traffic in my peripheral vision before Ridge's hands gripped my arms—hard. He spun me to the side and pushed, toppling me to the ground. A white van screeched, missing the turn in the intersection and barreled closer. I watched in virtual slow-motion as Ridge launched himself into the path of the oncoming van.

His palms landed with force against Colton's shoulder blades. The little boy lurched forward, the shove like a shockwave through his body. Colton crumpled in the grass at the base of a nearby front porch. I scurried toward him on hands and knees, pebbles grinding against a tear in the knee of my jeans.

I glanced toward the sidewalk as Ridge regained his balance. He teetered toward the safety of the grassy knoll. But he wasn't fast enough. I pulled Colton into my arms, shielding him as the van left the safety of the street, jumping the curb and skidding onto the sidewalk.

The impact slammed Ridge to the pavement. The weightless jostle of his body forever burned in memory. The scream clawed in my throat, sound echoing in my ears as the van crunched against a well-placed telephone pole, steaming to a halt.

My body vibrated. The lead in my muscles obeying the order to slide forward, crawling. Colton's arms clung around my neck as I called Ridge's name. A creak from above stopped me. The gasp of bystanders I hadn't noticed until that moment surged in unison. Another crack–long and destructive–sounded from overhead. A shadow fell over the patch of grass, the pole aiming for the ground around us.

I crab-crawled back to the safety of the knoll. The wooden post came to rest with a bounce between where Ridge lay and our own huddled forms. The white van creaked against the broken stump, one tire spinning in the air as if someone left their foot on the accelerator. I cradled Colton to my chest, his sobs turning to back-racking wheezes.

"It's okay, Colton, everything's going to be okay." The words played on my lips in a repeating loop. My eyes fixed on the wreckage less than ten feet away. The van's engine belched a cloud of gray smoke, engulfing Ridge's unmoving form.

The memory of my cousin, standing on the other side of his own car all those years ago–the vision that changed my life forever–filtered into my brain like fog.

"No," I said aloud, forcing the memory away. This would not end like that. I wouldn't let it. The hum of a growing crowd, their footfalls hard on pavement, voices loud, registered–a blessed distraction from horror plaguing from both my past and my present. My eyes stayed rooted, though, fixed and staring at the one corner of Ridge I could see–his left foot, unmoving beneath the hunk of steaming metal.

"Is the little boy okay?" a woman repeated after I finally realized her words were meant for me.

"I think so," I said, pulling Colton away from my chest long enough to check for injuries.

"I'm a nurse." She crawled toward me on all fours. Only then did I realize the lines of the downed power pole had us trapped in a triangle of live wire. "I can help," she said. "Can you pass him to me?"

Another sob racked Colton's tiny chest as the whir of a fire response team approached from a side street. The nurse looked their direction and backed away. "Just hold tight," she said. "They can help us with the lines."

I nodded, dragging my focus back to where Ridge lay on the pavement. Three men were helping a now conscious elderly man from the driver's side of the van. I scooted forward as far as the live lines would allow, Colton still clutched to my chest. They handed the man over to a paramedic before a rush of firemen descended on the driver's side of the wreckage.

One of the firemen's eyes caught mine. His gaze, warm understanding. He nodded and I shifted away, burying my face in Colton's blonde curls. "Please, God. Not this. Not now," I whispered, interrupted by the vocal demands of a first responder from my left.

"Ma'am. Are you hurt?"

I shook my head, only vaguely aware of pain radiating from my right knee.

"We've cut power to the lines." He held out a gloved hand. "Pass the child through to me and then crawl out this way."

He forced a cluster of lines apart and reached for Colton, who instinctively latched onto him, burrowing his head against the firefighter's jacket. The female nurse from before reached her arms for him and again Colton complied to the stranger's request. I kept my eyes planted on his blonde head, crawling my way through the lines toward the waiting group of first responders.

By the time I was out, two medics had joined the corps of firefighters, standing by on the opposite side of the van. The metal squealed against the tools they used, bucking as the van lifted enough for them to assess "the pedestrian."

The words echoed in my ears until one of the medics finally popped his head from under the van. "Anybody know his name?"

I stood, the pain in my knee crumpling me. "Ridge," I said, my voice hoarse and rough after the grating scream that tore through moments before.

"It's McCaffrey," one of the firemen yelled as a medic ushered me back into a sitting position.

"They'll get him out," the medic assured, her fingers pushed and prodded the area around my kneecap. I couldn't help but notice she only promised they'd break him free, not that he'd be okay.

I winced under the pressure of her fingers. She disappeared into the ambulance parked a few feet away and returned to wrap a stiff white brace around my knee "This will stabilize your knee for now, but you'll need x-rays to confirm there's no break, but my guess is a sprain. Did you twist your knee?"

"I don't know." Emotion added a wobble to my voice.

"It's okay," she said. "Tell me what you do remember."

"Where's Colton?" I asked, suddenly aware I'd lost sight of him.

"He's fine. He's in the back of unit 12 with a couple of my colleagues." She pointed across the side street now lined with onlookers. "We'll transport him to County Memorial just to be on the safe side, but other than being shaken up, he seems good." She hesitated. "Are you Mom?"

"No." A shudder of panic slipped through me. "Oh, God, Bridget."

"Bridget? Bridget is Colton's mom?"

"Yes."

"Do you know how we can reach her?"

"I don't have her number, but Ridge..." One emotion crashed into another and I curled against myself, hugging the knee that didn't pulse with panic-dulled pain. A sudden surge of adrenaline, part shock, all fear, loosened the grip of despair and I formed the words Colton needed for me to provide. "Colton's mother is Bridget McCaffrey, she lives at 337 Channing Way."

The medic ran her eyes over me and nodded a thank you. "We're doing everything we can." Her hand stayed firm on my shoulder. "You're Liv, right?"

I didn't remember ever telling anyone my name, but in the commotion I couldn't be sure. "I need to go with Colton. I can't let him go alone."

She looked me in the eyes. Her blue-green irises reflected the lights spinning on top of the fire truck that blocked the main road. "It won't be a problem," she promised. "You hang tight while I run this information over to Colton's unit, okay?"

I watched her trot away, meet another medic who stepped down from the back of the van marked with a gold number twelve. Her voice drifted into the background cacophony of vocal orchestration. Information delivered from one responder to another. The rumble of bystanders as they stood in a disarray of shocked semi-silence. The questions of police officers newly arrived on scene. The hum of the soundtrack broken by two words I'd been waiting to hear.

"He's out."

A thread of hope worked its way from the pit of my stomach as a medic ushered a backboard and gurney to the far side of the crash. I watched Ridge's foot for movement. But it remained still. Silence fell over the team of responders. Long seconds spread into minutes of excruciating silence.

"I've got a rhythm," one of the medics finally said.

A hand moved Ridge's foot from view and I heard the click of the gurney locking into place. I forced myself to a standing position, trying to glimpse the man on top, praying for some sign of life. Instead, I watched a medic use a bag to force oxygen into Ridge's lungs.

"Miss Sullivan? We're ready to transport Colton." The female medic had returned. "I can help you from here."

My heart fluttered in an irregular rhythm as I hobbled to unit 12. *You've got to be strong,* I coached on the walk over. *Colton needs you right now.*

I might have been able to take my own advice if the scared eyes looking out at me from inside the medical unit weren't a miniature version of Ridge's. If he hadn't held his arms open for me.

If he hadn't said, "Livvie."

And asked the one question I couldn't answer.

"Is Daddy going to be okay?"

51

LIV

T he only time I'd ever been in the children's wing at County Memorial Hospital was for a stay in the psychiatric ward after police found my best friend, Andrea Chase, face down in Cascade Lake and had no one else to pin it on but me. And to be honest, through the blur of emotions and drugs, I didn't remember a lot of it. But it was plain to see, no matter what part of the hospital you were in, every floor was just alike. Sterile, white catacombs that all looked the same. At least the pediatric wing had broad stripes of color lining the walls to help you know which way to go.

I sat in Colton's room with him, running borrowed matchbox cars over the rough fuzz of the hospital blanket. Colton was making crashing noises with his mouth and I was beginning to regret informing the nurse that Hot Wheels were his favorite toy. Thankfully, though, the medic had been spot on. Other than a scuff to the knee, Colton was physically fine. It was the fear I read in his big blue eyes, the subtle pricks of it in the air between us, that worried me most.

In the hour we'd been together, he must have asked the

same question at least eleven times, and right now, as Bridget's arrival was announced by the scurry of footsteps in the hall, he asked again.

"When will Daddy be back?" And for the twelfth time, it broke my heart that I couldn't give him a straight answer.

"He'll be here as soon as he can, okay buddy?"

"M'kay." Colton's eyes lit at Bridget as she swept into the room and snatched him from the side of the bed, holding him close.

"What happened?" she asked, before burying her head in Colton's curls. She hugged him long and hard while I moved from the chair, hobbling to the foot of the bed to give them space. She released him with a sigh, settling him back onto the bed to play with the cluster of cars.

She fixed her gaze on him as she moved to join me. She asked again, dragging her eyes away from her son to meet mine. The same fear I'd seen in Colton, now reflected in hers.

"I don't know." Tears tugged at the corners of my lips. I shook them away, forcing my mouth to comply with her question by repeating the same statement I'd given police.

For the second time that day, Bridget pulled me in for a hug, her words hot against my ear. "Ridge is strong, Liv. He'll pull through."

Her choice of words left me breathless, the seriousness of Ridge's injuries solidifying into a hard knot in the center of my chest. I returned the squeeze of her hand in mine and tugged free from her embrace.

"Thank you, for what you did for Colton. He needed someone and you were there for him. I can't thank you enough for staying with him." No truer words had ever passed through Bridget's lips, I was sure. "Now go." She eyed the rip in my jeans. "Get that knee checked out."

✦

I CHECKED myself into the emergency department. And after a detour through radiology, I was transferred to an exam room. Fingering the frayed edges of the lopsided hole at the knee of my jeans, I waited for the results of the MRI. Alone in the room I found myself with both time and silence, two elements that only ramped up the replay of the accident that screamed through my skull.

I palmed away uncontrollable tears as a young doctor slipped inside the exam room and introduced himself. He handed me a tissue. The letters on his gold name tag a combination of consonants that somehow blended to form a pronounceable surname. Albeit one that I had no hope of remembering under the circumstances.

"Would you like the good news or the bad news first, Miss Sullivan?" His dark eyes danced, sending a ribbon of hopelessness into my chest.

"Bad news." I forced the words into the air, shoving at the memory of the last time I'd been asked that question. What did they do, teach that line in medical school?

"You have a PCL sprain." He slid a tablet my direction, an MRI image loaded on the screen. With a pen he pointed out the assaulting ligament. "Fairly common with twist injuries. You said you were pushed to the ground?"

I could almost feel Ridge's grip on my biceps. The warmth of his skin against mine. I nodded. "Yes."

"Well, the good news is, you won't need surgery. We'll send you home with a brace to stabilize the knee. Give you a couple weeks to rest and refer you to an ortho for a follow-up consult, and you should be good to go. Sound good?"

"Perfect." The word felt sticky, unpronounceable. Nothing would ever be perfect again.

"Great. I'll send in a nurse and we'll get you out of here as soon as we can."

The silence of the room swallowed me once he left. I studied the posters hung on the door–the human body in muscular detail, pointing out the perils of opioid use for pain management, a purple colon cancer screening options poster, complete with smiling ColoGuard box. I was reading the statistics on the sign when the door reopened on a familiar face.

"Brian." Saying his name unleashed a rush of emotion. He closed the distance between us, wrapping his arms around me and holding tight.

"Are you okay?" He pulled away and scanned me from head to toe, eyeing my swollen knee.

"Just a sprain," I said. "How's Ridge?"

I saw the answer in Brian's eyes. "Skylar's with him. George just arrived."

"That's not what I asked, Brian." The words clogged my throat. "He made it through surgery. They're only allowing family with him now." Brian pulled a chair up to the bed.

"Surgery?" I asked as Brian took my hand, giving it a gentle squeeze. I searched for pulses of emotion, like I could feel when I was with Ridge, but they were absent–only roughened skin from too much dishwater slid against mine.

"It's bad, Liv." Brian's voice was quiet. His thumb traced an arc along the fleshy part of my hand. "He's got a concussion. They're worried about swelling in his brain. The main goal right now is to alleviate that. They gave him meds to keep him under, to give him a better chance."

At survival, I thought, sucking in a long breath to fight the rising tears.

"Other than that, he's pretty beat up–broken ribs, shattered ankle. They put plates and pins in his lower leg and ankle. He'll never go through airport security again without setting off the metal detector." Brian choked out a nervous laugh.

"He'll be okay," I soothed, for my own sake as much as Brian's.

The door swung inward again, giving way to a short woman, not quite as tall as my own 5'3". She forced a businesslike smile at us both and got busy manipulating a black splint around my leg.

"Doctor wants you taking it easy until you're seen by the ortho. Okay?" She raised a thick pair of eyebrows at me. "We'll send you with crutches if you request them, but I'll warn you now, insurance rarely pays."

"That's fine. I'll manage."

"You should get the crutches, Liv." Brian cut in. "It'll be hard to get around, otherwise."

The nurse eyed Brian. "Boyfriend?"

"Friends," Brian and I said the word at the same time. And the nurse shrugged, keeping whatever thoughts she was having to herself.

"Okay. I'll take the crutches." I had no money to speak of. All of my grandmother's inheritance was now locked in a trust, and the cash Adam had given me was still with the police in Bishop's Hollow. But I did have Mom.

The next ten minutes were spent fitting the crutches and showing me how to maneuver with them. Once the nurse was satisfied, she delivered my discharge paperwork. By the time we'd made it to the end of the hall, I was already winded and pain was radiating around my knee like a tourniquet tied too tight.

"They should've given you a wheelchair," Brian said, a smile playing at his lips. He trotted a few paces up the hall to a nurse's station and I watched as they wheeled a chair from around the corner. Brian pointed down the hall toward me and

I waved at the blonde nurse. She smiled and Brian trotted back, pushing the wheelchair in front of him.

"Here," he said. "It's the only way we'll make it to ICU before they kick everybody out at eight p.m."

"Do they really do that?" I asked.

Brian shrugged. "They did when you were here."

The past slammed into me. Brian as he hovered over me in Lyle Hunt's office, pressing against the gash in my gut as blood filled the back of my throat. "I'm sorry," I managed as Brian squatted in front of the chair, adjusting the footrest to support my injured knee.

"You've got nothing to be sorry for, Liv." His deep blue eyes locked on mine, shining acceptance I didn't deserve.

"I came back," I said, difficult truth taking over where conflicting anxiety left off. "This never would've happened if I hadn't come back."

52

LIV

Brian and I were outside the interior glass window of Ridge's room when one of the ICU nurses approached from behind.

"Excuse me, are you Liv Sullivan?"

I confirmed her suspicion with a questioning, "Yes."

"Beth Sullivan is in the waiting room for you."

I glanced at Brian. *Mom.* "Did you call her?"

Brian shook his head. "I came straight here when Sky got a call from the hospital."

I thanked the nurse and started to arrange the crutches so I could stand before Brian planted a hand on my shoulder.

"I got you," he said, wheeling me the short distance into the ICU waiting area. Mom stood along the row of windows looking out toward the sinking sun. Brian started to slink out, giving my shoulder a squeeze, but got caught midway to the door, my mother turning around. "Nice to see you, Beth," he said, nodding a goodbye as her eyes shifted onto me.

She closed the distance between us and lowered onto the

sofa next to my chair. My mother's dark brown hair hung to her shoulders, her blue eyes filling with tears.

"The man you call Sowards," she asked, "Did he do this?" Her voice was all warm understanding as she tucked a strand of hair behind my ear. She'd obviously overheard more than I thought.

"I don't know. Probably."

"Liv," she breathed. Worry replaced understanding as she eyed the brace around my knee.

"I'm fine, Mom. Twisted my knee, but I'll be good as new in a few weeks."

She wrapped her arms around me in an impromptu hug, the unlocked wheels of my chair rolling closer to the couch with the force.

"They said Colton is okay," she said.

"Ridge pushed him out of the way."

Mom wrapped her cool fingers around mine and the silence stretched. "I'm sorry," she said, finally. "I overheard Ridge talking on the phone when you were in the hospital. I worried something like this might happen. It's like a curse our family can't shake." My mother was blubbering, wiping at rivers of tears with an already soaked tissue.

"We'll get through this." The truth of her words sunk under my skin and lurked there. I leaned into another hug and stayed close. My lie the glue that held us together.

When Skylar and Brian entered a minute or two later, my mom and I were still wrapped in each other. George followed them in, and I pulled away, taking in Skylar's red-rimmed eyes and the worry carved wrinkles across George's brow.

"The doctor's coming in with an update," Sky said. She sniffled, wiping her nose on the back of her hand before Brian could pass her a Kleenex. She snatched it from him and sat on the sofa across from my mom.

George took a seat across the aisle, the heat of his stare boring into me. I glanced up, but he looked away, shifting his focus to his clasped hands.

Skylar's gaze took his place, landing on me, blazing. "You did this." She sniffed. "This is your fault."

"Sky–" Brian reached a hand to Skylar's knee. But she jerked away, standing as the doctor entered.

"Friends and relatives of Mr. McCaffrey, I presume?" The doctor's appearance called an unspoken truce and he pulled up a single chair, joining us as we all nodded like worried bobbleheads.

"I'm Dr. Williamson, the lead in Mr. McCaffrey's case." He made eye contact with each of us. "I won't sugar-coat this. The next forty-eight hours will be touch and go. We're doing what we can to make sure the swelling in his brain stays within check. That's priority number one. We've repaired the fractures to his lower leg and ankle. At this point, he is still unconscious, but his vitals are good. We're cautiously optimistic."

Dr. Williamson glanced around the room, checking in with each of us again before standing. "When you go in to see him, you'll notice bruising and lacerations from the impact. Be prepared. We'll be monitoring his heart and brain function in the coming days, but we'll know more once we get past this initial trauma period."

Brian was the only one who spoke as the doctor walked toward the door. "Can we see him?"

The doctor nodded. "Of course. Limit it to two at a time, but do talk to him. Studies show that patients can hear even when they aren't able to respond. Let him know you're here. And if you have any questions, please let one of the team know. I assure you. He's in good hands."

Brian nodded and thanked the doctor.

Skylar pushed past me, shoving the side of my borrowed wheelchair hard enough that my leg wobbled. I bit against the wave of pain that sliced through my knee.

She stopped, turning to face me. "That should be *you* lying in that bed, Liv. Everywhere you go, tragedy follows. You should have died in that cabin. He should have killed you when he had the chance."

My mother stood, her mouth hanging open in shock.

"Skylar–" George reprimanded. His blue eyes tired.

"You don't mean that." Brian reached for her elbow and guided her into the hallway. Skylar spun to face him. Brian's words were muffled, but clear. "I get that you're hurting, Sky. We all are. But taking it out on Liv isn't helping anyone."

"I'm sorry," George said quietly. He patted my shoulder. "Maybe you should come back in the morning."

George left my mom and I alone in the waiting room. I watched as he strode down the hall toward Ridge's room.

"Don't lecture me, Brian," Skylar said as George passed. "Ridge told me about the threats. She knew coming back was a risk. Her greed put my brother in that hospital bed."

"An *accident* put Ridge there, Skylar." Brian's voice rose, colored with the heat of anger. "Ridge wants Liv here, so don't go blaming her. Your brother needs this opportunity just as much as Liv does, maybe more."

"Well, he might not get that chance. Why should she?"

Skylar didn't wait for an answer before storming down the hall. She stopped at the door to Ridge's room, turned back, and eyed both of us as I worked my way to the open waiting room door.

"Get out. Both of you. I don't want either one of you near him. Understood?"

Brian opened his mouth, but no words came.

53

LIV

"Can I borrow your phone?" I asked, as my mother drove in mutual silence from County Memorial Hospital to Sullivan farm.

"Sure," she nodded. "Don't you have yours?"

"I dumped it before the flight the other night. Thought they might be tracking me."

"They?" Mom probed for clarification.

"Sowards, the legal team in DC, anybody really. Didn't seem worth the risk."

Mom nodded her head in a slow rock, evidence she thought I might be more than a bit paranoid.

"You don't have to worry about me," I said, hoping to soothe the unease I saw in her. "I'm just trying to work through what happened. Keep it from happening again–to someone else."

"It's not that."

"What is it then?" I watched the reflection of dashboard lights on my mother's face.

"You're taking this really well."

"What other choice do I have?"

My mother's silence beckoned threatening tears as I tapped in the number I knew by heart.

Mom turned her attention back to the road as the line clicked open, "Medici."

"Tony, it's Liv, can you meet me at the farm? I need your help."

"I'm already here." Tony clicked the line closed as Mom turned into the drive and wound her Mercedes up the driveway toward the farmhouse.

Mom's headlights tracked over Tony as he stood in the dark, leaning against the gray SUV.

"Are you sure you don't want me to stay?" Mom asked, her eyes locked on the hulk of a man making his way to the passenger side door.

I planted a kiss on the side of her head, assuring her I wasn't in the hands of the enemy, before Tony popped open the door and helped me out, fishing my crutches out of the back seat with a nod to my mom.

"I was waiting for your call," Tony said as we watched my mom's car disappear up the drive.

"No phone," I reminded him. The corner of his mouth crooked up into a half-grin.

"I thought that might be the case. Here." He pulled a cell from the pocket of his jacket. "It's just a burner. But you'll need some way to stay in touch."

I thanked him and started toward the front door, the key Ridge had handed me that morning pressed hard against me from inside my jeans pocket. I'd been in Cascade Hills just over twenty-four hours, and already my world had been blown apart.

"I KNOW you want to blame Sowards for what happened to Ridge, Olivia. But according to CHPD, it was an accident." Tony worked his way around the farmhouse checking for signs that someone was watching. He paced from living room to dining room, finally meeting me in the kitchen.

"Skylar blames me," I said.

"I spent all afternoon on this. Guy was a diabetic. A delivery driver for a local florist. Back of the van was full of arrangements at the time of the accident." He paused. Looked at me. "If it wasn't for Ridge's quick thinking, all three of you could be laid up in the ICU right now."

"Is that supposed to make me feel better?" I emptied two cans of Guinness into pint glasses, the first I'd had since coming back from Ireland. I handed one off to Tony. "I need you to find out what he wants."

"Liv, I just told you, this wasn't Sowards."

"Maybe it wasn't today. But Skylar's not wrong. Tragedy follows me, Tony. And we know Sowards is out, free to go with no repercussions for the pain he's caused. There's no way I can believe he's done."

Tony took a long swig of his Guinness.

My jaw ached, proof of the pain I refused to free. "When I woke up in Ireland after the explosion, they were gone. Did you know that? My abilities?"

Tony's gaze slid down the side of the pint glass. It was all the answer I needed.

"Michelle told you," I guessed.

Tony nodded.

"I need you to find Sowards, Tony. So I can make sense of this. Whether the accident was his responsibility or not, the people in my life are hurting, and that's because of me." I narrowed my eyes on him. "Please. I'm only asking for two things. Find out where Sowards is and protect that little boy."

"I promised Ridge I wouldn't let anything happen to you."

"Ridge isn't available for consultation right now, is he?" The words bordered on panic, biting the air between us.

Tony took another long swallow of Guinness.

"I mean it, Tony. Don't let Colton out of your sight."

"That's taken care of." Tony rose from the table and took his near empty glass to the sink. "I'll work on finding Sowards. But my gut tells me, he'll find you first."

Tony's comment unspooled a thread of fear. Fear which immediately turned to self-loathing. I worked to keep the roller coaster of emotion in check as Tony headed for the front door.

"Just one thing," he said, turning to face me. "What about Lombardi?"

"What about her? She's the one who took me to Ireland. She drugged me at the airfield. I haven't heard from her since. What else do you want to know?"

"I know enough. But you might want to know a few things," Tony shot the words at me. "I pulled your original flight plan. Lombardi had you landing in an airfield outside of Charlottesville. My guess is the PCP was to make sure you didn't notice."

"That's near where O'Malley's cabin was."

Tony nodded. "I'm digging around, trying to find a connection. Property Sowards owns–something–that can link him to what Lombardi did to you."

"She's working for him." The realization sank through my chest, pushing me hard against the dining room chair. "How does Colton fit into this?"

"I'm not sure he does. That's what I'm trying to say, Liv. Putting yourself out there for Sowards is the same as being complicit in whatever he's hoping to do next. Do you really want to help him relaunch the genetic program you came back to shut down?"

Tony locked his eyes on mine for a beat before jerking the door open and disappearing into the night. I twisted the glass of Guinness in front of me and took a sip, but it didn't taste like it once did. Cool froth turned bitter against my tongue. I forced a swallow, the knot of realization growing in my throat. Ridge might not make it. I couldn't save him. No matter what I did, the life I'd fought for was on the brink of collapse.

54

RIDGE

Ridge woke to the beeping of machines. His eyes fluttered. Voices, far away at first, grew louder. A penlight, shining in one eye, then another, blinded him to the fuzzy fog of the room. He lifted an arm, and then a leg, but his body was lead, arms and legs immobile. He attempted to speak, but something was in the way, stopping his words. Panic gripped his chest and the beeping to his left increased in tempo.

"Relax," a strange voice said as gloved hands slid over his skin. "Breathe."

Ridge followed the command, sucking in a breath over dry lips.

"Now cough."

Ridge did as instructed, and the blockage disappeared, replaced with the coppery taste of blood from the back of his throat.

"Nice job," the voice said. "Do you know where you are?"

Ridge licked his lips, ready to formulate an answer that wouldn't come.

"There was an accident," the voice said. "You're in the hospital."

Ridge squinted, an attempt to access a memory he didn't have. The fog in his vision began dissipating, revealing a crowd of faces.

"Can you tell me your name?"

He swallowed, and his throat burned, the interior of his mouth desert dry. "Ridge," he forced out over chapped lips.

"That's good. Can you sip?" came the next question.

The bed mobilized under him, forcing his torso higher. He locked eyes with the woman holding the plastic container of water, a thick plastic straw paused at his lower lip. He wrapped his mouth around the straw and sucked, something in which the woman next to him seemed to take great delight.

A second face popped from behind the first. And a slice of relief threaded into his core.

"Dad," he forced the word through still parched lips.

A hum of voices followed, and another recognizable face appeared. Skylar reached for his hand, gripping hard as he slipped back into the haze of sleep.

"Do you remember where you are?" An unfamiliar face in a white coat asked when Ridge woke again.

"Hospital," he croaked out. "There was an accident," he repeated the information provided by the nurse.

"That's right. Is there anything you can tell me about the accident?"

Ridge brought his left hand up to his forehead, scrubbing at the crease between his brows. The words broken and unsure. "I don't remember."

"That's perfectly normal." The doctor's lips twisted into a tight smile as he made a note in Ridge's chart.

Ridge squinted, as if that action would usher in some wave of memory that was just beyond his reach. Skylar looked over the doctor's shoulder expectantly.

"Was I driving?" Ridge asked. "Did I hurt someone?" The sudden possibility lurched through him.

"No, no," the doctor soothed in warm tones. "You didn't hurt anyone. In fact, we think you saved a couple people. But none of that is important right now. What's important is that you rest. Heal."

Ridge's day was a puzzle–broken snippets of time he'd have to stitch back together later. The sky outside his window moved from day back into night–the only way he had of marking time. It was still dark when a flash of memory lit inside Ridge's skull, accompanied by a hot slice of panic.

"Colton." The beeping machine to his left skyrocketed, mimicking the thunder against his sternum. Two women dressed in green scrubs filed in. One fiddled with the machine while the other held a stethoscope to his chest.

"I need to go home." Ridge attempted to sit, ignoring the persistent thump in his skull. He reached for the nurse's arm. "My son. Where is he? Is he okay?"

The nurse cocked her head and smiled. She was young, her blonde hair loosely knotted at the back of her head.

"Is this him?" She pulled a framed picture from the windowsill. "Your wife brought it earlier today when you were asleep."

"Wife?" Ridge asked, his mind fogging at the word. He took the silver frame from the nurse's outstretched hand.

"Her name is Bridget, I think," she said. A shadow of *maybe I shouldn't have said that* fell over her features.

"Ex-wife," Ridge clarified, and the girl's lips tipped up in relief. The second nurse excused herself while Ridge examined Colton's most recent school picture.

"His name's Colton." Ridge traced the outer edge of the frame with his thumb.

"He's fine. He's at home with his mom. I'm sure you'll get to see him soon."

Ridge scanned the nurse's glittering eyes. Panic eased its grip on his lungs and he lowered back onto the mattress.

"How long have I been here?"

"Three days," came the response.

"When can I go home?"

"That's up to the doctor to decide," she said. "But you're making great progress. You should be out of here in no time." She slid the photo from Ridge's hand. The happy tones of her voice drifted into the background. "Get some rest. Your family will be here to see you later today."

Maybe it was the drugs, or relief of knowing Colton was okay, but Ridge lost the battle with sleep. Drifting off to the memory of his palms against Colton's shoulder blades, the hard shove that toppled his son to the ground. He felt a tear leak from his left eye, but he was too tired to do anything about it.

RIDGE WOKE TO VOICES. The familiar tones of the doctor first. "It's imperative that he remain calm. That you don't ask too much of him in these first days. He may not remember things. Details, short term memory has undoubtedly been impacted. But he did remember his son."

Ridge blinked his eyes open. His dad and sister stood at the foot of his bed. "I'm right here, you know. I can hear you." The words strung like taffy in his mouth.

Skylar and his dad exchanged glances Ridge read as relief,

before the doctor responded. "I was just telling them that you asked about Colton last night."

Ridge nodded, his head heavy. "He's okay," he repeated the nurse's confirmation.

The doctor strode around the bed to Ridge's side. "You'll have some visitors today, but if you get too tired, just let one of us know. This is a marathon, not a sprint, and exhaustion is the enemy."

Ridge glanced down at his left foot, heavily wrapped and propped on a pillow at the foot of the bed. "I'm guessing there won't be a lot of running in my immediate future." His lips tipped in a smile and it felt good.

Sky and George both smiled. Bubbles of relief escaped in quiet laughter.

"Well, he hasn't lost his sense of humor, that's half the battle," the doctor said, patting Ridge on the arm. "I'll check back later."

Ridge thanked the doctor, glad to have the stranger out of the room.

"Am I allowed to ask about my foot?"

"You've got a plate and six screws in your ankle," Skylar said through tight lips. "You're lucky to be alive thanks to–"

"Sky–" George cut in.

Ridge rubbed his forehead, avoiding the spots that caused him pain, unable to process the expression that stretched across his sister's features as a newly stitched memory bloomed in his skull.

"Liv was there." Ridge's words were quiet. But the automatic clench in his jaw sent a pulse of pain throbbing through his temple. "Where is she?"

Panic climbed into his chest and the machine on his left responded, the tempo increasing as he glanced from George to Skylar.

"She's fine, son," George answered. "She's home." He shot a dagger stare at Skylar before stepping forward. "I'll let her know you're asking for her."

Ridge nodded.

"It's important to stay calm," George echoed what Ridge had heard the doctor say numerous times since he'd regained consciousness.

Ridge watched his sister storm out of the room. "Sky seems angry."

George sighed. "She had a bit of a falling out with Brian and Liv. Called off the wedding. It's been...interesting."

"What happened?" Ridge squinted, an attempt to piece together what his father was saying, his brain sluggish.

"I think I best leave that discussion for the four of you. Now, if you don't mind, I've got some phone calls to make."

George exited the same way Skylar had. The two of them disappeared down the hall while Ridge worked to make sense of reality on his own.

55

LIV

Skylar put Brian and I both on Ridge's disallowed list, which meant neither one of us had been able to check in on him for the last three days. Tony and Bridget were good about keeping me posted, but the inability to see him, let him know I was there, that I cared, was emotionally debilitating.

As if that wasn't punishment enough, she'd also contacted the local television stations and newspapers about my return, a few of whom now intermittently camped out on the lawn at Sullivan Farm, waiting for me to come out and give them a juicy sound bite.

Mom and Tony checked in daily. My mom spent most of her visits anxiety cleaning every bathroom in the house and fretting over the fact that I wasn't eating. I ignored her comments. It was hard to eat when nothing tasted good.

"I called Jack Reynolds," Mom said as she finished up her daily cleaning spree that third day. Jack Reynolds had been the Sullivan family attorney for as long as I could remember. "He's going to put together a petition for you to get your name back, your ID. Says it might not be easy, though. With the remains and DNA evidence it'll be an uphill battle. Says you'll need to have some bloodwork–genetic testing. I put the information on the table for you."

"Thanks," I managed, doing my level best to keep the eggs and toast she'd forced me to eat for breakfast from making a reappearance.

"Have you talked to Bridget? Heard anything?" she asked.

"Not since yesterday morning. I know she's busy."

Mom hesitated, wringing her hands in her lap. "Might be good to spend some time with her. The two of you might need each other if–"

"Don't." I flung the covers back and hobbled to the dining room where Mom had left the note from Jack.

My mom apologized and gathered her purse. "I just thought maybe she could talk to Skylar. Help smooth things over."

I knew what she was doing, trying to prepare me for the worst. She'd lost a husband–my father–suddenly. Never got a chance to say goodbye. She didn't want the same for me. Even if Ridge wasn't able to say it back.

"According to Bridget, Skylar's not interested in talking. She's angry. I can't say I blame her." I followed my mom to the front door. "I'd be angry, too."

My mother cupped my chin in her hand. "You wouldn't take away someone's chance at goodbye."

I lifted my gaze to meet my mom's.

"Face it, Liv. You've spent the majority of your adult life trying to help people–spirits–who never got that chance."

I sucked in a wobbly breath. I had no response. She was right. And now I was left with nothing–no spirits, no energy. The only man who even sparked a buzz of electricity now lay unconscious in a hospital bed.

Mom patted my cheek. "I'll see you in the morning."

TONY SHOWED up late that afternoon with Chinese take-out just as I was poised at the open refrigerator door about to settle on a bowl of cereal for dinner. It was the first time in two days the thought of food hadn't repulsed me.

"This is a thousand times better than Frootloops," I said. I dug into the chicken fried rice like I hadn't eaten in a week, hoping my stomach wouldn't retaliate later.

Tony smiled at me. "Glad to see you're feeling better."

"Any news?" I watched Tony over-chew his egg roll. He waited until he swallowed before responding.

"Ridge is awake."

"What?" I dropped my fork and it clattered against the dining room table. "Why didn't you—"

Tony held his hands up. "Let me explain. He woke up late yesterday afternoon. The doctors wanted to be cautious. Assess the damage. Take it slow."

The chicken fried rice lurched in my gut. "He doesn't remember."

"By the time Bridget and I got to the hospital this morning, he'd remembered that Colton was there. The doctors seem pleased with his progress." He paused, taking another bite of egg roll.

"But he doesn't remember me." My voice was a quiet declaration.

Tony lifted a shoulder. "He hasn't asked for you."

Tony's words hit me full-force. I worked to calm the roiling sea of nausea in my stomach. "But Bridget and Colton, he knows them?"

Tony nodded. His brows pinched over hazel eyes laced

with sorrow. "He's been kind of in and out of it. Bridget's only been able to see him briefly."

"And George and Skylar?"

"Yes." Tony pushed what was left of his dinner away from the edge of the table. "They've spent the most time with him so far."

My stomach churned again, forcing me from the chair. I crutched down the hall to the bathroom, lurching over the toilet just in time to lose what little bit of dinner I'd managed to eat.

Tony appeared in the doorway and stepped inside. He pulled my hair from around my neck and shoulders and held it as my stomach freed the last of its cargo.

Even with my eyes closed I could feel the back of Tony's hand against my cheek. "Are you sick?"

I gave Tony a gentle push and he stepped away, releasing my hair.

"I'm fine." I grabbed a washcloth from the towel bar and rinsed it in the sink, wiping my mouth before turning to sit on the now closed commode. "It's just stress."

"How long?" he asked. "Since you ate and kept it down?"

"I managed to keep Mom's eggs down this morning. That was the first time since the accident."

"Liv." Tony's voice was a web of concern as he kneeled in front of me, careful not to bump my knee. "It's not my place, so you don't have to answer, but..." he hesitated. "Are you pregnant?"

"No." The answer was instinctive denial, but the thought process that followed was anything but. Neither of us had been prepared for a rendezvous that first night in DC, Bishop's Hollow either for that matter. But that hadn't been very long ago, just two weeks by my count. I did the math in my head. Sure enough, I was three days late.

Tony must have seen it in my eyes. He stood with a curse

and paced the tiny two-piece powder room. Two steps one way, two steps back. His size added an element of comedy to the scene.

I put my arm out to stop him, my fingers latching around the muscles of his forearm. "It's stress," I said. "You can't say anything. To anyone. Not until we know for sure."

"Liv, what we found in that file. Your grandmother's warnings."

"Shut-up." I didn't mean for the words to slice through the air the way they did, push Tony back a step. I took a breath. "We don't know anything for sure. Besides, I can't think about this right now."

Tony nodded as his phone buzzed hard and fast from his pocket. He didn't reach for it, just stayed immobile, his eyes on me.

"Aren't you going to get that?"

Tony reached in his pocket and pulled the phone to his ear without checking the name. "Medici," he answered.

I could hear Bridget's voice in the background. "Are you with Liv?"

"Yes," Tony answered.

"Get her over here, Tony. Ridge is asking for her."

Hope fisted around my heart and squeezed.

"And tell her to ignore whatever Skylar says."

"We'll be right there, Bridget." Tony ended the call and turned to me.

"Bridget says—"

"I heard," I said, pushing past Tony. "Let's go."

56

RIDGE

R idge woke that evening to a soft voice and a tickle of touch along his right hand. A welcome reprieve from the too frequent wake up calls by overly attentive nurses.

"Ridge?" The voice came again. He fought through the dregs of medicated sleep to open his eyes.

In the fog of the morphine drip he could almost believe he was hallucinating. Had thought that was the case when the memory of Liv at the diner first bloomed. Other memories were more deeply rooted. The explosion. Her memorial service. His fight to find some emotional balance in the wake of it all. But as hours passed, his memory cleared. Liv was home. And she'd been with him the morning of the accident.

"Liv," he breathed. He reached for the remote, nudging the head of the bed higher. He shifted to see her face, lit by the amber glow of sunset. "God, it's good to see you." His words felt heavy and deliberate, but she smiled. And heat melted through his core.

"Is that from the accident?" Ridge asked, tipping his chin in the direction of the crutches she'd stowed against the wall.

"It is." Ridge sensed a flicker of pain in her eyes as she sat, replaced quickly by a spoken, "Just a sprained knee. Nothing major." She hesitated, eyes lowered as she laced her fingers through his. "I missed you," she said. "I was afraid you wouldn't wake up."

Her eyes welled with tears as a memory clicked into place for Ridge–the three of them at the diner. He smoothed his hand along the side of her face and she leaned into his palm. A tear cut loose from her eye, skimming her cheek before he could wipe it away with his thumb.

"How much do you remember?" she asked.

"Not much. But I think I'm doing better than the doctors expected." His lips curled into a smile and he traced Liv's lower lip with his thumb. She closed her eyes to his touch and a tingle of heat worked its way through tired muscles and into his core.

She curled closer, nestling her head against his shoulder. "Is this okay?"

Wisps of curl fell over his bare chest, the sweet scent of her working its way into his sense memory, reminding him how much he'd missed her.

"Better than okay," Ridge said. He pulled her hand to his lips and kissed the tips of her fingers, giving the spiral of want in his core a chance to grow. He needed out of here. Needed to be alone with Liv, somewhere they could talk–process through this accident and move forward.

"Was it Sowards?" he asked quietly. So much had come back to him in the time since he'd asked for her.

But Liv shook her head. "Not this time."

Commotion from beyond the glass partition caught Ridge's attention. Sky stood outside, poking Brian in the chest with an insistent index finger as he continued to retreat from her.

"I better see what's going on." Liv sat up, dragging her hand away from Ridge. "Sky's not very happy with me and Brian right now."

Ridge wanted to ask why, but in the flush of her skin against his, the word wouldn't come. Liv tucked the crutches under her arms and worked her way toward the door. Each step she took sent an ache of loss into his core.

"Liv," Ridge said, stopping her before she left.

"When you're done sorting out whatever that is, come back. I don't care what my sister says."

The glitter of fear and pain colored her eyes, and although he was sure a portion of that pain was physical, the emotional ache ran deeper.

"I will. I promise."

Ridge watched from the hospital bed as Brian and Skylar argued. Liv and Tony reached them at about the same time, a security guard the next on scene. His door hadn't closed all the way when Liv left, and he strained to hear.

"Why are you so angry with me?" Brian said, arms raised in self-defense.

"Because I found this." Skylar pulled a folded letter from her pocket and threw it at Brian. It bounced off his chest and hit the floor. But as soon as he looked down, the expression on his face changed.

"Where did you get this?" Brian stooped to collect the letter from the floor.

"Does it matter?" Skylar folded her arms across her chest, her head turned toward Liv. "Maybe we need to show Ridge, too, as long as we're clearing the air."

Ridge felt the immediate rhythm change in his chest. The machine next to him confirming the shift with a staccato beep. He sucked a long drag of air into achy lungs.

"Skylar–" Ridge's dad slid into view, planting a hand on Sky's shoulder, but she shook it away.

"You need to take this outside." The guard who'd approached directed them all to the nearest bank of elevators.

Liv started to follow Brian, but Tony turned, stopped her. "This is between Skylar and Brian. You stay with Ridge."

"Is it?" Skylar shot over her shoulder toward Tony as the guard ushered them away.

Liv was about to push back through the door to his room, when Bridget appeared in the hall outside, Colton's hand clasped in her own. An impromptu clutch of breath seized in Ridge's chest as Liv and Bridget hugged, speaking in hushed tones. Liv stayed in the hall for a moment, looking in, while Bridget and Colton pushed through the door.

Ridge worked himself higher on the bed, wincing against the pull in his lower leg.

"Take it easy," Bridget said. "We'll come to you." She smiled and hoisted Colton up off the floor, settling into the chair next to him.

"Daddy?" Colton's voice was quiet, a note of fear clipping the last syllable.

Ridge stretched out a hand to his son. "I'm glad you came."

Ridge watched as Colton's eyes scanned him from head to toe. Other than his bandaged foot, the worst bruising was along his left side, covered by blankets. But the lacerations on his face and chest remained in full view.

"Does it hurt?" Colton asked.

Ridge smiled. "It looks way worse than it is, bud. Everything's going to be okay. I promise."

Colton lurched out of Bridget's grasp and planted himself face-first on Ridge's chest. Ridge gritted through the knives stabbing from the inside. He caught his breath and wrapped his arms around his son.

Bridget reached for Colton, but he hung on like a leech.

"It's okay," Ridge took another deep breath and relaxed into the pain of relief.

57

LIV

Bridget and Colton sat with Ridge most of the evening. I'd been with him for less than ten minutes before the on-duty nurse ushered me out at Skylar's request.

"When can I come back?" I asked George on my way out. It had taken me three days to finagle my way in, I guessed it would take just as long to do it again.

"Give it a day, Liv. Stay home tomorrow. I'll let Ridge know this is Sky's decision, not yours."

I sucked in a breath. If I had to give Ridge's sister twenty-four hours to keep the peace, so be it.

Tony agreed to drop me off at Murphy's on his way to take Bridget and Colton home. He eyed me through the rearview mirror so often Bridget noticed. She squeezed his hand, asked if he was okay before Tony brushed her off.

Tony had been keeping his part of the bargain, following Colton everywhere in addition to checking up on me. But I had a sneaking suspicion his interest in Bridget and Colton had more to do with connection and less to do with duty. I hoped I was right. But neither one of them was talking, at least not in front of me.

"Any luck with that project you've been working on?" I asked, anything to shift Tony's attention from our afternoon conversation and onto something else.

Tony eyed me again. "Nothing yet," he said, but something in the tone of his voice told me he wasn't telling the whole truth.

We pulled into Murphy's parking lot and Tony got out to help me with the crutches. "Are you feeling okay?" he asked quietly.

"Better than I have in three days," I said. And it wasn't a lie. Yet another point for the "caused by stress" column in the anxiety versus pregnancy game I'd been running through my mind since that afternoon. If it hadn't been for the distraction of Ridge, I might have driven myself crazy.

"Be careful. No drinking. Call if you need a ride back."

"Thanks, Dad," I said with a smile, my words dripping sarcasm.

Tony just shook his head as I hobbled away from his SUV, stopping to smile and wave at Colton and Bridget from the front entrance of Murphy's. I swung open the heavy wood door and wound my way through the after dinner crowd toward Brian at the bar.

"Got a minute?"

The expression on Brian's face was unreadable. I couldn't tell if he was happy to see me or faltering along the lines of "Stay the hell away." Either way, I wanted to know what happened between him and Skylar. Especially since Sky somehow felt I was involved in whatever was keeping them apart. He nodded to his bartender, grabbed a menu, and followed me to an empty booth in the far corner of the pub.

"How'd it go with Sky?" I asked.

"She gave me the ring back, if that's what you're asking."

I swallowed against the bite in Brian's words and offered an apology. "Did I do something? It seemed like maybe–"

"Here." He tossed the folded letter I'd seen that afternoon onto the table between us and slid out of the booth. "That's why you're here, right? To snoop? See what the fuss is all about?"

"I'm here because I'm worried about you."

Brian let out a sarcastic huff and shook his head. "You want something to eat?"

"Fish and chips sound good," I answered before fully realizing that the grumble in my stomach was actually calling for sustenance instead of threatening the opposite–a good sign. He walked away without another word.

I fingered the folds of notebook paper, mulling over the option in front of me. By the time Brian made it back to the table with a Guinness I hadn't ordered and the fish and chips, the letter was still neatly folded exactly where he'd left it.

"You didn't read it."

"You didn't want me to."

"Jesus, Liv." Brian tucked the tray onto an empty table and slid back into the booth across from me. "It's this–shit like this– that made me write that letter. You don't know the impact you have on the people around you."

"Then enlighten me, because I have absolutely no idea what you're talking about right now."

Brian sighed and rubbed his hands down his thighs. "I don't know if Ridge told you, but after you–" Brian struggled to say the word.

"Died?" I supplied, picking at a french fry.

"Right." His eyes caught mine for a brief second before he pulled them away. "Anyway, I found this grief counseling group. And it helped, you know. Ridge wasn't the only one who lost someone that day."

"What about Skylar?"

"That's just it. Everybody expected me to be happy. And I was, but there was a hole. One I never expected. We were friends, Liv. Ridge deserved someone that made him happy. But once you were gone..."

A twist of anxiety unspooled in my gut as I realized where he was going.

Brian shook his head and picked up the letter. "This was one of the activities they assigned in the counseling group–to write to the person we'd lost and tell them all the things we never had a chance to say in life." His eyes locked on mine. "I wrote this for you."

"And Skylar found it."

The muscle in Brian's jaw clenched.

"What's it say?"

Brian's gaze traveled down my face, holding on my lips for an uncomfortable moment before returning to my eyes. He unfolded the paper and began reading from somewhere in the middle.

"There were so many times I wanted to let you know how I feel. Those moments at the farm after Jason died, and after the IED in the woods–I came so close to telling you. Feeling you pressed against me when we hugged made me feel alive in ways I'd never experienced. Being around you made the sun brighter."

Brian paused, checking my expression before moving on.

"I'm sorry I never got the chance to tell you how much you mean to me–not only as a friend, but as something more. Even now, I wonder what it would have been like to feel the heat of your lips on mine, the softness of your skin against me. Maybe, in another time, you would have chosen me."

"Brian–" It was all I could think of to say.

He folded the paper. "Don't, Liv. Don't say anything."

"I didn't know," I whispered.

"Would it have made a difference?"

"No." It was all I could do to force the word through the clench in my chest. As much as I loved Brian, I'd never considered him as anything more than a friend.

"Good," he said, pocketing the letter. "You should eat. Only sushi is good cold, and we don't serve that here." He scooted out of the booth and disappeared through the kitchen door.

I picked at the fish and fries, checking in with the turbulence in my gut, while the new information swam in my head. But the longer I sat, the angrier I became. Not at Brian or his repressed feelings, but at the fact he'd pulled Skylar into the middle of it, made her feel like she was his second choice. No woman deserved that. Heat built inside until I couldn't take it anymore. I slid out of the booth and crutched my way to the bar.

"Get'cha something?" Murphy's regular bartender asked with a smile.

"Him." I pointed to Brian who'd squatted to look for something underneath the counter. "And a water, please," I added.

"Bri? Someone here to see you," the barkeep said, filling a glass and sliding it to me before turning toward a pair of patrons.

Brian grunted, bumping his head on the cabinet as he stood. I might have felt sorry for him if I hadn't been so angry.

"You're an ass."

"Okay," Brian looked both ways across the bar. "Before you say anything else, can we take this outside?"

"Fine," I said, taking a long sip of water before following

him behind the bar and through the cacophony of the kitchen to the back exit.

He turned to face me as the door swung closed behind us. "Let me have it."

"If you truly felt that way about me, why did you ask Skylar to marry you?"

"First off, I don't feel that way. I love Sky. Truly. We have a great time together. She's fun, beautiful, patient, kind–everything I ever wanted."

My shoulders dropped as confusion overpowered anger. "Then why write that letter? At the very least, why keep it?"

Brian sank onto the top of the picnic table. "Sky asked me the same thing. And the truth is, I don't know why I kept it." He glanced at me. My irritation must have shown because he followed it up with, "Yeah, she didn't believe me either."

"Think about it, Bri. What if Ridge found it? How do you think that would affect him?"

Brian picked at a nonexistent speck on the table.

"That's it, isn't it? You wanted him to find it." Fury clawed its way back in. "Why would you do that to him?"

"It's not what you think. You didn't see him afterward. The break-up with Bridget was one thing, but losing you sent him off the rails. He self-destructed, Liv. I thought if he found that letter he could channel his anger. Move through the guilt."

"You thought you could get him to hate me."

"Something like that."

"So if the letter is just a fabrication, why didn't you tell Skylar?"

Brian stood, closing the distance between us. "I did. But she needed proof and I couldn't–" Brian stopped short.

"No. You don't get to shut me out, Brian. Tell me what happened."

Brian's eyes darkened. "Ridge would kill me if he knew I told you."

I glared at Brian. "I don't do secrets anymore, Brian."

He held my gaze for a beat. His shoulders slumped with a sigh. "I found him at Sullivan farm on the anniversary of the night you two first met. He wasn't answering his phone. So, I went looking for him. There he was, sitting in his car, nose-first toward Cascade Lake. He had his foot on the brake, a fifth of Jack, and his handgun, complete with one hollow point in the chamber. It was pretty clear what his intention was that night."

Brian's words shoved me back a step.

"Skylar doesn't know."

An image of Ridge taking his own life, drifting into Cascade Lake as blood leaked from a wound in his head tore through me, seizing my lungs like a vise. "But you never gave the letter to Ridge."

"I tried. More than once. Put it in places I'd knew he'd see it. But he never did." Brian dragged a hand down the back of his head and turned away. "Once he started cleaning up, going to counseling, everything started to shift. The way he spoke about you–this lifeline of memories he went to whenever he needed a fix. I couldn't take that from him. So I tucked the letter away."

"But Sky doesn't believe you." I guessed.

"Would you?"

I didn't know how to answer that question. Truth was, under the circumstances, I understood why Sky was angry with both of us. My sudden reappearance resulted in nearly killing her brother and jeopardizing her engagement. Even if there was no truth to the latter, it was no wonder she wanted me as far away as possible.

58

RIDGE

"Where's Liv?" Ridge asked Bridget as they ate lunch together in his room. "I'm guessing Sky told her she couldn't come."

Bridget nodded, but stayed quiet. And quiet was rarely a good thing where Bridget was concerned.

Ridge lowered his fork. He'd been cleared for solid foods yesterday and he was ravenous, even if the mashed potatoes and chicken pot pie all tasted the same, congealing into an unappetizing gelatinous mass on the plate before him.

"Spill it, Bridge, what's going on?"

"It's nothing. Just a...feeling."

Ridge cocked an eyebrow at his former wife. "Don't tell me *you're* psychic now, too."

He smiled, but the words stung, an unintended mockery of Liv who wasn't even here to defend herself. He didn't mean it.

"Glad your sense of humor is intact," Bridget said. She paused, pushing pieces of lettuce around on her plate. "I'm worried about her."

If Bridget was worried about Liv, there was more to all of

this than he knew. "I'm stuck in here, Bridge. Sky's lost her mind. Why? She still won't tell me. Brian doesn't even bother to try to see me. Tony's in and out, but he doesn't say much. If there's something I should know, I'm relying on you to tell me."

"Liv's been having private conversations with Tony. I know she talked to her lawyer. They can't move forward with her petition to get the declaration of death lifted because of the DNA from the remains. He sent her for genetic testing. Liv's desperate. I think she might have asked Tony to find Sowards."

Ridge's last bite stuck in his throat, and he swallowed again. "She wouldn't do that."

"Tony's been poring over all kinds of files. Talking to friends from the Bureau."

"How do you know all this?"

Bridget pushed her plate away, her gray eyes finding Ridge. "He's been staying with us."

Ridge sucked in a breath. "You're seeing each other," he clarified.

She nodded. Bridget's admission didn't have the sting it once would have.

"Does Colton know?"

"It's not like we ever sat him down and talked about it, but I think he has some idea."

Ridge let the bubble of laughter escape from his chest. "Just take it easy in front of him, okay? He is a pretty perceptive little guy."

"Gets that from his dad," Bridget said, smiling. "I'll keep it behind closed doors." She pointed at Ridge's tray. "Done with that?"

Ridge nodded and pushed the food away as Bridget swept the tray clean and tucked it back alongside the bed, and out of the way. "Tony got a call this morning. Said he wouldn't be back until this evening."

Ridge tried to ignore the sinking feeling in his gut, that sixth sense that even he possessed to let him know when something wasn't quite right. Agent intuition he used to call it. "If you're so worried about what he's doing, why haven't you asked him?"

Bridget shrugged. "I don't know." She crossed her arms across her chest and leaned against the bank of windows. "Maybe I'm afraid of what he'll say."

"Tony's a good guy, Bridge. He's not going to do anything to hurt you."

Bridget ran a hand through a length of her raven hair. "I lost a guy once to Liv, just don't want it to happen again."

Ridge smiled and shifted on the mattress, letting his legs dangle from the side of the bed.

"Bridge, you know as well as I do that Liv never stole me. Besides, you and I make way better friends than lovers."

"I know." Bridget smiled and ruffled Ridge's hair. "You need a haircut."

"And a shave," Ridge said, scratching at the start of a beard. "It's a wonder Colton recognized me."

"I'll bring some supplies tonight, get you cleaned up for Liv's visit tomorrow."

Ridge thanked his ex-wife and resituated himself in the bed, propping his achy foot on the mound of pillows.

"Today's field day, right?" he changed the subject. "I thought you were going to chaperone."

"I signed us both up, actually. But that was before." Bridget waved at Ridge's bruised and battered body.

"Hey, don't blame me. Yesterday I walked from one end of the hallway to the other. I could definitely manage a game of wiffle ball with four-year-olds." He smiled, forcing the creep of darker thoughts away.

"Yeah, well, I figured the PTO Posse could handle it."

Ridge laughed at the unexpected response. The muscles around his midsection seized, intensifying the ache in his torso. He held an arm over his ribcage and leaned forward until the pain subsided.

"Note to self, don't be happy," Ridge said, readjusting his position for the umpteenth time that day.

Bridget chuckled quietly. "Looks like my time's up," she said, nodding toward the doorway.

Ridge turned to look just as Skylar popped her head inside.

"Thanks for coming, Bridge."

She bent to kiss him on the top of the head and started away.

Ridge caught her hand. "Hey, bring Colton tonight, okay? Maybe check in on Liv, tell her I miss her."

Bridget smiled and squeezed his hand. "I will. I'm sure the feeling's mutual," she said as Skylar sidled up beside her.

Bridget left without a word to Skylar, and Ridge waited in silence until she'd pulled the door closed behind her.

"I don't know what happened, Sky. But you owe me an explanation."

"Somebody's feeling better today." Skylar lowered into the chair next to Ridge's bed.

Ridge let his eyes comb over his sister. Dark circles lined sad eyes. Her cheeks looked pale and hollow. She ran her right hand over her left, the ring finger now bare. "Is it that bad?" he asked.

"They aren't who you think they are, Ridge. I'm just trying to protect you. You'd do the same for me."

The ominous sensation Ridge had felt earlier returned, settling into a light buzz along his right forearm. He didn't need this now. Not here. He sucked in a long combat breath and released, putting an end to the vibration.

"Brian never loved me." Skylar's voice laced tight with hints of jealousy and hurt. "He loved *her.*"

"Who?" Ridge didn't try to hide the confused scrunch of his eyebrows.

"Liv." Skylar nearly knocked the chair down as she jumped from her seat, eyes blazing. "Are you blind?"

Ridge attempted to keep the laugh inside but didn't have the strength to do it. It came anyway. The pain surged through his torso, stifling his initial reaction.

"Why are you laughing? Are you kidding me, right now? This is not funny. I'm supposed to get married in less than a month and I find out my fiancé has feelings for my brother's girlfriend?"

"Let me guess," Ridge started, catching his breath. "This is about a letter. Dated, oh, three months ago?"

Skylar lowered into the chair. "You knew about it?"

"I've read it," Ridge admitted, dragging a hand through his hair. "Look, Brian wrote that to talk me off a ledge–literally."

Skylar narrowed her eyes at him. A silent request for more information.

"He wanted me to find it so I'd be mad enough at Liv to stop blaming myself and start blaming her. Come on, Sky. You saw how I was after I lost Liv. Brian did what good friends do–whatever it took to help me." Ridge hesitated. "And I'm guessing Brian told you this already."

Skylar tipped her chin down. A tear slid over one cheek and Ridge reached to brush it away, but Skylar batted away his hand.

"Why didn't you ever blame her?"

"Why would I? If she had wanted to be with Brian, she would have been. The opportunity was there–more than once. And I sure treated her like shit enough to give her reason to go running. She didn't. She stayed." History clogged in his memory, images of his mistakes marching through like enemy soldiers.

"But that doesn't mean Brian didn't have feelings for her."

Ridge swallowed. "No, I guess not. But I do know he never made a play for her. Not once, Sky. He made a play for *you*. And if you don't believe him, ask Liv."

Silence stretched between them as Skylar processed what he'd said.

"I hate you sometimes," she said. "You and that stupid logical brain of yours."

"You mean the one that almost got splattered across Humphrey Boulevard a week ago?" Ridge smiled at his sister. "Now, shut-up and go get Liv," he said. "And apologize to Brian. You've got a wedding to plan."

I hired an Uber for the trek to the geneticist's office. Housed in a twelve story building on the outskirts of nearby Columbus, it was the easiest choice. My mom already had plans with her local bridge club, which I knew she'd be happy to cancel, but I didn't want to ask. More accurately, I didn't want to answer questions I wasn't ready for in the off-chance the geneticist could tell me if I was, or was not, pregnant.

I thanked the driver as he pulled up to the medical complex and hobbled out of the car. I was crutch-free now, but not limpless.

My heart raced as they took my vital signs.

"There's no reason to be nervous," the nurse said with a smile. Her happy grin broke into dimples that only served to remind me of Ridge.

"Do you have any questions before we get started?"

"Yes," I somehow managed to speak. "Is there any way to tell through this procedure if I'm pregnant?"

The nurse cocked her head to the side, her smile fading.

"We can check for that, but I recommend you see your obstetrician for any kind of prenatal testing. Are you worried about an abnormality?"

"No." That was a lie, but getting into my family history with a complete stranger wasn't a subject I was willing to broach right now. "I just realized that the possibility is there, and I was coming here, so..." The words were making less and less sense as my heart thumped heavy in my chest.

The nurse smiled again. "No worries. I'll pull some blood and have our in-house lab run it right away. We should have the results in a couple hours."

THE RETURN UBER had just dropped me off at the house. One of the reporters followed me all the way to the porch before I turned a bottle of pepper spray his direction, threatening. I closed the door behind me and punched in Skylar's number. She wouldn't listen to Brian, so I doubted she'd listen to me, but it was worth a shot if she'd call off the hounds.

Her line rang once before going to voicemail–a clear indication that she was declining my call. I sucked in a breath and hobbled to the sofa. I sat on my makeshift camp on the living room couch at Sullivan farm and rubbed the ache from my knee. Images swirled through my head–Ridge's lifeless body drifting in Cascade Lake, the white van crushing him, Brian's arms around me on the nights he'd mentioned in the letter, the possibility of a new life growing inside. I picked apart each scenario until my phone broke the silence–exactly two hours from the time I'd left the geneticist's office–not that I was counting.

"Miss Sullivan?" If I had to guess, the voice belonged to the same happy nurse that I'd met at the office that morning.

I identified myself and she launched into her spiel. "I thought you'd like to know that your bloodwork does indicate an elevated presence of hCG consistent with early pregnancy. You'll want to follow up with your OB, of course. I hope this has been helpful."

My body hummed as I worked to formulate an appropriate response. But an insufficient, "Thank you," was all I could muster.

I'd barely slid the phone from my ear when it vibrated, dropped out of my shaky hand and onto the coffee table before skittering to the side and onto the floor. I reached too fast, feeling the pull in the side of my knee before I could do anything to stop myself. I groaned through the slice of pain and pulled the handset to my ear.

"Olivia Sullivan," the voice on the other end asked as soon as I'd uttered hello. "I hear you're looking for me."

"How did you get this number?" I managed. Whatever shock was left fell away, replaced with the plunging sensation of fear. His voice hadn't changed. Low, with the gravelly undertones of a smoker. I'd recognize it anywhere–Marcus Sowards.

"Did you know today is field day at St. Stephen's Preschool?"

I swallowed the wave of sick that churned in my gut.

"This isn't about him," I said. "Leave Colton out of it."

"How do you know it isn't about him?"

I hobbled to the front door, my fingers trembling as I reached toward the secretary for my keys. I slipped through the door, keys jingling, ignoring media still camped outside my house.

"Where are you? We can meet. Just tell me where."

"Well, it certainly can't be Sullivan farm, can it? Not with the reporters staked out front." *He was watching.*

"Then where?" A few of the journalists surged toward me, shouting questions that got lost in a blur of panic as I pushed toward my car.

"Panera. Across from the school. Alone."

The line clicked dead and I revved the engine of my Mustang. Throwing gravel and ignoring the tearing pain in my knee, I sped out of the driveway and toward Colton's school.

SOWARDS SAT IN A CORNER BOOTH, watching the kids across the street through the plate glass window of the restaurant. I scanned the mob of preschoolers, picking out Colton's blonde curls as he and another boy hopped their way to the finish line in a potato sack race.

"How's the knee?" Sowards asked as I bent to slide in across from him.

"What do you want?" I asked.

"Funny." He raised his gray eyes to meet mine. "That's exactly what I was going to ask you."

"I want the same thing I wanted two months ago, Sowards. Answers."

"That's it?" He looked genuinely surprised.

"I want you to leave us alone."

"Ah, there's where it gets tricky. I can't."

"Why not? You got away with it. You're free. You buried Liv Sullivan under someone else's remains. I don't know how, but you did. She's gone. You don't need me anymore."

Marcus Sowards twisted his cup of tea and brought it to his lips, sucking the cup empty with a slurp. "That's where you're wrong, Olivia. I do need you. I made promises. Promises I intend to keep."

I expected to be afraid. I expected the memories of what

he'd done in the cabin to come surging back–hands around my throat, slamming me against the rough sawn boards until I could see nothing but stars. But instead, all I felt was hate. Burning hatred at the man who'd abducted Ridge's sister and used her as a means to pull me into his web. Hate at the man who'd paid Adam to lock me away, an ocean from Ridge, my mother, Brian. Hate at the man who was using an innocent little boy to pull me right back in.

"What was supposed to happen?" I asked. "Once I was in Ireland. What was the plan?"

"Oh, Liv." Sowards leaned back against the seat, a slight groan in his words. "Can't you see that what happened at the cabin was for the best? You'd be dead if Adam hadn't pulled you out."

"I'd be dead because of *you*." His thumbs against my windpipe, digging, squeezing, were the last memories I had of O'Malley's cabin.

Sowards locked his eyes on mine for a moment before tracking to the side, out the window toward the kids.

"I knew Ridge's mother. Did you know that?" He cocked his head, returning his gaze to me. "Violet. We went to school together." Sowards leaned forward. "She was one of Grace's firsts, you know."

"You're lying." They were the only words I could force free from the vise grip in my chest.

"Test me," Sowards said. "Sic your bodyguard on Vi's information. I know you feel it when you're with Ridge. You know there's something more between you–a connection you can't explain." Sowards smiled a sinister smile. "And I'm not the only one who knows. If you want answers, start with Vi."

He slid out of the booth without another word. I jerked to follow, but my knee throbbed, buckled against the force of the quick movement.

"Wait," I said, ignoring the faces in the room–staring, judging–as they picked at their salad bowls and quinoa.

By the time I freed myself, Sowards had pushed through the double doors. I watched as he trotted across the road and stood on the sidewalk, raising his hand in a jovial salute to a group of kids near the swing set. Most of the kids stood and stared, eyes wide. Only one child waved back. Colton.

60

LIV

S owards pulled away in his car, the same black Lincoln he'd had when I'd met him last year. I slipped into mine and followed, my knee throbbing in time to my inner critic who screamed at me to stop, turn around, go home. Instead of listening, I pressed harder on the accelerator.

I trailed Sowards out of town, weaving in and out of traffic, until I lost him in a surge of rush hour traffic on the northbound freeway. Only then did I realize I was crying–sobbing, really. The traffic around me blurred into blobs of metallic pinballs.

I took the first exit after that, pulling off to the side of the road as my chest heaved and stomach tumbled. My fingers gripped the steering wheel too hard, my knuckles white against the black leather. Flips of anxiety in my gut morphed into unmistakable nausea. *"This is stupid,"* I said aloud to myself. I peeled my fingers from the wheel and rested my forehead where they'd once been.

I reached for my phone with trembling hands. But I didn't make it through three digits before the gut flip of nausea took over. I shoved open the driver's side door, lurched out of the car and spilled a puddle of sick onto the roadway. I was still sitting there, doubled over with my door open, when the crunch of tires on gravel sounded from behind.

"What the hell are you doing?" Tony was angrier than I'd ever seen him. Evan had always been the angry one. Tony the calm voice of reason.

"How did you find me?" I asked, wiping spit from the corner of my mouth.

"Your phone. You weren't answering anyone's calls. When I had Ridge call and you didn't answer, I knew something was wrong."

"I'm sorry," I managed. I squinted, trying to make sense of his information. I'd had my phone with me all day. Had answered every call that came through.

Tony squatted in front of me. "How did you get here? Are you sick again?"

"I followed Sowards. And I'm pregnant."

Tony was silent for a long beat. "Come on." He wrapped his arms around me and lifted me from the car. "Let's get you in the SUV."

I lay, my cheek against the cool leather of the backseat while Tony drove my Mustang to a nearby parking lot.

"We'll get it tomorrow," he said, buckling into the driver's seat of the Jeep. "I've got your phone and your wallet. Was there anything else you needed?"

I shook my head slowly, careful not to disrupt this nausea-free moment.

"Where did you meet Sowards?"

"Panera," I answered each of Tony's questions with a short response. Filling him in on the details of the morning.

"When did Ridge call me?" I asked, once the interrogation was over.

"See for yourself." Tony chucked the phone into the

backseat. I scrolled through the missed calls. I hadn't added anyone as a contact on the burner, but I found his number easily. The one call I didn't find, though, was the one from Sowards.

"It's not here."

"What's that?"

"The call from Sowards." I sat up too quickly, launching another roil through my gut.

"If you're gonna be sick, use this." He emptied a plastic grocery bag and handed it to me.

I breathed through the wave. "I'm okay," I said. More for myself than for Tony's benefit.

"Can I see Ridge?"

"That's where we're going." Tony glanced at me through the rearview mirror, an unreadable expression in his gold-flecked eyes. "Just relax. We'll be there soon."

We drove in silence until I couldn't take it anymore. "Sowards told me to ask you about Violet McCaffrey, Ridge's mom. He said they were classmates. Did you know that?"

Tony was quiet.

A trickle of fear threaded through my core. "You don't believe me, do you?"

"It doesn't matter what I believe." Tony flicked the turn signal to turn into the hospital parking lot.

"I'm serious, Tony." I reached for his shoulder as he pulled to a stop in a parking space. "You think I'm making this up."

Tony took the key from the ignition and turned to face me. "I think you've been through a lot."

"What is that supposed to mean?"

"It means..." Tony struggled to find the right words. "No. I don't believe you."

"I swear to you, I'm not making this up." My words shifted into panic mode, too high-pitched for the confines of the car.

"Liv, listen to me. I don't believe you because it can't be true. Sowards is dead, Liv. He hanged himself last night. I found out this morning. It's why I was trying to find you."

Breath built up in my lungs as my lips worked to find something to say. I felt myself shaking my head. "That's not possible," the words came out of my mouth in a whisper. "I saw him."

I followed Tony to Ridge's third floor hospital room in a fog–uncertain and afraid.

"I won't tell anyone if that's what you want," Tony said as we waited for the elevator doors to open.

All I could do was nod. Even when my abilities had been in full swing, I'd never hallucinated a vision. Not once. The visions, even daytime ones, had always been surrounded by a sort of light blue haze, reality dissolving into the background for the duration, not becoming part of the scene. It scared me–blurring the line between what was real and what was not. And I didn't know what to do.

Ridge was sitting on the edge of his bed when we arrived. The first I'd seen him sit up under his own power since the accident.

"Liv," his body relaxed as he said my name, as if my being gone was a rod through his spine, forcing every muscle to attention.

I folded into his open arms and breathed him in.

"Where have you been?" he asked against my ear.

"Can I tell you later?" I asked, glancing at the group–Tony, Bridget, George, even Skylar–gathered near the foot of Ridge's bed.

"Come on, folks," Tony's voice boomed from the corner. "Show's over, Liv's here, let's give the two of them some space."

61

RIDGE

L iv's skin was cool and clammy to the touch. Her face pale, hair disheveled. He skimmed the back of his hand over the side of her face and she closed her eyes, leaning into him.

"Am I hurting you?" she asked.

"No." Ridge gripped Liv tighter against his chest–a challenge to the stabs of pain assaulting him from beneath the skin.

"How's Colton? Where is he?" Liv asked.

"Home," Ridge said, smoothing Liv's hair. "Brian's sister picked him up from school. She's watching him until Bridget can get back. He's fine."

"Is it true?" Liv pulled away and looked up at him, eyes wide, confused. "Is Sowards dead?"

"Tony got word this morning. Went to Charlottesville himself to check it out. He's gone, Liv. He can't hurt us anymore."

Liv sucked in a wobbly breath, her hands moving from his

shoulders to his face. The corner of her lip tipped into a forced smile. "You shaved."

"Haircut, too. Thanks to Bridget."

Liv ran the tip of her index finger over the dimple in his cheek. Ridge caught her hand and pulled it to his lips, pressing a kiss along the pads of her fingers. "What happened, Liv? Where'd you go?"

The silence stretched between them, pulling on pain-dulled patience.

"Jack set up an appointment with a genetic testing lab. I was there all morning."

"Bridget mentioned something about that. How long until you get the results?"

"A week or two." Liv hesitated, stepping out of Ridge's embrace. "I need to sit."

He watched her jaw clench as she reached for the chair behind her. She pushed out an even breath, gaze lowered. Her hands gripped the sides of the plastic chair with force, turning her knuckles white.

That same sinking feeling he'd had when Bridget was telling him about Liv returned, this time with a vengeance. "What's going on, Liv? We said no secrets. Please."

"It's nothing, Ridge."

Even through a healing concussion, he didn't believe that for a moment. "Damn it Liv, talk to me. It's bad enough I'm stuck in here. I can't have you shutting me out, too."

"I'm not shutting you out. There's nothing to say," Liv shot back, meeting his gaze in a silent challenge.

Swirls of repressed thoughts swam in his skull. Possibilities brought on by Skylar, even Bridget, and stoked by Liv's absence. "Is there somebody else?"

Liv leaned against the back of the chair, eyes that had blazed indignance a moment before now widened by shock.

A plunge of regret sucked through his chest. He reached for her as she stood but she pulled away.

"There's never been anyone else." A lone tear tipped over the rim of her left eye. "Is that what you think of me?"

A spiral of panic swirled in his chest, emptying into his gut. "Of course not," Ridge managed, hating himself. "Sky and Bridget just got in my head." He rubbed his forehead, hoping for some semblance of clarity.

"Bridget?" Liv's voice got quiet. Pain streaked across her features and straight into Ridge's heart.

"Liv, please. I never should have said that."

Liv took a few steps and turned, her voice soft, but clear. "I made a mistake. I never should have come home."

"Wait," Ridge eased himself to the floor next to the bed, using the mattress as a crutch. "Don't go."

Liv stopped at the exit. "I saw him," she said, running a finger along the edge of the door handle. "That's what happened today. I saw Sowards."

Breath caught in Ridge's chest.

"I watched him wave to your son. And I followed him until I lost him somewhere north of Columbus. Then, I found out he was dead."

Liv twisted the door handle as Ridge stood frozen, unable to give voice to even a simple word.

"And since we're being honest, there's one more thing you should probably know." Liv's eyes locked on his. "I'm pregnant."

She swung through the doorway as understanding dawned on Ridge. A hot slice of panic rising through him.

"Wait," he called again, stepping forward. Pain rocketed from his ankle through his leg and into his spine. He gripped the foot of the bed, but it was too late. The door clicked closed behind her and agony crumpled him to the hard tile floor.

His own yell was cut short by the grind of his teeth. Stars danced in his vision as her words echoed in his ears. Nurses rushed inside, admonishing him with curt words while helping him struggle back into bed. All he wanted to do was run. Run after Liv, bring her back and wrap her in his arms. Apologize. Tell her he was wrong, that he understood–even if he didn't.

"She told you, didn't she?" Tony's voice broke through the effects of the pain meds administered by the nurses. "Everything?"

Ridge looked up but didn't answer.

Tony pulled the chair to the side of Ridge's bed and sat with a resigned sigh. "This'll blow over. I'll keep an eye on her. Whatever she thought she heard or saw, I'll figure it out."

"And the baby? You gonna figure that out, too?" Ridge heard the accusation in his own voice. "I assume you were the first to know."

Tony scrubbed a hand over his close-cropped hair. "She's been sick. I happened to be in the right place at the right time. Nothing more than that."

Anger started a slow creep through Ridge–misplaced though it was. He only had himself to blame. He was the one confined to this place, unable to be there for the one person who needed him most.

"I want proof," Ridge squinted against the remaining fog in his brain and pushed himself higher on the bed.

"Proof she's pregnant?" Fingers of shock penetrated Tony's voice. "Ridge, that's hardly my place."

Ridge shook his head. "Of course not." His jaws ached from the angry clench he'd set them in. "I want proof Sowards is dead."

I t was after ten by the time the Uber rolled down the farm driveway. The windows of the three story house dark and foreboding. I scanned what was once the barn lot. The clutch of reporters that had become a staple over the past week, now conspicuously absent.

I waved at the driver as he backed up the drive, my mind spinning. In the last twenty-four hours, my life had changed irrevocably. And I'd managed to dump it all in the lap of the one man who didn't need to add my shit to his list of things to deal with. Maybe George was right. Maybe I was crazy.

I worked my way to the door, my knee poking and prodding with each step, scolding me for the day's overexertion.

"I figured I'd find you out here." A woman's voice drifted toward me from the darkened porch. I squinted to make her out, but deep down, I was already sure. I stood, frozen, as Amanda Lombardi stepped into the dusky light of the full moon.

"How's the knee?"

"Fine." I stayed rooted to the cracked cement walk, a dagger of panic pressed against my sternum.

"And Ridge?" Amanda stepped forward, the first porch step creaking under her weight. "I trust his health is improving."

"Why are you here?"

She took the second step. "I think there's been a misunderstanding, Olivia. I owe you an apology."

She descended the final step and started up the path toward me. "What happened at the airport, that wasn't me."

I wanted to believe her. I didn't know why, maybe it was the flash of understanding I'd felt when her skin brushed mine. The idea that we were part of a shared experience.

She smiled, stopping feet in front of me. "You know I was there that night, in the cabin, waiting for Adam to bring you to me."

"Adam said the cabin was empty. He left me alone."

"I waited for him to leave. Bit of a boy scout, Adam."

"Why should I believe you?" Her hand skimmed my arm and the flash of memory returned, imprinting on me. I jerked away from her touch.

"I know this is scary. These abilities you thought were gone forever, now suddenly returning."

"They aren't," I refuted. The image of Sowards, sitting across from me at Panera Bread, watching Colton, waving, flickered in. I closed my eyes. This was all just a figment of my imagination. I sucked in a breath. That's all this was.

But when I opened my eyes. Lombardi was still there.

"Come on. Come up to the porch so we can talk." She motioned toward the front of the house as the hint of a breeze blew across Cascade Lake, lifting my hair and twisting it. I pushed it off my face and followed her, limping up the steps.

"Is Michelle with you?"

Lombardi waited for me to settle into the rocker before lowering into her own. "Michelle has never been *with* me, Liv. We have very different goals, she and I."

"And Sowards?" I ventured into territory the lifted hairs along my arms and legs warned against. "Is he really dead?"

Lombardi's eyes combed over me–assessing. "Do you trust him?" she asked, instead of answering my question.

"Who?"

"Who told you Sowards was dead, Olivia?"

"Tony," I answered.

Lombardi rocked back, her head against the headrest. "And do you trust him?"

It was a question I'd flirted with since the beginning. I trusted Ridge, and Ridge trusted Tony. Trust by proxy, if that was a thing. I didn't answer.

"I'm guessing he also told you that the accident had nothing to do with Sowards."

My jaw squeezed.

"That's what I thought. But guess who owns the floral shop, Liv." Amanda sucked in a breath of the sweet summer air, continued her rock. "Hunter Enterprises. A shell company I can trace to one Marcus Sowards. And, coincidentally, the same company who owned The Hunter Steakhouse."

She stopped rocking, waited for her words to register.

"Lyle Hunt's restaurant," I confirmed. I carried the reminder of my run-in with Lyle daily, the scar embroidered across my side now faded to a dull pink.

"That's right. Although, he was really just a pawn. All of them have been–Lyle, Jason, Michael, even eccentric little Herman Mayhew–all of them paid by divisions of Hunter Enterprises."

"And Tony?"

"What do you think? Who did you have lunch with today?"

The tear spilled from my eye without warning. I wasn't crazy. He'd been there. Which meant one thing. Colton was in danger.

"I'll make this brief, Olivia. Ridge might not be dead, but he is out of commission. And that gives Sowards the perfect opportunity. What happens next is up to you."

"You drugged me, tried to put me on a plane to Charlottesville. Why should I trust you?"

"I'm trying to help you do what's right." Amanda glared at me, the corner of her lip tilted in a half-smile. "Think, Liv. Where did that nugget of information come from?"

The slow creep of panic worked its way up my spine. My brain raced, sorting through details—what had come from Tony and what had not.

"The drugs weren't Tony," I managed.

Lombardi sighed and turned to face me, pausing the sway of the rocker. "Fine. You want the truth? I paid off Adam. Transported you to Ireland. Waited for you to heal so Sowards and I could start a new generation of GenLink. But then, you started digging. Once you were home, it was obvious Sowards wanted an all-out attack. I had to do something to convince Sowards I was on his side."

"Why didn't Sowards come after me himself? He had a chance today."

"He wants more. Revenge. To punish Ridge for walking away from GenLink."

"Sowards destroyed GenLink," I almost shouted. The hard edges of my voice echoed in the darkness. "There was nothing left to walk away from." A ribbon of anxiety clawed its way from my gut to take up permanent residence in my chest.

"If I go to Sowards, give myself up?" I gripped the armrests of the chair, fighting nausea. "Will he leave Colton alone?"

Lombardi stopped rocking and zeroed in on me. "I can't

make any promises. Sowards is angry. He knows Ridge would never give up fighting for you. Taking Colton gives him leverage."

"Leverage for what? You're telling me he'd hurt a little boy just to get back at Ridge?"

Amanda's voice was calm, steady. "Think of all he's done so far, Liv. Sowards faked your death. Tried to kill Ridge. The only way to protect Colton is to give Sowards what he wants. Turn yourself in. Push Ridge away before Sowards does something that can't be undone."

Anger leaked out and I lurched forward, forgetting about my healing knee until shooting pain wrapped around my leg and squeezed, doubling me over and onto the decking.

"Take it easy," Amanda said. She reached down to help me.

I pressed my fists against my eye sockets, forcing away the threat of tears.

"I can't do this. I can't just disappear. Not after..." I stopped myself. This pregnancy would be one secret I would keep from Sowards. "I owe Ridge an explanation. I need to warn him."

"Don't," Lombardi's voice was firm. "Warning him will only make things worse. Sowards will know."

"How much time do I have?"

My heart raced as silence closed in on us, the distant lap of water against rocky shore the only sound between us.

"Not long," Amanda finally said. She twisted in her chair, eyes glistening in the moonlight. "I know this isn't what you want. But sometimes what we want and what's right are two different things. Ridge needs his son. You have to be able to see that."

"Why does Sowards want me?" I choked out, pressing against the weight of her comment. "If he's planning another GenLink, I'm useless to him. My grandmother's research proves it."

"Does it?"

I could tell from the way her eyes lit on mine, the arch of her brow, that she knew more than she was letting on.

"Yes," I forced out through tight teeth.

Amanda leaned back, relaunching the rocker into motion. "Regardless of what the files say, you're still the only one genetically capable of making GenLink work."

"And you've worked for Sowards? This whole time?" I held my breath, waiting for the confirmation I knew was coming.

Amanda didn't answer right away, rocking in silence. "It may not feel like it, but I've only ever tried to help you, Olivia."

"Help me what?" Seething anger gnawed at my insides. "Disappear?"

Amanda jerked toward me, eyes blazing. "You chose to come back. You chose this life. You put Ridge in a position to pay for your sins. Look at what you've done. He nearly died. Colton is in danger. *You* did this." She paused. Took a breath. Her voice calm indifference when she spoke again. "Sowards will destroy every person you love if that's what it takes to relaunch GenLink. If you love Ridge, don't jeopardize the one thing he has left."

Lombardi stood, smoothed her jacket and started down the steps.

"Say goodbye, Liv. Be thankful. Some people never get that chance."

She walked on, hesitating at the end of the cement walk, turning back with an afterthought.

"Oh, and you don't have to trust me. But you'll know when you need me."

63

RIDGE

By the time Ridge was released, he was stir-crazy and admittedly grumpy. Every call he'd made to Liv's cell had gone unanswered and she hadn't been to the hospital since dropping the bombshell on him two nights ago. All of which only exacerbated the loss of the morphine drip and ensuing inability to get his pain under control.

Now that they had, he was more than ready to be home. To have a conversation with Liv without an audience. Not to mention the added advantage of not being poked, prodded, and otherwise kept like a zoo animal. The only benefit of the extra twenty-four hours was one more session of intense physical therapy. And, while it sometimes made him want to crawl out of his skin, it also made him feel halfway human again.

His dad wheeled him out of the elevator onto the fourth floor of his apartment building into a waft of deliciousness.

"Someone's having something good for dinner," George remarked.

As they rounded the corner, Ridge was both surprised and relieved to see Liv holding the door to 1400C wide open. He breathed in the intermingling scent of chicken and home cooked goodness that permeated the hall from inside.

"You did this?" Ridge asked as George pushed him closer.

"Bridget sent a cherry pie. Said it's your favorite." Liv shrugged, her eyes darting away. "Which, I didn't know. You can blame me for the chicken and noodles."

Liv's attempt at self-deprecating humor sent a stab of hurt through Ridge's chest. Over the last couple years, the girl he'd met in the driveway of Sullivan farm had morphed into a self-assured woman, and it hurt to watch her retreat into her shell.

"I'm sure it's delicious," he said, pulling her hand into his.

"We thought the two of you needed some time alone, so I'm just here to push you in, and then you kids are on your own." George smiled, his gaze shifting between Ridge and Liv.

Liv waited in the doorway. A cloud of gloom behind her eyes sent a spike of apprehension through Ridge's core. What if she wasn't ready for this? Didn't want to start a family? Where would that leave him? He cleared the web of thoughts as his dad shoved the chair forward.

"Wait." Ridge stopped George before he could pass over the threshold. "I'm walking."

George lodged his complaint but knew better than to think he could change Ridge's mind. A streak of worry crinkling Liv's brow was the only thing that gave Ridge pause. George and Liv stood close while Ridge pushed himself from the wheelchair. With the help of physical therapy, he'd learned to maneuver in the walking cast pretty well, at least over short distances.

Liv took a bag of meds from George and retreated to the kitchen as Ridge lowered back into the chair and said goodbye to his dad. She lined his meds up on the counter, giving him a rundown on dosage for each one. It had only been two weeks since the accident, but somehow his whole world had changed.

⬡

"Dinner was delicious," Ridge said as Liv stacked dishes in the sink. They still hadn't talked about Sowards or the fact that the two of them would soon become three. The latter of which was eating Ridge from the inside out. He stood. "Can I help clean up?"

Liv's gaze caught him right in the chest. "You can watch me clean up from the couch over there." She tipped her head in the direction of the living room sofa. "Don't overdo it, Ridge. You'll regret it tomorrow."

Ridge did as he was told, following Liv with hungry eyes as she finished washing the pots and pans. "You didn't eat much," he said, hoping for a segue into a real conversation.

She held his gaze for a beat before answering. "If I manage to keep down the little bit I did eat, I'm going to call it a win."

There was a bite in Liv's words that Ridge couldn't interpret—a mixture of unsettled fear and anger that turned the warm tones of her voice to ice. It took everything in his being to force the next sentence. His chest ached with every syllable. "Liv, if this isn't what you want, I understand. It's still early. This is your decision."

Liv stopped washing, braced her hands on the sink surround, eyes cast toward the linoleum floor. Ridge's heart squeezed—breath imprisoned in his lungs. Is this what she'd been waiting for? Permission to end the pregnancy?

He pushed off the couch, ignoring the slice of pain through his calf and into his thigh as he worked his way toward the kitchen. The whole time, she never moved, frozen in front of the sink. It wasn't until he was on the other side of the island that he could tell she was crying.

"What is it? What do you want?"

Liv pushed back from the counter and cleared her throat, wiping wet cheeks with the backs of her hands. "I want you to sit. You'll hurt yourself."

"I'm not worried about me." Ridge leaned against the counter, taking the weight off his injured leg.

"I'm scared."

"You're supposed to be scared," Ridge said. "We both are. It's part of the process."

Her gaze locked on his, all wide-eyed fear and helplessness. "You're going to think I'm crazy."

"Because of Sowards? Of what you saw?" Ridge shook his head, reaching across the island to trace Liv's cheek with his free hand. "You're psychic—genetically—I signed on for that, remember? O'Malley's drug may have stripped it away, but it's bound to come back. Maybe that's what happened."

"He was there, Ridge. It wasn't a dream or a vision. He was there—flesh and blood—right in front of me. And he'll be back."

Ridge wasn't sure how to respond. Telling her she was wrong would put her on the defensive. But he wasn't a psychologist. Playing into her delusion seemed therapeutically unconscionable, no matter what the reason.

"I asked Tony for proof." Ridge admitted. "I've seen the ME's report."

"You can't trust him," Liv said, her voice quiet. "Don't ask me how, I just know."

Ridge's leg trembled under him. He shifted against the counter, but Liv noticed.

"Sit," she ordered, helping him to the loveseat.

"We promised when we got back to Cascade Hills there'd be no more secrets between us. I get that you're scared, but don't let fear jeopardize everything we've worked for."

"What are we working for, Ridge?"

Her question caught him off guard. He leaned forward, gripping her waist and pulling her in. He flattened his palm against her lower belly. "This," he said, daring her to look away. "Our future."

64

LIV

Ridge's words hit the air between us with force, sparking heat. I was supposed to be saying goodbye. My face grew hot. Underneath his hand, my belly tingled, a warm sensation soothing the near-constant tumble of my gut. No matter what Amanda Lombardi said, I couldn't do it. I couldn't push him away.

Ridge tugged me closer, his eyes asking for permission as his hands shifted, roaming to find flesh under the hem of my shirt.

"I need you," he breathed. "I need us."

His lips found the soft skin of my torso and I closed my eyes against the hungry pressure of his lips against bare skin.

"I'll do whatever it takes to make that happen."

He slid his fingers over my hips and watched as my body responded. I arched against his touch, tucking the lower corner of my lip between my teeth, pain rooting me as Ridge worked his way northward, pushing my sweater up as high as he could manage from his position on the couch. I took over, ducking my head through the draped opening and dropping the top onto the floor beside us.

He bent forward to kiss the fading scar across my abdomen and unzipped my skirt, his hands skimming my legs as he pushed it to the floor.

"We're not supposed to be doing this," I said. Amanda's words skittered like pinballs through my mind. But I deserved this, didn't I? One last night of ecstasy before Sowards pulled me back in? I slid a hand through the side of Ridge's hair. "Doctor's orders, remember?"

Ridge pulled back. His eyes combed over my body, but his hands stopped exploring. "It's okay if you don't want to."

A tickle of disappointment surged in my chest.

Ridge traced the lace of my bra with his index finger. "We can just talk," he said, but his body told a different story.

I leaned closer, sinking onto the couch with my good knee. "Promise to tell me if it hurts."

Ridge tipped his head back and nodded as I skimmed my hand from his hair down his jaw and onto his chest, methodically working the buttons on his shirt.

Ridge closed his eyes as my hand sunk lower, his body still bruised and battered from the accident. I paused. I'd done this. Sowards had tried to kill Ridge because of me. If I stayed, it would only be a matter of time before he did it again.

"Don't stop," Ridge whispered, guiding my hand lower until he rose against me–unleashing a growl from his chest.

I lost myself in the moments that followed–all well-placed hands, lips and hot breath. Grinding pressure took us both to the brink before a key in Ridge's front door cut the heat like a sliver of ice.

I swiveled in shock. Unable to maintain my balance, I tripped over the forgotten skirt and toppled to the floor–muffling a pained yelp as the door swung inward.

"Ridge," his sister exclaimed, turning her back to the living room in a well-executed spin.

"Jesus, Skylar, don't you knock?" Unsatiated hunger roughened Ridge's voice. A thread of anger seeped alongside, dulling the glow of the last thirty minutes.

"You just got home. I was trying not to make you come to the door," Skylar shrieked in response.

I managed to shrug into my top in record time, but the skirt proved more challenging. I sat crumpled on the floor, trying–without success–to free the garment from the Velcro of my knee brace.

Ridge reached for me, untangling the skirt and providing another hand as I struggled to my feet. I moved away, ignoring the shooting pain along the side of my knee.

"Liv," Ridge called after me as I slipped out onto the balcony. I sucked in a breath of the cool night breeze, listening as he lit into his sister. "What the hell, Skylar?"

"I thought she'd be gone."

I watched Skylar turn to face Ridge, her eyes red-rimmed and puffy.

"What's going on, Sky?" Ridge's voice softened on his sister.

"It's Colton. He was playing on the trampoline in the backyard."

"Is he hurt?"

I peeked inside as Skylar ran to the couch and flung her arms around Ridge's neck. Her voice a shocked wobble. "Someone took him, Ridge. Colton's gone."

65

RIDGE

B ridget wrapped Ridge in a hug as he fumbled his way up the steps to her front door. Her eyes were red and swollen, makeup non-existent. She was dressed in a pair of jeans and an old t-shirt he'd left in a drawer once upon a time. The woman who'd once won his heart peeked out through a veil of tears.

"I'm so glad you're here," she sobbed into his neck. "I don't know how to do this." Her fingers clawed at his shoulders, and he loosened his grip on one of the crutches to pull her into him.

"Everything will be okay, Bridge. I swear. I won't let anything happen to him."

Bridget pulled away, her features twisting. "Something already *has* happened, Ridge." She shoved him with both hands and he winced, catching himself with the toe of the crutch.

Bridget sucked in a scared breath and her hand flew over her mouth, covering the curse and apology. Her eyes went wet, filling with another wave of tears.

"Take it easy, Bridge," he managed, pulling her into him. "I probably deserve it."

The living room was set up exactly as he expected it to be. Officers manning a recording station in case the kidnapper made contact with demands. Techs in and out of Colton's room, searching for anything that might indicate what had happened in the hours he'd been missing.

"How long has he been gone?" Ridge asked one of the officers as Bridget sidled up from behind, her hand skimmed the back of his arm.

"Estimate is two hours now."

The automatic clench of Ridge's jaw sent a shooting pain into his skull. The internal fire of blame stoked in his chest and it was all he could do not to unleash on Bridget. But the questions fired through his mind just the same. *Where had she been? What time did she last check in on him? Who was she with that was more important than her son?*

He forced fury away as she tugged on his arm, urging him to follow her away from the buzz of the kitchen and living room and down the hall to the privacy of the family room.

"Were you with Tony?" Ridge asked as soon as they were alone, unable to stave off the urge any longer.

"Yes," Bridget answered. Her voice barely audible. "But this isn't my fault." She spat the last words at him.

"Bridge, I know. I'm not blaming you. I'm just trying to get a picture of what happened."

Bridget sank onto the muted taupe couch. The same couch he'd sat on with Liv as she'd combed through the contents of her grandmother's humidor just a little over a year ago. He forced the memory aside and lowered into the adjoining easy chair.

"Tony came over for dinner. Colton was playing outside afterward." She sniffed and wiped her nose on the back of her hand before Ridge could pass her a box of tissues from the end table. "I was doing the dishes. And when I looked up..." She stopped talking, the words visibly painful.

"He was gone," Ridge finished.

Bridget nodded and sniffed.

"Was Tony still here?" He wasn't sure why it mattered, but if it gave him something to focus on besides the disappearance of his son, he'd take it.

Bridget nodded. "He called the police." She wrapped the tissue around her index finger and pulled it tight. Guilt, Ridge realized.

"Bridge, you didn't do this. They'll find him."

"What do they want, Ridge? Whoever took him must want something."

Ridge stared at the carpeting under his feet. The full understanding of what he was about to admit slithered down his spine like a constrictor. "They want Liv. Me, maybe."

Bridget was quiet. Ridge could feel her eyes on him. Waiting for him to meet her gaze. He gave in and glanced up. The thunderstorm swirl of his ex-wife's gray eyes pulled at him, issuing silent blame.

"Where is she?" Bridget asked. "Did Liv take Colton?"

"Jesus, Bridge, of course not. She was with me."

"Then what the hell do you mean? Is this about the threats? You told me there was nothing to worry about."

Ridge swallowed and wrapped his arm around his ex-wife.

Bridget pushed away. "Our son is missing. And you're telling me your girlfriend might be the reason why?" The heat of Bridget's breath landed square against Ridge's jaw. Hot puffs of emotion. "Find him, Ridge. Bring him back to me. Whatever it takes. You need to fix this."

Ridge stood. "I'll try, Bridge. I swear to you." The choke of emotion came without warning. His internal monologue mocked with an irrepressible *I don't know if I can.* He stumbled backward, pushing through a wave of painful unbalance to steady himself.

Bridget turned away, settling onto the couch and wiping her cheeks with the heel of her hand.

Ridge moved for the door. "I'll be back," he said, stopping. "I'm going to talk to the detectives. I promise you, Bridget. We'll get Colton back. No matter what it takes."

Ridge slipped around the corner and into the hall bathroom, splashing water over his jaw to combat the swirl of frustration, anger, and if he was honest with himself, guilt. He jerked the towel from the nearby rack and held it over his face.

Steps in the hall outside sent an unwelcome pulse of adrenaline into his chest, squeezing as he prepared for what would certainly be another test of his composure.

"Give me a minute," he said through the towel.

The footsteps stopped. But there was something else. A vibration, maybe, that made him remove the towel and peer through the reflection and into the hall just beyond the door. A flash of auburn curl was all he caught.

"Wait–" Ridge leaned through the doorway.

Liv turned and relief sucked the air from his lungs.

"I don't want to be in the way," she said.

"You could never be in the way," he whispered, limping into the hall and wrapping his arms around her. "I'm glad you're here."

Silence passed between them as they stood. When she spoke again her words were soft, pained, and burrowed their way into his soul.

"He was supposed to take me," she said. "Just me."

Ridge tangled a hand in her curls, breathing her in. Until that moment he hadn't realized just how much he needed her right now.

"We'll find him," he promised. "And you're not going anywhere."

66

LIV

I stood in the hallway of Ridge's former house. His arms wrapped around me, warmth trickling from his body and into mine. And I could almost forget the conversation with Lombardi, her warnings, Sowards' revenge.

Ridge slung an arm around my shoulder and the two of us hobbled down the hall like invalids. He poured us both a glass of iced tea and showed me to the patio out back. We tried not to look at the empty trampoline at the back edge of the yard.

"The detectives will want to talk to you," Ridge said. "I already told them you were with me all evening, but they might ask about..."

I turned away from the sizzle of anger that darkened Ridge's expression.

"Sowards," I said.

Ridge nodded.

"Okay," I breathed. *Tell him this is your fault,* the words taunted from the back of my brain, *for not saying goodbye.* But this wasn't about me—not for Ridge. This was about a missing little boy. A little boy Ridge would only get back if I disappeared, and to do that, I had to keep him in the dark.

We talked a little while longer, downing our glasses before Bridget's voice cut out onto the patio.

"Have you seen Ridge?" she asked an officer standing inside the sliding glass door.

Ridge turned to me. "I should go. Promise me you'll stay. Don't go home alone."

I nodded, fighting the words I wanted to share. This was not the place, and my time was up.

The corner of Ridge's lip tilted into a pseudo-smile. The best he could do under the circumstances, I guessed. "Are you sure you're okay?"

"I should be asking you that." I managed.

Ridge looked away. "We'll get him back," he said.

I WAS SITTING ALONE on the patio when George slipped out of the house late that night.

"Liv," he said by way of hello, sliding into one of the gray plastic patio chairs. "Ridge said I might find you out here."

I glanced behind him at the house. "I'm just trying to stay out of the way."

George gave a grunt of understanding and pulled a cigarette from his jacket pocket. "Mind if I smoke?"

"Didn't know you did."

"I don't—anymore. Only in times of great stress." He held the cigarette between his fingers, waiting for permission.

I forced a smile. "Just blow it that way."

He laughed and lit up, sighing through the first exhale. "I thought maybe you and I should clear the air."

I focused on the man next to me. An older, less-fit version

of Ridge, down to the worried crinkle between his brows.

"Some of the comments I made when you were in Bishop's Hollow were hurtful. And I'm sorry. But in light of recent events and conversations I've had with Ridge, it's important to me that you know the things I said were out of concern for my son."

I didn't respond right away, lingering fears and questions about Ridge's mother still swirled near the surface of my thoughts. "Why didn't you ever tell Ridge about his mother?"

"I know your hulk of a bodyguard has been digging into Vi's life. And, frankly, I'd appreciate it if you called him off." George sucked in a drag of his cigarette. "I know you believe in these things, Liv, but no matter what Mr. Medici may have told you, Vi was not *psychic*."

George finger quoted the word, and a tendril of irritation crawled up my spine.

"Ridge's mother was diagnosed with paranoid schizophrenia after she tried to kill both herself and Riley." George studied the burning cigarette. "Gave her too much NyQuil and sat in a closed garage with the car running until they both passed out. If I hadn't come home early from the job site that day, Ridge would've lost his sister much earlier than he did."

"Did you ever ask your wife why she did it?"

George stubbed the butt into the patio pavement and turned to me. "Do you think there is any explanation that could have helped me forgive her for that?"

"I suppose not." But I could think of some. Maybe not any that George could understand, or even Ridge. But after what Sowards said, I could imagine why she'd want to protect her daughter from a life twisted by GenLink, even if it meant taking their own lives to do it.

"I've said it before, and I'll say it again. I see her qualities in you. Emotional. Impulsive. At times, paranoid." George shook his head. "Do you know what it's like to lose a child?"

I didn't answer.

"I didn't think so. Ridge was just beginning to move on with his life when you came back. I watched what losing you did to him. I can't stand by and watch you destroy him again."

"I have no intention of destroying anyone, George. Least of all Ridge."

George's blue eyes lit on mine, darkened by flecks of fury. "If you are who Ridge claims you are. You can end this."

Amanda's accusations echoed in my mind. Colton's wide-eyed innocence fell in behind, haunting from the depths of my brain. I didn't need George to remind me that all of the guilt rested with me.

"I don't know if I can." The words were hard in my throat.

"Ridge told the detectives about DC, the threats. He thinks you're the one Sowards wants. If that's the case, you sure as hell *can* do something about it."

George left me in silence, slamming the sliding door closed with enough force that I jumped. I let the first tears fall in quiet darkness. If George hadn't been right, the conversation would be easy enough to ignore–the insult of a grieving grandfather. But instead all he'd done was speak truth. Truth too painful to hear.

I pulled my phone from my pocket and turned it over in my hands, watching as the screen came to life and darkened again with each shift in position. I swiped the screen and tapped the phone icon, punching in the only contact number I'd bothered to store.

The other end of the line rang twice before the familiar voice broke through, sending a twist of fear-laced acceptance down my spine. "Lombardi."

"Amanda? It's Liv. Help me end this."

67

RIDGE

Ridge stayed with Bridget until they both fell asleep late that night. The throb in his leg squeezed him awake before the sun came up the next morning. A check with the still present officers proved what he already suspected. There'd been no contact from an alleged abductor.

Ridge checked his watch–2:30 a.m. They were going on nine hours now. Long enough for his son to wake up in a strange place, with a strange person, and wonder where his mom and dad were. Long enough for Colton to feel fear. The idea of it shoved hot and heavy against his sternum.

He'd only dealt with one child abduction case in his time in law enforcement, and it had been while undercover in Cascade Hills. The memory of it surged now. The father battling emotions of anger and blame while the wife hung quiet and fearful in the background.

At the time, the father's angry outbursts had irritated Ridge, but after Liv's abduction last year he'd begun to understand them completely. Now, faced with the same situation, he fought with every ounce of his being to keep them in check.

Ridge swallowed the knot of repressed anger and made his way toward the front of the house, looking for Liv. The patio where she'd sat the previous evening was empty. He didn't blame her. Sitting around, waiting for word that never came, was trying on everyone. And he certainly hadn't made it any easier on her, drifting away to soothe Bridget's fears and leaving Liv to battle her own. Ridge sucked in a breath and let it go, shifting his focus on the deserved pain in his leg instead. Radiating from his ankle and into his thigh, it proved almost unbearable after three missed doses of pain killers.

The hum of a couple officers conversing at the far end of the kitchen stopped as he entered. "Any news?"

"No new leads," one of them said. "The department is organizing a search. Plan to start about eight a.m."

Ridge only nodded, breathing through the speech inhibiting clench in his jaw. "Did Liv Sullivan get a ride home last night?"

"I took her," the younger cop said. "Out to the old place on Sullivan Road."

"Thanks." Ridge nodded.

"You need a ride home?" the same officer asked.

"I'll manage." Ridge's patience was thin, and spending a car ride cooped in a cruiser with the human reminder of his son's abduction was more than he could handle right now.

The rookie nodded and went back to his conversation.

The belt around Ridge's chest tightened. Pinpricks of anxiety crawled up his right arm. He flexed his fist to ward them away, working his way from the house to the curb to meet the Uber driver. Each hobbled step ratcheted the vise around his lungs one notch tighter—the unrelenting lock of helplessness.

RIDGE'S PHONE launched into a full-blown explosion around three that afternoon. Shrugging out of the sleep-deprived coma he'd medicated himself into wasn't easy. The cocktail of pain killers and prescription strength sleep aids weren't unleashing their grip without a fight. He groaned and pressed his pillow over his head, comprehension of what could be on the other side of his ringtone too far beyond his reach.

The phone silenced, and Ridge fell back into a dark dreamless sleep until the knocking on his door kicked in. Before he knew it, Brian was in his room, followed by Tony.

Ridge blinked the fuzz from his vision, the two men coming into focus. Worry etched across Brian's brow while Tony wore a scowl of resigned aggression.

"Get up," Brian said for at least the third time that Ridge could remember. He jerked Ridge's arms forward and the dregs of sleep finally released their hold.

"Fine, fine. I'm up." Ridge coerced his legs over the side of the bed.

"Tony went to check on her this morning. The house is empty." Brian's sentences were a string of panicked chunks. He tore an envelope from Tony's hand and shoved it at Ridge. "This was under your door when we got here."

His name in Liv's hand scrawled across the front of the white envelope, a leftover from her own mail Ridge realized from the typewritten address. He pulled the flap loose and tugged out the letter-sized piece of paper. One side was a letter from Jack Reynolds outlining all the necessary steps Liv needed to take to petition for removal of Olivia Sullivan's declaration of death by absentia.

"The back," Brian said, pointing.

Ridge flipped the letter over. His eyes skimmed the first two lines before Tony commanded, "Read it out loud."

Ridge could feel the wobble in his voice as he read. "I wanted to tell you in person, but maybe you're still at Bridget's. These past weeks have been a rollercoaster of highs and lows. And as I sat on that patio last night, I realized how wrong I've been. How selfish it was to put your family in jeopardy. I never should have come back. So, I'm doing what I should have done from the beginning. I got you into this. I put Colton at risk. And I will do whatever it takes to make your family whole again."

Ridge stopped reading, the vise around his midsection squeezing. "Where is she?" he asked.

"We were hoping you could tell us," Tony answered.

Ridge blew through a leveling breath. His eyes skimmed silently ahead as a choke rose in his throat.

If this has to be goodbye, please know that every moment we've spent together has made an indelible mark on my soul. And no matter what happens, promise me that you'll forgive. Forget about Sowards. GenLink. Me. Rebuild your life. Share the love you have to give, and trust that I'm at peace with this decision. You've been my protector since the beginning. Now it's my chance to be yours.

Always,

Liv

68

LIV

I t was noon by the time I turned into the farm driveway off Sullivan Road. My hands still shaking. The lines of the letter I'd slid under Ridge's apartment door ricocheted through memory, slicing and digging. Both what I'd said, and all the things I'd left unsaid, like razor blades in my mind.

"You did the right thing."

I wasn't surprised to see Amanda propped up against the brick near the porch steps. "Where is he?" I managed through the surge of adrenaline that tightened my throat.

"Can you walk?" she asked, ignoring my question. "There's something I want to show you."

My body hummed, buzzing like a thousand ants crawling under my skin. Her presence thickened the electricity in the air and it pulsed between us, sending a flush of heat over my cheeks and through my extremities. I forced one leg forward and then another, fighting the sparking vibrations.

Amanda tipped her head, nutmeg curls falling to the side as she squinted against the glare of midday sun.

I nodded and she motioned toward the lake. A small motorboat was tied to the usually empty cleat along the west side of the dock. I followed as she picked her way across the overgrown yard. Breeze picked up the sleeve of my shirt, flapping against my upper arm, raising gooseflesh in spite of the humidity in the air.

"Where is Colton?" I asked again as we reached the wooden dock.

Amanda smiled—the same kind smile I'd first seen the day we met at George's house. "Just come." She stretched her hand for mine and helped me down into the boat, steadying me as it rocked against the nearby pilings.

"You didn't answer me." I said as she motored out into the open lake, staying as close as she dared to the rocky northern shore.

"He's safe." She pulled her phone from her pocket and held it between us, a live feed displayed on the tiny screen.

I leaned closer. Colton's body curled across a thin mattress. His cherub lips open and eyes closed. Amanda yanked the device away and shoved the phone into her pocket.

"Is he okay?" Colton's sleeping face ramped the surge of adrenaline inside me. She shrugged and the sudden urge to shove Amanda Lombardi into Cascade Lake washed over me. Only the understanding that she was my only link to that little boy stopped me.

"He's fine. For now. We gave him a mild sedative."

"I'm doing what you asked. When are you taking him home?"

"That's not up to me, Olivia."

I sat motionless. Attempting to quell the flip of sickness that took root in my gut as Amanda guided the boat into a cove near the back corner of Sullivan farm.

"Come on," she said, tugging me from the bow. "Do you remember this place?"

I hadn't been in this inlet for almost twelve years. Not since the night my best friend, Andrea Chase, went missing, her body pulled from the lagoon two weeks later.

"It's the deepest part of Cascade Lake," she continued, turning to me with a sinister smile. "But you already knew that, didn't you?" Amanda wrapped the rope around the cleat and tipped her head into the woods. "See that hump of earth, up there?"

I looked where she was pointing. Several yards into the woods a mound of earth jutted up between the trees. An old bomb shelter according to my grandfather.

"That's where we're going." Amanda grabbed my arm. "I need your phone."

I started to refute, but she yanked me sideways, unleashing a stab of pain through my knee.

"Your phone. Now." She bent close, her breath hot against my ear. "Remember why you're doing this, Olivia. I can feel your fear."

I tried to jerk away but her grip tightened, her free hand sliding a knife from a sheath at the small of her back. The *shink* of metal tore through me, activating a memory that sent a shiver up my spine.

"All it takes is one text message to end him, Liv." She twisted my arm behind my back and held the knife to my cheek without ever taking her eyes away from mine.

"You wouldn't do that."

"Is that a chance you're willing to take?"

"In my back pocket," I managed. Her lips curled into a smile and she tugged the phone free. Her grip on my arm relaxed.

"Knives aren't your favorite, are they?" Her brow quirked

up as she examined the blade. Shadows from the whispering trees played on her face.

"Just get this over with, Amanda." I fought the rising clutch of emotion in my throat. "Colton deserves to go home."

Amanda smiled. "Just like my sister got to go home?"

Breath left my lungs in a panicked huff as realization hit. Andrea's sister had been in the military for the extent of our friendship. I could only remember meeting her once, and it had been brief, at a party, no less.

"I didn't hurt Andrea."

Lombardi shoved me forward, up the decrepit dock and toward the shelter. With every step, my body buzzed, vibrating with warning. Images of Andrea diving below the surface of Cascade Lake, never to resurface. Of Colton curled on a dingy mattress.

"You have to believe me."

We were almost to the door before I tore from her grip, twisting to the side with enough force to pull free. But I wasn't fast enough to run, not yet. My knee buckled with every third step as I stumbled my way through about twenty feet of overgrown woods, grabbing and pulling at trees and branches to keep my balance. I tucked behind a tree, pulse thumping in my ears, straining to hear Lombardi as eerie silence closed in.

"Do you want him to die?" a voice seethed. An arm wrapped under my shoulder, jerking me from the damp forest floor and hoisting me upright. I stared into Adam's eyes, tried to speak, but it was too late. He pulled me against him mid-scream.

"You're making this harder than it needs to be," he said.

"Why are you helping him?"

Adam's gloved hand forced a rag against my mouth.

"Just breathe."

I struggled against him, but he was too strong, too well-trained. I coughed, tasting the sweetness before the scent ever registered.

"Stop fighting, Liv. I don't want to hurt you. We want the same things here."

The buzz in my extremities faded and my eyelids drooped. The trees around us blurring into a sea of green fog. My fingers clawed without injury against Adam's arms. I sucked in one last breath, let out one final muffled scream before the world dimmed into black.

69

RIDGE

The knock on the door came before Ridge could make sense of the letter. Tony pulled the front door open, Ridge's heart hammering in his chest.

"Tell me you know something," Ridge said to the two detectives at his door.

They looked at each other and then to the ground. Ridge's first clue that the only reason they were here was to badger him about Colton, and now Liv.

"May we come in, Mr. McCaffrey?"

Ridge nodded and hobbled to the sofa. He wasn't sure if it was the news that both Liv and Colton were now missing, or the cocktail of drugs still swimming in his brain, but the room around him fuzzed. Voices of the detectives as they spoke to Tony and Brian, dipped in and out of his grip on understanding.

"When was the last time you saw Miss Sullivan?"

Ridge was pretty sure that was at least the second time the detective posed that question before he managed to answer.

"Last night." He rubbed his forehead, hoping to clear the fog. "She was at Bridget's."

"But you've had no contact with her since then?"

Ridge shook his head. "I came home, mixed pain killers and sleep aids. Now what you see is what you get."

Brian took a seat next to him, offering a glass of orange juice. Ridge sucked the glass empty in three long swallows, hoping to stave off the remaining fuzz.

"We have no further developments to report in your son's case," the older of the two detectives, graying at the temples, said. He meandered around the room as if he was searching for something. "But we are doing everything we can."

"And Liv? Are you doing everything you can to find her, too?"

The detectives glanced at each other. "We have reason to believe she may have been involved in the abduction of your son."

"You're wrong." Anger cut through the remaining fog. "The same person who has Colton, has Liv. I promise you that. And like I told you last night, that person is Marcus Sowards."

The pair lowered onto the opposite sofa in unison. "Marcus Sowards is dead."

"I don't have time for this."

"Excuse me?" The female detective stood.

Ridge met her narrowed gaze. "I don't have time to explain to you the million reasons why you're wrong."

She put her hands on her hips and stepped forward. "Why don't you start with one."

"Marcus Sowards faked Liv's death, not once, but twice. First with an explosion, and most recently by planting DNA in remains at a crime scene, making it impossible for her to reclaim her identity. He is more than capable of fabricating his own death."

Tony's phone buzzed from his pocket and Ridge glanced his direction, watched as his ex-wife's lover slipped out the door and into the hall. Maybe Liv was right.

"Your father mentioned that Miss Sullivan was once in an inpatient program at a mental health facility. Is that true?"

Ridge suddenly regretted every conversation he'd ever had with his father regarding Liv.

"That was a misunderstanding."

"She wasn't diagnosed with a mental disorder?"

"She was," Ridge admitted. "But she never should have been there. She's psychic, not mentally ill."

Ridge ignored the loaded exchange of glances between the two detectives.

The young detective approached, her voice calm. "I understand your need to protect her, Agent McCaffrey. But if she's done something to jeopardize the life of your son, is it worth it?"

"She hasn't." Ridge forced himself onto two legs.

"What kind of relationship does Olivia have with your son?" the second detective asked. He mirrored Ridge's movements, joining his partner in the center of the room.

"Liv's great with him. Colton loves having her around."

"But she hasn't been around for long, is that right?"

Ridge launched into the explanation that sounded crazy even to his own ears only to be cut off.

"We've been briefed on the history," he said. "Agent Medici was very forthcoming."

"Medici," Ridge repeated.

"Yes. He was with your ex when they discovered Colton was missing. Initiated the all-points bulletin on Miss Sullivan himself."

"You filed an APB on Liv?"

"She's a person of interest."

A crash of pain materialized behind his eyes, and the room shifted and blurred. The cold heat of panic washed over him.

"She's not a suspect. She's a victim," Ridge managed. Liv had been right–from the beginning. Tony was no more trustworthy than Lombardi or Rogers. He closed his eyes and pushed against the pain in his forehead with the heel of his hand.

"Mr. McCaffrey, are you okay?" The graying detective came forward. "If there's something you think we should know, now's the time."

"I think you should know she's the target of a madman. A man who will do anything to get her under his control, including abducting my son."

"So you admit you believe she could have some involvement with your son's disappearance."

Ridge read the accusation in the detective's voice.

"No. That's not–" Ridge leaned over and rummaged in the end table drawer. He tugged the file Tony had brought from underneath the stack of magazines.

"Medici brought me these a few weeks ago. Before the accident." He met the detective's gaze. "I may sound crazy. But you can't make this shit up. I was a Special Agent under Marcus Sowards within the GenLink Program before I left last year. Dig deep enough and you'll find him."

"Yes, we're familiar with your history." Ridge detected contempt in the hard edges of the detective's voice as she leaned over her partner's shoulder, surveying Liv's GenLink file. "Inappropriate conduct with a Bureau asset," she parroted the declaration on Ridge's dismissal paperwork.

"The same Bureau asset who's unaccounted for at the same time as your son, Mr. McCaffrey. You'll excuse us if the timeline seems suspicious."

Ridge exhaled a curse, managing a wobbly stagger toward the apartment door.

"Believe me or don't, that's up to you. But I need you to find my son," he said. Tipping his head in the direction of the door, he pulled the knob inward, dismissing the detectives without another word.

BRIAN STOOD in the bedroom doorway as Ridge tossed the t-shirt he'd worn for the last fifteen hours in the laundry basket and yanked a fresh one from a drawer. He balanced against his dresser and pulled the shirt over his head.

"You know this is crazy, right?"

"Yeah, well, according to my dad, it runs in the family." Ridge tugged a lone shoe from under his bed and slid into it, bending to tie the laces.

"Come on," Brian stepped forward. "We've done what we can. I know it's hard, but we need to wait, let the police do their job."

"And arrest Liv in the process?" Ridge pushed into Brian's space. His insides roiling. "I left her to fight alone twice, Brian. I won't do it again. Besides, finding her means finding Colton."

Ridge pushed past Brian and into the hall, stopping at the linen closet to unearth a gun safe from under a pile of towels. He could feel Brian watching as he placed his fingers along the glass pads of the biometric lock, hesitating until it clicked open.

"Seriously Ridge, this isn't a good idea."

"If the police think Liv is involved in Colton's abduction, they won't be afraid to use force," Ridge said, shrugging into a leather shoulder holster before turning to face his friend.

Brian dropped his head and exhaled a curse, his lips

twisted, readying to ask another question, but Ridge cut him off with the weight of his next words.

"Liv's pregnant. How long do they have to be gone before it's okay for me to do something about it?"

Brian stepped out of the way as Ridge loaded his Sig, tucking it into position under his left arm. He swiped the plastic Vicodin bottle and hobbled, crutchless, through the kitchen, stopping to slide his jacket into place.

"What about your leg?" Brian asked.

"What about it?"

"Who knows what kind of damage you're doing. You've been on it too much, Ridge. I was there when they released you, remember? I'm pretty sure the words, 'Take it easy,' don't encompass a rogue search for a known assassin."

"Assassin, huh?"

Brain shrugged. "What else would you call Sowards?"

Ridge paused, taking in his best friend. "Bri, if this goes bad, just promise me you'll take care of Sky, okay?"

"I'd feel better if you'd just promise me it wouldn't go bad at all. Can you do that?"

Ridge folded Brian into a hug. "I'll do what I can."

70

LIV

The room was pitch black. The earth hard against my cheek. I blinked, trying to focus on something, anything, but there was nothing.

"Hello?" I managed into the darkness, pushing onto my hands and knees.

"Welcome home, Olivia."

Sowards' voice startled me. The gravel of it sunk into my gut, vibrating through every muscle with each open O that rolled over his tongue. I turned, crab-crawling backward until my spine hit concrete block. The wall was damp, cold, as I scuffed my hands along the seams.

"Your grandmother built this place. Did you know that?"

I heard the flick of a lighter, its flame pulsing–small then big–in the inky blackness. The flicker reflected on Sowards' face as he puffed a cigar to life.

"Actually, the tunnels were here long before. Part of the underground railroad, or so the stories go."

I swiveled my head, taking in the tiny room.

"People lived and died in these tunnels, fighting their way

to freedom. Seemed only natural this is where you do the same."

An involuntary squeak of panic escaped my lungs. I dug my fingers harder against the cinderblock.

Don't be afraid." Sowards pocketed the lighter. "This is what you wanted."

I stood. Blinking through the blackness to find my aggressor.

"This was never what I wanted."

The tiny red dot at the end of Sowards' cigar glowed as he puffed. The only indication I had of his location. He remained silent until a soft click bathed us in the glow of a single low wattage bulb. I blinked in the glare. The light swung from the ceiling, shadows dancing around the room as its pendulum swing slowed. Sowards stepped into the light.

He tilted his head, dark eyes shining. "Your grandmother birthed the plans to GenLink in this very room, Olivia. This is where secrets were kept. Lies told. Plans made. Lives destroyed."

"Where's Adam?" They were the only words I could tear free from the threat of tears. "Colton?"

Sowards laughed, white teeth gleaming in the near darkness. He took another measured step toward me. "Don't you see? None of that matters anymore, Olivia."

I forced a wobbly exhale. "What do you want from me?"

My body buzzed as he closed the distance between us. I was acutely aware of the four stone walls that hemmed me in, the only visible door on Sowards' side of the room. He reached for me. His hand gripped the side of my head, fingers unyielding, magnifying my small insignificance.

"Ah, yes. Classic misunderstanding. What is it you think I want?" His thumb drifted lower, tracing the line of my quivering lips. "Hmm?"

"GenLink," I answered.

Sowards grabbed a handful of hair and jerked, spinning me against the wall and holding me there. I yelped. The *shink* of a blade ricocheted against cement block. The cold of the knife pressed against my windpipe.

"I don't know what Amanda told you, but I take what I want, Olivia. No one has ever *given* it to me."

He twisted the knife, the blade biting at the flesh under my jaw.

"What if I want to watch you bleed out, stain the very earth where your grandmother once stood?" Sowards' breath fell hot and fast against my face. "I've dreamt of that moment."

"You need me," I hissed through clenched teeth.

"Do I?"

My neck stung, the blade slicing flesh. A warning before he pulled it away, releasing me.

"Did you ever think you and I would have such similar goals, Olivia?"

Stagnant air chilled the dribble of blood down the left side of my neck. A pool dampened the collar of my shirt before trickling southward, drying hard against my chest.

"Don't ever make the mistake of believing you have the upper hand just because of who you are," Sowards said. "You are nothing to me."

"If that was the case, you wouldn't be here." I taunted.

He stared at me for a moment. His eyes sparked in the glow from the naked bulb. "What's your offer?" he asked.

He pulled a handkerchief from his inside jacket pocket and wiped the blood from the blade of the knife. Streaks of pink and red on a white background.

"Colton goes home. Once that's done, I'll come with you. Do whatever it is you need me to do for GenLink."

"Whatever it is," he mocked, his mouth twisting into a wicked grin. "You have no idea what I want, Olivia."

"Then tell me."

He laughed. His hand wrapped around my throat where the blade had once been, holding me in place. "Revenge. But experience tells me everyone has a line they won't cross. Especially people like you, people who believe they are the righteous ones. The moral fortitude." He cocked his head. "What's your line?"

"Leave Ridge and his family alone. I'll never hurt him."

"That's what I always liked about you. Ridge was sent to protect you, but you've been his savior from the start."

I swallowed. "Tell me about Hunter Enterprises." I stepped to the side, but Sowards followed, the thin fabric of my shirt no protection against the rough block walls.

His brows pinched, even in the low light I could see the flash of confusion. He didn't answer.

"What would you do to protect them? Would you agree to torture?" Sowards asked, clutching tighter. "Murder?"

Again I shifted to the side and he followed, the wall with the door almost within reach.

"Abduction?"

The same dance again. This time he cornered me–my back against one wall and my shoulder against another. I had nowhere to go. I wrapped my hands around his wrists, fighting his hold, but his grip only strengthened. I coughed–breath stuck in my chest.

"Rape?" He whispered the word, breath hot in my ear. His leg slipped forward, spreading my thighs.

I screamed. My unheard voice dissolving into an array of stars as I fought for breath. I steadied on my braced leg, ignoring the pain, and lifted the right, landing a solid blow against my intended target, doubling Sowards over.

"You seem to forget, you've already acclimated me to all four," I huffed through sucks of renewed breath and rushed for the door.

I heard the curse aimed my direction. Felt the wave of wind before the thrust of an object landed hard against my shoulder blades, knocking me to the ground.

"GenLink is not why you're here," Sowards seethed from behind. "You've got it all wrong."

I fought to fill inoperable lungs. My chest seized–aching–as I climbed onto all fours. Bile surged from my stomach and I spit a glob onto the dirt. I reached for the handle of the door–fingers splayed. Sowards' voice rang in my ear before the second blow caught the back of my head in a blinding flash of white.

"Nothing you do can protect him now."

71

RIDGE

R idge jammed himself in the passenger seat of Brian's Charger and headed for the farm. He ignored the knives traveling through every nerve ending in his leg, clustering in a knot of agony at the base of his spine. By the time Brian pulled into the driveway at Sullivan farm, the lot near the house was crammed with cruisers. Ridge pulled the crutches from the back seat and used them to hoist himself out of the car. Two hops on his good leg was enough to hike the sticks under his arms and propel himself forward. He congratulated himself for only stumbling once in the gravel on his way to the front porch.

He left Brian outside and crutched his way into the house, watching from the foyer as a group of techs sifted through a stack of mail on the dining room table.

"Good to see you." Ridge's former boss, Captain Frank Wallace, approached from behind and clapped him on the shoulder. "Wish it wasn't under these circumstances. Didn't expect to see you up and around so soon. You look good."

Wallace's hand on his shoulder unleashed the first wave of

true fear Ridge had allowed since hearing about Colton's disappearance the day before. The harsh reality that both of them could be gone forever reared into existence.

"They find anything?" Ridge asked in lieu of responding with the looming anger that taunted him, threatening to break free.

"No sign of a struggle. But we've got shoe prints leading to the dock. Two sets." Ridge followed Wallace in his gimpy half-walk through the grass to the edge of Cascade Lake. Even without the circling techs and Wallace's narration, it was obvious someone had been there. Crushed grass, footsteps apart, and muddy prints on the dock were visible without the tools of the BCI team.

The tech saw Wallace and spoke. "Found some hair, natural red by the looks of it." He held up a cylinder with a few strands of auburn curl.

Wallace nodded at the tech and addressed Ridge, his tone flat, detached. "We're dragging the lake."

Ridge's stomach plunged.

"We don't expect to find anything. There's no evidence to suggest Colton was here. I've reported as much to the special victims team." Wallace sighed. "But they were happy to share their theory."

Ridge nodded. "They think Liv took off with him."

Wallace apologized. But it wasn't his fault. And as hard as Ridge tried, he couldn't blame the detectives on Colton's case either. It was damn suspicious. He only hoped he could find Colton, get to Liv, before it was too late.

Ridge narrowed on the boards hovering a few inches above the water. He pointed. "Did you get a sample of the paint? I don't remember that being there." Truth was, he wasn't sure he'd ever paid that close attention to the streaks of barely visible hues dashed along the edge of the dock, but if there was even a minuscule chance that a paint chip could lead them to Liv and Colton, it was worth a shot.

The tech nodded and got to work on the roughhewn pine.

"He's using Colton as bait," Ridge said to Wallace. "Sowards knows Liv wouldn't do anything to jeopardize Colton. I need to know where he could take her."

"We're working on it, Ridge. I've got State, County, and even the Feds in on this one. We'll find them."

"We should talk," Tony said as soon as Ridge got to Bridget's a few hours later.

"I should see how Bridget is doing." Ridge had no desire to have a friendly chat with the man who only days ago made Liv believe she was losing her mind. Maybe if Tony had listened, paid more attention to her claims, she wouldn't be gone. Ridge was overreaching, but it felt good to blame someone other than himself for a change.

"Her sister just got in from Denver. She's with her, so we have time."

Ridge swallowed his irritation and followed Tony down the hall and onto the back patio, sliding the door closed behind them.

Ridge lowered into a plastic chair with a groan, rubbing the shooting pain stabbing through his thigh.

"You doing okay?" Tony asked, tipping his chin toward Ridge's boot.

"Fine," Ridge managed. Brian was right. He was doing damage he might not be able to undo once all of this was over, but what choice did he have?

"Liv was right about Sowards," Tony started. "I found

footage from the street cam outside the school the day Liv met him. I've got him on video waving to Colton."

Relief trickled through Ridge's core like someone had turned on a faucet. "You showed this to the detectives?"

Tony nodded. "That's not all. Liv asked me to do some digging." Tony hesitated, his gaze firm on Ridge. "Into your mom."

"Don't tell me you're on the Liv-must-be-crazy bandwagon now, too."

"Actually, the opposite."

Ridge hadn't noticed the file in Tony's hand.

"Just, be prepared."

The cover was the same blue-gray that Liv's un-redacted folder was, except, rather than a name, it was labeled with only a number. The steady stream of relief in Ridge's gut ceased mid-flow as he worked his way through the genetic reports. He felt his shoulders slump, the slack in his own jaw as he gave voice to the words. "My mom was part of GenLink."

Tony nodded. "Pretty early on, before they had a training program in place." He nodded toward the file splayed in Ridge's lap. "Keep going. Her psych files are in there. Someone must have added them after she was hospitalized."

"You mean after my dad had her committed?" Sarcasm dripped from Ridge's voice. He couldn't process this right now. As far as he was concerned, his dad gave up on his mom. He tossed the file back to Tony. "Give me the short version. What does this mean for Liv?"

"I'm actually more concerned by what it may mean for Colton. Genetically, he could be a carrier. Maybe Sowards isn't using him to get to Liv. Maybe he's using him because of who *he* is."

"Jesus Christ." Ridge ran a hand through his hair. "So that's it then. He's got both of them, and there's no reason for him to give either one of them up."

"I don't know, Ridge. This is all speculation." Tony scooted an Adirondack chair close. "Maybe Liv can convince him she's worth more."

"What are you saying?"

"Liv's genetic makeup is still more potent. Colton's would produce psychic tendencies in one of every four offspring."

"This is my four-year-old son we're talking about here."

"Age isn't important to Sowards. This isn't sex, Ridge. It's science. He needs an X chromosome to replicate Liv's perfect genes. As long as he has Colton he can create that, at least twenty-five percent of the time."

The puzzle pieces started clicking together in Ridge's skull—the picture of a future he couldn't yet face. "But if Sowards knows Liv's pregnant, his gamble turns into a sure thing."

"As long as he knows the baby's yours," Tony mumbled, head bowed. "I'm sorry."

Ridge eyed the man in front of him, his trust meter wavered like a tennis ball on a court, pinging between would-trust-him-with-my-life and wouldn't-let-him-watch-my-dog. He pressed the heel of his hand against the middle of his thigh, pushing pain away. The little black and white cat Colton had adopted from the farm, wove between the medical boot and Ridge's shoe. Ridge reached down to scratch between the cat's ears as Dewey mewed.

"She'll tell him," Ridge said, choked by the strangle of emotion. Dewey launched into a full-blown purr. "If she knows that's what he's after, she'll do it to save Colton."

He felt a release—a trickle of warmth worming its way from the logic center of his brain.

"Don't worry buddy, Colton's coming home," Ridge whispered to the cat.

Desperation gripped Ridge's chest, like claws gutting his insides, leaving him empty and raw.

"Make sure the cat gets back inside," Ridge told Tony, pushing himself from the chair.

"Where are you going?"

"If I'm going to lose her, she's at least going to know I didn't let her go without a fight."

WHEN RIDGE RETURNED to the farm the police presence had multiplied. The sun was on its final descent behind the tree line, silhouetting at least two recovery boats on the lake. Ridge forced away the thought of what they might find.

He hobbled out of his Shelby, ignoring the knife-like reminder from his leg that he had no business behind the wheel of a car, especially one with a manual transmission. A police helicopter whirred overhead, sweeping the woods with a bright white spotlight.

"Wallace around?" Ridge asked one of the officers standing in the reeds at the edge of the beach.

The *thwack* of the screen door at the rear of the house echoed in the night and Ridge turned. Captain Wallace trotted down the steps, intercepting Ridge.

"You shouldn't be here," he said, leading Ridge away from the beach and back toward his car.

Ridge shouldered out of his grip. "Where the hell am I supposed to be?"

Wallace's blue eyes held on Ridge, ferocity morphing to understanding.

"How well do you know these woods?" Wallace asked.

"Better than any other cop you got out here right now."

The muscle in Wallace's jaw ticked. "We found a structure on the far north end. Know anything about it?"

"It's an old bomb shelter," Ridge answered. "Sealed up for years."

"You've never been inside?"

Ridge shook his head. "Why are you asking me this? What'd you find?" A surge of panic pulsed through him, jacking his heart rate into a rapid thump against his sternum.

Before Wallace could answer, the quiet soundtrack of chopper beats and officer conversation was broken by the rapid fire echo of gunshots. The radio in Wallace's hand buzzed to life. "Shots fired. I repeat, shots fired. Northwest Sullivan woods."

Before Wallace could respond the pilot broke in. "I've got visuals on the scene. Victim down, approximately twenty meters north-northwest of structure. Suspect headed north on foot. Will pursue."

Wallace put his hand on Ridge's chest and spoke into the mic. "10-4. All units respond with caution." He dropped the radio to his side and turned his attention to Ridge. "You're in no shape to be crawling through the woods. Stay here."

"Like hell I am," Ridge said, limping toward Wallace's cruiser. "There's an abandoned access road at the north end of the property. Let's go."

72

LIV

I thought I heard crying. Soft sniffles interspersed with unintelligible words. I blinked to make sense of my surroundings. The single bulb remained lit, casting eerie shadows on the walls. Something warm and thick pooled at the back of my head. I reached to touch it, coming away with fingertips of blood.

I curled to the side with a groan I didn't intend, and the crying ceased. My bones ached. The earth beneath me cold, hard, and unyielding. Footfalls in the hall thumped through my brain–too loud. I closed my eyes and the sound stopped.

"Show time." Sowards' voice broke into my consciousness. But I couldn't respond. "Look at me." He shoved my shoulder with his foot. His voice louder this time–demanding.

I squinted upward. Sowards' form blocked the incandescent glow. My eyes not yet able to adjust, his body split into mirror images before meeting again and solidifying into one. I looked away, blinked, trying to make sense of the visual disruption–a concussion, no doubt.

"Learn anything from last night's adventure?" he asked.

An involuntary moan slipped through my lips as I gained enough understanding to realize Sowards was lifting me. I squinted, trying to make sense of the space as he walked. But nothing made sense. Walls of cinderblock turned black and inky. The air grew cold and damp. The back of my head ached. And the soft crying grew closer.

"Colton," I managed, my mouth dry and sticky.

I forced my eyes to focus. The Sowards-shaped shadow laughed, lowering me onto the ground. The space here was black. No naked bulb to light it. I forced my muscles into motion, pushing at Sowards' hands as he fastened a cuff around one ankle with a *clink*. I scrambled away, my leg pursued in the darkness by a snake of metal.

"Where are we?"

Sowards pushed a blood soaked piece of hair away from my face and I jerked from his touch. A slicing pain stabbed through the back of my skull.

"You're getting what you want, Olivia," Sowards answered. "Freedom. You can thank me on the other side." The echo of his voice drifted into oblivion, leaving me in a shroud of darkness.

I pushed my hands against the damp ground–a combination of stone and earth. Wetness soaked through my jeans and into my skin, and I screamed. Over and over again for long minutes. My voice turned hoarse, the pulse at the base of my skull thumping with panic and exertion.

I listened to faraway sounds. Angry voices–one female, one male–diminished and died. I walked my fingers down the length of chain attached to my ankle. I guessed three feet before it reached a metal plate screwed to a hunk of stone at the base of the room. The only sound, the gentle lap of water against the shores of Cascade Lake.

The walls were stone for as far up as I could reach. While

the first room had been built, this one was natural. The boulders uneven and broken in some places, forming small piles of fragmented shale along the uneven ground. I imagined a cavern enclosing me, some rocks slick with a glaze of damp history, while others were rough, calcified by time.

I closed my eyes, sinking to the floor. All the time I'd spent at this farm. Days of solitude, running from my parents' expectations and the dreams that haunted my sleep. This farm had been the only place I'd found solace. And all the time, this prison had been here, lurking, waiting. I only wondered who had come before me.

Minutes passed before three muffled pops reached me. I strained to hear, pulling myself up to standing. The rise and fall of a faraway siren. More quiet thumps. Muted voices. My own renewed scream echoed against the rock in the cave, numbing my own ears. By the time I stopped, there was nothing but silence–and waves.

73

RIDGE

Wallace's cruiser was the third on the scene at the northern edge of Sullivan farm. The radio had been a constant buzz in the car in the sixty seconds it had taken them to make the trip to the access road.

"Stay here," Wallace demanded, sliding from the driver's seat and out into the night. The helicopter hovered overhead, illuminating the scene.

Ridge stayed where he was, listening to radio transmissions and working to calm the belt of panic that had a firm grip on his lungs. Besides, Wallace was right. He couldn't run. He could barely stumble on solid ground, let alone the overgrown back forty of Liv's farm. He'd be a liability.

He rocked his head against the headrest and sucked in a breath, fighting the pinpricks of anxiety in his arm.

"I've got eyes on the vic. GSW to chest. Unresponsive, but I've got a pulse. Need a bus." The voice fuzzed through the radio in the cruiser.

The speaker went silent for several long seconds before

another officer radioed the words Ridge had been waiting to hear. "Suspect in custody. Marcus Sowards."

Ridge watched from the cruiser as the detectives who had only hours ago blamed Liv for Colton's abduction, walked his former boss from the woods.

Sowards' eyes latched on his, lips twisting into the hint of a smile as they led him past Wallace's cruiser and into an unmarked sedan.

When Wallace returned, there were beads of sweat across his nearly bald head. "You need to come with me."

Ridge hobbled after Wallace, climbing through overgrown brush pounded down by emergency response. He was out of breath, the pain in his leg morphing into homicidal stabs, by the time they made it to a clearing. The crime scene unit was taping an area off, collecting evidence to the left of a patch of blood.

"It was Miller," Wallace started. "Looks like Sowards shot Adam Miller."

Ridge didn't bother to hide his shock. He didn't have any emotional energy left to hide anything. "Do we know why?"

Wallace pounded, open-palmed, on the rear door of the nearby medic van. The one Ridge assumed housed Adam. The door swung open and Ridge glanced inside.

"We think Miller was trying to protect him."

Ridge grabbed the door to steady himself. Both legs on the brink of failure.

"Daddy?" Colton said from inside. His tiny chin wobbled.

"I'm here, buddy," Ridge said as the rest of the world fell away.

He hoisted himself into the unit and wrapped his arms around his son. He sat, Colton curled against his chest, whispering, "It's okay, buddy. I've got you."

With his son nestled against him, for a brief moment all

was right with the world. Ridge breathed him in, swaying with him in his arms, until his son's sobs evened out. His breathing slow and steady–sleep.

Only then did he turn to the waiting paramedics. "Is he okay?"

A young brunette smiled at him. "Cold, scared, a little dehydrated, and a bit of shock. But he's a trooper." She ruffled the curls on top of Colton's head.

"Could someone call Bridget?" Ridge asked to the small cluster of people standing around the back of the van.

"Already done," Wallace said.

RIDGE STOOD with Bridget in the doorway of Colton's room, watching him sleep.

"I'm glad you were there," Bridget said. "Do you really think Adam rescued him?"

Ridge had been over the possibility in his mind a thousand times. "That's what Colton says. I believe him." Ridge rubbed Bridget's shoulder. "We'll know more when Adam wakes up."

"If he wakes up," Bridget reminded him.

Ridge sucked in a breath and Bridget apologized.

"Any word on–" Bridget stopped. She'd yet to say Liv's name since meeting Ridge at the hospital three hours ago.

"You can say her name."

Bridget turned to face him, ran a hand down his face. Pity tumbled behind stormy eyes.

"I should go," Ridge managed. "Tony's outside if you need anything."

"Ridge, it's five a.m. you haven't slept."

"Sleep's not really an option right now. They're searching the farm. I'll be with Wallace."

Bridget nodded and tossed a, "Be careful," in Ridge's direction as he gimped up the hall, holding back tears until he slid behind the wheel of his Shelby.

"Thank you," he managed upward, grateful to a god he'd only recently given much thought. Kids had a way of doing that to you–grasping at any and every possibility when the threat of losing them hovered near. He bowed his head against the steering wheel offering up one more desperate prayer.

"Please help me bring her home."

74

LIV

I don't know what time it was when the water started leaking in. It woke me. Slow at first, it gained momentum, moving from a trickle into a steady stream. Flowing from somewhere high, it splashed onto the floor, soaking me with spray.

I shivered against the cold lake water and screamed again. My throat was raw, my voice no longer sounded like my own. I paused to listen. There'd been sounds not long ago. Hushed voices I couldn't understand. But they either couldn't hear me or were ignoring me, either way, my vocalizations had done nothing but cause me pain.

I jerked and pulled at the cuff around my ankle, wrenching it this way and that, ready to crush bones if it meant breaking free. But there was nothing close enough or heavy enough to bash bone.

Water pooled around me, soaking through the leather cuff around my ankle, darkening it to a rich mahogany, the color of Ridge's hair. I tipped the back of my head against the wall and unleashed another desperate scream. This time, his name.

Tears fell, dripping into the swiftly rising current, cold and biting against my skin. My body quaked, teeth chattered. Gooseflesh rose on exposed skin. By the time the water reached my knees, I knew. This was the way I would die.

75

RIDGE

Ridge met Captain Wallace at the county jail at the request of the special victims team that had hauled Sowards away. He'd rather be at the farm with the crime scene techs, but he knew as well as Wallace did, he had no business either place, so he'd take what he could get.

"He'll only talk to you," the lead detective said.

"I'm a civilian. Couldn't that jeopardize the case?" Ridge refused to do anything that would play into Sowards' future acquittal.

"You're former LEO, and I'll be in there with you. We'll make sure everything's done right."

Ridge followed the detective to an interrogation room and waited while the guards brought Sowards in, pushed him into the seat across from Ridge.

Sowards was the first to speak. "I can tell by the look on your face you haven't found her yet."

Ridge was unprepared for the surge of hate that blasted through his core. "Tell us where she is," he seethed.

"I'm only doing what her grandmother would have

wanted." Sowards clasped and unclasped his hands, the cuffs jingling.

"Grace never wanted Liv to be part of GenLink. She told me that herself–information I then reported to *you*. In case you forgot."

"But Grace," Sowards started, leaning forward, eyes latching on Ridge. "Grace never knew about *you*. She thought you could take Liv away from this life. Protect her. She didn't know you were Violet McCaffrey's son, that GenLink material flowed through your veins."

"That's bullshit, and you know it."

"Is it? Tell me you don't feel it. It's more than attraction and you know it. My guess is you've felt it from the first time you met. It's why you begged me to take you off the case." His eyes held on Ridge, a challenge. "From where I sit, I'm doing Grace a favor. I'm setting Olivia free. Ending the program just as it should have ended at O'Malley's cabin."

Ridge sat back against his seat, fighting for clarity against the hatred crawling through him. He glanced at the detective, who sat in the corner with a notebook, pen poised, waiting.

"You need Liv," Ridge said.

"That's where you're wrong. You think I planted that mandible, but I didn't. I didn't know Liv was alive until my lawyers told me."

"What about Adam Miller?"

"Miller took Colton from the bunker. I shot him. That's true enough. Might have gotten him back if it hadn't been for your eyes in the sky. But Miller always thought I was the bad guy. Thought I wrote those letters. Forced him to live with the guilt of dumping Liv for the last seven months. But you both need to check your facts, McCaffrey. Only one person had the means to harvest the DNA and plant that evidence. One person was alone with Liv long enough to do it."

"Lombardi," Ridge said.

Gray eyes locked on his, the twist of a smile playing on Sowards' lips. "I might be a killer. But at least I do it for the right reasons."

"That's enough," the detective broke in. "Whose murder are you admitting to?"

Sowards tipped his head in the detective's direction. "You really should bring your detective up to speed."

Ridge leaned over the table. "Tell me where Liv is, Marcus."

"And let you rescue her? Carry this pregnancy to term? Propagate a whole new generation of GenLink? Because whether you realize it or not, that's exactly what you're doing. No way. GenLink dies. Past, present, and future." Sowards glanced at the clock. "And it dies today."

"Where?" Ridge demanded.

Sowards hesitated. Breathed a long sigh. "I hid her from Lombardi. They're flooding the dam this morning. You're too late."

"It's Lombardi," Ridge said over the phone to Tony as he floored it from the county jail to the farm. "Lombardi is the one who wants to reboot GenLink. Find her."

The more Ridge thought about it, the more it made sense. Why else would Sowards invite him to the scene, let him take Liv's ring home with him, grant him a hefty severance package. There was only one reason—guilt. Sowards was a monster. There was no doubt about it. But he was a monster with a conscience.

Ridge made it to the farm in record time, followed the whole way by Wallace.

"I've got Tony looking for Lombardi. He might need backup," Ridge said as they worked their way down to the entrance of the old bomb shelter.

"We searched the whole thing, Ridge. She's not down there."

"Get the team down here and search again. I want divers in the lagoon. The water's already up five feet."

Ridge shoved through the door and pulled out his flashlight, sweeping it back and forth around the circular entrance room.

"It works downward from here, through that doorway," Wallace said.

He hung back as Ridge shouldered into the next vacant room. His beam flashed on the cinderblock walls before coming to rest on a yellow evidence marker to the left of the door.

His heart seized. "Blood? When were you going to tell me about this?" He was astonished by the level of calm in his own voice.

"We sent a sample to the lab. We don't know that it's hers."

Ridge turned on his once-superior, gripping his collar. "Who the fuck else would it be?"

Wallace held Ridge's gaze until his fist relaxed, dropped from Wallace's collar. His eyes went back to the puddle. It was a lot of blood. Too much. Wherever Liv was, she'd be weak, hurt, possibly unconscious. He pushed past Wallace and soldiered on down the hall.

The lower they went, the more the sound of water echoed in the space. At the end of the tunnel, both men stopped.

"That's it. That's all there is. The team searched every room. They found nothing."

Ridge stopped, planted a hand on the wall next to him and leaned back–momentary relief for his overused ankle. "I need a minute," he said to Wallace.

Ridge watched Wallace comb his way back up the hallway. His mind spun. He had to be missing something. He pushed away from the wall. Cool hit his back. His shirt soaked where he'd been leaning against the rocks. He skimmed his light over the tightly packed rock.

"What's behind this?" he hollered to Wallace.

"Earth," Wallace replied.

"No way. It's too wet." Ridge dug his fingers against the rock, working to shift the boulders.

Wallace's radio buzzed to life. "Diver's in."

"Tell him what section we're in," Ridge's heart kicked an uneven rhythm as Wallace relayed the coordinates to the dive team.

Ridge put both hands against the wall and closed his eyes, forcing his surroundings away. He focused on his hands and waited. He was just about to give up, his inner skeptic calling him every derogatory name in the book, when a gentle buzz, like the snap of an electric fence, hummed through the index finger of his left hand.

"She's here." The words were a whisper. "She's here," he repeated, louder.

"Ridge." Doubt permeated Wallace's response.

"Behind this wall. I swear to you. I don't know if she's alive. But she's here."

76

LIV

I swam against the weight of the shackle to keep my head above water. My arms and legs ached and the split on the back of my skull throbbed, pushing me to the brink of unconsciousness more than once. The slosh of water had long drowned out any other sounds with the exception of my own panicked sucks of breath when my head bobbed above water.

I clawed at the wall with my fingers and toes, trying to give my muscles a break. But the force of water filling the cavern created a vacuum of current, breaking me free and pulling me under. I drifted underwater until my lungs burned and my head pounded–pulse thumping. That's when I felt it. An imperceptible vibration that started in my fingers and worked its way up my arm. The familiarity of it forced me upward, gasping at the ever decreasing space near the ceiling of the cavern. Ridge was here.

I called his name. But my lungs were weak, my voice a hoarse echo of what it had once been. The vibration continued for a moment longer, drifting away as if the water swept it down the drain.

"No," I said to the silence. Emptying my lungs and replacing the air, I jerked again at the tether. I gripped the wall, pulling with all my might as the water slopped over my head. My length of chain no longer sufficient to gain a gasping breath.

The hole where the water flowed in was visible now, the tiniest glow of sunlight somehow worming its way inside. But it was too far away. I reached for it, pulling against the chain until I felt the snap. I glanced down, half-expecting to see my foot jackknifed to the side, but instead, the leather cuff, a metal shackle broken, floated downward into the darkness.

I kicked up, sucking in air until my lungs were no longer on fire. But the water continued to pour in. I shoved at the rocks in the hole, working to dislodge them. Pulling oxygen from ever decreasing air pockets near the ceiling every chance I got.

A rock shifted. Drifted away. I shoved an arm through, but the hole was too small. I shouldered against another rock and it tipped forward. I returned to the ceiling for air, but the pocket was gone, replaced by water. My heart hammered in my chest, my hands groping the ceiling for air.

The irrefutable urge to draw breath, the siren song of all drowning victims, preyed. Sunspots of black peppered the edges of my vision as my malnourished lungs gave into an involuntary suck.

My body turned weightless, muscles useless as I gulped, reaching one last time for the too small hole. The thump in my ears and chest slowed. Tangles of hair floated around my face, obscuring my vision as the blue-gray water turned black.

77

RIDGE

Ridge arrived at the edge of the lagoon as the diver broke radio silence.

"I've got visuals. She's in a cave. Behind a wall. I can't get to her." The last sentence of the transmission pulsed in Ridge's ears.

"No, no, no, no, no." He heard the word on a loop, not completely certain whether it was reaching the air or not, as he hobbled onto the ancient dock.

Jumping in was more instinct than plan, but what he hadn't counted on was the dead weight pull of the boot around his leg. He unbuckled the plastic cast and pushed it off, watching it disappear into the depths below. He scissor-kicked upward, adrenaline dulling the sting of pain.

Ridge joined the suited diver at the rock ledge of the lagoon. They dug with both hands, scooping rocks from the opening. His lungs burned by the time he caught a glimpse of auburn hair in the dark water beyond the wall.

Lightheadedness seeped in and the diver motioned him upward. The fire in his lungs nearing explosion by the time he reached the surface. He gulped a lungful of air and dove back under, resuming his claw at the cave entrance. A pale hand reached toward him from the space they'd created, fingers splayed as if she knew he was there. Ridge reached for her, lacing his fingers through hers. A surge of hope ignited in his core and he dug faster. He'd die before he let her go.

Rocks fell, a silent tumble, to the bottom of the lagoon. Ridge's lungs burned. The diver pulled at his shoulder urging him to the surface. But Ridge refused, kicking the final rock free as the last bubble of oxygen escaped from starved and aching lungs.

They broke the surface of the water together. With strength Ridge didn't know he possessed, he hoisted himself onto the dock and dragged Liv's body from the water. Training kicked in, overtaking panic. The rhythmic compression of his palms against her chest followed by the push of air into saturated lungs. Seconds extended into minutes.

Footfalls against the wooden dock registered as medics arrived and pushed Ridge out of the way.

"What's her name?" one of them asked. The words still far away to Ridge's ears.

Wallace answered their question, pulling Ridge from the scene. "Let them work," he said, voice quiet.

Ridge sat, helpless, at Wallace's feet.

"How long was she under?" came the next question.

"Unknown," the diver answered. Ridge glanced at him. He'd forgotten all about the diver.

"She's hypoxic," the medic said.

The second medic stabbed a needle into Liv's shoulder while the other continued CPR. Time moved like molasses, stretching and pulling. Tremors worked their way through Liv's extremities. The EMTs looked at each other. Ridge knew that look, the expression of someone about to give up.

"Please." Ridge grabbed the shoulder of medic number one. "Keep trying. She's pregnant."

Contact with the air weighted his words, and Ridge choked on the threat of emotion that gripped his chest. He felt Wallace's hand on his shoulder.

"Come on, let's go. This isn't over yet." The second medic said, launching into another round of compressions.

They let him hold her hand once the convulsions stopped. And Ridge knew it was because they'd given up. He traced her fingers. Liv's skin cold, blue against the healthy tan of his own.

Ridge's chest ached. Maybe from his extended time underwater, but more likely from what he was watching Liv go through. He listened as the medics counted, stopped to assess, and counted some more—a prelude to certain death.

Liv jerked. The rhythm interrupted. The blessed suck of water-logged lungs followed by uncontrolled coughing. Her hand slipped from his as they rolled her to her side. Pain spiked through Ridge's heel and into his thigh as he shifted position.

"Okay to transport." The medic radioed, breathless, wiping the sheen of sweat from his brow with a forearm. He moved away from Liv, setting his gaze on Ridge. "She's asking for you."

Ridge hadn't heard a thing, but he crawled to her side. Bloodshot green eyes blinked, slow and deliberate, focusing on him.

"Colton?" Her voice was no more than a whisper.

"We found him. He's fine. He's with Bridget."

Liv closed her eyes and sucked in an uneven breath, curling onto her side for another wave of wet coughs that ended in a spew of lake water.

She groaned and he could hear the dregs of raw destruction from her throat. A fist wrapped around his heart and squeezed. How long had she been there? Fighting. Screaming. Unheard and unseen.

He leaned down and breathed her in, pressing his lips lightly against her forehead as the medics arrived with the backboard. "We're going home, baby. Hang in there."

Ridge was curled against Liv when the first shot split the silence. The hot spray of blood spatter speckled the back of his neck, sending flecks of red onto the dock around him. By the time he turned, the EMTs were already assisting Wallace, the captain's body sprawled a few feet away next to a growing puddle of blood.

The diver radioed a frantic call for backup while Ridge scanned the surroundings for the shooter. The woods were silent, the water calm. Long seconds stretched before the boat came into view. The second shot rang out and he flattened himself against Liv.

"It's okay," he whispered. But it wasn't.

Her breath came in uneven puffs against his skin. She needed transport, not to be locked in a firefight in the middle of an abandoned dock in an undiscoverable lagoon.

"Step away," came the command. The boat sidled up to the dock with a *thunk*. Lombardi stepped onto the aged pine, gun pointed at Ridge. "This wasn't supposed to get messy."

Lombardi wasn't alone. A man Ridge recognized, Evan Thurber, climbed off behind her. He corralled the medics and diver into the boat, his Colt M4 a ready threat.

"This could have been easy," Lombardi said. "She almost came willingly. But you couldn't let her go, could you?"

Ridge hovered over Liv, taking his right hand off the dock in a slow reach for his Sig.

"Hands where I can see them, Agent. Or you'll both die right here."

Ridge swallowed against the threat. Liv's eyes had closed. A thin trickle of blood pooled on the boards under her head. An ache of desperation clawed through him. The diver had made the call before Evan took control of the radio. Backup was on their way. He just needed to play Lombardi's game for a minute, two tops.

"She's hurt, Lombardi. If she doesn't get to the hospital she won't be any good to either of us."

"Do you know how long it took them to find my sister's body after Liv killed her?"

Pain tore through Ridge's ankle as he shifted to make eye contact with Amanda Lombardi. "Andrea Chase was your sister?"

The corners of Lombardi's lips tipped into a smile. "Liv took her from me and it's taken me the last twelve years to figure out how to get her back. How to destroy her world–her family–just as she destroyed mine."

"Liv's not the monster you think she is," Ridge said, maintaining focus on Lombardi, buying time. "If you want to find out what happened to your sister, do it the right way. I'll help you. But don't take innocent lives down with you." Ridge gestured to Wallace, gurgling on the dock less than ten feet away.

"I know what you're trying to do, McCaffrey. It's honorable, really. But it's too late. I've made my decision. And I know what I need to make it happen." She closed the distance between them, stomped on Ridge's injured ankle and shoved, toppling him off the dock.

Ridge caught himself on the edge, fighting off the flashes of stars dancing in his vision. His bad leg dangled, slices of pain so intense it bordered on numb. He hoisted himself back onto the boards, scrambling toward Liv and cursing the scream of pain that slowed him.

He reached for his gun, but it was gone, lost in the depths of the lagoon, most likely. Lombardi barked a laugh, unsheathing a high-gauge needle. She rolled Liv onto her back, piercing the soft skin on her belly.

Ridge lunged for Wallace's sidearm, thumbing it free from the captain's holster as the third shot of the morning ricocheted through the trees.

He jerked back, expecting his worst nightmare. Instead, the close range bullet exploded through the back of Lombardi's skull, crumpling her body on top of Liv.

He heard the motor, voices from the other side of the tree line as Liv twisted free, toppling Lombardi's body into the water. Ridge's own Sig P227 remained locked in the trembling grip of Liv's right hand.

Ridge crawled to her. Numbness giving way to renewed shards of pain. Evan's heavy steps echoed from behind. Ridge swiveled, the priming click of the M4 registering as he pulled the trigger on Wallace's Glock. Evan stumbled, finger catching on the trigger as he hit the ground.

Ridge waited for the sting of automatic rifle fire. But the rounds went over his head, unaimed into the atmosphere. He reached for Liv. She sank back onto the dock, breath hiccuping in a full-body sob. Scared eyes met his, warming skin pressed against his lips as he kissed her forehead.

"Everything's okay," Ridge whispered. He gripped the needle, sliding it–slow and steady–from her abdomen. It was embedded farther than he expected. He took his eyes from hers long enough to notice the bubble of blood seeping from the puncture wound.

He slid his gun from Liv's grip, pushed it and Wallace's Glock over the scuffed boards. He raised his hands, complying with the command from the police boat as it rounded the jetty and motored toward them, sights set on Ridge.

LIV

T he medics, shaken from the run-in with Evan, flanked me in silence as the team of SWAT officers stepped off the boat, shouting demands at Ridge.

"No," I screamed voicelessly, fighting to pull myself into a sitting position with muscles jellified by exhaustion and shock.

Ridge kneeled on the dock, empty hands crossed above his head. He answered too loud questions with calm responses as one of the officers pulled Ridge's hands down. The *click* of metal cuffs registered, kicking a pulse of desperation loose in my chest. I willed him to look at me, but he kept his eyes low.

"Tell them he didn't do it," I said to the medics, my voice raw, barely audible over the commotion of boots and police chatter descending from both directions–water and land.

"Don't try to talk," the medic closest to my head said. His hands shook as he wiped blood spatter from my face.

Ridge winced as the officer jerked him to his feet, his eyes glanced off mine and onto the medic next to me. They exchanged a barely perceptible nod before Ridge stumbled. He hopped on his good leg to catch his balance before two officers helped him off the dock and into a boat. I watched until the blur of tears made sight impossible.

"Where are they taking him?" The words were barely past my lips before pain rocked through my belly. It fisted and twisted inside, curling me into the fetal position punctuated by a silent guttural yell.

Tony was the first to arrive in my hospital room. His gold eyes reflected uneasy sadness as he pulled up a chair next to the bed.

"How are you?" he asked.

I sucked in a lungful of air, trying hard not to cry. I didn't have an answer to that question. "Did they arrest him?"

Tony bowed his head, reaching a hand for mine. "They've got one dead WITSEC agent, a PI from the US Attorney's Office, and a precinct captain in critical condition. Ridge pulled the trigger. The D.A. had no choice."

"I killed Lombardi," I whispered, ignoring the slices of pain in my throat that accompanied every word. "Ridge was trying to protect us."

Tony nodded. "They'll sort it out, Liv. He's lawyered up. It's just going to take some time."

I blinked long and hard, a tear leaking from the corner of my eye. I was too tired to wipe it away. "Did they find Sowards?"

"He's been in custody since early this morning. Claims Lombardi was the one set on building a new generation of GenLink. And you were right. According to Sowards' confession, he knew Violet McCaffrey. They had an affair. Ridge would've been young—four or five, maybe. Blames her involvement with GenLink for her diagnosis."

"Does Ridge know?" It was all I cared about. I imagined

him learning the truth about his mother. Her involvement in the same program that had already stolen so much. I should have been there.

Tony nodded, but he didn't speak right away. His lips twisted and relaxed as if he was chewing over a decision and not a stick of gum.

"She's dead. Institutionalized outside of Charlottesville until her death last year, complications of a drug interaction. Likely what caused Sowards to go off the deep end–rope you in, try to end things."

A slice of understanding slipped through my core, tightening around my lungs. "He told me we were after the same thing. I didn't know what he meant."

"Sowards promised Vi he'd do what it took to destroy the program. That's why he sought out Ridge in the first place. Why he used O'Malley's drug to end the assets. Rigged the explosion at the cabin. It was his effort to make good on his promise to Vi. His lawyer is already prepping for a psych defense."

My breath wobbled. "Does that mean it's over? GenLink is done? Colton's safe?"

One side of Tony's mouth quirked up in a forced smile. "We've still got some pieces to put together–Adam in particular. But yes. You can breathe, Liv. You're free." He patted my hand. The simple act unleashed a wave of emotion I could no longer combat.

"I think I lost the baby." The words gurgled through the breath of half-shed tears.

Tony leaned into me. "Ridge told me what happened on the dock." His brows scrunched together and his eyes welled with moisture I'd never seen in him. "I'm so sorry, Liv." His hand on mine tightened, the pressure of it sinking into me.

"Why did you do all this? Chase down records, search for truth that's been buried for over a decade? Why?"

Tony pulled his head up to look at me, a brute of a man brushing away a rogue tear. "Your case landing on Michelle's desk was never an accident. You have more friends than you think you do."

I wanted to ask him who, but the raw burn of my throat stopped me. Instead, I waited. Tony's jaw tensed. I imagined the gum between his teeth trapped in a cinnamon clench.

Tony's eyes were wary by the time he met my gaze. "Your sister, Ashlyn. She called me the night you confronted her. Told me you were coming home, that you were going after Sowards."

"How?" I mouthed the word, my voice absent.

"She and I were partners in an op once upon a time. Did you know she trained at Quantico?"

I shook my head. There was so much I still didn't know about my sister.

"Anyway, I promised her I'd do what I could. I passed your case along to Michelle. I knew she could help you. None of us knew about Lombardi though."

His hand gripped my forearm with that statement, eyes locked on mine. He was telling the truth.

Tony sucked in a breath, his shoulders slumping. "I had a wife once. Emily. I was still in the Corps then, stationed at Camp Lejeune. She was six months pregnant when she got caught in the crossfire of a Bureau operation gone bad." His eyes landed on mine. "I know what it's like to lose someone. To live with the what-ifs. And I know what it's like to blame." Tony pulled back, sliding the palms of his hands over his thighs with a sigh. "When Ashlyn called, asking for help, I promised myself I wouldn't get personally involved. But I couldn't watch you get caught in the middle. You deserve better than that. Both of you."

He didn't need to say more. I understood completely. Guilt and blame were two sides of the same coin. A coin Ridge and I had carried far too long.

"I'd better get back to the precinct. I promised Ridge an update."

"Tell him I'm fine," I managed. "Don't tell him I–"

"I won't," Tony broke in, saving me from having to say the words.

I thanked him as he slipped out, holding the door for Mom and Brian who broke the calm of my room with a tumble of are-you-okays and what-happeneds.

My jaw ached. Clenching against the swirling pool of emotion and exhaustion that clawed from the inside. The two of them huddled over me, asking questions my voice wouldn't allow me to answer. I'd never been more thankful to have our visit interrupted, dark-suited detectives standing at my door.

EPILOGUE
RIDGE

3 months later

Ridge stood under a wooden arch, the sand gritty beneath his shoes as he watched Liv walk down the white runner toward him. The corner of her lips tipped into a smile, eyes holding his, as Brian's groomsman kissed her on the cheek.

They broke away from the procession, tucking into position. The groomsman stood beside Ridge, while Liv stepped onto the platform behind Skylar's maid of honor. She was beautiful, standing there. The gentle breeze lifted tendrils of hair tied away from her face, exposing the curve of her neck. Not one day had gone by in the past three months that Ridge didn't thank God for allowing her to stay in his life.

Colton was already halfway down the aisle by the time Ridge looked back. Satin pillow clutched in hand, he moved much faster than the measured steps Skylar had insisted on during rehearsal. Ridge reached a hand for his son, directing him onto the step below.

"Awesome job, buddy," he whispered, giving Colton's shoulder a squeeze.

He glanced at Bridget, sitting with Tony in the third row, and exchanged a knowing smile. Both of them glad the dirt patch on Colton's shirt–the result of an impromptu excursion into the woods–was hidden by the uncomfortable black jacket.

The music shifted, the string quartet's version of Pachelbel's Canon in D moving into Wagner's Bridal Chorus. Skylar appeared at the edge of the short-trimmed grass and the crowd turned. His father joined her, walking between rows of white plastic chairs decorated with lavender tulle, yellow roses, wisteria, and baby's breath.

Ridge glanced at Brian. His best friend's blue eyes focused fully on his sister. Ridge felt the tug at the corner of his lips as she walked forward, passing arrangements placed that morning during a last-minute decorating spree.

His father planted one last kiss on his sister's cheek, ushering in the memory of their long overdue conversation after Ridge's release. George had known about Vi's affair. Had tried to get her help before the incident with Riley that sent her to the local psych ward. Unlike Liv, Ridge's mother had been damaged by a program without resources to help her. She hadn't known how to make sense of the visions, and therapists and meds only exacerbated her paranoia.

George had to do what was necessary to protect his family, even if it meant turning one of them away. And for that, Ridge couldn't blame him. He refocused, shifting toward the pastor as Brian led Skylar forward.

The ceremony moved like clockwork, Ridge's eyes flicking to Liv every chance he got. By the time the recessional started, he was more than ready to be out of the sightline of the hundred and fifty or so guests.

"Any news on Adam?" Ridge asked Tony, joining him on the front porch after the ceremony.

"Closing arguments are Monday. Michelle is confident he'll walk with some mandated therapy."

Ridge nodded. "I've got a lot to thank him for."

"We all do." Tony shifted gears as one of the bridesmaids ran past them and into the house. "How's the new job, Detective McCaffrey?"

Ridge laughed. "Better than I expected. Wallace has been good to me. Bridget tells me congrats are in order for you, too. Your transfer to the Cincinnati field station came through?"

Tony smiled, tapping his fingers along the wooden support post. "Yeah, well. I think I have you to thank for that, don't I?"

"My friends might not be as high-ranking as yours, but I still have a few." Ridge shrugged. "It was the least I could do."

"You all set for tonight?" Tony asked, the question punctuated by a crack of gum.

The smile took over Ridge's face. "I've been ready," he said. He clapped Tony on the shoulder and hopped off the porch, following Skylar's voice as she corralled all the groomsmen for pictures.

LIV

WATER LAPPED against the moonlit shore of Cascade Lake, cool on my toes. The last of the music wafted from the dance floor, handmade by Ridge and Brian and installed over the scorched swath of earth where my grandparents' barn once stood.

The wedding had been beautiful. Skylar's simple bohemian style perfect against the backdrop of the lake. But I was glad to be on the tail end of the celebration as festivities dwindled.

"I hoped I might find you out here." Ridge's voice cut through the still of the night. "Mind if I join you?"

I smiled his direction. The sight of him had its usual effect, sucking the air from my lungs. He'd shed his jacket post ceremony and his white tuxedo shirt was unbuttoned at the collar, tucked into custom tailored black pants.

"Sky and Brian just left. Shouldn't be long before we have the whole place to ourselves again." Ridge pressed against me from behind.

His breath fell warm against my neck, fingertips skimming flesh as he pushed my hair out of the way. His lips worked along the asymmetric neckline of my bridesmaid's dress.

"This dress looks amazing on you," he said between kisses.

"Ask me how long it took to get it zipped." I turned in his arms, the gauzy fabric twisting around my bare legs. I lifted on my toes to taste him, hot and salty from a day spent in late summer humidity.

He cocked an eyebrow, the dimple in his cheek appearing as he slid his hands to my waist, the dress taut over the newly visible swell of my belly. He bent to plant a kiss below my bellybutton. "However long it took, it was worth it. I like that I can finally see her."

The music in the background ceased. I tried to ignore the tickle of panic that surged up my spine at the mention of our daughter, but it came–uninvited.

"I can feel that, you know," Ridge whispered against my ear.

He'd told me about his experience in the tunnel, and his abilities had grown since then–from sparks of random energy when we touched, to pulses of identifiable emotion. I'd be lying if watching it manifest in him didn't freak me out a bit, making me more grateful for the acceptance he'd shown when I'd first shared my own capabilities.

The more we learned about Vi's involvement in GenLink, the visions she reported to George and staff at the mental health center, the more it made sense. Ridge had the genetics to support a psychic link, he just hadn't allowed it through before now, which only made me wonder what Skylar was hiding.

I'd helped Ridge along the way, teaching him how to decipher one emotion from another, while my own abilities came trickling back. But now it meant he knew when I was anxious, worried, or otherwise upset—which had yet to be a bad thing.

"Just like I can feel you," I reminded him. A bead of anxiety worked its way between us, sparking in the air like an unseen firefly. "You're hiding something."

"Fair enough." He tugged his jacket from the ground a few feet from where we stood and pulled something from the pocket. He returned, tucking whatever it was behind his back. "I have something I need to ask you."

He sucked in a breath and kneeled. A sea of nerves and uncertainty tumbled behind his eyes. I tried not to smile, my lips twisting with the effort.

"As my father likes to remind me, we've been apart more than we've been together over the past eighteen months. But we've been through more than most couples go through in a lifetime. We've kept secrets, cried, lied, died and everything in between. But one thing has never changed..." He pulled my hand into his. "...how I feel about you."

Ridge paused, tracing his thumb in an arc over the back of my hand. Electric pulses of nervous energy collided with my skin.

"You came back to a broken man. And you managed to put those pieces back together. You make me whole, Liv." The clouds of anxiety cleared from his eyes. "You'll always be my one."

I may have sensed this moment was coming, but the perfection of his words forced me back a step. My toes sunk into the sand, a clot of emotion building in the back of my throat.

He dropped my hand and withdrew a red box from behind his back. He popped it open, the moonlight glinting against the diamond inside.

"Olivia Grace Sullivan…" His voice sunk through me, low and deep. "Will you marry me?"

I sunk to my knees with an uneven breath, wrapping my arms around his neck. My lips on his–kissing–long, hard, and deep, toppled us both to the side.

"Is that a yes?" he asked.

"Yes," I managed, breaking our embrace. My chest ached, expanding with a swell of happiness.

"I wouldn't have waited so long, but I was under strict orders to wait until you had an actual verifiable identity." He smiled at me, tucking a windblown curl behind my ear.

The letter from Jack Reynolds sat on the secretary in the entryway of the house. I hadn't even told Ridge about it yet. "I only got confirmation this morning."

Ridge shrugged, pulling the ring free and tossing the box aside. "Wallace says I make a pretty good detective."

He slid the ring on my finger, slow and easy.

"I had it made. The jeweler used parts of your grandmother's Claddagh. She's the one who brought us together, after all." His eyes caught on mine. "I hope that's okay."

The cushion cut diamond winked from my hand, the setting a combination of platinum and gold, the hands, heart, and crown of the Claddagh fully visible in the gallery.

"It's perfect," I breathed.

Ridge pulled me close, hands cradling my face. "Friendship, loyalty, and love." His voice spiraled through me, the meaning behind the three elements of the Claddagh. He leaned in for a kiss. "Forever."

"Took you long enough to get that second one down," I teased, ruffling a hand through his hair.

Moonlight reflected along Ridge's jawline as a breeze picked up the hem of my dress, molding it to my body. Ridge's hungry gaze dragged over me, sending an ache of need through my core.

He pulled back, eyes suddenly serious. "You saved me." His skin pulsed with need-wrapped relief.

"From what?" I asked, but I already knew.

"Myself," he answered. "Guilt. Blame. The monsters of the past."

I leaned forward, my thumb trailed his lower lip as I breathed him in.

"We saved each other." I guided his hand low, pressing his palm against my belly. "And we're setting her free."

He kissed me—gentle, hungry—and I melted into him, pulling contentment from his skin.

I ignored the tickle of uncertainty climbing my spine, the breath of the wind as it whispered over my shoulder, *"It's not over yet."*

DEAR READER

Thank you for following Ridge and Liv on their journey and reading Inherent Fate, the third installment in the Blood Secrets series.

This series, despite its many twists and turns, is a story about love, trust, and the ability of those qualities to overcome even the most insurmountable circumstances. These characters have been on a wild ride and I hope you've enjoyed the journey.

Before you go, please consider leaving a review at your retailer of choice. Even if it is only a line or two, it truly makes a difference and is the best gift a writer can receive.

Enjoying my unshackled suspense? Stay up to date with new releases, appearances, and exclusive reader extras by signing up for my newsletter. I hope to get to know you better.

Sign up today

www.AliciaAnthonyBooks.com

AUTHOR'S NOTE

Over the course of this series, Liv Sullivan has endured her share of trauma. And although she managed to come out the other side relatively unscathed, it is not my intention to make light of any of the situations depicted in these books. In fact, my intent is quite the opposite.

As I type this, RAINN (Rape, Abuse, and Incest National Network) reports that 1 in every 6 American women has been the victim of an attempted or completed sexual assault. The ramifications of these crimes are life-changing for the individuals that endure them. If you or someone you know has experienced a sexual assault, there is help. Don't suffer in silence.

1-800-656-HOPE (4673)

You can also help by donating. Donations to RAINN support victims and the many programs the organization offers.
www.rainn.org/donate

ACKNOWLEDGEMENTS

Every book presents a writer with distinct challenges, and this one was no exception to that rule. From the very beginning, I had an idea where Ridge and Liv's story was headed, but navigating all the twists and turns along the way was an emotional roller coaster I wasn't always prepared to deal with. My friends and family kept me sane.

It takes a village to produce a book and I have a million people to thank for their help and inspiration as I worked through Inherent Fate. First and foremost, my family, from whom I disappeared for long stretches during marathon writing or revising sessions. They did laundry, took care of pets, and kept the household going without ever making me feel guilty about locking my office door. So, Doug and Jillian, thank you.

To my Golden Heart® Persisters and Omegas, your valued advice and encouragement will always be one of the best parts of this journey, and I can't imagine taking it with a better group of people. Here's to our next Zoom conference!

On the business side, it takes a team to make all this work, and I'm blessed to have Cameron Yeager and Aurora Publicity in my corner rooting for me and helping me keep my head above water. Without Cam, and her magnificent powers of organization, I'd undoubtedly be drowning.

I'd also like to thank the wonderful Holly Ingraham for her editing prowess and ability to make me feel like Wonder

Woman, even when the manuscript is a mess. I'm truly in awe of your skills and am happy to have you on speed dial.

Finally, I'd be remiss not to mention my parents—particularly my mother—who continues to support this dream of mine even when I'm deep in edits and ignore her phone calls. Thank you for your forgiving nature and your constant love. I am who I am today because of you.

ABOUT THE AUTHOR

Alicia Anthony's first novels were illegible scribbles on the back of her truck driver father's logbook trip tickets. Having graduated from scribbles to laptop, she now pens novels of psychological suspense in the quiet of the wee morning hours. A full-time elementary school Literacy Specialist, Alicia hopes to pass on her passion for books and writing to the students she teaches.

A two time Golden Heart® finalist and Silver Quill Award winner, Alicia finds her inspiration in exploring the dark, dusty corners of the human experience. Alicia is a graduate of Spalding University's School of Creative & Professional Writing (MFA), Ashland University (M.Ed.) and THE Ohio State University (BA). Go Bucks! She lives in rural south-central Ohio with her amazingly patient and supportive husband, incredibly understanding teenage daughter, two dogs, three horses, a plethora of both visiting and resident barn cats, and some feral raccoons who have worn out their welcome.

www.AliciaAnthonyBooks.com